78

ford

Tupelo

Mississippi

82

45A

50 Miles

WHERE SOUTHERN CROSS THE DOG

Allen Whitley

EMERALD
BOOK CO.

Published by Emerald Book Company in Austin, TX
www.emeraldbookcompany.com

Copyright ©2010 Allen Whitley

Distributed by Emerald Book Company

For ordering information or special discounts for bulk purchases, please contact Emerald Book Company at PO Box 91869, Austin, TX 78709, 512.891.6100.

Design and composition by Greenleaf Book Group LLC
Cover design by Greenleaf Book Group LLC

Cover image uses photo ©AGStockUSA / Bill Barksdale
CD compilation by Allen Whitley and Jim O'Neal, copyright 2010 by Stackhouse Recording Company and Drop Top Music. Library of Congress procedure has been followed to make good faith attempts to contact performers on this compilation by U.S. mail, using address information provided by the Library of Congress.

Cataloging-in-Publication data (Prepared by The Donohue Group, Inc.)

Whitley, Allen (George Allen), 1960-
   Where Southern cross the Dog / Allen Whitley. -- 1st ed.

   p. ; cm.

   ISBN: 978-1-934572-41-2

1. Murder--Mississippi--Fiction. 2. Murder--Investigation--Mississippi--Fiction. 3. Lynching--Mississippi--Fiction. 4. Espionage, German--United States--Fiction. 5. Mystery fiction. I. Title.

PS3623.H585 W45 2010
813/.6   2009942927

Part of the Tree Neutral™ program, which offsets the number of trees consumed in the production and printing of this book by taking proactive steps, such as planting trees in direct proportion to the number of trees used: www.treeneutral.com

TreeNeutral™

Printed in the United States of America on acid-free paper

10 11 12 13 14 10 9 8 7 6 5 4 3 2 1

First Edition

To those blues musicians and singers who took the hollers from the cotton fields and created America's greatest art form, bestowed upon us the imagery of history and culture in their lyrics, and taught us how much fun we could have on a Saturday night.

For me, this work of Southern fiction would never have been complete without the complement of music. The blues is such an integral part of the spirit of Mississippi that I was bound to share its powerful message that I have been fortunate to experience.

In the back of this book you will find a CD of recordings, most of which have never been heard except by a handful of people who knew the artist. With Jim O'Neal, noted blues researcher, at the helm, we journeyed down the road of discovery and relished in the findings for this compilation. The tracks, most of which were recorded near Clarksdale, Mississippi, in the early 1940s, include prison work songs, oral history narrations, and a few songs with very little instrumental accompaniment.

Listen, at least once, knowing that you've heard something that is pure and newly rediscovered, and that until our voices join theirs, we will always have occasion to sing the blues.

Here is a listing of the tracks:

1. Lewis (Billy) Bell: "Levee Camp Holler (Got Me 'Cused of Forgin')" (2:23) Sherard, 1942 (AL)
2. Convicts, state penitentiary, Parchman: "Can't Pick Cotton, Can't Pull Corn" (2:25) Parchman, 1936 (JAL)
3. Convicts, state penitentiary, Parchman: "Dem Long Summer Days" (2:30) Parchman, 1936 (JAL)
4. Convicts, state penitentiary, Parchman: "If You White Folks Want to Learn to Play Poker" (2:55) Parchman, 1936 (JAL)
5. Jesse James Jefferson: "Walk Around" (2:33) Clarksdale, 1942 (JW)
6. Irene Williams: "Come On Oar" (1:50) Rome, 1940 (JAL & RTL)
7. Walter Whitehead: "Last Night and the Night Before" (0:21) Drew, 1940 (JAL & RTL)
8. Two girls [sic]: "I Met Brother Rabbit" (0:24) Greenville, 1939 (HH)
9. Doretha Cook and Bessie Lee Huffman: "One Year Twenty-Four Years Ago" (0:32) Greenville, 1939 (HH)
10. Bessie Lee Huffman: "Jump Po' Rabbit" (0:44) Greenville, 1939 (HH)
11. Mrs. A. Williams [Annie Williams]: "Shout For Joy" (3:48) Friars Point, 1942 (AL)
12. Emma Jane Davis & Group: "Little Sally Walker" (0:36) Friars Point, 1942 (AL)
13. Emma Jane Davis & Group: "Shortenin' Bread" (2:16) Friars Point, 1942 (AL)
14. Turner Junior Johnson: "Preacher Let Your Heart Catch on Fire" (2:50) Coahoma County, 1942 (AL)
15. Asa Ware: "Levee Camp Song (Before I Go)" (0:50) Hopson Plantation, 1942 (AL)
16. Houston Bacon [with Elias Boykin]: "Lining Track or Calling Track" (12:13) Clarksdale, 1942 (AL)
17. Unidentified Negro: Toast ["You Shall Be Free"] (1:29) Sherard, 1942 (AL)
18. Will Starks: Interview (14:04) Clarksdale, 1942 (AL)
19. Will Starks: "My Old Mistis Promised Me" (3:11) Clarksdale, 1942 (AL)
20. Will Starks: Toast ["Doodley Doo"] (1:46) Clarksdale, 1942 (AL)

The folklorists who recorded the tracks include: Alan Lomax (AL), John A. Lomax (JAL), Ruby T. Lomax (RTL), Herbert Halpert (HH), and John Work (JW).

ACKNOWLEDGMENTS

I HAVE MANY PEOPLE TO THANK FOR ASSISTING ME along a journey where the lessons were discovered during the voyage, not at the destination.

First, thanks to the following people who provided resources, information, connections, and such: Dean Blackwood, who always took my calls and provided names and contacts of people who were invaluable to the project. Ed Komara, a wonderful resource at The State University of New York at Potsdam who was instrumental in recommending Eric Sackheim's *The Blues Line: Blues Lyrics from Leadbelly to Muddy Waters* and Michael Taft's *Talkin' to Myself: Blues Lyrics, 1921–1942*. I took the chapter-opening epigraphs mainly from these two sources, attributing some lyrics to the actual writer and other lyrics to the artist who recorded the song. Ed Young, founder of AGStockUSA, Inc., and photographer

Bill Barksdale, who provided what turned out to be an incomparable cover photo. Jeff Sayers, Mississippi born and raised, who reestablished distant relationships for my benefit.

A special thanks to Jim O'Neal, founder of *Living Blues* magazine, who was responsible for finding the wonderful music, narrations, and work songs accompanying this book. Without the music, this project is only half done.

A big round of thanks to the Greenleaf Book Group's production and consultation team: Matthew Donnelley, Neil Gonzalez, Justin Branch, Alan Grimes, Chris McRay, Theresa Reding, and Katie Steigman, who brought the concept to Greenleaf. Their professionalism was refreshing and much appreciated.

Special thanks to my editors, each of whom provided unique perspectives and worked tirelessly to help me craft what I meant and not what I wrote: Mindy Reed, Jerry Davis, Susan Figliulo, Jay Hodges, and Linda O'Doughda, my sponsor into the mutual admiration society.

Thanks to Kevin Chapman, astute attorney, rancher, and friend, who provided insights and guidance into the intricacies of legal procedure and kept me within the confines of reasonable legal behavior.

I'd like to express a sincere indebtedness to Don and Marcus Brown, who reduced my degrees of separation from Katie, someone who understood and cared about my vision.

Writing is a terribly selfish pursuit. Alone and away from distractions, the cocooned author creates an imagined world that plays out all around him and temporarily substitutes for the real one. There are no actual casualties of the flesh, but there are sacrifices all must bear. Time spent mulling over fabricated lives is never recovered, and those lost moments of connection and closeness are forever abandoned. Once again, my selfishness has stolen what cannot be reclaimed. No penance to amend the sin of forsaking. To those I've neglected—loving wife, faithful daughters, supportive mother, and generous father: Kathi, Kara, Emma, Arline, and George—I can only offer my sincerest gratitude and love.

CHAPTER 1

No power on earth dares to make war upon it.

Cotton is king!

—*Senator Hammond of South Carolina, 1858*

THE ROAD—A COMMON MIXTURE OF PACKED REDDISH clay, pebbles, and stones, dry and sharp—stretched out in front of Travis Montgomery for what seemed like a hundred miles. The breeze stirred gently that afternoon in mid-August, 1938, just enough to lift the top layer of dust off the road and into Travis's face. The grit stuck to his skin and intensified his thirst as the blistering sun beat down on him.

An old farmhand had once told Travis that when he was thirsty, he should place a pebble or a piece of clay in his mouth, like chewin' tobacco, until his craving subsided. Travis had tried it several times, but having swallowed a small wad of clay on the last try, he decided to forego the practice. Now he stared at a pebble in the road and tried to imagine it quenching his thirst. Remembering his resolution, however, he stepped squarely on it as he continued his journey.

Travis looked at the fields bordering both sides of the road, where row upon row of white-tipped cotton plants grew. To the twenty-one-year-old who had never left Mississippi, the patchwork landscape of brown and white looked like pictures he had seen of springtime in New England, when retreating snow exposed the earth and rock below. The bulbous plants swayed gently, reminding Travis first of legions of soldiers marching in a parade, and then of jaunty white pom-poms waved by fans at a football game.

What lay before Travis was more than just a crop or a commodity; it was treasure, cared for and cultivated more tenderly than many of the people who lived within a three hundred-mile radius of this very spot. This crop was considered God's greatest creation, and the Lord himself had granted a select few the divine right to cultivate it as they saw fit, often at the expense of all others. Deep down in the Mississippi Delta, this was King Cotton.

In his mind's eye, Travis visualized his journey across the rectangular state: it bordered the Gulf of Mexico at its southern edge, Louisiana and Arkansas to the west, Alabama to the east, and Tennessee to the north. He could see the foothills in north central Mississippi dwindling, like a roller coaster easing into the end of its run, into the productive and provocative Mississippi Delta. Dark, rich land once covered with thick forests was cleared when the earliest settlers— *his* forebears—realized the farming potential of the New World's earth. Each time the Mississippi River had overflowed its banks, it deposited yet another layer of soil throughout the Delta, increasing the land's fruitfulness. Twenty years after the War Between the States ended, the Mississippi's waters were at last tamed by levees— long mounds of dirt piled high upon the riverbanks—in hopes that they would impose some genteel Southern manners upon the unruly river. The Delta became an agricultural holy land, a fertile mecca stretching to the horizon.

Geographers, historians, and cartographers might delineate the Delta as the oval-shape "island," 250 miles long, between Memphis and Vicksburg. But Travis knew what book learning could never impart: The Delta didn't exist merely in geography, an area defined by landmass within natural borders. No, the Delta existed somewhere a little more obscure. More than a place, the Delta was a spirit.

For the past four years, Travis had been attending Millsaps College in Jackson, about 150 miles south of Clarksdale, a town founded in 1848 and nestled near the head of the Sunflower River's deeper waters. Each time he returned home, the serenity of the Delta overcame him anew. Even with his eyes closed he was always able to tell that he was home.

The sun was beginning its descent when Travis heard the familiar rumble of a truck carrying cotton pickers headed north toward Clarksdale. Travis stuck out his thumb, hoping for a ride. The truck's brakes squealed; it slowed to a stop, and Travis ran up along the driver's side and put a foot on the running board.

"Headed to town?" Travis asked.

"Yeah, boy," the driver said, never taking his eyes off the road before him. A cigarette dangled from his lips, and he pulled it out and flicked it past Travis's head. "But you're going in back, with the darkies."

Travis clenched his fist and felt his nails dig into his palm. He wiped the stinging sweat from his eyes and looked past the driver. Another man sat motionless in the front seat. They could have made room, but Travis wasn't going to argue. He smiled his appreciation and climbed onto the truck's bed.

The pickers moved only slightly as he settled on the outer edge, facing the passenger's side. His right leg hung off the back and his right arm crossed his body to grab a slat for support. His other leg was tightly bent, his knee jammed under his chin. He didn't have to sit in this contorted position, hanging off the end of a truck barreling down the road. He could have, if he liked, forcibly made room for himself anywhere, with no worry of retribution. But he didn't.

The passengers were quiet, exhausted after a day spent picking cotton, and Travis tried to avoid meeting their tired eyes. Their shirts clung to their bodies like skin, sweat still oozing from their pores. Some dozed; others stared aimlessly into the darkening sky. The backbreaking work of picking cotton every day for several months every year would silence anyone. The monotonous task pared a person's acuity, robbing life of the vitality that God bestowed upon it.

"Hard day?" Travis said.

"Every day's hard, suh," one of the men said.

The drone of the engine and the bumpy ride lulled them into a semiconscious state; a quick meal and sleep was on everyone's mind. The darkness that immediately precedes the dawn would come too soon.

The truck chugged along, halting often, slowly unraveling its tangle of riders. They jumped from the truck bed, the driver barely stopping, until only Travis was left.

Night had fallen by the time they reached the edge of town. Travis hopped down, waved an arm in thanks, and walked the last quarter-mile home. He crept in the front door and immediately made his way to the kitchen after a wave of hunger overcame him. He didn't bother to turn on the lights; after living in the same house most of his life, he could walk around with his eyes closed. He prowled the counter, searching for one of his mother's freshly baked cakes or pies and didn't notice the figure sitting at the kitchen table.

"Well?"

Travis jumped and took a step back. "Gee, Dad, I thought everyone had gone to bed early," he said, his voice slightly shaky.

"No, everyone's not asleep," Bill Montgomery said.

"All done. I got everything packed up and sent. I'm officially a graduate even though it took an extra summer to do it."

"It was nice they let you go through ceremonies in the spring. Anyone ask you what your plans were?"

"No, sir. I think most everyone was ready for a quick break before fall classes begin. Campus was quiet."

Mr. Montgomery rose and stepped to the sink. He washed the remaining milk out of his glass, dried it with a towel, and placed it in a cabinet. "Well, I'm going to bed. See you in the morning?" he said, cinching up the belt to his robe.

"You'll see me tomorrow, sometime. Good night, Dad."

Travis listened to the creaks of the old stairway as his father climbed the stairs. He looked around for something to nibble on, then realized his exhaustion trumped his hunger. He didn't have the energy to make a sandwich or even to pour a glass of milk. He tip-toed upstairs and stopped in the bathroom to wash off the parts of Mississippi he had brought home with him. Then he went to his bedroom, undressed, and slid into bed. He stared at the ceiling, muttered the prayer he had said every night since he could remember, and reflected on the day—especially the field workers. Picking, eating, sleeping. He'd been around them all his life but still couldn't imagine how they could go through that routine, day in and day out.

His body felt heavy, and Travis sank further into the soft mattress. His mind blurred. With a last gust of breath, he slept.

CHAPTER 2

Graveyard going to be my bed.

—Red Nelson

AS THE SUN CREPT OVER THE HORIZON THE NEXT morning, Sheriff Frank Collins turned his county police car off the road onto a dirt path heading toward the Sunflower, the small river that ran through Clarksdale and continued south, eventually meeting up with the Yazoo River northeast of Vicksburg. He drove straight for 150 yards, and then he veered left off the path into a pasture and drove parallel to the bank.

He continued on for another 30 yards before stopping the car. He stared at an oak in the distance. The surrounding grass had grown several inches high and started to turn a dingy brown because of the lack of rain. He turned off the ignition, squeezed his robust torso out of the car, and leaned against the roof.

Collins removed his thick-rimmed glasses and reached into his shirt pocket for a cigarette. "This doesn't look good," he mumbled, striking a match and inhaling.

The sheriff lumbered over to the tree. The sweet smells of late summer hanging in the air took him back to his youth in the Delta. Here at the river, just yards away, he had spent endless days as a child, swimming and playing. Today's Clarksdale was different, and like the rest of the South, it was changing. The Great War, the colored migration to the North, the Depression, and the New Deal. People liked to believe that the sovereignty of the Old South was a constant, but in truth, the only real constant was turmoil and change.

As he approached the oak, the air began to thicken with the acrid stench of melted flesh and gasoline. When he was about five yards from the tree, Collins could see a half-burned, mutilated body lying on the newly charred dirt. He took a step back, looked away, and gagged into his handkerchief. He spit to get the taste out of his mouth.

He walked back to the car and radioed the office.

Barely fifteen minutes later, Bill Montgomery, the county coroner, was standing next to the sheriff, looking down at the horrific sight.

"Kind of warm out for a suit," Collins said.

"A little," Montgomery agreed, removing his brown coat and placing it neatly on the grass. "How'd you hear about it?"

"Same as before. Edna told Betty, and Betty told me at breakfast."

"Edna say how *she* found out?"

"Not really." Collins shook his head. "Always a phone call from somebody who passed by or heard some noises or something like that. You know Edna. She's getting old. Sometimes she gets things mixed up. Heck, we're lucky she remembers anything at all."

"So this makes four," Montgomery said.

"In six weeks. You ain't tired of autopsies yet, are you?"

Montgomery stood motionless, Collins to his right, and looked down at the corpse. He wished he had stayed home, chatted with Travis, and had a leisurely breakfast. Instead, here he was, staring at another body that offered few clues as to what might have happened or what he should do next.

"Somebody said they saw Travis get back late last night," Collins said, not taking his eyes off the body.

"Yeah, when I left the house this morning, he was still in bed," Montgomery said, looking up at Collins who stood a couple of inches taller.

"What's he going to do this fall?"

"What everybody else does: pray for the price of cotton to go up."

"What about after that?"

Montgomery shrugged his narrow shoulders. "I don't know, but he better be making money or making progress. One of the two."

The coroner moved away from the sheriff and began to circle the body. They had done this so often lately it was routine.

"Well, we know it wasn't an act of passion over a card game or a woman," Montgomery said, not bothering to look at Collins. "Of course, neither were the other ones. Looks like our killer spent some time making the victim pay for whatever he did. The mutilation is extensive, a real mess."

"And nobody called me about coming out to watch a lynching," Collins said, only somewhat kiddingly.

"Frank, if this *had been* a lynching, you know the perpetrators would still have been standing around patting each other on the back when I got here," Montgomery said. They both smiled uneasily because it was true.

Montgomery leaned over and opened the coroner's bag he had brought with him. He took out a pencil, a notebook, and two sample jars. He continued to study the body and look for any clues while Collins leaned back against the tree and puffed away at another unfiltered cigarette. He'd need the final report for Sam Tackett, the district attorney, as soon as Ruth could have it typed up. Eventually, the sheriff, the coroner, and the district attorney would meet to discuss the findings and develop a course of action for this and the three previous homicides.

"Recognize him?" Collins said.

"No," Montgomery said. He assumed that, like the other victims, this one had drifted into Clarksdale looking for day work in the fields. If someone wanted to work, this was the time to do it in the Delta. This victim may or may not have found work, but he certainly found the fastest way out of the Delta. Some would say he found salvation and freedom from the chains of a dirt field. That what God hadn't given him in this life, he was sure to get in the next.

Montgomery bent over the body and carefully scooped up some charred, gas-soaked soil with a small spoon, then emptied it into one of the sample jars. He capped the jar and returned it to his bag. Then he stood up and walked around the tree. He continued to walk circles, enlarging them with each pass, hoping to spot anything that might provide some answers.

The body lay in an oddly peaceful configuration. The victim's hands were at his sides, palms facing up; his legs were stretched out as if he were dozing, and his feet were bare. His head had been battered and numerous bruises were evident. His left eye was swollen shut and his jaw was broken. Portions of his clothes were torn and burned, although his filthy charred shirt and pants covered him adequately. His left wrist showed cuts and abrasions, evidence of having been bound. It would have been nearly impossible to set fire to an untied man unless he was already dead.

Collins tossed his cigarette to the ground, mashed it into the dirt with his foot, and moved closer to the body. He peered intently at the dead man's face.

"Look at this," Collins said. "Why the hell is there dirt in his nose?"

Whether because of the burns, the bruises, or the morning's shadows, neither man had noticed the dirt and mud until then.

"I don't know," Montgomery said. He took a knife from his pocket and unfolded its thin, narrow blade. He knelt, placed one hand on the dead man's forehead, and gently scraped at a nostril. Then he flipped the knife and used its handle to gently pry open the victim's mouth. Dirt had plugged his nostrils and partially filled his mouth.

"What do you think, Bill?" Collins asked.

Montgomery stood up, wiped the knife with his handkerchief, folded the blade away, and returned it to his pocket. "I don't know," he repeated. "But he certainly wasn't able to breathe very well with all that dirt in there."

"Very well? Maybe not at all." Collins wiped his brow and glanced up at the blazing sun as it began to burn away the morning clouds.

Montgomery walked toward the river, mentally listing what was known. Only a few similarities linked the county's four recent deaths. First, all of the victims were colored men, apparently day laborers who had drifted into Coahoma County and met a terrible end. The crimes were not of an overtly sexual nature, and the victims had been found with small sums of money, eliminating robbery as a motive. There seemed to be only one motive: to inflict a painful death. A shooting, a stabbing, a drowning, and now this—a sadistic combination of beating and burning. Four homicides in quick succession were unusual in this Depression-stricken county in the cotton patch, but not improbable. The sheriff and the coroner had considered calling the state police, or even the feds in Jackson, after the third body had been found, but they had decided against it because they didn't want the commotion of outside law enforcement officials traveling all over the county, stirring everybody up and overriding local jurisdiction.

Now, it might be impossible to keep them out.

"Are we done?" Collins called out to Montgomery. Sweat was dripping from his forehead into his eyes and trickling down his neck, staining his tan shirt.

"Just about," replied the coroner, turning back to the sheriff. "Let me get a photograph and we'll go."

Montgomery took a large camera from his car and carefully snapped a picture. Then he and Collins walked back toward their cars.

"Bill, why don't you stop by after the autopsy and let me know what you find," Collins said. "Then we'll meet with Sam early next week."

"Sure," Montgomery said, rubbing his hand through his thinning hair. "I think we have time. Sam can't indict until he has at least one suspect." Montgomery knew the district attorney wasn't looking forward to explaining this new development to Judge Bertram Long, the sitting county judge.

Collins reached inside his vehicle for the radio. "Yes, Sheriff," said the dispatcher on the other end of the radio.

"Send out the body buggy. I got someone needs a ride."

CHAPTER 3

When you get to Clarksdale.

—Muddy Waters

TRAVIS WAS AWAKE LONG BEFORE THE COFFEE'S AROMA wafted upstairs. The groans and rumblings of the trucks headed to the cotton fields and the wagons hauling cotton to the gins had started shortly after dawn, rousing him from a deep and satisfying sleep. But he hadn't gotten up. Now, however, he could smell bacon, eggs, potatoes, coffee, and biscuits. He lay in his bed, enjoying visions of breakfast the way he used to daydream under the magnolia in the backyard. Then he heard his sister Rachel tiptoeing down the hall. Her footsteps slowed, and he sensed her arm rearing back with a tight fist. Three loud bangs on his door shattered the silence.

"Breakfast is ready!" Rachel yelled. "Hurry up before it gets cold!"

Travis smiled, pleased that he was already getting to her so early in the day. "Thanks, Sissy," he said. "I'll be right down."

Plopping his feet on the floor, Travis got out of bed and pulled on a white robe. He looked at himself in the mirror above his chest of drawers. His dark eyes stared back as he picked up a brush and pushed his thick brown hair back to the right, keeping a crooked but discernible part on the left. His walk yesterday had left a touch of sunburn on his forehead and nose, but in a day or two, the red would turn a deep brown like it always did.

He headed downstairs, smiling again as he listened to his mother ask Rachel, as she had for years, to please knock quietly on Travis's door the next time. Rachel was already at the table, picking through her eggs and fried potatoes while the radio played softly in the background.

"And that was 'Deep in a Dream,' by Artie Shaw," the radio announcer said. "That song is sure to be one of the most popular hits of 1938. It's been one of our favorites, and our listeners' too, for over eighteen weeks now. We'll be back in a moment."

"Good morning, Mom," Travis said, leaning down and lightly kissing his mother on the cheek as she stood in front of the stove.

Margaret gently pushed back her curly auburn hair from the sides of her face so she could see her son's face better. "Glad you're home safely."

"Got your favorite radio station on?" Travis said.

"Of course," she smiled, setting a plate down at Travis's usual spot, then wiping her hands on the beige apron that covered her maroon dress.

"Morning, Rache," Travis said as he sat down. His sister cut him off with a glance, and he turned his attention to the breakfast before him. He sized it up, deciding what to sample first. He took a sip of his coffee, and then broke a perfect, glistening egg yolk with his fork.

Travis looked up from his plate at Rachel. She was fifteen, no longer the childish girl he once knew. Even as she glared at him, her green eyes and jet-black hair were almost magical. Her complexion was a nutty brown that radiated, as it always did, from the first days of summer until almost Christmas.

The clothes she wore were in no way provocative—Travis's parents would have none of that—but they hung on her in a way that hinted at her athleticism, confidence, and femininity. The day Travis would have to scare off countless unacceptable suitors was approaching. Shortly, his sister would be a woman of the South. Not a belle, but a woman. She could cook, tend house, mix drinks, and do everything her mother could. Well, almost. Her cooking skills needed a little fine-tuning, but not much.

Travis mused about Rachel in silence. It wasn't that Travis and Rachel didn't get along; rather, that Travis, like so many sons of the South, was the recipient of a mother's abundant adoration and attention. Rachel believed this would corrupt Travis so that no woman could ever measure up, and she considered it her unenviable task to ensure that Travis always had one foot grounded in reality, even if she had to put it there herself.

"Rachel, dear, would you like to tell your brother good morning?" their mother said.

Rachel looked at him and grimaced. "Thanks for dressing for breakfast."

"Where's Dad?" Travis asked.

"He was called in to work very early," Margaret said.

"Do you know what he wants me to do today?"

"Well, I think he wants you to meet him down at the courthouse. He should have a list of things for you to check on by then. He also asked how those applications to Mississippi, Virginia, and Emory were coming."

Travis winced at the thought of poring over the dreary questions on law and medical school applications. He was procrastinating, at the least, putting them off indefinitely if he could.

He finished his bacon, methodically making his way around the plate, eating one thing at a time. His biscuits were next.

"Just eat it," Rachel moaned as she watched his ritual.

Travis ignored her. "Okay," he said casually, "I'll go down to the office after breakfast." He purposely neglected the topic of his applications, hoping his mother would forget she mentioned it.

"Can Travis take me to work?" Rachel asked.

Travis had hoped she wouldn't make the request, but his mother nodded, and he was instantly obligated.

"Your father left the car at the courthouse for you, so you can walk over with Rachel, take her to work, and then go back to the courthouse," she said.

Travis sopped up the last bit of egg yolk with a biscuit and realized that he had once again eaten too much. He finished his coffee and pushed his chair away from the table while motioning for Rachel to pass her plate to him so he could take it to the sink.

"I'll get it myself," Rachel snapped. She rose from the table.

Margaret leaned over and took her plate. "I'll get all this. Y'all get ready to go. You don't want to keep your father waiting."

Travis went back upstairs, dressed quickly, and returned to find Rachel waiting outside on the porch. He stood for a moment, taking in Clarksdale, listening to the bustling activity of harvest time in the Cotton Belt.

"Ready," he said, stepping off the porch.

They walked to the sidewalk in front of their house, turned left, and headed down Clark Street. Clark and nearby John Street were lined with the large and stately homes of Clarksdale's most prominent and well-to-do families. Huge oaks, magnolias, elms, and dogwoods adorned the front yards of houses distinctive yet similar to their neighbors. Some, built in 1919 during one of King Cotton's heydays, were representative of that era's extravagance and the excesses that often accompanied a surge in cotton prices. Others dated to a more conservative period, their simple frame structures a clear indication of less prosperous cotton seasons.

The oldest houses included the home of John Clark, Clarksdale's founder and brother-in-law of James Lusk Alcorn, a noted Mississippian who had been at various times a Confederate general, a U.S. senator, and a governor of Mississippi. Alcorn, a moderate Republican, was known as the sage of Coahoma County, and during Reconstruction he had been Clarksdale's leading citizen. Begun a few years before the War Between the States, the two-story mansion, which overlooked the town's river, was moved on logs in 1916 to make room for the Cutrer home, an Italian Renaissance villa, whose owners, Clark's daughter and her husband, desired the property for its view.

The Montgomery family home was one of the smaller ones on the block, a wooden, two-story house with just three bedrooms and an outside porch that wrapped halfway around the house. Because he was an elected county official, Travis's father thought it prudent to live in such a home. He always said that when taxes pay your salary, it's better to live modestly—unless, of course, you were a judge.

Travis and Rachel turned left onto John Street, passing the big house that stood on the corner. It was the former home of Governor Earl Brewer, who had built it upon returning to Clarksdale from Jackson after his term as governor from 1912 to 1916, and it was one of the finest homes in Clarksdale. Travis had been inside only once, while playing with one of Governor Brewer's grandchildren. In a house of that size, hide-and-seek was a popular game, and Travis had once hidden for more than two hours. He was eventually found sleeping in a closet.

The brother and sister then turned right onto First Street and headed for the west side of town, where the city hall, county courthouse, and county jail were located. They passed Issaquena Avenue on their left and peered down the street at its many shops.

"Looks busy today," Travis said, though they both knew the Delta was always busy this time of year.

Farther down Issaquena stood the train depot along the Illinois Central line. Past the tracks was the other Clarksdale: black Clarksdale.

Travis and Rachel turned onto Sunflower Avenue, and they easily spotted their father's car. Travis reached under the driver's seat and felt around for the keys. The car started right up, and they traveled south down Sunflower Avenue, which ran parallel to the Sunflower River. Travis turned right onto Highway 61 and drove for a few miles until he reached the Gilman plantation. Although it no longer operated like the plantations of an earlier century, many Southerners still liked to refer to the old farms as such, taking rebellious delight in all the connotations that accompanied the word.

They drove past the cotton pickers, bent at the waist, some appearing to crawl as they half-carried, half-dragged their canvas sacks, slowly filling them with cotton. Most of those men and women in the field were sharecroppers, but Travis knew it was just another name for legitimized slavery. Abandonment was their only escape.

Travis pulled up to the plantation's commissary, a small store where most of the tenants and sharecroppers bought food and day-to-day necessities. He turned to his sister. "You want me to pick you up this afternoon?"

"Okay. Why don't you come back around five o'clock?" Rachel said. "Do you know if Mom wanted anything from the store?"

"She didn't say anything to me about it."

"See you later," said Rachel by way of thanks. She stepped from the car and slammed the door. She walked up a couple of stairs, opened the commissary door, and was gone.

Travis cautiously backed up, watching carefully for pedestrians, and pulled onto Highway 61. He accelerated toward town past a steady flow of trucks rolling in the other direction, headed to the gin. He had always lived in town, never the country. The plantation owners—their habits, politics, and thinking—were simultaneously comprehensible and foreign to Travis. He usually felt uncomfortable here, beyond the rules of fair play and a town's scrutiny. It seemed to Travis that on the plantations the rules were like those in any card game where the house plays a hand. Rule Number One: The house wins all ties. This always gave the house a slight advantage. And Rule Number Two: Don't ever forget or try to change Rule Number One.

CHAPTER 4

Lord, I've got a trouble in mind.

—*Mississippi John Hurt*

CONRAD HIGSON KICKED ASIDE A SMALL RUG ON THE floor of his bedroom. He bent down and, with both of his thick hands, grasped a short rope tucked into a six-inch slot on what looked like a floorboard. He tugged at the rope, and several boards rose together with a reluctant creak. He rotated the small door 180 degrees on its hinge and laid it down.

Then he gingerly climbed down the stairs that led to a tiny study underneath his bedroom. He had to stoop as he made his way to the desk in one corner of the room, although once he sat down, his balding head was about two feet below the ceiling, giving him ample room in which to work.

When Higson first came to Clarksdale, he had looked for a house built on the highest piers he could find. After he moved in and paid rent for two months, he had constructed this room—his laboratory, as he called it. Since the piers were so high, he had only needed to excavate two feet of soil. He had shored up the sides of the small room with boards and put in a floor. The boards also helped seal the room from the Delta's pervasive dampness. Outside, shrubs and latticework surrounded the perimeter of the house and concealed the room from view, even when someone was standing in the yard.

The house itself was isolated, about four miles outside of Clarksdale, stuck in the middle of several crop fields with only one small road leading in. It was like his own private island: he could see anyone driving or walking through the surrounding fields toward the house.

It was close to noon when Higson sat down at his desk. He turned on a light and placed a blank piece of paper in his typewriter.

August 20, 1938
General Herman Schnor
Ministry of Public Enlightenment and Propaganda
Leopold Palace
Berlin, Deutschland

Dear General Schnor,

It has been several weeks since my last correspondence, and I am eagerly anticipating the resolution of my application for reinstatement. I hope it will come soon, as I am growing tired of the warm Southern climate.

I have been working furiously and recently entertained several professors from some very prestigious universities in Oxford, Mississippi. They were very knowledgeable about the new generation of engines being used in mechanical harvesters very similar to the one I am building. They provided some fascinating drawings and research results, which I have already forwarded.

In addition, another of my colleagues is making great advances in the manufacturing and machining of high-strength, lightweight materials, which will have many agricultural applications. He has promised to send me several papers they are preparing for publication. I shall translate these and forward them to you as soon as possible.

In a few weeks, I am attending the Texas Cotton Association's annual conference in San Antonio, Texas. I shall send all papers and other materials that I collect. And later this fall, I plan to visit the University of Tennessee to review their agricultural research facilities. This trip should be quite informative.

Please tell the Chairman and the other members of the review committee that I have learned much here. I am prepared to bring this knowledge back to Germany and stand ready to serve in my best and most useful capacity.

This is my hope and my plea. I beg for a quick approval of my reinstatement application.

Respectfully,

Professor Conrad Higson

Clarksdale, Mississippi

Higson slumped back in his hard chair and read through the letter. Then he folded it precisely into thirds, typed an address on an envelope, and sealed the letter inside. He placed the envelope on top of a large box, also ready to be mailed, then climbed out of his laboratory.

Later in the day, he loaded the box into his car, placed the envelope in his coat pocket, and drove north to Memphis. The whole way, he prayed that the wretched Southern landscape would soon be a vague and nondescript memory.

CHAPTER 5

I walked around this world.

—*Memphis Minnie*

TRAVIS ENTERED THE COURTHOUSE AS TWO ELDERLY women were exiting. "Good morning, ladies," Travis said, holding open the heavy door as they passed by. He walked to the stairwell and ascended to his father's second-floor office. He opened the office door and greeted his father's longtime secretary.

"Morning, Ruth," Travis said. He thought her white hair made her look much older than she was, although he had no idea how old that might be.

"Oh, hi, Travis. How are you doing this morning?" Ruth asked, looking up at him with a smile.

"I'm fine, thank you." Her posture was so erect it looked pain-ful.

"Why don't you have a seat in your dad's office? He'll be up in a minute. He's finishing an autopsy. You want some coffee?"

"No thanks, I'll just wait inside." Travis slipped inside and left the door cracked so as not to be rude.

"Holler if you need anything," Ruth said, turning back to her typewriter.

"Yes, ma'am, thanks."

Travis circled his father's desk idly, stopping to look at the diploma on the wall. "Millsaps College," it read, and underneath, "Bachelor of Science." It was dated June 1914, twenty-four years before Travis's own graduation. Travis had followed in his father's footsteps at the small liberal arts school, earning a bachelor's degree with a double major: English and chemistry. He knew his parents wanted him to attend either medical or law school. Travis wasn't so sure about either, but he hadn't come up with anything more promising.

A door opened in the outer office, and Travis heard his father's voice. "Ruth, I'll have the autopsy results ready for you by the end of the day."

"Copies for Sam and Frank?" Ruth asked.

"Please," Montgomery answered.

"Travis is waiting in your office," Ruth said, as Montgomery pushed open his office door. "He hasn't been there long."

Travis was surprised to see his father looking so grim at this early hour. "Good morning, son, did you get Rachel to work all right?"

"Yes, sir," Travis said. "I'll pick her up tonight on my way home." His father's pants were dirty, and his shirt had sweat stains. "Are you doing an autopsy today?"

"Almost done," he said. "Another strange one. Young colored fellow, burned and beaten. Somebody made a special effort to prolong his pain. Poor man."

"Was he badly burned?"

"Mostly on his arms and legs. But I don't think that's what killed him."

The county coroner sat down at his desk, while Travis continued to stand.

"Recognize him?" Travis asked.

"No," replied his father, "but he was a field hand. Strange thing, though, there was dirt packed into his nose and mouth."

"Where was the body found?"

"By the river."

"What killed him?"

"It looks like he might have gone into shock. He must have been alive after the beating. If not, why burn him? The killer probably put dirt in his mouth to shut him up, keep him from screaming, but it may have suffocated him instead. Let's hope so. Considering the evidence, it's the least painful alternative."

Travis pondered his father's world: nothing but deaths, and so many of them. Why would anyone want this job? He couldn't do it.

"Well, what have you got for me today?" Travis asked, leaning against the desk as his dad shuffled papers and made some notes. Although Travis thought having to perform autopsies was revolting, there was a part of his father's job that appealed to him: driving around the county and delivering and retrieving documents from county officials and other prominent citizens. Sometimes he even traveled to other towns. He enjoyed being outdoors and working independently; it sure beat a desk job.

Mr. Montgomery handed Travis a slip of paper on which he had listed tasks for the day. "Here, son, you go ahead and take the car, and I'll meet you at home tonight. Judge Stamps said he'll leave the package outside his front door, and Mrs. Yule needs the past three years of some county property records. She said you could leave it with Celia."

Travis carefully reviewed the list, making sure he had no other questions for his father. "Why does Mr. McPherson want a list of the county's registered voters?"

"I don't know. You can get the list downstairs from Gene."

"And what do you want me to do at Mr. Hollingsworth's?" Travis asked, looking back at his list.

"Hollingsworth wants you to pick up some paperwork. Why don't you ask him if he wants me to send over the new John Doe we picked up today?"

"Yes, sir, will do." He folded the paper and tucked it into his shirt pocket. "See you at home."

Travis dispatched his duties easily throughout the late morning and afternoon. He drove out to Friars Point and then to Bobo. In Stovall, at the home of Mrs. Ruby Simpson, he ate two pieces of pie, drank a large glass of milk, and enjoyed a good half hour of conversation just for delivering a will. Everywhere, people asked him about his future plans and aspirations. Travis's last stop of the day was at Hollingsworth Funeral Home in Clarksdale. No cars were parked outside, so he assumed no families were gathered to discuss funeral arrangements. Relieved that he would not be disturbing any mourners, he parked the car and went inside.

Travis knocked lightly on Hollingsworth's office door.

"Yes, good afternoon," a familiar voice rumbled from within. Travis opened the door, and George Hollingsworth rose from behind a filing cabinet and stepped toward him. "Oh, Travis."

"Good afternoon, Mr. Hollingsworth," Travis said. "Dad sent me over to pick up some paperwork?" Travis stepped forward and extended his hand. He knew better than to make this gesture in public, but, in the privacy of the funeral home, he felt protected. And it was just good manners.

"Yes, yes," Hollingsworth said in a voice hoarsened by a lifetime of smoking. He leaned toward Travis and the two men shook hands.

Hollingsworth didn't have to lean far; his body had begun to stoop, the result of too many formative years spent in the fields. His step was still youthful, however, for a man in his sixties.

One of the county's most respected and successful Negro men, Hollingsworth had grown up in Clarksdale, sharecropped with his father, and also worked in the funeral home of a family friend. He turned out to have a knack for the business and eventually opened his own funeral home, which became very successful.

One reason for that success was the prevalence of burial insurance among the colored population of Coahoma County. Poor as they might be, whether sharecropping a patch of land out in the country or working as a domestic in town, everyone who could afford it—and most everyone could—paid a small premium of 20 or 30 cents every week for burial insurance. It was the first thing bought and the last given up. Most of the South's Negroes had few earthly possessions; their final reward, like Heaven itself, was a nice $100 funeral.

"How have you been, Travis?" Hollingsworth asked, moving to his desk and shuffling through some papers. "Very well, I hope."

"Fine," Travis said. "I'll be busy this fall with my county work, and possibly back in school by the spring, or at the latest, next fall. My dad prefers spring."

"Well, that's an excellent idea, Travis. Sounds like your father has the right idea. You should heed his advice and guidance, because most people don't have someone like your father helping them plot out a steady course. Where are you applying?"

"The—" Travis began, breaking off his answer as he heard the front door open and then two timid knocks.

"George? You here?" a voice asked.

"We're in the office, Richard," Hollingsworth called.

A rather imposing man soon appeared from around the corner, striding gracefully into a hallway leading to the office. He stopped abruptly, some ten feet from Travis, and looked from Hollingsworth to Travis and back.

"Afternoon, George, I didn't know you were busy." The man was dressed impeccably, defying heat and dust in a dark gray wool suit and a white shirt. He obviously had not expected to see a white man in the office.

Travis immediately stuck out his hand, "Good afternoon. My name is Travis Montgomery. I work for the county coroner."

"It's all right, Richard," Hollingsworth said quickly. "Travis and I are old friends. He's just picking up some paperwork." He cast a wink at Travis.

The man lifted his arm to shake hands with Travis. "Hello, I'm Richard Morgan. Pleasure to meet you."

"Richard's in the insurance business, Travis," Hollingsworth said, "so we see each other quite a bit. And since Travis works for the coroner, well, I see him quite a bit, too. "

Travis nodded his acknowledgment as he shook Morgan's hand.

"We're almost finished," Hollingsworth said to Morgan.

"Please take your time," Morgan said. "I'm in no hurry."

"Speaking of your father, Travis, how is he these days?" Hollingsworth asked, turning back toward the younger Montgomery.

"Oh, he's fine," Travis answered. "Very busy. I don't know whether you heard or not, but there was another murder last night. He conducted the autopsy today."

"Yes, I certainly did hear about that," Hollingsworth said. "When Mr. Winston stopped by to drop off a suit, he mentioned it. Do they have any idea who did it?"

"Well, if they do, nobody's saying anything," Travis said, resting against the back of a chair. "I think they're still unsure. I didn't hear anybody talking much about it at the courthouse this morning."

"What about those other murders? Doesn't anyone suspect they're related?" Morgan asked, folding his arms and joining in the conversation.

"I think Sheriff Collins does," Travis said. "But there doesn't seem to be any evidence to support it."

"It would be pretty surprising if they weren't somehow con-nected," said Hollingsworth, placing his gathered paperwork neatly in a folder and turning to Travis and Morgan.

"What about the Klan?" asked Morgan.

"Could be, I guess," Travis said. "They just don't know."

Hollingsworth sat down in a chair and sighed. "I wonder if we should have a meeting, Richard. Get a few folks together at the church and decide whether we should discuss the situation with the sheriff. We don't want people thinking there's some murderer running loose."

"Wouldn't hurt," Morgan agreed. "Folks could become too scared to go outside or walk to work. Clarksdale might shut down. And during harvest time, that would affect everyone."

"We'll talk about it Sunday after church," Hollingsworth said. "Maybe ask the reverend what he thinks." He held out the folder for Travis. "Here you go, Travis. Thanks for stopping by to pick these up."

"No trouble at all," Travis said, taking the folder. "And if you want my opinion, I think you should let the sheriff know about your concerns. You don't want him thinking you're just getting people stirred up."

"That's a good thought, Travis," Hollingsworth said with the barest trace of a smile. "We'll do that."

Travis shook hands with both men. "Nice meeting you, Mr. Mor-gan," he said.

"It was nice meeting you, too."

Travis walked down the hall but turned back to the men just before stepping out of sight. "Oh, by the way, Mr. Hollingsworth. Do you want my dad to send over the new body?"

"By all means, Travis. Everybody's got to be buried."

CHAPTER 6

Down in sweet old Dixieland.

—Robert Lee McCoy

EARLY MONDAY MORNING, DIVISION CHIEF RUSS Kalman opened one of the two heavy doors to a large old building in downtown Jackson. Inside, he greeted those he knew and continued to a spiral stairwell in the center of the first floor. He ascended the stairs to the second floor, turned right, and walked halfway down the hall to a door that was half wood and half opaque glass. The first line of lettering on the door read: "Federal Bureau of Investigation"; beneath it were the words "Mississippi Division."

Kalman opened it and went inside.

"Good morning, Russ," said the secretary who greeted everyone who entered the office.

"Morning, Sally. Where's Bob?"

"They're all in the conference room. Been there fifteen minutes already."

Kalman hurried past rows of desks to the back of the office. He could hear muted voices as he approached the conference room.

"Hey, there he is," someone said as Kalman opened the door. He breathed in the familiar smells of coffee and cigarettes. The door was solid oak; there were no windows. The bulb in the single overhead fixture provided fewer watts than the room needed. Around a square table in the center of the room sat Bob Thompson and Dan Mulevsky. Their chain-smoking didn't help with the illumination.

The division chief approached a second table in the corner of the room, poured himself some coffee, and took a seat with the others. He grabbed a pack of cigarettes, pulled one out, tapped it on the table, and lit it. All four men stared at their coffee cups and blew smoke in the air. No one spoke.

Kalman looked at his senior agents, both G-men. All dressed— just as he was—in a white shirt and dark tie. It was the uniform that wasn't a uniform. Finally, he asked, "What have we got today?"

"Well, Chief, where should I start?" Thompson said, the number two, yet oldest, man in the office.

"I don't know, how about the first one?" Kalman sighed, his cigarette dangling from his lips.

"Robbery in Vicksburg," Thompson said. "They got away with $3,000 and killed one uniformed officer. Local authorities have no idea where to start the search."

"That's not too bad."

"I'm just getting started, Chief. There were two other robberies in Natchez and Meridian."

"Large amounts?"

"No," Thompson said.

"People are still hurting, boss," Mulevsky said. "And it doesn't look like the economy's getting any better."

Kalman rubbed his temples, as if it would somehow enlighten him. These cases could make or break his career. He had come a long way from the police department in Wheeling, West Virginia. A long way from the striking miners who had killed the police chief and from the mother who had sent her young son out on a frigid night to make sure it was true.

Every day Kalman thought about that night; every day it haunted him. Time and maturity had eased the fear he felt that night, but the pain was still there. Although he had been in Jackson for only a year, he was starting to wonder if these Mississippi cases would be what he needed to earn a promotion and thus a return to Washington.

"Keep going," said the division chief.

"There was a murder in Greenville," Thompson said. "Actually, that was a lynching. Seems like the Klan is getting active up there."

"That's the third one this year around Greenville," Kalman said.

"But we couldn't link the others to the Klan," said Mulevsky. "So they weren't recorded as lynchings, just homicides."

"Just," Thompson said.

"Continue," Kalman said. He lit another cigarette.

"And one in Hattiesburg," said Thompson.

"All last week?"

"Last two weeks," Thompson said.

"Busy couple of weeks," Mulevsky said. "But we've had worse."

Thompson flipped a page in his file. "Oh, and I almost forgot," he said. "There was another one in Clarksdale."

"Anyone want more coffee?" Mulevsky said. He got up and walked to the table in the corner.

They all shook their heads.

"How many does that make in Clarksdale?" Mulevsky asked.

"Four in a month and a half," Kalman said.

"You want us to head up there and find out what's going on?" asked Thompson. He threw the files back on the table.

"We already know what's going on." Mulevsky smirked.

"What's that?" asked his boss.

Thompson rose from the table, walked over to the door, and leaned against it. "Most likely a bunch of peckerwoods," he said. "I'll bet you a month's pay. Or maybe it was just some bad blood over a card game. It's cotton-picking season. The money's flowing, people are feeling pretty—what's the word—uppity. We can drive up, if you want."

"No," Kalman said. "We've got too many other investigations. Let Collins and his gang handle it. They prefer it that way. What could we really do anyway?"

"Probably nothing," Thompson said. "And if we start asking questions, we won't get another witness to anything, ever. Collins will gag that town so fast. We have to look at the long-term implications of getting involved. Down here, murders occur periodically, and no one ever thinks twice about it. If we start getting involved in this investigation, Collins will be in front of the local judge complaining, and you think any judge is going to side with us? We'll never be able to investigate in Coahoma County again."

"We could get a federal judge," said Kalman. "We've got the authority."

"Not worth it," Thompson said.

"What if we just start with the blacks?" continued the boss, sipping his coffee.

"Come on, Russ," Thompson said. "The first person who talks will be the last. People will know we're in the county before we open our mouths."

"What about bringing them to Jackson?" Kalman asked.

"Who?" Thompson said. "Everybody who thinks they might have seen something on some particular night? We'll have everybody in the county visiting at our expense."

"My first instinct was right. It's Collins's investigation," observed the chief as he extinguished his cigarette in a coffee cup on the table. "Let's break up this little social—we've got work to do."

Thompson opened the door.

Kalman squinted as the bright sunlight burst in from the outer office. He took a breath of the fresh air pouring into the room. Then he walked out of the small, smoky conference room into an office buzzing with phone messages and secretaries beckoning for him to come here or go there. He couldn't tell his men all that he knew about Clarksdale—not just yet.

CHAPTER 7

Going down to the courthouse.

—Sam Collins

A FEW DAYS LATER, AFTER THE REPORTS HAD BEEN written, Bill Montgomery and Sheriff Collins walked the short distance to the district attorney's office. Sam Tackett had practiced a few years in Jackson before moving to Clarksdale. On a whim, and at the advice of a friend, he had run for DA on a platform focused on the planters' agricultural concerns. He won by a landslide and was halfway through his term.

They opened the door labeled "District Attorney" and proceeded past the secretary, whom they acknowledged with a brief hello.

They took seats at the small conference table in Tackett's office. Copies of the various documents and findings were in front of each seat. Tackett quickly rose from his desk and joined them at the table. He wasn't sure if he was ready for this meeting.

"Well?" Tackett asked.

"Well, what?" the sheriff said.

"We've got a hell of a problem."

"There's no doubt about that."

"We have four homicides, and no suspects or leads," Tackett said. "What was the cause of death on the last one?"

"Well, he certainly experienced trauma from the burns and contusions," Montgomery said, "but it's hard to say exactly what killed him. He had a significant amount of dirt in his nose and mouth so I reported asphyxiation."

"I suppose it really doesn't matter exactly how he died, or how any of them died," Tackett said. "The point is, they're dead, and they were murdered."

He sat back in his chair and folded his hands behind his head.

"Well, I'm inclined to just leave this one alone," Collins said. "So we got four black bodies. Who cares? We can't get all wrapped up in some investigation and be concerned with who did what, when, and where. The fact is, we're probably never going to know who did this, and we're better off spending our time doing something else. If we had some leads, that'd be one thing, but we don't have anything. How do we know it wasn't just a few lynchings?"

Tackett stared out the window, his hands still interlocked behind his head.

"We don't know anything, and that's the problem," Tackett said. "We need some answers."

"Sam's right," said Montgomery. "We need an investigation. There are just too many bodies to ignore."

"Too many bodies?" Collins said. "Are you kidding me? There aren't near enough for my taste."

"Frank," Tackett said, "as Clarksdale's district attorney, I'm expecting you to do your job. I don't want to have to do it for you. I've been elected to do *my* job, remember, which is to ensure that justice is done, regardless of someone's color or religion, regardless of whether they are rich or poor. I think these dead souls need some peace, and we should do our part to help them get it."

"We have any more homicides in this county, Frank, and something tells me we'll be hearing from community leaders—black and white," Montgomery said. "We don't need that problem in addition to what we already have."

"That's right," Tackett said. "We help ourselves in a number of ways by getting started on these cases."

Collins looked down at his shoes to avert Montgomery and Tackett's gaze. "I don't know. Seems to me, for as long as I can remember, a few darky field hands in the wrong place at the wrong time was nothing to get all worked up about."

"Times change, Frank. Besides, it's especially important to keep the peace during harvest," Tackett said. "You know as well as anyone that your boss and mine, those planters out there, will make our lives miserable if they can't find enough folks to work in their fields and clean their houses. They're already mad they have to send recruiting agents out to get hands. If they think some killer is keeping their day labor from getting to Clarksdale or, God forbid, chasing them North—because they're already fuming over all the hands they've lost to Yankeeville—and if we could've done something about it—well, then, your tenure as sheriff and mine as district attorney will be considerably shorter than we'd like."

Collins sat in silence, looking out the window, his arms folded across his burly chest. "All right," he said, "we'll look into it, but I'm not guaranteeing we'll find anything."

Tackett sensed the dissatisfaction beneath the sheriff's acquiescence.

"I'm only putting one man on the job," Collins said. "Don't figure on the whole office working these cases."

"But he's got to get out and talk to folks," Montgomery said. "He can't just sit and review the files for eight hours a day."

Collins grabbed his hat and stood up to go. "I don't like this, boys. They just black, that's all."

"Maybe we'll get some leads, and we can wrap this thing up quickly," Tackett said. "Oh, by the way, did either of you two speak to anyone down at the paper? Did you see the short article on the murder?"

"I saw the article, but I didn't talk to anybody," Montgomery said.

"You don't need to ask me, do you?" said Collins.

"Someone down at the paper is getting information that only a few people know," Tackett said. "I didn't think much about the first couple of articles on the other murders, but if we're going to start pursuing this, we can't have the details of our investigation published in the paper every day. I'll go down and have a talk with. Wilson this week to see if he'll stop printing stories about the homicides."

"That's a good idea," Montgomery said. "We don't want anything getting out too early. We need to kill the source—so to speak."

"I'll make sure to keep it quiet on our end," Collins said. He opened the door and left.

Tackett saw Montgomery to the door. "He always comes around."

"Yeah," Montgomery said, "but he makes it so hard."

That night, after the offices were closed and everyone had gone home, Moses Hooperman stood at the side door of the courthouse, tossing his keys around in his hand looking for the one that unlocked it. The door led to a small room that held his cleaning supplies. Finding the key, he opened the door, went inside, and then locked the door behind him.

He changed into his work clothes: his stained shirt bore a few small holes, the result of ashes dropping off his cigarettes; the knees of his pants were torn beyond mending.

Moses had been the night custodian of the courthouse for a dozen years. Usually, he came in at eleven at night and worked until about five the next morning, when county workers began to arrive. He always liked to be out of the building before the first one got there.

Starting on the top floor and working his way down, Moses diligently emptied trash cans, mopped the floor, cleaned the restrooms, and swept the seemingly endless hallways.

A little after midnight, he entered Bill Montgomery's office and started to dust. He passed his dust rag over the desk and noticed a report dated the previous day. He finished dusting and started to mop the floor, beginning in the far corner. Halfway done, he set the mop aside and returned to the desk. Making careful note of where the report was and how it was situated on the desk, Moses picked it up, read the cover, and leafed through the pages, reading a few thoroughly and scanning the rest. He laid the report down, picked up the phone, and dialed a number.

After two rings he heard, "Hello."

"Mr. Murphree," Moses said, "I'm down at the courthouse. You might want to come down and have a look at something."

"I'll be down in a minute," was Murphree's immediate reply.

Murphree hung up and staggered to his feet, still half asleep. He squinted at the clock. Two-twenty. He dressed quickly, grabbed his briefcase, and headed for the stairs.

"Lewis? Be back soon?" his wife murmured, barely stirring in the bed.

"Soon," he said. After ten years of marriage to the newspaper's assistant editor and chief reporter, she was accustomed to these late-night outings. He descended the stairs and quietly shut the front door behind him.

Murphree walked the short distance from his house on Court Street to the courthouse. A block away, he made a detour so that he could approach the building from the rear. He crept in the shadows, ensuring that no one saw him, and slowly made his way to the side door where Moses had originally entered. He glanced around, making sure his presence was still unnoticed, and tapped on the door.

From the other side came a familiar voice: "Mr. Murphree, that you?"

"Yes," came the whispered reply.

Moses shut off the light in his small room and gently opened the door. Murphree slipped in, and Moses closed the door behind him.

The two men exchanged greetings and started up the stairs to the coroner's second-floor office.

"How'd you find it?" was the reporter's first question.

"I was cleaning up and there it was, big as life, just lying on the desk. I'm always surprised folks don't lock things up, or at least put things away. They ought to try and be a little more careful."

"Well, lucky for us they're not."

"Most people know I clean the courthouse. Don't they think I might see something on somebody's desk? I guess they just forget I'm here. Like I'm invisible or something."

"They probably don't know you can read."

"Now that's true," Moses said. He grinned at Murphree. "Yeah, I try to keep that a secret. Between you and me."

"And we'd better make sure that's how it stays. We'd sure have a lot of explaining to do if someone found out different."

They approached the office and picked up their pace. Moses had left the door ajar, and he pushed it aside as they stepped in. He pulled it nearly shut so he could listen for noise in the hallway. They walked past Ruth's desk into Bill Montgomery's office.

"It's on the desk, there on the left," Moses said, pointing to the report.

Murphree picked up the document and started to read. After a moment, without removing his gaze, he opened his briefcase, removed a pad of paper and a pencil, sat down, and began to make notes. Moses picked up where he had left off cleaning the room.

"Find anything good?" Moses asked after a few minutes.

"Oh yeah, there's always something good in these reports. It's just a matter of finding what we can print and what we can't."

The newspaper reporter continued reading and taking notes for another ten minutes, hastily paging back and forth among various sections of the document. Finally, he closed the report and placed it back on the desk, exactly as he had found it. Moses moved it slightly.

"Well, that was certainly interesting," Murphree said, still sitting in Montgomery's chair. "Seems like we have a pattern. I wonder what they plan on telling the public?"

"Which public?" Moses said, as he gathered his cleaning supplies near the door.

"Good question."

Murphree stood up and rearranged the chair as he had found it. "I don't know. Maybe another story in the paper will get the sheriff moving a little quicker on this. It's pretty clear somebody needs to do something before things get out of hand, because this surely isn't what we typically see in Clarksdale. I think I can help speed up the process. Whether that's what they want or not, I guess we'll find out."

Both men entered the hallway and made the short trip back to Moses's storage room. Murphree pulled out a few dollars—compensation equal to at least a few days' worth of monotonous janitorial work—and pressed it into Moses's hand, who closed a tight fist around the money and smiled.

"Thanks, Moses, and let me know if you find anything else," said the visitor.

"Yessuh, Mr. Murphree. You know I will."

Moses turned out the light and slowly opened the back door.

Murphree slipped out, walked home, and crawled back into bed. He lay awake for an hour, writing the story in his head. He finally fell asleep but was up two hours later for work. He yawned all through breakfast, but his wife didn't ask any questions. She understood it was better not to.

Two days later, Sam Tackett picked up the morning paper and read a second article describing the most recent murder, complete with details only a few people knew.

"Son of a—. Where are they getting this information?"

He read about the crime scene, the use of gasoline in the murder, and several theories relating to the case. In his anger and frustration, he almost picked up the phone and called Emmett Wilson, the senior editor and owner of the paper, to condemn the reporter's irresponsible release of sensitive information during an ongoing investigation.

Then he reminded himself that talking to editors never helped. The reality was that Wilson's reporter would continue to embarrass him until he solved this case.

CHAPTER 8

The Mississippi Delta begins in the lobby of the Peabody
Hotel in Memphis and ends on Catfish Row in Vicksburg.

—David L. Cohn

THE HECTIC DAYS OF HARVEST PASSED BY QUICKLY while Travis continued his duties as the runner for the county courthouse. Whether the task took him to the farthest reaches of the county or to an office down the hall from his father's, Travis relished the independence of the work and its complete lack of real responsibility.

One lazy Thursday afternoon, Travis picked up a magazine and sat back on the couch across from Ruth's desk. He was a paragraph into the first article when the phone rang.

"Bill Montgomery's office," Ruth said.

Travis reread the paragraph as he listened to Ruth.

"Sure, Rachel, he's in." She covered the receiver and called out, "Bill, it's Rachel."

"Hi, Rachel," Montgomery said, answering the phone.

Travis looked toward his dad's office.

"Yeah, I think he's here. What time do you need him?"

Travis knew he'd have one last chore before his workday ended.

"Couple of hours? He'll be there." Montgomery hung up and raised his voice a little. "Ruth, is Travis still out there?"

Travis quickly put his finger to his lips.

Ruth looked at him and smiled. "Yes, sir," she said, rearranging her grin into a disapproving look.

"Travis, can you pick up Rachel today?"

"Sure," Travis said.

"She needs you at Gilman's place in two hours."

"Okay. I'll leave in a little while."

"If you leave now, you can watch some of Professor Higson's experiment. He's testing another cotton harvester this afternoon. Sheriff Collins will be out there with some other folks if you want to go."

Travis tossed the magazine on the table next to the couch. "I'll see you tomorrow, Ruth," Travis said. He stepped into his father's doorway. "See you at home, Dad."

"Don't be late for dinner."

Travis pulled off the road in front of the Gilman commissary and saw that Rachel was not outside waiting for him. He looked down the road and saw a half dozen cars and two trucks parked on the shoulder about two hundred yards away. In the field directly in front of the cars was a strange contraption. It could only be one thing— the harvester.

He walked over and recognized Sheriff Collins in the small crowd.

"Afternoon, Sheriff," Travis said, approaching the group.

"Travis," Collins said.

"Hello, Travis," said Wilson.

"Hello, Mr. Wilson," Travis said. "Plan on writing an article for the paper?"

"Not just yet. The professor says it's still experimental. Don't want to get everyone excited for nothing."

"What are you out at Gilman's for?" Collins asked.

"Picking up Rachel," Travis said. "But I'm early, so I thought I'd take a look at the harvester."

"Not much to see," Collins said, removing his cap and wiping his forehead with his sleeve.

They watched as Professor Conrad Higson, perched on the monstrosity, requested tools from his assistants and made the final mechanical adjustments to his harvester.

"When was the last test?" Travis asked.

"It's been a while," Wilson said.

"Couple months at least," Collins said.

"I think he's been up in Oxford conducting some research," said Wilson. "I also heard he was doing a little work with the Agricultural Extension Service in Starkville."

Finally, Higson stood up on the machine and turned to the gathering. "Well, all right, chaps," he began, his peculiar accent and word choices a result of having spent part of his youth in England before his family returned to the coal mines of Germany. "We're going to start it up and see how we do."

Hank Gilman walked over and stood next to Wilson. His arms were folded across his chest. "If Higson doesn't get this thing to work—" Gilman said, shaking his head.

With help from an assistant on the ground, the professor turned the ignition, and the giant machine sputtered to life. It backfired once or twice at first, which caused a few in the crowd to flinch, but it finally settled into a low growl.

Higson pressed on the gas and the engine roared a little louder. He raised a hand with his thumb in the air, then reached for the gearshift. The harvester bucked into motion and started down a path parallel to the rows of cotton.

Travis watched the machine slowly rumble through the field, its massive width stretched across five rows of cotton. The stalks passed underneath the machine, and the cotton bolls were fed between two arms that yanked the bolls from the stalks and tossed them into a hopper attached to the rear of the harvester.

At ten yards, the harvester appeared to be cleaning the stalks fairly well, but at fifteen the crowd heard metal grinding on metal. Before Higson could shut it down, the arms were entangled with one another, twisting and bending in every direction. Finally, the harvester locked up and quit moving forward.

Higson turned off the ignition and stared at his newly spun web of steel. "Well there, I guess that just about does it for today. Wouldn't everyone agree?"

His assistants rushed to the harvester trying to piece together exactly what happened. The crowd let out whistles and murmurs of exasperation as it began to disperse.

"He's never going to get that thing working," Gilman said. "This is the one thing that could change the face of the South, and our friend Higson can't make it work. I'll be paying someone to work my doggone plantation 'til I die. You know how much money I've sunk into this?" Gilman didn't wait for an answer. He waved his hand at the professor in frustration and stomped off.

"He's obviously none too happy," Collins said as he, Wilson, and Travis watched Gilman get in his car and leave.

"Yep," Wilson said. "Seems he wants to get rid of his sharecroppers and day laborers once and for all."

Collins stared down the road at Gilman, pulled out a notepad and pencil, and wrote something down. "They sure are a heap of trouble," he said, nodding. "Of course, we got someone trying to do that for him." He chuckled at his own joke.

"Got to have 'em, though," Travis said. "Else that cotton's staying in the field."

"But not all of them," Collins said. "That contraption will work one day, and then all those pickers won't have any pickin' to do, and they'll head north. Save us all a lot of trouble."

Collins and Wilson each got in their cars and headed back into town. Travis walked back to the commissary and went inside to let Rachel know he had arrived. He was instantly engulfed in the day's-end frenzy, people scurrying in and out with their purchases.

"Excuse us, sir," two young girls said, bumping into Travis on their way out the door.

"Have a good evening," Travis said. They quickened their pace, startled at his civility.

Travis looked around for Rachel but didn't see her. Most of the patrons were Gilman's sharecroppers, most of the help Gilman's family or friends. Rachel got a job because Bill Montgomery and Hank Gilman knew each other from college.

"Hey, Travis," one of the employees shouted from behind a counter.

Travis replied with a nod and a wave.

The store was stocked with a large variety of provisions to ensure that the laborers would not have to go anywhere else to shop. It was also the only store where tenants and sharecroppers were offered credit. Although the prices were high and the 20 percent credit terms usurious, the plantation laborers' options were limited. All debts were settled at the end of the year, when the cotton crop was in.

Travis strolled through the store, looking at shelves of canned foods, bags of sugar and flour, sewing supplies, and some toys. He glanced around for Rachel every so often. Eventually, he made his way behind the wide and deep counter and peeked in the back for her.

Out of the corner of his eye, he saw Raymond Wilkins recording a customer's order. Travis had known Raymond since they were kids, and he had never cared for him. Raymond had grown up in town but decided he liked it better out here for some reason. After high school, he took a job at one plantation and then another. Recently, he had been hired at the Gilman plantation as the store's assistant manager. Raymond was a bully—always had been—and life on the plantation offered him the opportunity to flourish.

Travis eased along behind the counter until he was just a few feet from Raymond, who was still busy ringing up some purchases. The buyer was a widow Travis had met once when Rachel introduced them. She was about seventy years old, and her children worked the land her husband, their father, had worked. Because she didn't produce crops, the widow's balance was always added to her children's account at the end of the year.

Travis peered over Raymond's right shoulder while the clerk noted the widow's purchases in the tenant-transaction ledger. "These cans all together are thirty-four cents," Raymond said, while writing down the amount in the ledger, then picking up another item. "These are twenty-three cents."

Travis watched closely. Raymond recited a price for each item, but for a few, he wrote a different—higher—price in the book.

"Twelve cents," Raymond droned. Travis watched him write twenty-one cents.

"Whoa there, Raymond," Travis said.

Raymond jumped a little, startled.

"You said twelve cents, like on the label, but you reversed the numbers when you wrote it."

Raymond picked up the can and compared its price to the number he had written.

"You wrote twenty-one cents," Travis said. "It should be twelve cents."

"Oh, I guess I did write down the wrong number," Raymond said, putting the can down to erase his last notation.

"And you did it here and here," Travis said, pointing to two more lines in the book.

"Thanks, college boy. Or maybe Aunty should thank you."

The old woman nodded her head in Travis's direction when Raymond looked away.

Travis acknowledged her with a smile. "There's no need to thank me. I'm just trying to help out."

Raymond scowled as he corrected the other numbers and gave the woman her purchases. Travis turned away. He knew Raymond was furious.

At last Rachel emerged from the back of the store.

"Where've you been?" he said. "Let's go."

"Okay, just a minute."

"C'mon, Rache, let's go now!" Then she disappeared again.

Travis walked back outside to the car. A couple of minutes later Rachel came out, carrying a paper sack and accompanied by a young woman. Travis guessed she was almost his age.

"What's in the bag?" Travis asked.

"I'll tell you in the car," Rachel said. "Get in. We're going to give someone a ride home."

"Okay."

They all got in, Rachel in the front, and their guest in the backseat. Travis had pulled onto the highway and was headed back toward town before his sister spoke.

"This is Hannah Morgan," she said. "Sometimes she works at the commissary with me when they need extra help."

"Hello, Hannah," Travis said.

"Hannah," she continued, "this is my brother, Travis."

"How do you do, Travis," Hannah said.

An awkward silence held for a few moments as the setting sun cast a long beam of light into the car. It filled the backseat, dancing around Hannah's face and hair, its brilliance enhancing her beauty. Her skin was flawless, her eyes bright, her features matchless.

"What's in the bag?" Travis asked again.

"Oh, these are some books for Hannah," Rachel said. "She can't get all the good ones she wants down at her library, so I've been checking some out for her. But we don't like to let anyone know what we're doing. You know—"

"What do you like to read, Hannah?" Travis asked.

"Mostly the classics," she said. "Shakespeare, books like that. Some poetry, too."

"Hannah's father is in the insurance business," Rachel said.

"Is his name Richard?"

"Yes, it is," replied Hannah, somewhat puzzled.

"I met him the other day at Mr. Hollingsworth's funeral home. He seems very nice."

"I'm sure he is, but he's still my father. My view is somewhat different."

"You haven't been in Clarksdale long, have you?"

"No. We moved down a few months ago from Philadelphia, to be near my grandmother. My parents were worried about her health, although she's never been sick and doesn't seem to be now. She used to visit us when we lived in Atlanta, and she lived with us up North for a little while. But she wanted to come back home."

Silence fell again. Finally, Hannah broke it. "It's nice living near my grandmother. She's the one who got me interested in books. She taught me to read."

"You came from Philadelphia?" Travis said. "You don't usually hear about people moving to the South from up North. That's the wrong direction for most people in the Delta. Were you in school there?"

"At Cheyney University," Hannah said, still gazing out the window. "I'm helping my grandmother now. I'll go back to school next year, closer to Clarksdale."

Travis entered the city limits. "Where do you live?" he asked, trying to keep his voice calm, though he knew perfectly well what side of Clarksdale Hannah Morgan lived on.

"Do you know where the Brickyard area is?" Hannah asked.

"Yes," Travis said.

"We live on Mississippi Avenue."

To get to Brickyard, Travis first had to drive through Roundyard, a neighborhood immediately south of Brickyard next to the Sunflower River. They looked out the windows at Roundyard's small homes, many adorned with dry flaky paint and drooping roofs.

"Most of these homes are rentals," Travis said. "You'd think the owners on the other side of town would at least throw some paint on them every once in a while."

"Why should they?" Hannah said. "They don't have to live in them."

Once in Brickyard, the houses became larger and better kept, their yards manicured and their paint fresh.

"Do you have indoor plumbing?" Travis asked.

"Absolutely," Hannah said quickly. "It's a newer house, so the plumbing was in when we bought it. But some of those bigger, older homes up there don't." Hannah pointed straight ahead between Travis and Rachel. "Anyway, my parents would never have moved back if we didn't have indoor plumbing."

Travis drove slowly down Mississippi Avenue.

"It's two houses up on the left," Hannah said.

Travis stopped in front of the house. White with brown shutters, it sparkled from a fresh coat of paint, and it stood out as the nicest house on the block.

Hannah got out of the car and walked to the passenger's side window, where Rachel sat.

"Thank you for the ride," Hannah said. "I hope it wasn't too far out of your way."

"Not at all," Rachel said. She passed the bag of books to Hannah through the window.

"And thanks again for the books."

Hannah sauntered in front of the car and up the walk to the front door. Travis's mind was racing. What could he say? "Maybe we can give you a ride again sometime."

"Maybe," Hannah said. She walked up the porch steps, gave a casual wave, and was gone.

Travis stared for a moment before shifting gears. Mechanically, he drove through the neighborhood until the car crossed the railroad tracks. Then he headed for home.

"What was all that about?"

"What do you mean?" Travis said. He hadn't heard a word, only the sound of his sister's most nosy tone.

"You're usually not that forward."

"Oh, I didn't mean to be," Travis said. "She just seemed nice. We have a lot in common."

"Like what?"

"I like the classics as well."

Rachel made a sound of disgust while rolling her eyes. "Okay, I'll remember that at Christmas this year. But you better be careful. You're not the one who would get in trouble. She may not think anything of it since they lived up North, but you know it's different down here."

They made the rest of the short trip home in silence.

CHAPTER 9

And she's tailor-made.

—*Willie Brown*

THE WORKWEEK'S ACTIVITY REVOLVED AROUND farming, commerce, and business, but Saturday afternoons were devoted to recreation. Although some fieldwork was done on those mornings, around noon the streets of Clarksdale began to fill with people prepared to enjoy themselves by partaking of the Delta's few pleasures. Coahoma County residents came to the county seat from all parts of the city and country to shop, visit, and relax for a few hours. By four o'clock, downtown Clarksdale was overflowing. And at no other time was the area's racial disparity more apparent. Two-thirds, even three-quarters, of the people in town were black.

Travis slept in late Saturday morning and did a few chores around the house after he got up. By two o'clock, he was ready to venture downtown and see if anyone he knew might want to go to a movie.

"Bye, Mom," he called as he headed out the door.

"Hold on," his mother said. "I need you to get me a few things."

Margaret handed him a slip of paper on which she had written a list of grocery items in perfect penmanship.

"Is that it?"

"That's it. Have a good time."

Travis made his way to his favorite soda shop along the north end of Issaquena Avenue. On the southern end was the hub of Clarksdale's black business sector: Fourth and Issaquena streets was an intersection where, weekday mornings, day laborers waited for trucks coming from the plantations to pick up workers and, on weekends, folks socialized. Only one other Clarksdale corner was more famous: the intersection of highways 49 and 61, where young Robert Johnson was said to have made a pact with the Devil, trading his immortal soul for temporal virtuosity on the guitar. The Devil took his due when the wandering bluesman was twenty-eight.

Both Fourth and Issaquena were lined with small black-owned shops: a grocery, a cleaning and pressing shop, a soft drink stand, a cobbler's shop, a few eating establishments, a poolroom, and a barbershop. And Clarksdale had one amenity most towns didn't: a black-only movie theater.

Travis passed two police officers standing near a street corner. They acknowledged him with a nod.

"Mr. Crow coming out today?" Travis overheard one mutter to the other. Travis knew he was referring to the famous 1896 "separate but equal" doctrine, so named after a famous white minstrel popularized a song and dance routine in the 1820s that was originally performed by a stableman named Mr. Jim Crow in Louisville.

"He'll be out strolling today, no doubt," the other said.

Travis came to a building with a large sign over the door that read "Saul's Retail." He pushed open the door and walked into the only Jewish-owned store on Second Street. Saul Zlato's Russian accent was undiminished by a quarter-century in the American South. "What brings you to my store? Something for your mama?" he said to Travis.

Just then, however, Saul spied a new customer and politely excused himself. His father, a rabbi, had served as Saul's model for devoting attention to customers. Everyone who ever had a problem—Jews, Catholics, Protestants, and Greek Orthodox alike—came to see Rabbi Zlato for advice. Instead of selling salvation like his father, however, Saul sold an assortment of items from clothes and shoes to housewares and gardening tools. If he didn't have something in stock or if someone wanted a specialized piece of hardware or clothing they'd seen in a catalog, he'd order it for them.

Three customers later, Saul returned while Travis was picking through a barrel of hammers, screwdrivers, and pliers that were marked half off.

"You need some tools? I saw you looking at them. For you, half price."

"They're already half off," Travis said.

Saul let out a booming laugh, then once again looked to the door. This time Travis also turned and watched as Hannah and two of her friends walked into the store.

"Saul, I know them," Travis said. "Can I wait on them?"

"I don't know, they shop with me almost every week. Are you sure you know what to do?"

"I've watched you a few times. I think I can manage."

"What's our motto?"

"I don't care whether they're black or white, I'll take their green."

"Yes, good. Okay, you are ready."

Travis's legs felt wobbly as he walked toward Hannah and her two friends, an anxiety he was usually immune to. He noticed that all of her friends were dressed like Hannah: neatly, in laundered and pressed dresses that were newer than what most of Clarksdale's women wore. They were all members of Clarksdale's black elite, a small group whose members segregated themselves from others of their race through education, chastity or marital fidelity, a patriarchal family structure, and, sometimes, snobbery.

They were huddled near the women's shoes, Hannah's back to Travis. Her friends noticed him approaching but said nothing since they didn't know him.

"Good afternoon, ladies," Travis said. "What can I help you with today?"

Hannah turned. Her quiet confidence mixed with a little surprise, she answered: "I'm fine, Travis. I didn't know you worked here, too?"

Travis grinned a little foolishly. "I don't. I was chatting with Saul when we saw you come in. He said I could wait on you, but not to scare you off since you're such good customers."

Remembering her manners, Hannah said, "Travis, these are some friends of mine, Mary and Delia."

"Good afternoon," Travis said. They each responded with a nicety.

"I see you've already been shopping," Travis said, noting each one's parcels.

"We started early today," Delia said.

"What'd you buy?"

"Just some things to go with our dresses for tonight."

"Special occasion?"

"We're attending an out-of-town party," Mary said.

"That sounds like fun," Travis said. "Where's the party?"

"Memphis," Hannah said. "We're taking the train so we're very excited. But we have to be ready to go by four o'clock sharp."

Travis glanced at his watch. "You don't have much time if you have to change and get down to the station."

"We're heading home right now," Hannah said. "But we wanted to stop by and check on Saul's shoes."

"See anything you like?"

"No, not today. I think we have everything we need."

"But I need to sell you something, or Saul will regret letting me help you."

"Do y'all need anything?" Hannah asked her friends.

They shook their heads.

Hannah shrugged her shoulders as if to say sorry and reached over to a rack and picked out a pair of socks. "I'll take these," she said.

He took them from her and they walked to the counter.

After Hannah paid, Saul placed the socks in a small bag and heartily expressed his thanks for her purchase as though it were a twenty-dollar dress made of the finest silk. To Saul, any amount of green was good.

The girls chorused good-bye in unison as Travis opened the door for them. "It was nice meeting you. Have fun tonight."

Hannah took a few steps and then turned and walked back toward Travis. "There's a picnic next Saturday out at the old Stuart plantation. Why don't you come out and join us?"

"Us?"

"Meet me there around six. Do you know where it is?"

"Before I answer, I want you to remember that it's not the same in Clarksdale as it is in Philadelphia. We have a set of rules."

"I know about those rules."

"Sounds like I'll watch out for the both of us."

"Six?"

"At the Stuart plantation."

Travis was startled by her invitation, but he liked her directness. She certainly wasn't like most of the girls he knew. He wanted to say something else, but Hannah was already four paces down the sidewalk by the time he could think of anything.

Travis turned to say good-bye to Saul.

"Bring your mama next time," Saul said. "I'm getting some nice dresses in next week."

"Okay, I'll tell Dad to bring her. Maybe she'll buy two."

CHAPTER 10

Lord, have mercy on my wicked soul.

—Son House

"I THINK THEY GOT HIM!" EMMETT WILSON CALLED out as he hung up the phone.

"Who?" Lewis Murphree said from his desk, where he was enjoying his morning coffee and reading the day's paper, checking it for errors and omissions.

"The killer," Wilson said, rushing out of his office. "The one they've been looking for. If not, he knows a heck of a lot about the murders."

"Hold on, hold on. What's his name?"

"Luke Williams. Some sharecropper."

"Any more detail than that?"

"Not really. He came in late last night and started talking about the killings. Someone said he pretty much confessed to them all. Said he'd rather be in jail than having to keep killing folks."

"*Having to?* Are you sure that's what he said?"

"That's what I heard. Sounds a little crazy to me. But get down there and see what you can find out. We'll need to run a story by tomorrow at the latest. You can drop everything else you're working on. I'll get Buddy to finish up your other stories."

Lewis hurriedly gathered his notebook, pencils, and a couple of files and stuffed them into his briefcase. He slipped on his jacket, slung his camera over his shoulder, and then set out by foot for the county jail. He assumed Luke would still be there.

The inmates were just starting to stir when Lewis slipped into the jail. He walked to the guard's window and recognized one of the jailers by sight, but not by name.

"Mornin'," Lewis said casually. "I'm Lewis Murphree from the paper."

"Good morning, Mr. Murphree," the guard said. "Isn't it a little early to be visiting the jail?"

"Maybe," Lewis said, the man's name nowhere near his tongue. "Anybody brought in late last night?"

"Let me check the log." The guard took out a large book and scanned it, searching for any new names. "Here's a new one. Came in 'bout midnight."

"What's the name?"

"Ah, let's see," said the guard. "Luke. Luke Williams."

Lewis steadied himself to ask the next question smoothly. "Can I see him?"

The guard looked back in his book. "The note says no visitors. Sheriff Collins hasn't had a chance to talk to him yet. No, can't let you see him."

"Oh, I don't want to talk to him. I just want to look at him."

"Look at him." The guard was puzzled. "What for?"

"Do you know why he's here? What he's in for?"

The guard looked at the logbook again. "No, it don't say."

Lewis decided to play his trump card. "They think he might have killed a bunch of people. You know, the ones in the paper."

Suddenly the guard was interested. "All by hisself? That's a whole lot of killin' for one man."

"Sure is. I want to see the face of a man who killed that many people. That's a lot of hate."

"Well, let me call the sheriff's office and see if we can go peek at him."

"No, no, no," Lewis said hastily. "Let's don't bother the sheriff with this. Let's just go down and see him. You and me."

"I don't know if I can do that. Who's gonna watch the door?"

"We'll only be gone a minute." Lewis could feel the guard's ambivalence. Duty was battling with curiosity. "If someone shows up, we'll tell 'em you went to the toilet. Come on, let's go."

The guard put the book away, walked out of the admitting office, and locked the door behind him. "We've gotta hurry. I'll get in trouble if I'm gone too long."

They walked quickly through a set of double doors, the guard leading the way, then down a set of stairs and into a hallway. The jail was old and dingy, and even so early in the morning it was hot. The thick, dank air, mixed with stale smoke from an endless supply of cigarettes, choked Lewis; he could scarcely breathe in the airless hall. It took him a couple of minutes to get acclimated to the smell.

They walked down the hall, and Lewis looked out of the corner of his eye into several cells. Most men were still asleep, but a few stood in the dim light staring at the guard and Lewis. They didn't make a sound, but Lewis felt their stares.

"He's around the corner," the guard said.

Lewis peeked around the corner, and saw a cell occupied by a motionless man. Luke Williams was awake, sitting on the bed, his knees pulled up to his chest. His eyes were open; he stared straight ahead, cigarette smoke hanging heavy around his head. Luke was pale, like he had never worked a field. He also looked like he hadn't slept—perhaps hadn't even moved from this position—for days.

Lewis stared for a few seconds and tucked his head back around the corner. He looked around the corner a second time. If Luke heard Lewis, he made no sign. "Let's go," Lewis said to the guard.

As they retraced their steps, a voice rose in the half-light of the jail. The raspy chant echoed down the hall, seeming to come from the walls themselves.

Been down this old road before,
Been down this old road before,
Don't want to go there anymore.

Look up and I can see the sky,
Look up and I can see the sky,
Look up 'cause I'm sure I'm gonna die.

Oh Lord, there's things I gotta tell,
Oh Lord, there's things I gotta tell,
Those things they'll send me straight to hell.

When they reached the front door, Lewis thanked the guard for his kind assistance and headed over to the courthouse, which was just beginning to come to life. The hallways were filling up, and people were lingering outside their offices, chatting over their morning coffee.

Lewis spied Sam Tackett outside his office.

"The reason we called you down, Lewis," Tackett started, "was to make sure that what went on this morning gets reported accurately. We don't want to read anything in the newspaper that is conjecture or speculation. We want the facts stated clearly and precisely. We have a lot of people in the county to think about, Lewis. And making sure they clearly understand what has transpired is important."

"You know I always try to report objectively and to research stories thoroughly."

Tackett grinned as he looked Lewis in the eye. "Now, you know," he continued, "that we're holding Luke Williams in the county jail."

"Yeah, I heard that."

"He came in late last night and gave a short statement to the deputy on night shift. The deputy wasn't sure whether he was confessing or just telling what he knew about the murders. But he's willing to give a full statement today and to be questioned about the events and circumstances. This is our first break, and we need to be careful how we ask the questions and what he admits to. We don't want him to walk, because he's the only thing we have except a bunch of dead bodies."

"I'll do the best I can."

"I hope so, for your sake, Lewis, because we can always do this without you."

The interrogation room was hot and lit by a string of lights suspended over a square table that was surrounded haphazardly by several rickety chairs. Four other chairs were pushed against a wall near the door.

Collins was seated at the table by the time Bill Montgomery arrived. The deputy from the night before took a seat near the door, and Dan Mulevsky and Bob Thompson from the FBI, who had rushed up when they heard the news, were also in attendance. The Feds couldn't be accused of meddling if a suspect was already in custody. Lewis sat in the back by the deputy.

They chatted amiably until Luke was escorted into the interrogation room. He was handcuffed, and a deputy led him to a seat in front of the sheriff.

"Take the cuffs off," Collins said, thinking that if they got him relaxed maybe Luke would talk all day.

The deputy removed the handcuffs, placed them on the table, and stood against the wall directly behind Luke's chair.

Luke rubbed his wrists over and over again where the handcuffs had dug into his skin a little too hard.

"Luke, you know why you're here, don't you?" Collins asked.

"Yeah."

"You're our only witness, Luke, and we want to get your full statement today. Do you think that'll be okay?"

"Yeah, that's fine."

"There's no reason to be worried or concerned. We just want to find out what you know."

"Got a smoke?" Luke asked.

Collins drew a cigarette from a pack on the table and handed it to Luke. Montgomery slid some matches across the table.

"Now, you still don't want an attorney, is that right?" Collins said. "You mentioned that last night, remember?"

Luke shrugged his shoulders. "Yeah, I guess so. Maybe later."

"Is that a yes or a no?"

"Ask me again in ten minutes."

Collins didn't think this would take long. They knew most of the details because they had seen the bodies, been to the crime scenes. They needed a confession. Collins started with the basics. "State your name and address, Luke."

"Luke Williams. I live outside of town, northwest, toward Stovall. No address to speak of."

"And your occupation?"

"You know what I do. I'm a sharecropper. I'm what you city folks call a peckerwood. But don't call me that."

"Married?"

"Yeah."

"Kids?"

"Three."

"Ever killed anyone?"

Everyone perked up.

Luke didn't respond.

Collins thought he'd catch him off guard.

Luke continued to puff.

Collins pushed his notepad across the table to Luke. "Read the top line for me, Luke."

"I don't read."

"Anyone in your family read?"

"No. The reverend reads. Maybe if I did read, I wouldn't be farmin'." Luke pushed the notepad back to Collins.

"We want to hear," Collins said, "in your own words, what you know about the murders. Just like you told the deputy last night. Why don't you start with the first one?"

"Ain't much to tell. I know this guy was walking along the side of the road. Maybe he was hitching a ride, maybe not. Somebody asked him if he needed a ride, and he said sure. So he hopped in, and they drove down the road aways. Stopped after a little while, then they got outta the truck. The hitchhiker waited by the truck while the other one was doing something or other."

"Where'd the truck come from?" Montgomery asked.

"Borrowed," Luke said. "From a neighbor, maybe."

"Then what?" Collins continued.

"Then the driver walked up behind him and shot him in the head."

"What'd he do with the body?" Collins asked.

"Dumped him where you found him, behind the gin out near Mills Road."

Collins scribbled some notes while Luke took a drag from his cigarette.

"What about the second one?" Collins said.

"Which one was that?"

"Stabbing."

"Oh, yeah," Luke said. "Another guy looking for a ride, I heard. The driver and him disagreed about something, and they fought pretty hard. The driver left the guy lying on the ground then grabbed a knife from his truck and went back and stabbed him."

Collins looked over at Montgomery in disbelief. "Any witnesses? Someone who drove by maybe?"

"No."

"How many times was the victim stabbed?" Collins asked.

Luke smiled. "Once, that's all it takes."

Collins sat back and pulled out a cigarette for himself. He motioned at Luke for another, and Luke grabbed two.

"And number three?" Montgomery said. "Do you know any-thing about that murder?"

Everyone waited. Luke paused to recall what he had described the night before. His lips moved, but he didn't say a word as he used his fingers, which nimbly held the cigarette, to figure which two he had already discussed and which two he hadn't.

"We got a shooting and a stabbing, Luke," Collins said. "Who was next?"

Luke looked coolly at Collins then finally said, "Drowning."

"What happened?"

"I heard this guy was fishing and a black fella came up and started talking to him and carrying on. He was loud and wouldn't stop talkin'. Just kept yammerin' 'bout nothing. The sky, the weather. I guess the guy got fed up and shut him up for good."

"Where'd he drown?" Collins asked.

"In the Sunflower."

"Why?" Montgomery asked.

Luke waited a while, slowly inhaling and blowing smoke into the air.

"Why the Sunflower?" Luke repeated.

"Yeah," Montgomery said.

"I guess 'cause the Mississippi was too far away," Luke said. "You guys ask some funny questions."

Collins glanced around the room. Everyone was waiting on him, but they had all heard what they needed to about the murders. He needed a confession, not a summary.

"And the last victim, Luke."

"Somebody beat and burned him. Just that simple."

"Do you know why he had dirt in his mouth?" Montgomery asked.

"To keep him quiet," Luke said, his voice louder than before. "Man don't scream so loud with a mouth full of dirt."

Collins got up and stretched, then paced around the room. Luke had spoken in the third person the entire time. He hadn't confessed to anything yet, just admitted knowing some of the facts. Was it enough to get the indictments? Maybe, if Tackett could convince the grand jury that only the murderer or an accomplice would know these details. But a confession would seal it. "Why do you think these men were killed?"

"Could be to get some respect," Luke said. "Could be them Negroes thought they were better than other folks. Better than white folks, better than you and me. But that just ain't so. I'd say we're all the same, but that ain't true neither. They're dead. No way they can mouth off again. Gotta watch yourself in Clarksdale, especially if you ain't from here. No tellin' what can happen to a man that disrespects."

"Did they disrespect you, Luke?" Collins said.

"Maybe. Can I get another cigarette?"

Collins passed him the whole pack. "What else do you know?"

Luke stared down the length of his cigarette. "I know that killing a man doesn't make anything any better. It doesn't take away the pain or make your life any easier. And I know that sometimes it's bad luck to be where you are. Like those poor bastards."

"Did you think it would?"

"Would what?"

"Take away any pain."

"I don't know," Luke said, staring off in the distance, smoke swirling around near the light just over his head.

"Do you know who killed these men?" Collins said.

Luke let the cigarette hang from his lips while he ran his hands across the table.

"Let's everyone take a break," Collins said. "Why don't you think about things, and we'll come back in ten minutes or so. Then we can talk some more."

Collins and Montgomery stepped out, followed by everyone except the deputy, who stood behind Luke's right shoulder about four feet away from him.

Luke hummed an old gospel tune that had popped into his head and puffed on his cigarette without removing it from his mouth. He drew figure eights on the table oblivious to his surroundings until he felt the cold steel of a gun barrel behind his ear.

"Now, peckerwood, you listen up," the deputy said quietly into Luke's ear. "You're wasting everybody's damn time, and I'm getting a little tired of it. I've been waiting thirty minutes for you to confess, and all we got is a bunch of stories. You better tell the sheriff what he wants to hear, or I'm gonna do a little killing myself." The deputy pressed the barrel harder against Luke's head. "I'm just going to ask you this one time before they get back. And then you're going to repeat it for them."

"What do you want to know?" Luke said out of the corner of his mouth.

The deputy stepped forward to Luke's right side so he could look him in the eyes. "Did you kill all those people or not?" he said.

"Weren't you listening?"

The deputy pulled the hammer back and the click reverberated off the walls in the empty room.

"You sure you want to do this?" Luke said.

At that instant, the door started to open, signaling the others' return. The deputy glanced up, inattentive for just a moment, and with a single move, Luke swept the revolver to the ground. The gun discharged and everyone turned away at the sound, not knowing where the bullet would lodge.

Then Luke grabbed the handcuffs and kicked over the table, putting it between him and the door. He was not a big man, but he had lean strength from years of fighting mules in cotton fields. As the deputy drew back a punch, Luke drove the handcuff's sharp edge into the deputy's head near his eye. Blood instantly gushed from the jagged gouge, and the deputy shouted in pain. He fell to his knees.

Luke grabbed the deputy's baton and reared back, but before he could strike the downed man again, Thompson tackled him and both men tumbled to the floor. Luke was quickly on his feet, standing back over the deputy raining one— two— three blows on him.

Another gunshot and the baton flew from Luke's hand, bouncing several times before coming to rest on the concrete floor. He grimaced but never cried out. The shooter, Dan Mulevsky, stared down the barrel at Luke. Peace quickly settled over the room as the smell of gunpowder filled the empty space.

Luke held his arm and watched the rivulets of blood start to trickle down his forearm. Thompson pushed him to one knee and kept his hand on his shoulder.

Collins helped the deputy to his feet and immediately applied a handkerchief to his reddened eye.

Montgomery checked the deputy's wound. "You'll be okay," Montgomery said. "Let the hospital know we're coming," he yelled toward the hallway, where a crowd was already gathering. Montgomery stepped over to Luke and inspected his arm. "Let's get something on it and head to the hospital."

Thompson relayed a roll of gauze from someone in the hallway to Montgomery, who wrapped Luke's wound several times and tied it off. Once Luke was bandaged, Collins placed handcuffs on him.

"You going for number five?" Collins asked as he locked the cuffs around Luke's wrist.

"Another minute, and he'd been dead," Luke said. "That's all I needed. Couple more good blows to the head."

"Should we throw in an attempted murder charge?"

"Do what you want," Luke said.

Collins held Luke's arm and started toward the door. Passing the deputy who had put the gun to his head, Luke spat at his feet. "Yeah, I killed 'em. But I wish it was you."

"Killed who?" Collins asked.

"While you were out of the room, I asked him if he really killed all those people," the deputy said.

"Looks like we got a confession," Collins said.

Across the street by a large oak, two men watched Luke being led from the jail to an awaiting car.

"What do you think, Ned?" the taller one said, a matchstick between his lips.

"I don't know," Ned said, "but what I do know is Luke's no criminal."

"Not at all," came the reply.

"And if the law can't figure that out, then maybe they're going to need a little help."

Ned's partner looked over at him satisfied. "I been waiting for something like this. It's about time we took back this town. When do you think?"

"Soon," Ned said. "Soon." Ned started to walk away, but stopped and turned. "Come on, Bo, let's head out."

Bo watched as the car Luke was in neared. Just as it passed he made eye contact with Luke and winked. "Don't worry. It won't be long."

By the morning of the next day, Tackett was amused at the stories sweeping the town. A number of people had heard on good authority that he and the deputy had been killed, even though he wasn't there. That explained the strange looks he got on the way to work. What wasn't gossip or exaggeration was that Luke Williams, sharecropper and killer, was Coahoma County's most infamous resident. It was Tackett's job to ensure that justice prevailed—even if that meant jailing a white man for something that wasn't often considered a crime in Mississippi.

Tackett removed two books from the case behind his desk. He skimmed the pages looking through old cases and murder convictions. With a confession, all that remained was to figure out a possible sentence that he could recommend to the judge. Then he could put all this behind him.

Elma Williams placed a dirty pan in the sink and then went to answer the door for the fourth time this morning.

"Hello, Elma, how are you today?" a faintly familiar voice asked.

"Anita?" Elma said. "Anita Thornton?" Although the woman attended the same church that Luke and Elma did, she lived several miles away. Elma had met her only once.

"That's right," the woman said brightly. "And I know we haven't spoken much lately, but I heard about your predicament, and I wanted to bring you a few things. Is that all right?"

"Of course, that would certainly be appreciated."

Anita turned back to the truck parked in front of the house. "Boys, bring in those boxes," she called.

Two thin, tousled-haired boys emerged from the truck, unloaded one box each, and carried them onto Elma's porch. Then they went back and got two more. All four were filled with food and clothing.

Elma stared down at the boxes. "Anita, this is just so much," she said, shaking her head. "I can't take all this from you. What'll you have left for yourself and your kids?"

"Don't you worry about that. I've still got a man at home. He'll provide for us. Has anyone else been by?"

"Oh gosh, yes. More than I can count."

"Well, people know how it is when something happens to your husband. Either he gets killed or runs off. Or runs off and then gets killed." She laughed and touched Elma's arm. "And while Luke isn't dead or gone very far, you're still without a husband. What about the preacher?"

"Yes, he's come by a coupla times."

"I know he keeps part of the collection every week for times like these, so don't feel bad about accepting what he offers you."

"And he said a prayer with the family."

"Prayers are what you and Luke need right now. The reverend's right: if you say your prayers, everything will work out just fine."

"I'm sure you're right."

"Well, I better be going," Anita said as she patted Elma's shoulder. "Hank'll be coming in from the fields soon, and he'll wonder where I am."

"Anita," Elma said, dazed, "thank you again for being so generous. I don't know how I'll repay you."

"Don't have to." Anita smiled. "That's what neighbors are for."

As Elma watched Anita drive off, her children started rummaging through the boxes, which contained an assortment of canned food, clothes, and some candy.

This generosity, along with help around the farm, even a little spending money—it was all so much. She had never seen such abundance. She loved her husband, still did, and she didn't want to feel better without him. But she couldn't help it.

A few days later, one of the guards stopped by Luke's cell.

"Hey, Luke," he said.

"What is it now?"

"Your preacher came by. Told me to give you a message."

"You mean my wife's preacher."

"I guess."

"What'd he say?"

"He said you shouldn't worry about Mrs. Williams. The neighbors were helping her quite a bit with food and clothes and all."

"What about my crops?"

"Your neighbors got that taken care of, too. Shoot, they're not even going to miss you." The guard walked away grinning.

Luke lay back on his bed. He felt better about what he had done. Everything would be okay.

CHAPTER 11

Down in the levee.

—Lucille Bogan

TRAVIS WOKE UP EARLY ON SATURDAY AND BUSIED himself around the house for most of the morning. He helped his dad in the yard and pulled weeds from his mother's vegetable garden.

By five o'clock, though, Travis was antsy. He wanted to get going, but he didn't want to arrive at Hannah's picnic too early and appear overly eager—especially since he wasn't sure who would be attending the event. Just her friends, or Hannah's parents too? What he did know was that he couldn't wait to see her again.

Travis dressed nicely, though not in a suit, and combed his hair neatly. His father had agreed two days earlier to let Travis borrow the family car. At exactly 5:50, Travis announced that he would be leaving for the evening.

Opening the screen door, Rachel called with elaborate indifference, "Where are you going?"

"Out," Travis said.

"Who are you going with?"

"Maybe Petey and Max," he said, mentioning two of his friends whom Rachel knew but not well enough to contact.

"And when are you coming home?"

"Good-bye, Mama," Travis called out, past his sister, as he was closing the door.

Travis took the long way out to the old Stuart plantation. Most of its acreage had long since been broken into smaller plots of land and sold off to whomever could afford them. Now, the old Stuart house was surrounded by only about a hundred acres, and shabby homes dotted the surrounding landscape. Bad management and greedy family members had reduced a sizable fortune and business to a run-down house with a scrawny patch of cotton in its formerly lush front yard.

Travis drove around the plantation for awhile searching for the gathering. Eventually, he stopped to ask for directions.

"Excuse me," he said to a man tending a garden in front of a little house.

The man turned and looked at Travis.

"I'm looking for the Morgan family gathering," Travis said.

"Oh, that's probably at the old Stuart church," the man said.

"Where is that?"

"You're almost there. Just keep going that way until you get to a crossing. Turn left and go about half a mile. There will be a little dirt road on your right. You can barely see it, just two ruts for your tires on a little path. Go down that path 'til you see the levee."

"The levee?"

"Don't worry, it's the old one. Hasn't been used for twenty years. The church is right next to it."

Travis thanked the man and followed his directions. Before long, he pulled up to the front of the church, where two other cars, a truck, and several buggies were parked in the sparse shade. The horses had been unhitched and were tied to posts at the side of the church.

Travis stepped out of the car and looked uncertainly toward the group gathered under a cluster of trees about fifty yards from the church. Nobody had seen him pull in, but when he emerged from his car several people turned and stared. His first fear was that Hannah had neglected to ask her father if it was all right for him to attend; his second was that she hadn't arrived yet. Both of these fears tempted him to get back in the car.

Of the thirty or forty people at the gathering, half of them were under the age of ten. He heard one of the adults shout out, "Do that over there, not around the tables," as a group of squealing, laughing children chased each other.

Just as he stepped away from his car toward the picnic he saw Hannah wave and motion him forward. Travis breathed a sigh of relief. He picked up his pace, and she met him halfway.

"Hi, Travis, I'm glad you could make it," she said, lightly touching his arm, the sweetness of her voice and the softness of her smile immediately putting Travis at ease.

"You forgot to tell me about the church," he said, his tone somewhere between teasing and accusing. "Was that intentional?"

"Did I? Oh, well, I knew you'd find it all right."

They walked toward the crowd. "Does your family know I was invited to the picnic?" Travis asked.

"Of course. My father hesitated at first, but then he remembered you from Mr. Hollingsworth's. You remember my father, don't you?"

"Yes, but it was a very short visit."

"He remembered you."

Travis wasn't sure what that meant.

"And there wasn't a problem with—"

"You being white? No. Remember, we lived in Philadelphia for a while. Some things are different north of the Mason-Dixon."

"I still feel a little out of place."

"Feeling black, are you?"

Travis had to laugh.

Hannah's father stepped forward as they approached. "Hello, Travis," he said. "Nice to see you again. We're all glad that you could join us for supper."

Travis took up the man's formal demeanor. "Thank you for having me, Mr. Morgan. I certainly appreciate the invitation."

"Hannah, why don't you get Travis a drink?" her father said.

"What would you like, Travis?" Hannah asked.

"Tea's fine."

Hannah walked off, and Morgan turned to Travis. "I heard someone confessed to the murders?"

"A man named Luke Williams," Travis answered. "I don't know much about him except that he's a sharecropper."

"Well, that'll make George feel better," Morgan said. "Now he won't have to have any of those meetings we were talking about. I know he wasn't looking forward to them."

Hannah reappeared quickly with a glass filled almost to the top. "Here's your tea," she said, handing it to Travis.

"Thank you." Travis quickly took a sip.

"Dad?" Hannah said. Her father turned to her. "Let me guess. You're asking him what his future plans are? Especially since his father's the county coroner."

"Not yet, but I was about to." He shot a grin at Travis.

"He always does this," she said to Travis. "Don't feel singled out."

"Does that mean you bring a lot of men around?" Travis asked.

Mr. Morgan laughed out loud.

"I think I'll introduce him to a few more people," Hannah said, guiding Travis toward the shady area where adults sat in conversation.

"Good-bye, Mr. Morgan," Travis said.

Mr. Morgan smiled and nodded. Hannah and Travis slowly circulated, visiting along the perimeter of the group, talking about the weather, school, and the harvest. One by one Travis met the other members of Hannah's family. Her mother was nice, he thought, but very formal and not very talkative. Casually, but repeatedly, Hannah assured everyone that she had invited him to the party, and her father had approved.

They had spoken to nearly everyone when Hannah said, "Travis, there's one more person I'd like you to meet."

"Only one more? You promise?"

Hannah escorted him to an elderly woman seated in a rocking chair by one of the tables. She smiled as Hannah approached. Hannah reached down and took the woman's hand gently.

"Travis, this is my favorite grandmother," Hannah said. "The other Mrs. Morgan."

Travis leaned down and extended his hand. She raised her hand slightly, but it trembled. He leaned forward until his hand met hers. "Very nice to meet you, Mrs. Morgan," he said.

"Hannah, you didn't tell me you were bringing someone to the party," she said.

"Well, Gami, I wasn't sure if he would come or not," Hannah said, looking at Travis.

"Why wouldn't he come?" Gami asked.

"Yeah, why wouldn't I come?"

Hannah smiled at them both. "Some people just aren't brought up right. They say one thing and do another."

"Travis," Mrs. Morgan asked, "what do you do?"

"I work down at the courthouse, ma'am. For my father, Bill Montgomery, the county coroner. I do odd jobs, deliver courthouse documents, things like that."

"Yes, I know Mr. Montgomery. Is that boring?"

"Gami," Hannah said, rolling her eyes.

"That's all right," Travis said. "You're right, it is a little boring, but it's something to do, and it puts a little money in my pocket."

"In my day we didn't have any time to dawdle. We had to keep working, at a good job if we could get it. Keep moving forward. Whether we were in school, working professionally, or helping out in the field, there was never any spare time. We just never knew how much time we had left. Had to make the best of it. Of course, if ever we did take a break, sit down and rest, somebody would call us lazy. If we behaved like you youngsters do today, well, I don't know what they'd have done to us. I know my daddy would have made sure we didn't think about it very long."

"Gami, he's our guest," Hannah said.

"No, Hannah, that's all right," Travis said. "She's right. I could be doing more."

"I wasn't being too hard on you, was I, Travis?" Gami said. "It's all young people. Not just you."

"No, ma'am. You're right. You were being just hard enough."

"I'm trying to impart a little wisdom to you children. I hate to see you waste your time. Most times, young folks don't always listen to their parents, but they sometimes listen to other adults. I was the same way in my day."

"Gami used to live on the Stuart farm a long time ago," Hannah said. "And still comes to church here sometimes."

Travis turned and looked over his shoulder.

"What happened to the levee?" Travis asked, turning back to face them.

"Years ago," Gami said, "the river decided she wanted to flow in a different direction. There was no stopping her."

"Didn't they think about tearing it down?" Travis asked.

"No, the preacher at the time thought that it might provide some shade at the end of the day since it's on the west side of the church," Gami explained. "He always worked it into his sermons. He used to say it was a constant reminder of man's futile attempts to alter God's will."

"Gami, Travis and I are going to mingle."

"Very nice to meet you, ma'am," Travis said, bowing slightly.

"Y'all walk around. But don't miss the dinner bell."

Hannah bent over and kissed her grandmother on the cheek. "We'll talk to you later, Gami."

A few steps away, Hannah looked up at Travis. "Gami always speaks her mind," she said. It was the first hint Travis had seen of anything but confident self-possession.

"Don't worry about it," he said. "She was right. I'm very fortunate to be able to sit around and ponder my choices. Sometimes having too many choices isn't necessarily a good thing."

"Supper's ready!" someone said.

One by one, the adults who had been visiting while the children played came to the main table. Without any prompting, each person reached out and took the hand of those to their left and right. Travis found himself between Hannah and her mother. The circle was now joined.

"Let us pray for God's blessing," Mr. Morgan said. His deep voice seemed to draw the circle together. "Lord, we thank you for seeing to our daily needs and watching over us. Let us live in peace with ourselves and our neighbors. Allow us to bring forgiveness into our lives and help us live the Lord's message with hope, faith, and love. For these and all our prayers, we beseech you, oh Lord. Amen."

Everyone echoed the "Amen" and released hands.

Travis looked at the food crowding every inch of the table. Sliced pork, fried chicken, yams, peas, black-eyed peas, corn, berries, mixed fruits, sauces, pies and cakes, and a dozen other choices

Travis hardly recognized. Some of the fruits and vegetables had once been canned but now were mouthwatering dishes. Everything was displayed in festive dishware, and the table was covered with decorative cloths.

"Come on," Hannah said, "let's eat."

They both took plates and joined the line at the food table. Travis gradually filled his plate, eventually realizing that his food was piled embarrassingly high. He didn't want to offend anyone by putting anything back or not sampling something, so he covered his plate with a napkin and followed Hannah to one of the children's tables.

"Hannah," her father called, "why don't you sit over here with the grown-ups?"

"We're fine over here," Hannah said good-naturedly.

While Hannah and Travis ate, the children entertained them with games and stories, and Travis made sure he was an enthusiastic participant. Hannah laughed as Travis invariably guessed the wrong answer or chose the incorrect hand. Before long, they were laughing uncontrollably, the children screaming with delight.

"Everything's all right," Hannah said, when one of the adults asked who was making so much noise. "We'll try to keep it down," she added, laughing between bites.

When they had finished, Hannah helped to clear the table, then returned to Travis. "You want to take a walk?" Hannah asked.

"Sure," said Travis. "It might help my digestion, because I definitely ate my share."

"Don't miss the fireworks," her father called after them as they strolled away.

"Fireworks?" Travis asked.

"You'll see," Hannah said.

They walked toward the church and circled around it, past an old graveyard that lay at the foot of the levee.

"So, do you have a lot of boyfriends?" Travis asked.

"Not really," she said. "My father doesn't care for boys. He tells me, when I'm old enough, I can date men. He thinks boys don't have much sense."

"I'm sure he's right."

"Is that so? Well, I'm not sure you or my father can tell the difference."

"Between boys and men?"

"That's right."

"Men are just boys with bad eyesight. And we're taller."

"Besides, I had some trouble when we first moved back. Now I think most potential suitors are afraid to ask me out."

Travis noticed that her tone had changed. He bent down and looked at a headstone that was well away from the cemetery near the church. "What happened?"

"I only know part of the story, so you'll have to ask my father about the details. But I doubt he'll admit to anything."

"Sounds bad."

"I guess you could say that." Hannah sighed. "I went to a party, and the hostess had invited all sorts of different people. Some of the boys were in school, and there were a few professionals, but somehow the word got out and some, should I say 'country boys'— uneducated, the rougher types—showed up. But we didn't know that until we got there."

"So there was an occupational mix of people at the party, not a racial mix?"

"Right, and I'm not against that, but there was a lot of liquor, and some of the guys were drinking quite a bit. Well, we were dancing and carrying on, and I lost track of time. I looked at my watch; it was quarter to eleven, and my curfew is eleven o'clock. I started asking around for a ride back into town. I had come with a girlfriend, but her fiancé was at the party and she wanted to stay longer."

"You didn't have much time to get home."

"No. And the last time I was late, my father kept me confined to the house for a month." Hannah sighed again. "This young man offered me a ride, and I asked him if he had been drinking. He said no, and because the music was loud, the room crowded and smoky, I couldn't tell any different. When we got in the car, all I could smell was cigarettes and liquor, but I figured he could drive, and I knew I had to get home.

"Let's go this way," she said, interrupting her story to steer Travis back toward the church. "We were about a quarter mile from my house when he pulled over. I said: 'What are you doing? I live a few more blocks away.' He started trying to kiss me, and I pushed him away. I told him I had to go home, but he wouldn't listen. I was trying to get out of the car when he grabbed my dress and ripped it off one of my shoulders. But I was able to push him away and get out. I ran the rest of the way home, and he drove off. I came into the house winded, crying a little, and trying to hold my dress up so my father wouldn't see that it was torn."

"But he was already waiting for you?"

"Yeah, and when he saw what had happened to my dress, he went a little crazy. I'd never seen him that mad. It scared me to death."

"Then what?"

Hannah hesitated. "I'm not sure what happened because I went to bed. I do know Daddy made a few phone calls and left the house about midnight. The next time I saw him was in the morning, when he came to breakfast."

"Well?"

"I spoke to a few people later on. The man who assaulted me had gone back to the party, and Daddy was able to track him down. On the way there, Daddy had picked up a couple of men from the local pool hall. When they got to the party, they dragged the guy out. They threw him into the trunk of the car and took him to some old shed a few miles away. I heard they held him down and Daddy took a hammer to his legs."

"How bad was he hurt?"

"Someone told me they saw him in another town on crutches."

"Maybe I should leave now, while I can still walk."

"You asked. Why don't we head back to the levee?"

Hannah talked about her upbringing and her future. She hadn't decided yet what she wanted to do, but her father insisted she enter one of the primary professions—nursing or teaching. He had high aspirations for all of his children.

They talked about the books that Hannah enjoyed reading, and Travis said he'd get some for her if she liked. He had never talked about books and other serious matters with a girl before, and he couldn't match Hannah's extensive literary background.

They started up the levee, and Travis noticed that several people from the picnic were already sitting at the top. "Where are we going?" he said.

"To the top."

Just then, Mr. Morgan shouted, "We're starting soon, Hannah. You two get a seat."

Travis followed along, still surprised to be included. Hannah pulled a blanket from a pile at the top of the levee and spread it out on the ground. She sat down and motioned for Travis to do the same. He sat down next to her.

Hannah suddenly asked, "Did I hear that someone confessed to all those murders? Have you heard anything?"

Travis was startled by her question. "Yeah, someone did. My dad said it was some sharecropper from up in the northwest part of the county."

"What did he say?"

"Confessed to all the murders. But he went crazy during the questioning. Beat up a deputy before they could get him under control."

"People do strange things. I'm surprised every time I read the paper."

"We'll just have to wait and see. Nobody really knows anything for sure yet."

"Oh, I almost forgot to ask you," Hannah said, turning to look closely at him. "There's a party in two weeks. Would you like to go?"

"Another one? Sure."

"It may be a little wild."

Travis nodded. "Okay with me. But not wild like your other party? My legs don't need any adjustments. I like the way they work right now."

"Well, that all depends on you." Hannah smiled at him.

Travis looked around but still couldn't figure out what to expect. He leaned over to Hannah and said, "What are we doing at the top of the levee?"

"Just watch."

A truck that had been parked by the church pulled up at the bottom of the levee. The driver got out and unloaded a small barrel, some burlap sacks, and some baling wire. Then he reparked the truck by the church.

"What are they doing?" Travis said.

"Ssshhhhh," Hannah said.

Six men whom Travis recognized from the picnic gathered around the barrel. Each one took a sack and carefully cut the burlap, rolling it into a tight ball. Next they took the wire and, working in pairs, wound the wire around the burlap and tightened it with pliers. Then the balls were dropped in the barrel, which seemed to contain some kind of liquid. Just as they finished rolling the sixth and final ball, the last vestiges of sunlight winked and disappeared. It was pitch dark now. No moon, no lights of any kind.

The picnickers' voices slowly lowered to whispers and then drifted away altogether. "Is everyone ready?" a voice shouted from down below.

"Yeah!" everyone yelled, especially the children.

Travis saw the single, small flame of a match, then the area below the levee erupted in an explosion of light and fire as each man took a burlap ball from the barrel and ignited it. When the last one was lit, the whole area was ablaze.

The children screamed with delight when the balls were lit, their excitement rising by the second. The men formed a ring and tossed the balls between them, throwing them higher each time.

"How do they do that?" Travis asked in astonishment.

"The burlap was soaked in kerosene."

"No, how can they hold onto them?"

"They're farmers. Their hands are so callused they can't feel the heat, and they don't hold the balls long enough to burn themselves. A couple of them are probably wearing gloves. These are homemade fireworks."

The flaming balls flew in arcs through the night sky, like falling stars racing in the heavens. The sight was breathtaking.

Travis turned and looked at Hannah. Her face was beaming with delight. The light of the blazing spheres and their fiery tails flickered and danced in her eyes. Only she was more beautiful.

Travis grabbed her hand. "Thanks for inviting me."

Hannah smiled and squeezed Travis's hand in return, never taking her eyes off the spectacle.

In his subterranean laboratory, at close to three in the morning, Conrad Higson spread the broken and disparate pieces of various metals onto a cloth that covered the entire surface of his desk. He picked up the first one and held it in both hands. The curved blade, thirty inches long, was one of a dozen that had made up the mechanism of his nonfunctioning harvester that chopped off the top of the cotton stalk. The blade was made from a material being tested extensively at the University of Illinois. It had several military applications, including tank treads, ship decking, and, possibly, helmets. Higson meticulously examined each piece of metal, scribbled down a number of calculations, and handwrote a comprehensive analysis in his scientific journal. His notes included detailed formulas for estimating the strength-to-weight ratio, shear strength, and ductility, among other material properties; likewise, he included potential causes of failure and comparisons to other materials.

His analysis continued past daybreak and into midmorning. When he was finally done, he placed his journal, drawings, and a short letter in a box, which he then sealed and addressed to his contact in Washington, who would make sure it was delivered to the right Nazi official in Germany.

Higson was very pleased with himself for conceiving the idea of using the mechanized cotton harvester as a research tool for Germany's war effort. He hoped the reinstatement committee would also think it was clever.

It was nearly noon when the professor climbed out of his laboratory, placed the box on the kitchen table, and collapsed on his bed, where he slept for ten uninterrupted hours.

CHAPTER 12

Got me accused for murder.

—Roosevelt Sykes

JUDGE LONG RETURNED TO HIS CHAMBERS FROM THE county courtroom and removed his robe, hanging it carefully in a small cabinet. He opened a desk drawer and removed a bottle of bourbon and a glass. He filled the glass one-third full, capped the bottle, and placed it back in the drawer. He took a sip, and sat back in his chair. It had been another hard day on the bench.

He gazed out the window, daydreaming. Breaking his reverie, his secretary poked her head in the office. "Judge, Mr. Tackett is here to see you."

"Did he have an appointment?"

"Yes, sir. He's here at your request."

"Oh, that's right," the judge said without taking his eyes off the scene outside his office window. "Send him in, please."

"Come in, Sam," Judge Long said after hearing him knock gently on the door.

"Good afternoon, Judge," Tackett said.

The judge stood up to greet him. "How are you doing?"

"Fine, sir."

"I heard about the scuffle," the judge said, while shaking hands. "How's the deputy?"

"He's recovering. Nasty little gash, but he'll be all right."

"Have a seat," the judge said. He motioned toward a high-backed leather chair to his left.

"Thank you, sir."

"Would you like a drink?" He held up his glass.

"No, thank you, Judge."

The judge sat behind a large mahogany desk that seemed to stretch almost the entire width of the room. It was sparsely decorated with a lamp, an ashtray, three pictures, and several stacks of papers.

"Why don't you give me a few details," the judge said. "What went on down there the other day during Luke Williams's statement?"

"Sheriff Collins and Bill Montgomery were taking his confession, and he got a little agitated. They got things under control pretty quickly. I wasn't actually in the room when it started."

"Agitated? It was a little more than that, wasn't it?"

"Yes, sir."

"He ever ask for an attorney?"

"Collins said he didn't want one."

"But he could have provided him with one or at least some help. All I know is I've had several calls from folks wanting to know if Luke had some legal assistance. And a slew of others who said we're not sentencing a white man for what he's done without a trial. In fact, Congressman Morley called to make sure we're having a trial and that he gets fair representation. I assured him we were. Some folks even think Luke may have been justified." The judge took a sip of his drink.

"We wouldn't normally provide any legal counsel to—"

"It doesn't matter, Sam. I've taken enough calls already. We're not going to argue about this. Everyone in the county who's aware of this thinks he should have had some representation. And that's good enough for me."

There was another knock at the door. "Sir, Charlie Usher has arrived," the judge's secretary announced.

The judge motioned for her to send him in.

Charlie Usher entered and the three men exchanged handshakes and greetings. Charlie sat down in a chair across from Tackett.

"Drink, Charlie?" the judge asked, pouring a little more bourbon into his own glass.

"No, thank you, Judge," Charlie said.

"You still wearing those old dark suits, Charlie," the judge said, "and keeping that hair short?"

"It's hot out, Judge. These suits may be thin from too many cleanings, but they're cool."

"I'm glad you're here," the judge said. "We were just about to get to you." The judge sat up in his chair and picked up a pencil. "Here's what I'm going to do. I'm appointing Charlie as Luke's attorney for the trial."

"Luke Williams?" asked Charlie.

"That's right," the judge said.

"But Judge—" Tackett said.

"I don't have time to debate this. We're not sentencing a white man for killing a black in this town without a trial, confession or no confession. Not now and not while I'm taking calls from congressmen. Got it?"

"Judge, one question about the trial," Tackett said. "Will the confession be admissible?"

"I don't know yet. We'll have a pretrial hearing to discuss it."

Charlie protested. "I've never defended in a murder trial, Judge. I have very little experience in this area."

"Did you go to law school?" the judge asked.

Charlie nodded.

"Then you'll do fine. A trial's a trial."

Tackett and Charlie both grimaced.

"Charlie, you understand what I need from you?" the judge said, finishing his bourbon.

"I think so."

"Well, in case you don't, let me explain it clearly. I need you to defend this man and see if you can get an acquittal. That should be easy enough, right? A lot of people will be watching this trial, so you need to represent Luke adequately." Judge Long slid a file across his desk. "Read this; it'll tell you what you need to know for now."

Charlie picked up the file and jotted down notes.

"Sam," Judge Long continued, "prepare the paperwork. I want the grand jury convened tomorrow morning at eight and the indictments issued. We'll arraign at one in the afternoon." He stood to leave. "Now, gentlemen, I'm going home. I'll see you tomorrow."

"Judge," Charlie said, packing up his papers and preparing to leave. "Which indictment will we try first?"

"Sam, got any preference?" the judge asked.

"How about all together?" Tackett said.

Charlie laughed. "Never."

"Pick one," the judge said. "And let us know soon."

All three men exited the courthouse. The judge said his good-byes and left them on the front lawn.

"You better talk to your client tonight," Tackett said. "Tell him what to expect, and why we're having a trial."

"*I'm* not even sure what to expect."

At precisely 7:05 p.m., the jailer rattled his keys against the bars that kept Luke Williams from the rest of the world.

"Wake up in there," he said.

"I'm awake," Luke answered from the darkness. His voice was scratchy and hoarse.

"You've got a visitor," the jailer said.

"Who's that?"

"You'll see."

The cell door swung open, and Charlie Usher stepped from behind the jailer and entered the cell. He held a chair, which he placed in front of Luke's bed.

"Do you need me to stay?" the jailer asked, closing the cell door but not locking it.

"No," Charlie said.

"I'll check back in a few minutes."

"I'll need about thirty."

Charlie had checked the cells on either side of Luke's, and they were empty. If they spoke softly their voices wouldn't travel far. Charlie wanted to meet where Luke was most comfortable. It would keep him calm. "'Evening, Luke," Charlie said.

"Who are you?" He sat up and hung his legs over the side of the bed.

"I'm Charlie Usher, your lawyer." Charlie held out his hand. "Appointed by Judge Long to represent you."

Luke reluctantly shook it. "What do I need a lawyer for?"

"Like I said, I'm going to defend you at trial. Did you think you were gonna defend yourself?"

Luke looked at him suspiciously. He pulled a cigarette from a small pack, scratched a match on the bed frame, and drew deeply. "But I already told them everything."

"Yeah, I know, but you need a lawyer anyway. Speaking of what you told them, did you ask for a lawyer when they were taking your statement? When you were telling them about the murders?"

"Kind of. I knew they wouldn't get me one. I told them to ask me later, but later never came."

Charlie angled his legal pad to catch the small amount of light coming from the hallway. "Well, someone thought you were serious, so here I am."

"How do I get rid of you?"

"You can ask the judge to appoint you a new one, but I don't think he will. You're better off just sticking with me for now."

As he wrote, Charlie could feel Luke's stare through the smoky haze. He knew he was Luke's only option for legal representation—with or without Luke's approval. "Tomorrow we go to court, and you'll be formally charged with the murders. Then we'll enter a plea of not guilty."

"How can I do that? I already said I did it."

Charlie shifted in his chair. "That's okay. We can still plead not guilty. We're going to ask that the confession be ruled inadmissible. I think we've got cause. Did you know the FBI is involved?"

"No. Am I famous?"

"A little."

"They were there during your statement. Saw what went on. In fact, one of them shot you."

Luke held up his arm.

"And of course the victims themselves. They're drawing some attention."

"'Cause they're black."

"Yeah. Lot of people don't think a white man should go to jail for something like that."

"What do you think?"

"Doesn't matter what I think. My job is to defend you against the charges. So, are we going to plead not guilty?"

"What if I don't?"

"Well, it works like this. If you plead guilty to the murders tomorrow at the arraignment, there is no trial. The only thing a judge will do, a few days to a week after the arraignment, is to convene a jury, which will determine your sentence. Could be a prison term or the death penalty. But if you plead not guilty, then we'll go to trial to determine whether you're guilty or innocent. If you're guilty, again, you could get a prison term at Parchman Farm or the death penalty. But they find you innocent, you go free."

Charlie watched Luke think about his choices. He leaned over and grabbed one of Luke's cigarettes. "I'll bring you some more."

The cell remained silent.

"Honestly," Charlie said. "I don't think a jury from this county will impose the death penalty for these crimes. A judge might, if he could, but not a jury. If you plead not guilty, we'll get a fresh start."

"What about the confession?" Luke said.

"Like I said, we'll have it thrown out. I think it was taken under less than ideal circumstances. Look at your arm for God's sake." Charlie pointed to Luke's arm. "Is that the way the Coahoma County sheriff usually conducts his interrogations?"

"Do you think the judge will throw it out?"

"We'll see." Charlie watched Luke carefully in the dim light.

"The jury wouldn't give me the death penalty?"

"That's a reasonable assumption," Charlie said. "Coahoma County juries look favorably on their own. But that's only if you're convicted. You could go free."

"I wasn't really thinking about dying," Luke said, staring into the darkness, a confused look on his face.

Luke lay back on his bed. Charlie knew this certainly wasn't what Luke had in mind when he went into the sheriff's office that night and confessed. But Luke couldn't turn back now. He couldn't walk out of that jail and do whatever he'd been doing before he'd confessed.

Charlie heard the jailer approaching the cell and stood up. "I'll be back in the morning to discuss your decision. We meet with the judge right after lunch."

Luke didn't say a word as Charlie carried the chair into the hallway and closed the cell door.

At a quarter to one, spectators started gathering outside the courthouse, avoiding the courtroom until the last possible minute. After a big noonday meal, no one would be able to keep their eyes open sitting still in the steamy room.

Sam Tackett entered the courtroom, walked to the prosecution's table, and unpacked some papers and a pen. He sat alone.

A few minutes later, Charlie Usher strolled in and took his place across the aisle from Sam.

The rows were now filling quickly with spectators, including Travis, who had postponed one of his errands so he could watch the arraignment. Finally, Luke Williams was escorted in by two bailiffs and seated next to Charlie.

Sam knew Charlie had told Elma Williams not to attend. The trip was too far, and the arraignment wouldn't last but a few minutes. She said she planned on seeing Luke in a few days anyway.

Sam looked around. If it was this crowded for the arraignment, what would it be like during the trial? He glanced at the balcony. Nobody was there yet, but they would be. Everybody wanted to see if a white man would go to jail for killing a black man—*four black men*. And the altercation during Luke's questioning had only increased people's curiosity.

Judge Bertram Long entered the courtroom.

"All rise for the Honorable Judge Long," the bailiff rumbled. "The court is now in session."

The judge motioned for everyone to be seated.

He shuffled some papers and said, "The court would like to recognize for the record Mr. Sam Tackett, District Attorney of Coahoma County. He will represent the state in this matter. And Mr. Charlie Usher will represent the defendant. Are there any questions?"

Both Tackett and Usher nodded after being recognized. There were no questions.

The judge continued. "Mr. Williams, do you understand what we are doing today? The grand jury met previously and issued four indictments. This is your arraignment. Has your attorney explained what an arraignment is?"

"Yeah," Luke said.

"Mr. Usher, have you conferred with your client?"

"Yes, your honor."

"Well, will you please inform him that 'Yeah' will not be tolerated in my courtroom? He may say, 'Yes, your honor' or 'No, your honor' or 'I don't know, your honor,' but 'Yeah' won't do. Do you understand, Mr. Usher?"

"Yes, your honor."

"And do you understand, Mr. Williams?"

"Yes," Luke said. "Your honor."

"This arraignment has been convened to hear the indictments against Mr. Luke Williams, resident of Coahoma County, Mississippi. Mr. Williams is the defendant in the matter of the State of Mississippi versus Mr. Luke Williams. Are there any questions so far?"

Tackett and Usher shook their heads.

"If the defendant and his attorney will please rise, the district attorney will read the indictments and the defendant will answer with a 'Guilty' or a 'Not Guilty.' Is that clear?"

"Yes, your honor," Usher said.

Tackett, Luke, and Usher all stood.

"Sam, please read the first indictment," Judge Long said.

"Indictment number one, to the charge of murder of John Doe Number One. How do you plead?"

Luke looked at Usher and then Tackett.

Tackett stared back but had no idea what Luke would do. He wasn't easy to read.

"How do you plead, Mr. Williams?" the judge asked.

"Not guilty," Luke said. "Your honor."

Tackett could hear the slight hum of muffled voices in the court-room. He knew what they were saying. He continued to read the second, third, and fourth indictments. All murder charges, all the victims unknown. Luke answered to each, "Not guilty, your honor."

When the last one was read, the crowd noise rose. Judge Long tapped his gavel several times, casting a severe gaze around the hot room. The crowd quieted down.

"We've heard the pleas. Now counselors, I'm going to set the trial date. How does three weeks from today sound?"

"That's fine, your honor," Tackett said.

Usher concurred.

"We'll have a pretrial conference to discuss the admissibility of the confession. Will the prosecution's case be ready?"

Sam laughed to himself. He was ready right now. He had no other witnesses besides the defendant, and Charlie would never allow Luke to take the stand unless it was absolutely necessary for a self-defense argument; it was too easy for Luke to get misled or confused. And there was still the matter of the confession. If he could use it, this would go quickly. If not, he needed evidence, witnesses, weapons, something. "Yes, your honor," Tackett said.

"Mr. Usher, will you be ready?"

"Yes, your honor," Usher said.

"This concludes the proceedings," Judge Long said. "Court adjourned."

Judge Long stood up and walked back to his office and his bourbon. The bailiff came over to the defense table, took Luke by the arm, and walked him to the door.

Bob Thompson, an agent with the FBI who had been seated behind Tackett in the public seating area, leaned over the railing. "What's going on, Sam? I thought he confessed?"

"Yeah, but the judge wanted a trial. Says he's being pressured to conduct one. What's worse is I think he may throw out the confession because of what happened at the interrogation."

"A little unusual, don't you think?"

"Well, this case is already a little unusual."

"Let us know if anything develops in the meantime. We'll be back for the trial in a few weeks."

"See you then," Sam said.

Travis turned and watched Luke as he was escorted out of the courtroom. Who was this man? Did anyone recognize in this weathered sharecropper a vicious killer? What demons resided in the darkness of his soul? The severity of his alleged crimes made him appear much larger than his physical presence.

Travis turned to leave only after Luke had been escorted from the courtroom.

He walked out onto the steps of the courthouse and passed by two men he didn't recognize.

"Not another day," one man said.

"Then let's meet tonight at the cabin," the other said.

"See you tonight, Ned."

Travis walked past, thinking little of the interaction.

CHAPTER 13

Reap jus' what you sow.

—*Tommy Johnson*

THREE MILES OUTSIDE CLARKSDALE, IN A ONE-ROOM cabin deep in the woods, four white men—two sharecroppers, a handyman, and an unemployed gas station attendant—sat staring into a small flame that flickered in the fireplace. They themselves were embers, the hot remains of the Klan's fiery cross that had burned bright not so long ago. Now they were scattered and disorganized, their lofty intentions mutated by boundless hatred. But they found solace in small groups who met quietly and secretly, plotting their resurrection and the demise of local troublemakers.

Ned, the handyman, looked around the group and assessed the others. He wondered what they were capable of—individually and as a group.

"Well, what we gonna do?" asked Wyatt, the attendant, before swallowing a swig of homemade whiskey and then passing the bottle.

"What *can* we do? Luke turned himself in," Edgar, one of the croppers, moaned. "He's stuck."

"I don't care if he confessed," Wyatt said. "What he's done ain't a crime in Mississippi. They're gonna try to put him in jail for doing right. For what needed to be done."

"He's already in jail," Ned said. "What they're gonna do is try and keep him there. And we got to see 'bout that."

"You're right, Ned," said Edgar. "Luke ain't staying in jail. His family needs him."

"He's under a lot of pressure with his harvest and those kids," Ned said. "I'll bet if he was out of jail for just a little while, he'd be able to get things straightened out at home. Then, after the harvest, he can get right with the law."

Bo, the other sharecropper nodded his accord. "His crop'll rot in the fields if he don't get out of there."

All four men sat motionless, sipping the whiskey. Ned watched while the shadows from the fire danced on the cabin walls. The liquor had warmed his insides; his body seemed to be melting into the hot Mississippi night. His head felt loose on his shoulders, and he knew the liquor would bolster his friends' courage.

"Why don't we just march into that damn jail and tell 'em to let him out?" said Wyatt.

"I don't think that's such a good idea," Ned said. "Sheriff ain't gonna let him out just 'cause we ask." He watched them grow attentive. "Is there anything else we could do?"

They sat, seemingly stumped.

"I wonder what he was thinkin', turnin' hisself in like that," Edgar said.

"I bet he already decided that was a big mistake," Wyatt said with a grin.

"All right, I got an idea," Ned said. "Maybe we don't ask for his release, maybe we just take him." He knew he was lighting a powder keg among these hard-luck white boys.

They sipped more whiskey while Ned carefully laid out the details of the plan. "Edgar, I want you to drive," he said. "You're going to stay with the car while we're inside."

"I can't come in?" Edgar asked.

"No. Someone's got to be outside making sure we can get away fast. And letting us know if anyone's coming."

"What should I do?" Edgar asked.

"Honk, peckerwood," Ned said. "Just honk."

"What about me?" Wyatt asked. "What am I gonna do?"

Ned paused. "Wyatt, I want you inside watching the guards. I don't know what those fellows will do when they see what we're up to, but you're going to have to make sure they don't get any funny ideas."

"Will I have a gun?"

"Yeah. But I don't want you shooting up the place." Ned jabbed his finger into Wyatt's chest. "Just handcuff the guards. There ought to be two of them. After that, I don't think you'll have any trouble. Just don't shoot anybody, for chrissakes. We're there to do one thing."

"What if somebody shoots me first?"

"Then you'll be dead, won't you?" Ned said.

"I guess so," Wyatt said, looking slightly dejected.

"No shootin'," Ned repeated. "Bo."

Bo perked up noticeably.

"You and I get the keys from the guards after they're cuffed, find Luke, and get him out of there. Now, it'll be late and most everyone will be sleeping, so we can't make much noise." Ned looked at each man. "Does everyone understand what he's going to do?"

They all nodded their heads.

"Good. We walk in, get Luke, and get out in less than five minutes."

"Without Luke, they'll have to close the case," Bo said. "People will forget about those dead coons in a hurry."

"What about Luke?" Wyatt asked. "What are we going to do with him?"

"We'll see," Ned said. "Maybe he and Elma can take the kids to Arkansas. Nobody'll chase him there."

"Do we have to wear our hoods?" Wyatt said. "You remember old Clem, don't you? Riding along on that fine horse. Lord, that was a good horse."

"What happened to him, again?" Edgar said.

"His hood got twisted on his head, and when he went to fix it, his rifle went off. Killed that horse, just that one shot. Killed while he was a'ridin' it. He broke down and cried right there. A damn good horse."

"We've got to wear them," Ned said. "Don't want anyone recognizing us. Now don't ask again, or you're not going. And if anybody shoots the car, you answer to me."

Ned stared out the window into the Mississippi night, the moonshine washing over him. His men were full of notions of bravery and saving the white race. They had been on a few night rides, scared a few people after dark, but they had never done anything like this. He hoped they were ready.

"When do we go?" Bo asked.

"Patience, Bo," Ned said. "Patience."

CHAPTER 14

Preacher . . . meddle with every sister he meets.

—Henry Brown

TWO DAYS AFTER THE ARRAIGNMENT, ELMA'S minister, Reverend Coulter, gave her a ride into town. She had not seen Luke since the night he got out of bed and disappeared into the darkness. "I've got to do something," Luke had said.

"What can't wait 'til morning?" she had asked, her voice raspy with sleep. He had never answered. She stayed up and waited for him, an hour or more, before she fell back asleep. When she awoke the next morning, he was still gone. The pastor had arrived soon after and given her the bad news.

Now, she would have her first chance to ask what had happened that night. And to tell him that she loved him and the children missed him.

But the pastor thought otherwise. "Don't ask him about the confession or what he did," the pastor said. "He needs to talk about other things. Like the family and what's going on at home."

"I'll try," Elma said.

The pastor stopped in front of the county jail. "I'll be back in an hour or so. Be strong. He needs you."

"I know." The compassion her neighbors had shown her and her children had built a reservoir of strength that she would try and share with Luke.

Elma adjusted her hat, pushed down the wrinkles on her blue dress, and went inside. She signed in and was led into a small room partitioned into four sections that provided some privacy. There was a table with two chairs in each section. She sat down in the section farthest away from the door and waited.

A few minutes later, Luke—wearing handcuffs and leg irons—was led into the room, shuffling and rattling. The guard helped him into his chair across from Elma, removed the handcuffs, and walked to the door.

"I'll be right outside," he said. "If there's a problem, just holler." He closed the door behind him.

Luke and Elma stared at each other for a moment. He looked a little pale, but rested. Relaxed. He also needed a shave and his clothes were terribly wrinkled.

"Hello, Elma, I've missed you," Luke said. "More than I thought I would."

"Oh, Luke," Elma said.

"You look nice. I haven't seen you with a hat on in a while. Is that a new dress?"

"I didn't buy it. Someone loaned it to me."

"Blue always did look good on you."

She smiled.

"How are things back home?" He leaned forward and put his elbows on his knees. "How are the kids?"

"Everybody's doing fine. The kids send their love, and they want you to come home soon." Thinking about her kids without a father made her sad. She forced herself to remember her minister's suggestion to be strong for Luke.

"Do they know where I am?"

"Not yet. I told them you came to town to work on a job."

"What did they say about the crops?"

"Nothing really. I told them we'd get it done. With some help."

"Are folks helping you?"

"More than you can imagine." Elma barely knew where to start. "The reverend collected some church money for things that aren't donated. And we got some new beds, so no one's on the floor anymore. Then the neighbors have been giving us so much food we've had to start giving some of it back, or it'll spoil. I'm keeping all the canned foods, though."

She could see Luke's excitement over her new life in his face. She knew he longed to share in it. But she also knew that for it to exist at all required his absence.

"Sounds like things are going just fine. I'm glad."

"They are for now." She paused. "What happened?"

She didn't know whether he had an answer or not. "I don't know, Elma. I guess I just got tired of things the way they were. Tired of seeing the kids and you with nothing. Tired of spending every single day out in that dry, dirty cotton patch. Tired of letting you down. All that makes a lot of hate in a man."

"But it ain't your fault. It's nobody's fault."

Luke lit a cigarette. "Everybody gets through in different ways. I just got through my own way."

"Did you do it, Luke?" Her eyes started to fill with tears. "Did you do all that killing?"

Luke put his forehead in his hands. "I did what I had to."

Elma wiped her tears with a handkerchief. Be strong, she thought. She cleared her throat. "Well, they're saying there's a chance you might go free anyway."

"I don't know. I just don't know." He looked back up at her. "But I got a lawyer, and he's gonna do what he can."

"I want to come to the trial."

"Are you sure you want to sit through all that?"

"I'm sure."

"What will you tell the kids?"

"That I've got to do something in town. Or that I've got to run an errand. I'll get someone to keep an eye on them."

Luke sat back in his chair. "I'm sorry, Elma. I didn't mean to hurt you and the kids."

"I know," she said, putting the handkerchief back in her purse. "Luke, I've got to go. Reverend Coulter is waiting for me. When can I visit again?"

She watched him think it over.

"Next week? Unless it's too hard on you. The traveling."

It was the answer she wanted. "I'll be here next week."

"Good."

She felt her lip start to quiver again. She couldn't stop thinking about what her husband had been accused of. The father of her children. How could it be?

He reached out and grabbed her hand. "I'm sorry."

Looking at the floor so Luke couldn't see her eyes, she nodded her head gently. "I've got to go. Love you." Elma walked over to the door and knocked lightly. The guard opened it and Elma glanced back at Luke. He seemed so alone.

On the ride home, Elma was quiet. She looked at her bone-thin arms and hands. She felt worn and battered, and she wasn't even thirty years old. Too many stillborn babies, too many hungry mouths to feed in a house that had nothing. At least she was better off than her own mother, who died at thirty-two during the delivery of her ninth child. Yet now she was the wife of an accused murderer. She still couldn't believe it, even though she had seen her husband in jail—*in chains*.

"Where are we going?" she said, suddenly realizing they were driving down an unfamiliar road.

"A shortcut," the reverend replied.

Coulter continued on for a few minutes longer, turning left then right down out-of-the-way roads, before finally stopping at the dead end of a narrow path. The reverend turned the engine off and shifted around to face Elma.

"Elma, I want to speak with you about Luke," he said.

She was silent.

"We don't know what's going to happen," the reverend continued, "but from the looks of things it may not be good."

"But some folks are saying he may go free," Elma said. "There's still a chance things may work out."

"Maybe, but don't be too hopeful." He moved his arm so it lay across the seat behind her. "You've got to start thinking of life without Luke."

"Not just yet, I hope."

"You're still a young woman. You can have a full life without him." His hand brushed her cheek.

"But, Reverend, I'm—"

In one quick, startling motion, he shifted next to her.

She fumbled for the handle, but he grabbed her hand tightly and pulled it toward him. "Reverend, my kids are waiting for me."

"You're alone now, Elma. You need help. Let me help you."

He shoved her awkwardly onto her right arm, roughly pulling her legs onto the seat, and pinning her while he fumbled underneath her skirt.

She thought mentioning Luke might stop him. "What about Luke?"

But Coulter didn't stop. "Let me help you," he kept repeating, but Elma wasn't listening.

She lay there, his weight crushing her into the seat and taking the very breath from her body. She thought of Luke, hating him for leaving her alone. She closed her eyes and tried not to feel.

After a while the pastor moved aside and then started the engine again. When the car stopped in front of Elma's house, Coulter removed an envelope from his coat pocket.

"Here's something for next week," he said.

She looked at the envelope and back up at him. One of the kids came out on the porch and waved. He was wearing a new shirt.

Elma's hand trembled. She took the envelope.

"Take care, now, Elma," the reverend said.

She gathered her things and stepped out of the car.

"I'll check in with you in a few days. Or let me know when you need a ride back into town. Anything you need, let me or Helen know, all right?"

The kid on the porch came running toward the car. "Mom, mom. Look what I got! Look what I got!"

CHAPTER 15

I'll give you your last chance.

—*Gus Cannon*

GENERAL HERMAN SCHNOR WAS SEATED IN GENERAL Erwin Mauer's office in the Leopold Palace, which housed the Third Reich's propaganda machine. Each general had his own copy of the contents of Conrad Higson's most recent package. Included were the drawings he had sent, accompanied by synopses of the meetings he had attended, including details about who had been present and what topics had been discussed. New information immediately applicable to the war effort was underlined in red.

"Higson did an exceptional job this time, don't you think?" Mauer said.

"Yes, General, he did," Schnor answered his boss. "He always does excellent work." Reaching into his pocket, Schnor extracted a single sheet of paper. "I've also brought the letter that arrived at the same time his package did."

Mauer put on his glasses and slowly read the typewritten letter. Halfway through, he started shaking his head. When he was finished, he placed the letter on his desk and sighed. "Does Higson really want to return? He's been doing such a good job there."

"He's a very stubborn man, General. Moreover, I believe he may be turning into a security risk."

"Why?"

"He's been there so long. Two years, altogether, between his time in New York and now in Mississippi. The longer he stays, the greater the likelihood he makes a mistake. We've seen it before. If he's allowed to remain in the United States, I think he will eventually be caught. At that point, the American authorities will probably unravel our network. Diplomats will be compromised, in addition to our carrier routes. We might not get any more useful documents or information out of the country for quite a while. And we need those to keep moving forward."

"Yes, you're right. We've been lucky up to now. What do you have in mind, Schnor? He's your responsibility."

"Well, I think we must bring Higson home. Better to lose him than the entire network. What about his reinstatement?"

"It's not yet decided." Mauer picked up a file from his desk. "Where is he from again?"

"Born in 1885 in England, but he came to Essen when he was ten."

"And his background? Rich? Poor? What did his father do?"

"His father, German by birth, was an alcoholic coal miner. Worked on and off. Six children in all. Higson was the second youngest. From what I understand, he, along with his mother, was the target of his father's animosity, and the son became quite protective of her."

"It's a pity children must grow up like that. At what point did he enter the university?"

"I believe the mining company put him to work first. It was evident early on that Higson had extraordinary potential. A great intellect. The company eventually sent him to Hamburg University. He worked on some military projects, graduated, and then taught in Berlin."

"And why was he expelled?"

"He was classified as a political undesirable."

Mauer tossed the file on the desk and crossed his hands on his lap. "How so? Wasn't he a member of the Nazi Party?"

"Well, yes. But during a review by the Military Projects and Funding Committee, Higson got into an argument with General Kopf and belittled him publicly. When the expulsion list was being compiled, Kopf made sure that Higson's name was on it. He wanted him executed but settled for expulsion. Higson and some others were taken close to the French border and they walked the last ten miles into France."

"Sherry?" Mauer said, picking up a crystal decanter sitting on a credenza behind his desk.

"No, thank you, sir."

"How did Higson get to the United States?"

"Are you familiar with the Emergency Committee in Aid of Displaced German Scholars?"

Mauer poured himself a small glass, toasted Schnor, and took a sip. "Not that particular one, but I've heard of similar organizations."

"They contacted Higson once he was in France, and he entered the program. He already spoke perfect English, so it was easy to place him. He immigrated to New York, and then contacted the German embassy in Washington about passing classified documents. And he's been very clever while in the United States even though he's not located near any of the distinguished universities. He's using an agricultural machine, a harvester, to test materials and designs."

"But he's a security risk if he stays, especially if he should decide to turn. And he has no family, no sponsors here, except you. Is he worth all this trouble?"

"I think so."

"What do you suggest?"

"That we should arrange for his extraction from the United States and his transportation back to Germany."

"Is he still needed here?"

"What do you mean?"

"I mean, is he still valuable to the scientific community?" Mauer swallowed the last of his drink and placed the glass back on his desk. "Can he still contribute? Or has he done all he can?"

"We just agreed that he's done an excellent job in the United States."

"Yes, but gathering information in the United States and working on military projects here are two different activities. And don't forget, he's a political undesirable. Banished once already. I can tell you now that no one on the committee will want him working around matters of military importance. He's spied once already, he may do it again—possibly for the other side. It's in his nature now."

"I doubt that, sir," Schnor said hastily. "But it seems you've already decided his fate."

"I just know what the committee will say." Mauer walked to a window and gazed down on the square. "Make plans to reinstate him. Contact him and let him know. But I suspect the committee will want him in a concentration camp—*if* they allow him to return."

"Why a concentration camp?"

"I told you, too much risk," answered Mauer as he returned to his desk and sat down. "But don't worry about the camp. That's only if Higson returns."

CHAPTER 16

Hell going to be your brand-new home.

—King Solomon Hill

EDGAR PULLED THE CAR UP TO NED'S HOUSE AT 2:00 a.m. Ned and the others were waiting.

Ned leaned in at the driver's side window. "Got everything?"

"Yeah, I got it." Edgar said.

"Hoods?"

"Yeah."

"Your revolver?"

"Yeah."

"Full tank of gas?"

"Pretty near."

"Whiskey?"

"A pint, not much."

"Okay then, let's go."

Edgar got out of the car and opened the trunk. Ned, Bo, and Wyatt loaded their rifles, revolvers, and shells in silence.

The drive from Ned's to town took half an hour. Along the way, Ned went over what they were going to do one more time. They passed the small bottle of whiskey around while they rode.

The streets were dark and quiet as Edgar pulled into Clarksdale. Ned directed him to park near the jail, in an inconspicuous spot. Edgar found some stacked crates that obscured the car from view.

The four men stepped quietly from the car and gathered near the trunk. Edgar popped the lid and each man removed his weapon, checking once more to make sure the guns were loaded. "Keep your hoods with you until you need them," Ned said.

He turned to Edgar. "Wait in the car, not outside. If anything goes wrong, start the car and get ready to go. We'll meet you back here. Understand?"

"Yeah," Edgar said. He got back into the car, puffed on a cigarette, and watched the others walk away.

Ned was in front, Wyatt behind him, and Bo was last, with ten feet between each man. They hugged the rear wall of the courthouse, and as they turned the corner, they noticed a light streaming out from under a side door. Ned looked back and motioned them forward as if to indicate not to worry about the light. As Bo was about to pass the door, the light went out, the door swung open, and someone stepped into the night.

Startled, reacting out of pure fear, Bo dropped his weapon and plunged his fist into the person's head. The person fell to the ground, moaning.

Ned and Wyatt, who had moved ahead toward the jail, heard the commotion and looked back. Bo stood over his conquest not knowing exactly what to do next.

"Stupid peckerwood," Ned said as he grabbed Wyatt by the shirtsleeve and retraced their steps. "What the hell are you doing? Get him up."

Bo lifted the man to his feet and leaned him against the wall. The man slowly came to and grunted in pain.

"Who are you?" Ned said.

"Moses Hooperman," the man said.

"What are you doing in there?"

"I clean the courthouse at night."

"Put your hoods on now," Ned said to Wyatt and Bo. "This is all we need. And we're not even at the jail yet." Ned stepped closer to Moses and put his gun to Moses's head. "You want to do this easy or hard?"

Moses didn't reply.

Ned, Wyatt, and Bo were now hooded. Only their beady eyes looked out from their white masks. Ned grabbed Moses by the shirt.

"You didn't see any of us, did you?" Ned said.

"No, suh," Moses said.

"Anyone else in the building?"

"No, suh."

"If there is, you're a dead man. Let's go."

Bo grabbed Moses by the arm, and they half-walked, half-ran to the jail.

Ned opened the door to the jailhouse and was confronted by one of the guards, who was standing in the middle of the room, shotgun in hand, pretending he was shooting at something in the sky. "Drop it," Ned said.

The guard stood stunned, staring at Ned and the others. "Hey, Billy, it's the Klan," he shouted to a second guard.

"Oh yeah, what are they doing here?" Billy said.

Ned pushed Moses out in front of him and the others. "Drop it," he repeated.

The guard raised his shotgun and pointed it at Moses. "Ya know, I'm not sure he's gonna stop anyone from shooting you," the guard said, motioning toward Moses with his gun.

They all just stared at each other for a few moments.

"Okay," the guard said. "I'm not gonna stop y'all. We're supposed to be on the same side, ya know." The guard laid his shotgun on the floor.

"Back behind the counter with your friend there," Ned said. "Hurry up."

"Why is the Klan messing with us?" Billy said. "You're in the wrong place."

Ned didn't respond. He gestured to Wyatt to handcuff the two guards.

"What are you doing that for?" said the guard who had relinquished the shotgun.

"Shut up," Ned said. "Where are the keys to the cells?"

"I found 'em," Bo said, lifting them off the wall. "What do we do with him?" He pushed his weapon into Moses's back.

"Bring him," Ned said. "Where's Luke Williams's cell?"

"You know, coming in here and pointing your guns at us is one thing, but breaking someone out of jail is another," Billy said. "We could lose our jobs."

Ned looked at them indifferently.

"He's down the first row about midway," replied the first guard.

"Let's go find Luke," Ned said.

The men walked through the doors to the hallway that led to the cells. The hallway was dark, and they could hear snoring coming from a few of the prisoners. They peered into each cell looking for Luke.

"Luke, you in there?" Ned said. "Luke, where you at?"

There were no responses. They were almost to the end of the hallway when Ned guessed they had passed him. So he turned the group around and started back, opening each cell to check if the occupant was Luke.

"You want me to lock the cells back up?" Wyatt said.

"No. Let 'em all go," Ned said. "It'll cover our getaway."

At the fourth cell, the body in the bed moaned, "What do you want?"

Ned stopped and looked back at the bed, "Luke, that you?"

"Yeah, I'm sleepin'. Come back later."

"We need to get going. We're gettin' you out."

"Getting me *what?*"

Luke turned to face the cell door. He stared at Moses and the three hooded men. "What are you doing? And who are you?"

"We're the Klan," Bo said, pride evident in his voice. "You're gettin' released today."

"I can see you're the Klan, but—"

"Listen, we can talk about this later," Ned said. "Right now, we've got to get outta here."

Some of the other prisoners whose cells had been opened were poking their heads in Luke's cell to see what the commotion was about. "Good-bye, Luke," one said.

"I don't think I want to go," Luke said.

"What are you talkin' about?" Ned said. "Don't you want to get out and see your family?"

"My wife visits. And they'll really put me away if I make a break for it."

"Listen, we don't have time for this, Luke," Ned said. "We know what you did, but we don't think it was wrong. You shouldn't be in jail. Let's go."

"I 'preciate it boys, but I don't want to get in any more trouble than I'm in now. I'm goin' back to sleep. Y'all find your way out."

"Luke, we've got to go before we all end up in jail. Come on, there's a car waiting for us outside." Ned reached down and tried to lift Luke to his feet. "I said get up."

Luke shoved his arm away. "Go on," he said. He lay back down in bed.

"Bo," Ned said.

It was all that was needed. Several inches taller and fifty pounds heavier than Luke, Bo jerked the prisoner out of bed. Luke swung and missed. Bo smashed the butt of his rifle into Luke's jaw, and Luke crumpled to the floor.

"Get him up," Ned said.

Bo picked Luke up, slung him over one shoulder, and walked out of the cell.

"He was comin' one way or the other," Ned said. "No white man's going to jail for killing a bunch of cotton pickers. Speakin' of killing, what are we gonna do with *you?*" Ned looked at Moses. "Take him, leave him, or kill him, fellas?"

"Leave him," Wyatt said. "We don't want to have to drag him around."

"One more time, did you see our faces?" Ned said.

"No, suh," said Moses.

"Put him in," Ned said.

Wyatt pushed Moses into the cell, closed the door, and locked it. He lay down on Luke's bed.

"They'll find you soon enough," Ned said. "Have a good nap."

Ned and the others walked down the hall with their new prisoner. When they reached the entrance area of the jail, they found the guards still handcuffed together, back to back. They hadn't even tried to move.

"Find what you were looking for?" Billy said, unable to see them leave because he was sitting below the level of the sign-in counter.

"Yeah, and we left you a present," Ned said. He opened the front door to the jail and ushered everyone out.

"Thanks."

Ned closed the door quietly behind them, but it immediately opened again as several prisoners whose cells had been unlocked scampered out of the jail and into the darkness.

Edgar had the engine running when they turned the corner. The car doors and trunk were already open.

Luke was groggy, but stirring.

Ned pointed to the trunk. No telling what Luke would do when he woke up.

Bo put him in and closed the trunk.

"What happened?" Edgar asked.

"We'll tell ya on the way," Ned said. "Let's go."

Edgar hit the gas, and they sped off, taking the same route out of town they had used coming in. Clouds of dust billowed behind the car.

Ned looked out the window and watched the darkness roll by. Breaking Luke out hadn't gone exactly like he planned. Now here Luke was, locked in the trunk, and Ned wasn't sure what he would do when they let him out. Things hadn't gone well at all, but at least they got Luke out.

Ned recounted the events for Edgar on the drive. "Bo punched the janitor, who was armed with a mop, or was it a broom?"

They all howled.

"Do we have any more whiskey?" Wyatt asked.

"All out," Edgar said, having drunk the last of it himself while waiting.

Edgar pulled up to the cabin and shut off the car. It was still dark outside, but the moon produced enough light so they wouldn't need the group's only flashlight, which happened to be in the trunk. They all got out and stood quietly behind the car.

"Hey," came a voice from inside the trunk. "Open this thing up."

"Okay, Luke," Ned said. "But you've gotta behave. How's your jaw?"

"Sore."

"Is it broke?" Bo asked.

"I don't think so. Just sore."

"Sorry about that, Luke," Bo said.

"Okay, just let me out."

Ned motioned to Edgar, who opened the trunk and stepped back. Luke scrambled out, stood up, and dusted himself off. He rubbed his jaw and looked at Ned.

"What exactly is going on?" Luke said.

"I told you," Ned said. "We busted you out. No sense sittin' in jail if you didn't commit a crime."

"I think murder's a crime."

"Not when it's darkies."

Luke studied each man. They stood there, proud and defiant in their accomplishment. Luke could see Ned was the leader of a bunch of men just like himself: down on their luck, if they'd ever had any at all.

Luke turned toward the cabin. "You got anything to eat in there?"

Wyatt smiled. "You want something to eat? I'll get it for you." He hopped into the driver's seat. "Ain't much in the cabin, but I'll find something somewhere. I'll be back soon."

Ned said, "We needed some food anyway. You can stay as long as you want, Luke. Nobody'll find you here."

"What about my family?"

"You want me to get them?"

"No, not yet. Let me settle in first. Anyway, I think we better stay away from my family for a while. That's the first place they'll start looking for me."

"Yeah, you're probably right," Ned said. "Let's go inside. We got some extra clothes you can change into."

"How long do you reckon I should stay here?"

"We'll work on that later," Ned said as he walked toward the cabin.

Luke took that to mean Ned really had no idea what to do next. That was fine with Luke; he did.

CHAPTER 17

Bad luck done fell on me.

—*Lizzie Miles*

EARLY THE NEXT MORNING, THE FIRST PERSON through the door of the jail was Sheriff Collins. What he saw was Billy and the other guard, handcuffed to each other, sleeping on the floor.

Collins slammed his hand down on the counter. Startled, the two subordinates sat up, still half asleep. "What the heck are you two doing handcuffed to each other?"

"Somebody broke in last night, Sheriff," Billy said. "They were dressed like Klansmen, and they had guns and everything. I thought they might shoot us."

"The Klan broke in?" Collins said. "Who breaks *into* jail?"

"They were askin' about Luke Williams. Oh, and the other thing they said was that they left us a present."

Collins walked behind the counter. "Where's the key to the cuffs?"

"There's an extra one in that cup on the desk," Billy said.

The sheriff walked to the desk and called Sam Tackett. "Sam, we got a little problem down here," he said before recounting the scene, which looked more ridiculous than criminal. Collins was still chuckling when he hung up the telephone and retrieved the key to the handcuffs.

"You said they left you a present?"

"Yes, sir," the other guard answered, "that's what they said."

"Let's go see."

The sheriff and the guards walked back to Luke's cell, shutting the doors that had been left open on their way. Only three inmates were left, and they were found in a single cell, playing cards. Collins decided to leave them alone for the time being.

They arrived at Luke's cell and looked inside. A figure was lying on the bed facing the wall. Collins couldn't make out who it was in the dark.

"Is that your present or is that Luke?" Collins said, pointing at the body.

They shrugged.

"You sure this here's Luke's cell?"

"Yes, sir," Billy said.

"Hey, wake up in there," Collins said, rattling the keys against the bars.

The man in the bed moved.

"Get up," Collins said, a little louder.

Moses turned, looked over, and stared at the three men.

"Moses, what the heck are you doing in there?"

"The Klan put me in, Sheriff."

Collins unlocked the cell door.

Moses rose from the bed and stepped out of the cell.

"Did you recognize anyone?" Collins asked.

"They were wearing hoods, sir," Moses said.

"They didn't take them off at all?"

"No, sir."

"Is that true?" Collins turned to ask the guards.

"Yes, sir," Billy said. "They came in the front door wearing their hoods. We never saw their faces."

Collins looked back at Moses. "You wouldn't tell me even if you had seen them, would you?"

Moses was stone-faced. "Well, it certainly wouldn't be in my best interest. I've known folks that have done that very thing. Couldn't find them after that."

"Well, I reckon I wouldn't say anything either."

"You saw the guy that came out of this cell?"

Moses was quiet for moment.

"I know you must have seen him."

"I saw him."

"Recognize him?"

"No, suh."

"Sure this was Luke's cell?" Collins asked the guards.

"Yes, sir," Billy said.

"Anyone else gone?"

"I think so, but from what I can tell, only a couple of drunks. They were getting out today anyway."

"I'm going back to my office," Collins said. "We'll need to start looking for Luke, although most people probably don't care one way or the other. I know I don't. You going back to the courthouse, Moses?"

"Yessuh."

Collins opened the hallway door then turned back. "Billy?" Collins said.

"Yes, Sheriff."

"No more escapes. Hear me?"

Collins and Moses approached the courthouse, and Moses veered toward the door that led to his supply room. "I'm over this way, Sheriff."

Collins headed to the steps. "You let me know if you remember anything else," Collins said.

"Yessuh," Moses said.

He knew he wouldn't hear from Moses again.

Collins started up the steps. "And stay out of jail, Moses."

CHAPTER 18

If the river was whiskey, I'd stay drunk all the time.

—*Furry Lewis*

SATURDAY COULDN'T COME TOO SOON FOR TRAVIS, who was already tired by Thursday of Hannah's endless teasing about the upcoming party. And he still knew almost nothing about it, except that it would be held in some small shack near the river. Not the Sunflower River, like he had originally thought, but the big river, the Mississippi. Travis had heard stories about the rowdy house parties and juke joint get-togethers on the river, but he had never been to one.

Finally, the weekend arrived. Before heading home to get ready, Travis stopped by the local baseball field to watch one of the Negro teams from Louisiana, the Shreveport Black Sports, play a doubleheader against Clarksdale's local team, the Brown Bombers. The Negro field was located a half mile outside of town. When Travis

arrived, he noticed a handful of other whites who were also taking the opportunity to see some professional baseball in Clarksdale.
Travis sat between home and third base, ten rows up. After some
shadow ball, Shreveport led off. Travis ate peanuts and cheered for
his hometown team, but mostly he thought about Hannah. He left
after six innings of the first game.

When Travis arrived home with some groceries his mother had
requested, she was listening to Ella Fitzgerald wistfully singing her
most recent hit on the radio. His father was in the living room,
finishing the paper. Travis bounded upstairs, changed clothes, and
scrambled back down in less time than it took his mom to put everything away. He picked up an apple.

"When will you be home tonight?" she asked.

"I'm not sure," Travis said. "It'll be late. I might stay over at
somebody's house if I need to."

"Be careful, and tell your father good-bye before you leave. Are
you taking the car again?"

"Yes, ma'am."

"You'd better ask him first."

Travis sauntered into the living room. His father laid the paper
on his lap.

"You going out?" he said.

"Yes, sir."

"Where to?"

"I'm gonna head over to Conner's house, and then we'll go to the
movie or something. Can I use the car?"

"Sure. Can you put some gas in it?"

"Yes, sir. Thanks."

As Travis headed to the door, his father said, "Before you go, son,
I've been hearing rumors around town."

Travis nervously turned toward his father.

"What kind of rumors?"

"Just things."

Travis knew his father was being evasive. He didn't want to come right out and say it. Travis didn't want him to.

"You know, Travis," he said, "we have rules that are written down and enforced by law. Rules against murder, for example."

"Luke broke that rule."

"That's right. And then we have other rules that aren't written down. Those rules are more like customs, and we know them because that's what we're taught from our parents and from the people around us."

"Yes, sir, and for the past two years you've been bringing Hodding Carter's articles into our home, and we've been reading them, and you've been teaching us that some of those unwritten rules, well, they're just not right. You said Carter's the future of the South, and that if it's a foregone conclusion, then we ought to get on board now."

Travis could see his father pondering this fact. Neither of them looked away.

"And you're correct. Those are my thoughts in my house. But that's not how everyone outside these walls thinks. I can't tell them what to think and neither can you. If I tried, I'd be without a job. The rules, morality, and the actions must all be unified."

His father brought his hands together and interlaced his fingers. "Any one of those without the others just brings trouble."

"It's got to start somewhere." He shrugged his shoulders.

"You're a man now, and I'm not going to tell you what to do. You have to make your own choices. But what I will tell you is that even the unwritten rules get enforced. And breaking them carries a penalty."

"I understand, Dad. If I spend the night out, I'll make sure to be back for church. 'Night, Dad."

Travis drove toward the movie theater near Hannah's house. He arrived at 6:40 p.m. and parked across the street, exactly one block from the building where she had asked him to meet her. He could see the front of the theater and several blocks on the other side of it. He couldn't miss her.

At 7:05 p.m., he began to feel impatient. At fifteen after, he was concerned. Maybe she wouldn't show, had gotten into trouble, worked late, or any number of other possibilities. By twenty-five after, he thought about just driving home and forgetting the party.

"Hey, Travis!" Hannah said. She poked her head in the passenger's side window.

Travis flinched in his seat. "Where'd you come from?"

"I walked between those two buildings," she said, pointing over her shoulder.

Travis hurried out of the car and opened her door.

"Thanks," she said, pulling her skirt into the car and tucking it up under her legs.

"I never even saw you coming. Where have you been?"

"Oh, you know, it always takes a woman a little longer to get ready," Hannah said, settling into her seat and turning slightly to face him. "It also took a little longer than expected to get out of the house."

"Is everything all right?"

"Everything's fine."

"What time do you have to be home?"

"Tomorrow before church. I told my parents I was sleeping over at a friend's house."

"So did I."

Travis drove northwest out of town past the Stovall plantation and then back south.

"You know, we're only a few miles from the river, as the crow flies," he said, squinting ahead. "But we'll probably have to drive thirty to get where we're going. By the way, where are we going, exactly?"

"Just keep driving."

Travis kept glancing at Hannah. She seemed to glow in the light from the setting sun. She was wearing what appeared to be a new blouse and skirt. It was neither flashy nor prudish, and its color perfectly complemented her brown, flawless skin. Hannah was self-assured: she knew who she was and what suited her, and she never failed to capitalize on it. Travis realized he had yet to find any faults in her.

About ten minutes into the trip, Travis pulled a small flask from under the seat. Hannah looked down at it, then up at Travis. "I'm a little nervous," he said.

"Bourbon?" Hannah said.

Travis nodded.

"Where you'd get it?"

"There's a little storage room in the courthouse for confiscated contraband."

They passed the flask back and forth a few times as they chatted about nothing in particular. "You still nervous?" Hannah said a little while later.

"Maybe just a tad. But a few more swigs should help."

Around one corner, Travis took a turn a little bit wide, and Hannah grabbed the wheel and yanked the car back on the road. "Why don't I drive?" she suggested. "That'll give you time to sip. And I know where the party is."

Travis pulled over and stopped the car. They switched places and continued.

"I think I'm finally relaxed," Travis said after he capped the flask. "I only wish I had brought another."

"There's plenty more where we're going, so don't worry."

There was still some light in the sky when they reached their destination. Hannah parked the car about a hundred yards from a brightly lit cabin. Near their car were more cars, trucks, four wagons, and several horses tied up among the trees.

"We're certainly not the first ones to arrive," Travis said.

"I bet some of these folks have been here all day," Hannah said.

Travis's bourbon had done its work. He felt comfortable, relaxed—almost too much so. The smell of roasted meat wafted around the front yard and grew stronger as they approached the house.

"Ever been to a juke joint before?" Hannah asked.

"No, never. What's a juke anyway?"

"Juke? Juke, or joog, is Gullah. It means 'disorderly.'"

Just as Hannah stepped onto the porch, the cabin door opened and raucous chatter and laughter spilled out. The cabin was old, but there was still a roof on it in most places. Because of its odd layout, Travis couldn't tell right away whether the cabin had three or four rooms. It looked like two of the rooms had been an afterthought. One of these, near the front, housed the kitchen, where several women were cooking and serving food. Two boards were nailed across the doorway and served as an ordering window. There was never a line, just a steady stream of customers filling themselves in anticipation of the events to come.

In the back, one of the newer rooms held a noisy group of men shouting and cheering.

Travis leaned over to Hannah. "What's going on in there?"

"Cards, craps, sometimes a chicken fight," she said. "Always some kind of gambling in there."

In one corner of the main room stood an old piano with a guitar laid across its top. Travis knew it was just a matter of time before the instruments would come to life and the main room would be packed with people juking off the chains of their everyday lives.

Travis looked out onto the backyard through two doors that stood wide open. Most of the crowd seemed to be back there. Some sat at tables, some on blankets, and still others stood eating, drinking, and talking. Several men tended cooking meats over two open pits.

Standing alongside Hannah, Travis felt friendly because of the bourbon, but he knew better than to act familiar. He stayed close to Hannah but was careful not to appear possessive of her.

They approached the makeshift bar. It wasn't big, but it was functional. "Let me do the talking," Hannah whispered.

Travis nodded in agreement, trying not to stare at the bartender. He was such a huge man that Travis figured he must double as the peacekeeper.

"Good evening," Hannah said to the man behind the bar.

"He with you?" the bartender asked without greeting her. He was obviously offended by Travis's presence.

"He's with me," Hannah said.

"Is he staying long?"

"As long as I do."

"Is he here for business?"

"No, he's here just like you and me. For a little music, food, dancing, whatever."

"Maybe y'all can stay out the way. I've got regular customers."

Travis wanted to grab Hannah's arm and leave, but the moment his arm moved toward hers, the bartender glanced down at it. Travis redirected his hand into a pocket.

"We'll just stay where we stay," Hannah said, not backing down. "Can we have a drink now?"

The bartender jerked his head, indicating he was ready for their order but not happy about it.

"Whiskey. Two glasses," Hannah said. The bartender placed a small bottle on the bar. Hannah picked up the bottle and inspected the seal.

"Don't worry, our whiskey's good," the bartender said.

"Okay," she said to Travis.

Travis laid some money on the bar. The bartender took what he needed.

They walked away, and Travis said, "Let's hope we don't have to get another drink. But I definitely need one now."

They stood by the door while Hannah poured some whiskey into their glasses. She smiled at the first sip.

"Good?" she said.

Travis nodded. Hannah then turned to walk outside, and he followed. He could feel the eyes on him. She walked toward a vacant spot near an old fence line, and Travis followed slowly but deliberately, staring at the ground and choosing his steps carefully. When he accidentally made eye contact with someone he smiled, but didn't speak.

He felt out of place, like he was somewhere he shouldn't be, but was it any different for him than it was for anyone else here almost every day? Eyed suspiciously. Unwritten rules existed everywhere.

"Rebecca," Hannah called to someone across the yard.

A woman's hand went up. She smiled at Hannah, grabbed the hand of the man behind her, and walked toward them.

"I didn't think you'd make it," Hannah smiled, embracing the woman lightly.

"I thought we were going to Memphis this week but it's next week," she said. "I got the dates mixed up."

Hannah turned to Travis, "Travis Montgomery, this is Rebecca and Butch. They're friends of mine."

Travis felt paralyzed by the awkwardness. Should he extend his hand or just nod politely? He let Butch make the first move. Butch extended his hand, and Travis shook it vigorously. "Butch," he said. "Travis Montgomery, nice to meet you."

"Likewise," Butch said with a well-mannered smile.

Travis could tell instantly why they were friends with Hannah. They, like Hannah, were from Clarksdale's elite black families.

"Has the band started yet?" Hannah asked.

"No, I don't think so," Rebecca said. "But we just got here a little while ago."

"Isn't your father the county coroner?" Butch said.

"Yes—yes he is," Travis answered.

"Does he enjoy that line of work?"

"I think he does," Travis said. "He doesn't talk much about it. It's not always good dinner conversation, how people die and all the associated topics."

"Did he go to medical school?"

"No, he didn't. But he trained with coroners in Oxford. For Clarksdale, he's pretty well trained."

"Will you be following in his footsteps?"

"*We're* still deciding," Travis said with a grin, taking a sip of his drink. Butch also laughed, letting Travis know he understood the burden of family expectations. "What do you do, Butch?"

"I attend school up north. I'm just down for a quick visit. Helping with some family business."

"Coming to see me," Rebecca said, looking flirtatiously over the rim of her glass.

"Of course, that goes without saying," Butch said.

"It better not," Rebecca said. "You better say it often and with some enthusiasm."

"Do you like coming back to Clarksdale?" Travis said.

"You've lived in Clarksdale a while. Would you if you were black?"

Travis assumed the question was rhetorical.

"No, I can't say that I enjoy returning," Butch said. "I like to see my family, but that's about it. I try to stay around the house while visiting, or come to parties like this." Butch looked around the crowded yard. "I might like coming back when I'm older, but not now. There's a lot of youthful rebellion in me."

"In all of us," Hannah said. Travis knew she was protecting him—with good reason.

The moon was almost full, and Travis felt more at ease in the dim light. He lingered in the shadows, moving gradually during the conversation so that he ended up leaning against a tree: not hiding, just being discreet.

The conversation waned, and the foursome noticed that most of the people had started to go back inside the cabin. The strumming of a guitar could barely be heard above the hum of the crowd. The musician plucked a few notes, lazily practicing chords; then the sweet keys of the piano rang out, discordant against the guitar. A harmonica joined in. Finally, the beat of a drum emerged, a steady rhythmic pounding behind which the warm-up fell into step.

"Should we go inside?" Hannah said to the others.

"Sure," Rebecca said.

"It's probably a little hot in there right now," Travis said. "I think I'll wait 'til it cools down."

Hannah, Rebecca, and Butch looked at each other and then at Travis.

"It's not going to get any cooler tonight." Hannah laughed. She grabbed his hand and pulled him toward the door. "C'mon."

"Hold on," he said, pulling his hand from hers. He took a long drink, then refilled his glass from the bottle they had bought. He slipped it into his pocket. "Okay," he said, "I'm ready."

"It'll be fun, Travis," Rebecca said. "You'll see."

The four approached the door to the cabin just as the band started playing in earnest. What had been painful to hear a moment earlier now transformed into something the crowd clearly recognized, even if Travis didn't. Several people let out a shrill but controlled scream and a few whistled. Hannah picked up her pace.

The cabin was now packed. Everyone had crowded onto the dance floor in front of the band members.

Hannah led them into the crowd to get a better look at the musicians. Travis focused on the music. The drum pounded a beat while the piano player put his old but properly tuned instrument atop the rhythm. Several people had begun swaying to the music, but no one was dancing yet.

Travis passed through the mass of people and felt the stares. A stiff shoulder, a slight bump. He knew that everyone saw him as one thing—white. No matter what he thought or how he acted, he was white, and he was where he didn't belong. Suddenly, all he could think about was being the scapegoat for someone who had been cheated by a landlord or shopkeeper or boss earlier in the day. Why wasn't Hannah concerned?

Without stopping, the band moved into a much more upbeat tune. The guitar player joined the other three for a few instrumental bars, and then he started singing. The change in tempo brought the crowd into the beat, and the dancing began, slow swaying, picking up into a much more rhythmic and faster-paced movement. Travis watched and learned.

Hannah, who had been watching the band, turned to Travis and started to dance. Travis began to move but felt awkward because he was still holding his glass. He held it up to Hannah, who recognized his dilemma and held out her hand. Travis drank the remains and handed it to her. She turned and gave it to Rebecca, who set it on a table near the edge of the dance floor.

Travis's head was swimming. The heat and the bourbon were potent; he knew the next day promised a vicious headache and nausea, but he didn't care. It was Saturday night, and he was with Hannah—the only place he could imagine ever wanting to be.

He looked around the room and watched the others on the dance floor. Most were from the country, he surmised, and only a few came all the way from town.

Travis moved with the music while he made his way toward Hannah. Butch and Rebecca had danced themselves to another part of the room. Travis could barely see them now.

A few beats more and Travis stood right in front of Hannah. Their legs and arms touched intermittently while they danced.

Travis looked at her and she at him. She met his eyes then glanced away, drawing him toward her with each look, pulling and teasing with every motion. A brush of her arm against his became a clasp of her hand around his forearm. She steadied herself and used him for support, stepping up the intensity of her dancing. Finally, he dared to place his arm around her waist and pull her toward him. Her thighs brushed his, briefly straddling his leg and then moving away.

Travis and Hannah each sensed that there would be no more teasing, no more arm's-length courting. He was attracted to her, and she to him. His equal in education and upbringing, she was his superior in having worked to her station while he had only drifted into his. His birthright was her triumph. For Travis, Hannah was the only woman in the room.

He hardly noticed the rivers of sweat pouring down his face. He could see the shimmer of wetness on Hannah's neck and upper chest. They danced closer and closer, and she grabbed his arms to support herself while she rolled her body into his, and he into hers.

The band played song after song, and her arms moved around his neck. He locked both arms around her waist and pulled her tightly. Her moves echoed and then incorporated his; Travis had never danced like this.

At last the band took a break. Travis's shirt was drenched, and he looked like he had just spent all day in a cotton field. They stepped from the dance floor, Hannah clutching his waist, and walked outside on the porch to get some fresh air. His legs were tight from the dancing, and his arm ached from squeezing Hannah.

"Is it hot tonight!" Rebecca said. She and Butch were waiting for them.

"How long have you been on the porch?" Hannah asked.

"Just a few minutes. It was so hot in there."

"Did you have fun, Travis?" Rebecca said.

"I did, but I need to sit down," Travis said.

Travis slumped into the nearest chair on the porch. He propped his foot onto a deteriorated railing and pushed back slightly so that the chair rested on its two back legs. Three men, two younger and one older, were talking nearby.

"How's it going, Cap'n?" the older man said.

At first Travis didn't answer, his eyes wandering out over the fields in front of the house, but then he realized the man was addressing him.

"Fine," Travis said. "I just needed to sit down for a while. It's pretty hot in there."

The three men smiled.

"You by yourself tonight?" the man said.

"Oh no," Travis said. "I'm with her." Travis turned in his chair and pointed at Hannah.

The men gazed from him to her and back.

"Any of these your crops?" Travis said.

"No, sir. I live a couple miles down the road."

"How you doing this season?"

"All right, I guess. I might make a little. But mostly it's the vegetables to keep us fed."

"I know that Ag Act payments were stepped up this year," Travis said. "It's helped a few folks. You see any of that money?"

The three men laughed.

"The government money is for the voters," the old man said. "We don't vote."

Hannah walked up to the group. She leaned on the rail, just in front of Travis's chair. "What kind of lies are y'all telling?"

"Lots of them, and mostly about you," Travis said.

The men laughed heartily.

Hannah smiled and lifted her foot to the edge of Travis's chair, which was still tilted on two legs. She looked over at the men standing at the railing and just before Travis caught on, she pushed, and the chair and Travis went tumbling back.

This time the men didn't just laugh; they roared. Travis, still light-headed, scrambled to get up. He looked at Butch and Rebecca, who were laughing, too.

Travis stood up, slightly wobbly, and looked around for Hannah. The elderly man pointed out into the fields. Travis's eyes searched the darkness and finally found a lone figure running in one of the field's furrows. She was at least thirty yards away.

"Where's she going?" Travis said.

"What's it matter?" the man said, grinning. "When a woman runs like that, she wants to be chased. You better get moving."

Travis jumped off the porch, fell to one knee, and then started his pursuit while the three men yelled encouragement.

"Go get her, Cap'n. Don't let her get away!"

Travis caught sight of Hannah and ran to the furrow she was in. She was so far ahead he thought he would lose her in the darkness, but he ran, sometimes stumbling.

By the time Hannah reached the tree line that bordered the field, Travis was only twenty yards from her. "I'm right behind you," he yelled. Hannah let out a squeal.

The path through the trees was worn, so there were no low-hanging branches to slap them or tree limbs to trip over. Travis continued to gain on Hannah. He felt his heart pounding, and his breathing was heavy. He wasn't sure what he would do once he caught her.

The woods deepened, obstructing the moonlight so the path was almost completely dark, illuminated only by bright slivers that blinked through gaps in the trees. When Travis was about ten yards from Hannah, he could see her outline. And then, all at once, she was gone. By the time he started to slow down and look for her, he was hurtling out into midair, flailing his arms to keep himself vertical.

He was falling toward cleared earth, fully illuminated now by the moon. There were no trees to block the light, and he could see Hannah out of the corner of his eye as he plunged downward.

He didn't fall far, four or five feet he guessed, and hit the soft bank of the Mississippi River with a thud, feet first. Travis let out a wail as he fell backward, sprawling into a seated position. Hannah sat down, laughing and holding her stomach. Travis started laughing, too.

"What the heck did you do that for?" Travis said.

"Do what?" Hannah said, trying to look sheepish.

He scooted back and laid his head on a small log. The run had cleared his senses, and he was beginning to sober up. The air, though still thick with the day's heat, was cooler by the river. He glanced at the sky and then Hannah. He held out his hand to her. "Come closer."

She was just out of Travis's reach. She leaned over and grabbed his hand, and he pulled her to him. At first she lay down with her head on the log, but then she slid her head onto his chest and turned her body into his. She wrapped an arm around him.

Travis moved his head toward hers and breathed in her sensuality.

The small waves lapping at the shore were the only disturbance on an otherwise silent evening.

"Did you have fun tonight?" Hannah said.

"More than I expected, actually. Thanks for inviting me."

She paused. "What do you think changes things?"

"What do you mean?"

"Like people. The way they think, how they act."

He thought for a moment. "Time. Time passing creates change. It's slow, but change will come."

"It'll never pass fast enough for us, will it?"

Travis said nothing for a long minute. "Probably not," he murmured at last. "Not here."

He turned slightly and lifted her chin with his left hand until she was facing him. He looked into her eyes. A single tear coursed down her cheek. "But don't let that ruin it for us tonight. We can't change how fast time passes, but we've got now."

Then he leaned down and let his lips brush hers. She was motion-less. Quiet. His lips glided over her cheeks, kissing her salty tears, shed in frustration. She let him, never moving, never speaking.

He looked at her again, and her face shone while the moon's rays danced on it. "Hannah, you're the most beautiful woman I've ever met, and I'm falling in love with you. Nobody can take that away either. No matter what happens."

He pulled her tight and kissed her deeply. This night was theirs alone under that big Mississippi moon, the river flowing at their feet. She kissed him back. Her breath was hot and sweet, and he tasted her longingly. He pulled her onto him, her leg straddling his and his hands moving from her waist, down her hips, slowly mas-saging the side and back of her legs. She pushed hard into him, and her skirt inched up.

Travis lay back, breathing hard. She gave him a light kiss on the neck and lay her head on his chest again. He knew what he wanted must wait. The slow stirring of the water sounded like a lullaby, and he drowsily spoke to her in half-sentences and slurred words before they both drifted off to sleep.

The sun crept over the horizon, and Travis rustled. He opened his eyes, and it took him a full minute to remember where he was. His throat was dry, and his head throbbed.

Travis looked at his watch. "Hannah, get up, we've got to go."

She opened her eyes.

"Come on. You'll be late for church. And I certainly don't want your dad mad at me."

Travis grabbed her hands and pulled her to her feet. They ran back to his car hand in hand through the cotton field, he in one fur-row and she in another, lifting their arms over the crop, laughing heartily. On the cabin porch, they could see a few stragglers soundly sleeping off the evening.

Travis sped back to town, and they both were seated in their proper pews before the sermons began.

CHAPTER 19

I just can't stay here long.

—*Lemon Jefferson*

LUKE FINISHED A PLATE OF COLD BEANS AND TOSSED his dish into the basin. It clanged around and finally came to rest. Wyatt, who was settling in after lunch for a short nap, looked over at Luke.

"I'm gonna lay down for a while."

Luke looked at him disdainfully. How was this day different from any other?

Luke hadn't been left alone since the four Klansmen brought him to the cabin several days prior. He hadn't been broken out of prison so much as moved to a different one. Whether it was Ned, Bo, Edgar, or Wyatt, someone was here 'round the clock, day in, day out. It was clear they didn't know what to do with him.

Ned told Luke that Sheriff Collins had already been by to see Elma. Now there wasn't any chance of visiting her—at least not until the sheriff stopped watching who came and went from the house.

Luke had to admit, however, that Ned had found a good hiding place. Luke knew no one was going to find him in the middle of nowhere. He had wandered around the area a little without recognizing a thing. There was no water nearby, and the trees were cut back only about ten feet from the cabin. The road leading up to it was narrow, and Luke could see only twenty-five yards or so before the lane wound through the trees and was no longer visible.

He stepped outside on the small porch and listened. It was still. Nothing. He turned around and went back inside where Wyatt, true to his word, was napping.

What did fate hold for Luke now? Elma was a prisoner, held captive by a watchful sheriff, and he was confined at the cabin while that same sheriff searched all over the county for him. Safe hiding place or no, wouldn't they eventually stumble upon him? He was an admitted murderer. They weren't going to stop looking for him.

But being a fugitive holed up in the middle of the woods was no way to live. It didn't suit him. Besides, the meals in jail had been regular and the cooking better, and he knew his neighbors had watched over Elma while he was in his cell. Those same people wouldn't be so helpful to the wife of a fugitive.

Luke walked by Wyatt to make sure he wasn't merely resting his eyes. He shuffled his feet. Wyatt didn't move.

The car keys lay on a table near the fireplace. Luke picked them up and slipped out the front door. He walked to the window and looked in. No movement from Wyatt.

Luke knew that when he started the car Wyatt would hear the old motor rumbling and come running. Luke wasn't sure what Wyatt would do, but if Ned had told Wyatt to keep him here, then anything was possible. Luke considered running into the woods if it came down to it.

Luke stepped off the porch and walked over to the car, which faced the cabin. The quickest way out to the main road would be to back the car out 'til he could turn around. He wasn't sure how far that would be, but he did know he'd have to go slowly; if Wyatt came running out the front door, he might even be able to catch up with the car on foot.

Luke took a deep breath, started the car, and threw it into reverse. He backed out slowly at first, until he saw the cabin door move. He pushed down on the accelerator, and the car lurched backward down the narrow path.

He alternated looking to his rear, while he steered the car, and to the front. Wyatt had come out yelling. Fortunately, he wasn't carrying a shotgun. Still half asleep, he ran toward the car but tumbled over a pile of stacked firewood.

Luke backed up until he saw a small clearing. He turned the steering wheel forcefully and the car spun around, pointing him away from the cabin. Still, he couldn't speed up on this impenetrable path. He glanced into the rearview mirror but didn't see Wyatt. He wasn't sure how far the main road was from the cabin, but he recalled from his ride in the trunk that from the time the car turned off a paved road till they arrived at the cabin, it had been less than ten minutes.

Out of the corner of his eye, Luke saw something move. A blur. Suddenly, Wyatt landed squarely on the hood of the car. He flattened himself out, gripping the edge of the hood near the windshield. "Stop this car, Luke!" he screamed. "Get outta there!"

Luke sped up. Wyatt yelled, pounding on the windshield with his fist.

"Get off the car," Luke hollered, waving his arm at Wyatt.

Wyatt kept pounding.

Luke yanked the steering wheel from side to side, rocking the car. Wyatt became more frantic. With one final blow, he cracked the windshield with the palm of his hand and kept punching until the hole was big enough to put his arm through. He reached in and flailed wildly, smearing blood on Luke's face and shirt. Luke tried to push his arm away, but Wyatt hooked Luke's shirt with a finger and held on tight. He had no other choice; Luke slammed on the brakes. Wyatt flew from the car's hood and landed violently on the ground, tumbling over and over. Luke steered around him and sped away.

At last the car emerged onto the main road. Luke looked both ways. He didn't recognize the area. He turned left. He hoped Wyatt wasn't hurt badly.

Luke realized that everyone in three counties would now be looking for him. He drove fast, finally free. He considered Elma but wanted to keep her out of the mess he'd gotten himself into. She needed her peace. He could drive out of the county—hell, out of the state—if he kept going. It wouldn't take long; Helena, Arkansas, was just thirty miles away. Memphis was twice that. He looked at the gas gauge. He could probably make it.

But what then? More running? A new life? Where would he start? He had nothing—and no one.

He pushed hard on the accelerator and sped down the road.

CHAPTER 20

I lay down in my cell at night.

—*Joe Evans*

EARLY MONDAY MORNING, CONRAD HIGSON STRODE confidently out of his house, got into his car, and headed to Memphis at a leisurely speed.

He passed field upon field and row upon row of crops. He thought about the sharecroppers who worked the land, the landlords who owned it, and the struggle of both groups against the land, the elements, as well as each other. And of the coal mines in Germany where poor men fought the earth and the companies who owned it. What they harvested was the only difference.

He pulled over to the side of the road and sat for a while staring at the field hands. Watching the sacks slung over their shoulders sway while they shuffled through the rows, bent into the dirt itself where the white puffs hung, had a somewhat mesmerizing effect.

The drone of song heightened that effect as it arose from the field, lower and sweeter than the chirping of birds, the pickers singing against the heat, dust, and boredom.

The professor drove on, stopping for lunch at the small roadside restaurant he always visited on his way to Memphis. He sat at a small table in the corner and ordered the same thing he always did: ham, turnip greens, okra, and iced tea. For dessert he'd have apple pie.

"Best apple pie this side of Memphis," Higson would say to the proprietor.

"And the other side, too," the owner would yell from behind the counter.

They'd both laugh, and Higson would leave a little extra change. From the time he arrived until he paid his bill, precisely one hour would elapse.

As the professor continued his trip to Memphis, the Washington-bound parcel securely on the backseat, a car passed him going in the other direction. Though his features were indistinct because of the car's speed, Higson caught a glimpse of a broad smile on the man's face.

Later that afternoon, Luke drove into Clarksdale. The sun was smoldering and the streets were deserted. Everyone was hiding from the heat.

First, he stopped at the drugstore. "Let me get a meatloaf sandwich and a drink," he said to the waitress, pulling from his pocket thirty cents that he had won playing poker with Wyatt and Bo at the cabin. "Thanks," he said when his sandwich arrived, wrapped in crinkling wax paper, along with a cold bottle of Coca-Cola. He picked up his food and left. A few more hours of freedom would be nice.

Luke drove down to the courthouse and parked in front, under the hot sun. Then he took his lunch to the shade of a white oak on the courthouse lawn.

He sipped his drink and slowly ate his sandwich. He was going to miss meals like this. He watched the people come and go from the courthouse, scurrying as if they were squirrels storing up food for the winter. Two deputies walked from their patrol car into the building, never once looking at anyone but each other. Luke laughed to himself as he watched them enter the courthouse. Maybe nobody was looking for him after all.

He stretched out under the tree and laid his head back on a soft patch of grass. His eyes closed, and he drifted off to dream of freedom, his family, and men in hoods.

Luke felt his foot move. It wasn't a twitch; someone was kicking it, gently. Through his hazy summer slumber, he heard his name being called.

"Luke," the rough voice said. "Wake up. Hey Luke, get up."

Luke opened his eyes. The sun's harsh glare was shaded by the tree, but he still had difficulty seeing the face before him. The man came into focus, and Luke recognized him. He smiled. "Hello, Bill. How's it going?" he said.

"You know there's a few people looking for you. Where've you been?"

"Oh, here and there. Mostly there."

"Is that your car?" Montgomery said motioning to Luke's stolen transportation.

"Yeah."

"What happened to the windshield?"

"Rock hit it."

"One of the county employees mentioned the smashed windshield to someone at the front desk. Who does it really belong to?"

"Couple guys I know."

"Do I know them?"

"Doubt it. They're friends, not from around town."

Montgomery sat down next to Luke, who didn't move but continued to lie still on his back. His eyes were open wide now, and he was gazing up at the tree.

"Maybe they'll come back and get it sometime," Montgomery said.

"Maybe."

"What'd you come back for, Luke?"

"I don't know. Nowhere else to go, I guess. It seemed better than where I was at."

"And where was that?"

"Out in the woods somewhere. Playing cards and eatin' beans every day. Not doing much of anything."

"Who took you out there?"

"You know who. Same guys broke me out."

"Who was that?"

Luke looked at Montgomery. "Does it really matter? You know you'd be wasting your time messing with those fellas."

"We might eventually find out who they are. But whether the sheriff wants to arrest them, I don't know. I do know he was pretty upset that someone broke out of his jail."

"That's a shame he was riled." Luke smirked.

Montgomery paused for a moment. It was hot, even under the shade of the tree. "Why'd you break out if you were planning on coming back?"

"I didn't break out. I was broken out."

"Then I'll ask you again, why'd you come back?"

"I don't know. The sheriff was gonna get me soon enough anyway." He stuck a blade of grass in his mouth.

Montgomery wiped his forehead again. "Ready to go back in?"

"Can I finish my nap? I'm not going to see the sun again for quite a while."

"Yeah, you can finish your nap, Luke. I'll come and get you in an hour or so."

"Thanks, Bill."

Montgomery stood up and walked inside the courthouse.

An hour later, he and Sam Tackett went out to the oak and escorted Luke back to his jail cell.

CHAPTER 21

On the burying ground.

—Booker White

THAT AFTERNOON AROUND FIVE O'CLOCK, THE sheriff's office got a call. Someone had found a body hanging from a tree a few miles out of town. Sheriff Collins, Montgomery, and Tackett drove out to see it for themselves.

They arrived to find the field empty. The body was swaying gently in the distance.

"There're some tire tracks leading from the road to the tree," Collins said. "See how the grass is folded over?"

"Yeah," Tackett said, reaching down and running his hand along the bent grass.

"I wonder why someone made such an effort to bring him all the way out here?" Montgomery said.

The three approached the tree and each briefly inspected the body.

"Couple of stab wounds," Collins said.

"He was probably dead before they strung him up," Tackett said.

"They?" Collins said, glancing over at Tackett.

"You think one guy could have got him up there?"

"Depends—"

Tackett sighed, walked back over to the car, and sat on the bumper. He knew there was nothing else. Not a clue, not a bit of evidence. "We better go talk to Luke. Do we know where he and his friends were last night?"

"No, not really," Montgomery said. "He said he drove around till he got tired and then turned off the road somewhere and went to sleep. Finally drove into town after lunch. But he was by himself."

"Hey," Collins called from under the tree. "What do you want to do with this guy?"

"Get someone to cut him down and send him to the morgue," Montgomery said. "I'll take a look at him there."

On their way into the jailhouse, Collins glared at the guards who had been cuffed during Luke's breakout. "You guys gonna keep everything quiet tonight?"

"Yes, sir," they said in unison.

"I hope so," Collins said. "Give me the key to Luke Williams's cell."

One of the guards hurriedly passed Collins the key.

The sheriff, Montgomery, and Tackett walked down the hallway and found Luke lying on his bunk looking up at the ceiling. The sheriff unlocked the door and pushed it open. The three men stepped into the small enclosure. Montgomery leaned against the far wall, Tackett stood in the middle, and Collins stood alert by the door.

"Luke, we have a few questions for you," Tackett said.

"Okay, but do I need my lawyer?" Luke said. "Charlie Usher, remember him?"

"Yeah, I remember him, but you don't need him right now."

Tackett was surprised that Luke had asked the question.

Montgomery and the sheriff looked at each other. "Want a cigarette?" Collins said.

"No thanks," Luke said, still staring up at the ceiling.

"Can you tell us where you were and what you were doing the last few nights?" Tackett asked.

"I was in a cabin most of the time. Then I left. Drove around a while."

"What'd you do from the time you left the cabin to when you showed up this afternoon?"

"I want my lawyer."

"Did you meet up with anyone on one of those nights?" Tackett said.

"Where's Charlie Usher?"

"We don't need him yet."

Montgomery eyed Tackett for a moment.

"Did you see anyone?" Tackett asked.

"I saw a few people."

"You stop to talk with any of them?"

"I need my lawyer."

"Answer the question."

"And if I don't? What are you gonna do? Put a gun to my head like last time?" Luke turned over to face away from the three men. "Go ahead."

Tackett knew he couldn't go any further. "We're done." He turned to go, and Collins inched the cell door open.

"Good," Luke said. "And I'll need to tell Charlie about this."

"Don't worry," Tackett said. "We'll do it for you."

Collins closed the door behind them, and the three men walked back to Tackett's office.

"What do you think?" Montgomery said.

"I don't know," Tackett said. "But one more or less doesn't make any difference now. I've got to find some witnesses or something—anything—or he's a free man."

Outside the jail, Montgomery glanced over toward where Luke's car had been parked. He stopped. "Sam, Luke's car was right there a little while ago," he said, pointing to a space near the courthouse.

Tackett looked. "Well, it's gone now."

CHAPTER 22

A bird nest builded on the ground.

—Charlie Patton

SAM TACKETT WAS SITTING AT HIS DESK PORING OVER autopsy and crime-scene reports, sipping his morning coffee. His desk was littered with paperwork, all of which amounted to nothing more than a story with no ending. Three hard, quick knocks broke the silence of his office and brought him back to the present. He almost spilled his coffee.

"Come in," Tackett said.

The door creaked open, and a man stuck his head in.

"Good morning, Professor Higson," Tackett said, rising from his chair.

"Good morning to you, Mr. Tackett," said Higson, squeezing his body through the crack he had made even though he could have opened the door further. "Am I disturbing you?"

"Oh, no," Tackett said. The men shook hands. "Have a seat. Can I get you something to drink? Coffee?"

"No, thank you, I've got to get back to work soon. Can't stay long."

Tackett poured himself another cup and sat down behind his desk. "Speaking of, how is the harvester, Professor?"

"We're tweaking it. A few adjustments and we should be ready for another test. It needed quite a bit of work after the last run."

"That's what I heard."

"Yes, well, it didn't go exactly like I had planned. But we'll get it."

"I know there are a lot of people who hope you do. Agriculture is our lifeblood in the Delta. Anything that helps the farmer helps us all."

"Yes, that's certainly understandable." Higson shifted uncomfortably in his chair.

"You sure I can't get you something? Tea, maybe?"

"No, no. I've had two cups of coffee this morning already."

Tackett blew on his coffee. Steam rose up in front of his face. An awkward silence filled the room. Higson stared out the window with a faraway look in his eyes. Tackett could tell something was bothering him.

Tackett removed a blank sheet of paper from his desk drawer and placed a pen on it. "Would you like to discuss something, Professor?"

"Yes, Mr. Tackett. It concerns a picture I saw in the paper this morning."

Tackett didn't respond. He knew Higson would keep talking.

"Of a man."

"Who was it?"

"At first I didn't know his name. But I recognized his face, even though I wished otherwise."

"What do you mean?"

"That I had seen him before, under different, more dire circumstances."

"Circumstances? Where had you seen him?"

"At a hanging," Higson said rather unemotionally, still staring off.

"You mean the one the other day?"

"Yes. Unfortunately, I have some information I think I should share with you."

"Please go on."

Higson cleared his throat. "On the night of the murder, Sunday night I assume, I happened to be out walking near my house. Just a stroll. I take one three or four times a week. I was maybe a mile or two from my house, although if I'm not paying attention, it could have been several miles. These walks help me think. When I started home, I heard some commotion up ahead. I hurried toward the noise and crouched behind a small clump of trees, really bushes. I didn't know what it was, so I was being careful. I thought it might be an animal or something of that sort."

"And what was it?" Tackett said, picking up the pen.

Higson shifted again.

"Would you like to stand up, Professor?"

"No, thank you. I saw two men fighting. One was beating the other quite savagely. I think he had a knife. After they stopped fighting, one of the men was lying on the ground. I believe he was dead. He seemed so because he wasn't moving."

Tackett scribbled down some notes then looked up at Higson.

"Then the other man took a rope out of a car parked off to the side. He tied one end around the bumper, and he threw the other end up over a tree branch before tying it around the dead man's neck. He started the car and pulled the body up off the ground. Then he removed the rope from the bumper and tied it to another branch to secure it. The body just hung there, gently rocking back and forth."

"What else?"

"That was it. He drove away."

"Did you see the driver?"

"Yes, I had a pretty good look. The bushes concealing me were close to the road."

"Even though it was dark?"

"He had his lights on, and it wasn't completely dark. The moon was low in front of him so the light shone in his car while he was driving away."

"Did you see what kind of car it was or the license plate?"

"No, I'm sorry to say I didn't," Higson said. "I think it was— no, no, I couldn't see it. I didn't think to look at the license plate. He drove so quickly and everything was happening so fast. I was concentrating fiercely on the driver, and I was trying to stay hidden."

"What about when the car was parked by the tree?"

"Too far away."

"Did you try to help the man who was hanging from the tree after the assailant left?"

"He was limp. Dead. I've seen dead men before, Mr. Tackett. There was nothing I could do."

"Now, you saw the driver, but did the driver see you?"

"I don't think so, but I wasn't sure. If he had, wouldn't he have turned around?"

"Maybe. And that's who you saw in the paper?"

Higson looked up. His eyes met Tackett's. "Yes, that's him, Mr. Tackett. His name is Luke Williams, isn't it?"

"Yes. He's in custody now, and we're preparing to try him for some other murders. Why didn't you come forward immediately?"

"I was concerned for my safety. You didn't see what he did to that man like I did. And what would I have said? I could recognize him, but describing him in enough detail for you to find him would have been more difficult."

"So that night you just went home?"

"Yes. And yesterday I went to Oxford for the day. I would have come forward eventually, even if the picture hadn't appeared in the paper. I was just too scared at the time."

Tackett didn't know what to think. This morning he had a weak case against Luke Williams, and now he was chatting with a witness who had seen Luke commit a new crime. Just like that.

"Professor Higson," Tackett said, "would you be willing to take the witness stand and repeat what you just told me? To testify?"

"I'd like to, Mr. Tackett. Will I be in any danger if I do? From the perpetrator?"

"No, you won't be in any danger. But we can provide a deputy to escort you to and from the courthouse. The defendant will be in jail, of course, when he's not in the courtroom."

"Then I guess I should testify. Of course, I will testify, Mr. Tackett. It's my duty." The professor was facing Tackett now, excited by the prospect of testifying. "This perpetrator must be held accountable for his crimes."

"You're right. I'll let you know tomorrow when and where you'll need to be. Your coming forward kind of changes things, so I'll need to speak with the judge. You'll be staying in the area for a few weeks, won't you?"

"Oh, yes. I may go to Oxford, but I'll let you know if I do."

"Good."

"Is there anything else?"

"No, that's it for now," Tackett said. "I'd like to thank you for coming to see me with this information, Professor. It's very helpful, and to tell you the truth, we didn't have much else to go on."

"You're welcome, Mr. Tackett. I hope I've done the right thing."

The men shook hands and Higson walked out of the office. Tackett watched him until he disappeared down the stairs. Then Tackett returned to his desk and dialed Montgomery's number. Montgomery answered on the second ring.

"Bill, the car that Luke was driving on Monday when you found him. What was it?"

"A Ford, I think."

"If I got you some pictures, you might be able to identify it?"

"Possibly."

"And the license plate?"

"Never got it."

"That's all I needed to know. Thanks, Bill."

CHAPTER 23

Law gonna step on you.

—*Bo Chatmon*

THE FBI OFFICE IN JACKSON WAS IN ITS USUAL TURMOIL. Phones ringing, people shouting, the ping of typewriter keys striking paper and platen.

The news of the most recent slaying had made its way to the office, and Bob Thompson was thinking retirement was looking better every day as he paged through some reports.

Down the hall, Russ Kalman stepped into a conference room, dropped a pile of papers onto the table, and stuck his head out the door. "Bob, Dan," he called. "In the conference room. Now."

"What's up?" Thompson said, after they were seated.

"It's not good."

"We're used to that by now," Thompson said.

"I just received an update from Washington, and I want to share it with you. It concerns a Dr. Conrad Higson," Kalman continued.

"Who?" Thompson asked.

"Conrad Higson. He's made his way to Mississippi, and the bureau's been tracking him. From a distance."

"Where'd he come from?" Dan Mulevsky said.

"Europe, by way of New York," said Kalman.

"Looking for a little Southern hospitality?" Thompson said. "Or taking advantage of our sunny weather?"

"Neither. It seems some university professor—from Princeton, I think—suspects that Higson is passing documents and classified information to the Germans. This professor sent Higson some documents that were never returned, even after he contacted him several times. When Higson didn't answer, the professor contacted the FBI. But Washington already had their eye on Higson. The professor's report just confirmed things."

"Where is he?" Mulevsky asked. "In Jackson?"

"No, he's in Clarksdale," Kalman said.

"Clarksdale?" Thompson said. "Is everything we're investigating in Clarksdale? Maybe we should move the office up there."

Thompson could tell Russ wasn't interested in any snide remarks today. He didn't even look up.

"How long have you known about this?" Thompson asked. He didn't like bosses who kept secrets, particularly young ones with less experience than he had.

"Just a little while. Washington's been very quiet."

"When should we pick him up?" Mulevsky said. "While we're up there for the trial?"

"We won't be picking him up," Kalman said.

"What do you mean, Russ?" Thompson said. "We've got a known spy in Mississippi, and we can't pick him up? That'd be a first."

"Washington has asked us to hold off until they can determine exactly what Higson is doing," Kalman said. "If he's passing secrets overseas, he must have a network to get the information out of the country. There has to be more than one fish in this pond. The bureau wants to catch 'em all, not just one of the minnows. This is coming down from the top."

"What do they want us to do?" Thompson asked.

"Nothing," Kalman said. "Washington doesn't want us spooking Higson. Nothing changes. They're continuing to gather information, but until they have their case, we're not authorized to even be in Coahoma County."

"That's ridiculous," Mulevsky snapped.

"Those are the orders," said his boss.

"What about attending the trial?" Thompson said.

"Forget it. We don't know anything about him, his contacts, who he's working with. It's too risky."

"What about the sheriff's office?" Mulevsky said.

"Collins?" Kalman said.

"Yeah," Mulevsky said. "Call them. Have them keep a long-distance eye on him."

"You'd trust them to do that? Not me. We just stay clear until we're notified. If we screw this up and Higson walks away, and if the network remains intact or disbands without any arrests, I can guarantee you we'll all be fired, gentlemen. We stay away, period. Got it?"

No one responded.

He glanced around the conference table. "Good. If anyone wants to review the file, it'll be in my office. And I'll get a copy made and put in records."

He quickly left, slamming the door in his haste.

Bob watched him leave then looked over the top of his coffee cup at Dan. Their eyes met briefly, and then Bob looked back at the door.

CHAPTER 24

Mr. Judge, please don't break so hard.

—*Peg Leg Howell*

TWO DAYS BEFORE THE TRIAL, TACKETT ASKED TO MEET with Judge Long and Charlie.

"Judge," Tackett said. "We've had some luck with our investigation."

"Oh really," the judge said.

"We have a witness."

"To what?"

"The most recent homicide."

"Who do you have?" Charlie said, immediately concerned.

"Conrad Higson."

"You mean that professor who's been working on the harvester?" Judge Long asked.

"Seems he was out walking that night," Tackett said, "and saw the murder take place."

"Walking?" Long asked. "Credible story?"

"It checked out," Tackett said.

"And he identified Luke?" Charlie asked.

"Yes," Tackett said. "From his picture in the paper. No doubt about it."

"Well that changes a few things," Judge Long said. "What would you like to do?"

Tackett turned his chair slightly to face them both. "I'd like to delay trial on the four previous indictments. That should make you happy." He looked over at Charlie. "Then we'll have the grand jury issue another indictment, and we'll arraign and try Luke for the last murder. Depending on the outcome of the trial, we may or may not try the other indictments. Our primary evidence in the second trial, if we need one, will be the confession."

"Inadmissible," said Charlie. "Don't forget that. Judge, the confession was taken under duress, and we will not allow its use during trial. And you don't have a confession to the last killing."

"Judge," Tackett said, "Luke's initial statements were given willingly."

"Come on, Sam," said Charlie. "You know—"

"All right, boys," Judge Long said, "let's not get worked up. I told you we'll have a hearing to decide its admissibility. *If* we ever get to that point. We've got a lot to do before then."

"I want to speak with Higson," Charlie said.

"He's declined to speak with the defense until the trial," Tackett said. "You'll have to wait until cross-examination."

"Judge?" Charlie asked.

"It's Higson's prerogative," Judge Long said.

"Then what the hell are we trying Luke for?" Charlie said, standing up. "You're just wasting everyone's time. You've got a witness, a confession, and a string of murders. Let's send him to Parchman and be done with it."

Tackett looked to Judge Long to speak.

"I told you why," Judge Long said. "Folks want a trial. And we're going to give them one. If he's found guilty, then there's nothing anyone can say. We'll have done our part."

Charlie glared at the judge and Tackett, picked up his bag, and left.

"Do what you need to, Sam," Judge Long said. "We're staying on schedule."

Tackett plowed through his plan quickly. He prepared the paperwork, and the grand jury wasted no time in issuing another indictment for the fifth killing. Luke was arraigned again and pled "not guilty" to a single charge of murder.

On the day of the trial, Tackett met Montgomery and Sheriff Collins at his office, and the three men walked to the courtroom. There they struggled through a throng of people the size of which, folks later agreed, no one could remember having seen at a trial in at least fifteen years. Inside the courtroom, Tackett said his hellos and took his place at the prosecutor's table. He glanced at the jury box almost instinctively, but it was empty. The jury they had chosen so recently was still waiting outside, and even though representative of the county, the number of farmers bothered him. He had dismissed all he could. He opened a large briefcase and removed several stacks of papers and placed them on the desk, organizing them neatly for the day's work.

The room was filling up, and Tackett looked around at the gathering spectators: the white attendees found seats on the main floor, the black ones in the balcony.

Travis took a seat next to his father, several rows behind Tackett. Sheriff Collins sat near the back.

Charlie Usher entered the courtroom a few minutes after Tackett and sat at the defense table. Although his briefcase was the same size as Tackett's, its contents, once emptied, didn't add up to one-third the volume of papers Tackett had produced.

Tackett saw Conrad Higson slip into a back row.

Elma Williams sat two rows behind Usher. None of the children was present, but Reverend Coulter was sitting next to her. She wouldn't attend any other day of the trial. She was only here today because a friend of hers was testifying, and she was able to get a ride from the reverend. Tackett noticed the preacher was holding her hand; she looked pale and nervous.

Five minutes before the start of the trial, one of the jailhouse guards escorted Luke Williams into the courtroom. The buzz throughout the crowd picked up, and everyone's eyes turned to watch Luke take his seat next to his attorney. Tackett scanned the room, watching everyone except Luke.

The defendant was dressed in brown pants and a white shirt, which Charlie had loaned him for the trial. Both had been recently cleaned and pressed. Luke's shoes were also brown, and Charlie had made sure they were shined before he had them delivered to Luke's cell. After he had combed his hair, Luke looked like he might be about to attend church, not a murder trial.

He approached the table, and Elma gave him a fluttering wave of her hand, which held a handkerchief. Luke smiled in return.

After Luke was seated, the courtroom became quiet again.

At exactly 9:00 a.m., Judge Long burst into the courtroom through his chamber entrance.

The bailiff barely had time to call the court to order. "This court is now in session," he barked.

Banging his gavel once, the judge took his seat and began to arrange his notes. "Be seated," he said. "Does the prosecution or defense have anything to say before we get started?"

"No, your honor," Tackett said. Usher mumbled something similar.

"All right, show the jury in," Judge Long said.

The bailiff led the twelve white men to their seats. Tackett and Usher scrutinized them again, although they had seen them earlier in the week. The jurors took their seats, looking around the courtroom and at Luke. Tackett watched them carefully, looking to see what they thought of Luke's physical appearance. Did they seem sympathetic to him? Did they look at him like a stranger or a long-lost relative? The jury included only one sharecropper, but there were several farmers who knew well Luke's chronic plight. They'd be the ones to side with the defense.

But Tackett also knew there were a lot of murders on the table, although only one was being tried at this time. It would be easy to acquit Luke if he had killed just one man in the heat of the moment, if, perhaps, that person had given Luke any back talk or spoken disrespectfully to him or his wife, or if it was self-defense. But four other murders were looming like a cloak over the trial. There were just too many to rationalize.

The judge introduced the trial as the State of Mississippi versus Luke Williams, and then summarized the charge against Luke for the jury. After dispatching some administrative issues, the judge looked hard at Tackett, then Usher. "Are you ready to proceed with your opening statements?"

Both men answered in the affirmative.

Tackett stood first and spoke slowly and deliberately, sounding as though he knew that Luke was guilty, and he was sure he had several jurors believing it, too. He explained the murder, summarizing the graphic details, and captured the jury's and the courtroom's attention. He discussed the evidence—although it was little—the motive, and the opportunity. He intentionally alluded to the other murders, but the allusion was subtle.

"I intend to show you that the murders were committed by a single individual. And that man is sitting right over there." He pointed toward Luke.

The judge slightly raised an eyebrow, but that was all. Usher didn't seem to notice. He was busy rehearsing his own opening statement.

Tackett closed his remarks by thanking the jury, and then he sat down.

Judge Long looked at Charlie. "Are you ready?"

Charlie stepped up to the jury box and looked at all the members seated there. He looked over at Luke, and then out to the rows of people in the courtroom. Tackett had a witness, but he still had to prove guilt. Beyond a reasonable doubt.

"Members of the jury," Charlie began. "Today, I'm representing Mr. Luke Williams. I'm his defense attorney. I'm going to help show that Mr. Williams is no more a killer than I am. Or you are." He pointed a finger at them and raised his voice a notch. The jury sat up, attentive. "Now, what the district attorney has just told you is that Mr. Williams—may I call him Luke?" Familiarity would warm him to the jury.

Tackett stood up. "Your honor?"

"Mr. Usher," Judge Long said. "Please address your client properly in court."

"The district attorney has just told you," Charlie resumed, "that Mr. Williams committed a murder. One murder. And he's got a little evidence he'll show you to try and prove it. But does he look like a murderer to you? He surely doesn't to me."

Charlie began to pace in front of the jurors.

"Do you know what Mr. Williams does for a living?" he said, hoping none of the jury would try to answer. "He's a sharecropper. Any of you sharecroppers or farmers? Work in agriculture?"

Several jurors raised their hands.

"Good, good. I thank you for the delicious meals I get at home."
He chuckled, and a couple of the jurors nodded their heads with
pride. "Well, now, do farmers work half a day or a whole day?
Mornings or afternoons?"

No one answered, but they all looked curiously at Charlie.

"Well, the farmers I know work all day and into the night. And
when they're not working, they're preparing for the next day's work.
And when they're not preparing, they're so tired they can barely
stand up. They're exhausted from the endless days of backbreaking
work. Those the farmers you know? Those are the ones I know.
Mr. Williams has worked every day of his life, for as long as he can
remember. He told me that and so did his wife."

Charlie picked up a handkerchief from his table and wiped his
forehead. The fans weren't doing much to cool the room.

"Do you really think Mr. Williams had the time to plan and
carry out a murder? And if he could find the energy, how do you
think he got so far away from home without a car? The body was
found across the county, a long way from Mr. Williams's house. I
believe it's just not possible that Mr. Williams had the time or the
opportunity to commit this crime. And I think you'll agree with
me after you hear more about the murder, where it took place, and
how it occurred."

Charlie paused to sip from the glass of water on his table. Luke
looked at him inquisitively, and Charlie looked away.

"Now, what about the evidence?" Charlie said. "The evidence!
You've got to have some evidence to convict a man. That's what's
supposed to make the case against an accused man, isn't it? Where's
the evidence?" Charlie asked rhetorically. "Well, you're going to see
that there is little to no evidence. And don't you think that before we
sentence a man to death, or put him in Parchman for life, we ought
to have some real evidence? And a lot of it. I certainly wouldn't
want to be convicted on hearsay and rumor, would you?"

Charlie turned his head and looked into Sam's eyes. The district attorney stared back at him. He seemed to be taking this personally. Charlie returned to the jury.

"Finally, we've got to address motive. There has to be a motive for this murder. I mean no one kills a man without a motive. And we've got to hear one, or again, I'm gonna have a hard time believing that Mr. Williams is responsible. You know, people kill for all kinds of reasons—jealousy, hate, revenge. Some people are just crazy, and they run out and kill people for any old reason, even a made-up one. But whatever the reason, there is one. Has to be one. And that, along with evidence, is what the prosecution is obliged to show you and get you to believe. That Mr. Williams had a motive for what he allegedly did. It's the prosecutor's responsibility to show you that. And if he can't or won't, or you just don't believe it, then Mr. Williams has got to go free."

Charlie took another sip of water. "I hope I've made it clear what the prosecution has to do and what I have to do. You have a difficult task, but I know you'll make the right decision. For yourselves and for Mr. Williams."

Charlie stood for a moment, making eye contact with each of the jurors one by one. Then he turned away and sat back down at his table. Tackett would have to work for this one. Only after the final verdict was read would Charlie know what the jury believed and understood.

Luke leaned over just inches from his face. "That was pretty good," he whispered. "Maybe I'm glad I asked for a lawyer. But let's don't make it too good. I don't want to die, but cell life ain't bad."

Charlie looked perplexed. What did that mean? he asked himself. "Don't get overly excited. We've got a long way to go."

Tackett knew that Charlie wouldn't let Luke take the stand. He didn't even have to ask. Tackett's first witness was Mrs. Sarah Miller, who lived with her husband and children about a mile from the Williamses. She was about Elma's age, late twenties, and wore a simple beige dress that might have been borrowed, considering its good condition. She appeared nervous, almost trembling. Tackett would have to tread lightly. He didn't want her to cry. Didn't want the jury thinking he was bullying her.

Like Luke and Elma, Mrs. Miller and her husband were sharecroppers. They attended church together, and she praised Elma's singing talents. "She knows almost every song in the hymnal," Mrs. Miller said. She also mentioned the help Elma was receiving from Mr. Miller, her husband, and others.

"Since Luke's been gone, my husband has been helping Elma with her crops. Or, I should say, Mr. Williams's crops. She can't do it by herself, and Luke always raised a good crop and put food on the table. Once all the crops are sold, we're gonna split the money. Then next year, we'll do the same thing. We'll just keep going until he comes home."

Finally, Tackett inquired about what he really wanted to know, and asked Mrs. Miller if her family owned or had access to a vehicle. She said they did not but that their neighbors four miles away had one. Feeling he had achieved his goal of proving Luke had access to a car if he needed one, Tackett had no further questions for his first witness.

CHAPTER 25

Down to the churchhouse!

—Robert Petway

TRAVIS LEANED AGAINST THE CAR, WHICH WAS PARKED in front of the church. His foot rested on the car's running board, his fingers tapped rhythmically on the roof.

Where the heck was Wayne? He had known about this revival for two weeks. It was one of the last revivals of the season, and one of the best, especially if you'd never been to one. From what Travis had heard, the Church of Christ in God, or the "Holy Rollers" as nonmembers called them, was the most enthusiastic church in the black community.

Over the years, Travis had learned a lot about the black churches and their history. Methodists, Baptists, African Methodist-Episcopal, and Catholics all had one thing in common: their God was a maternal one who showed great mercy. In white churches, the ones that Travis had attended all his life, God was cast in the image of a father, a strict disciplinarian.

Tonight, Travis was eagerly expecting to see someone "get religion" or "get the Holy Ghost," but without Wayne he might not have the nerve to go alone. He should have asked Hannah to go with him, but it was too late now.

Travis watched as people continued to make their way into the church. It was filling up. After waiting for half an hour, he decided Wayne was not going to show up, and Travis climbed back into his car. But his hand paused on the ignition. He looked at the people streaming in. Why shouldn't I go in? he thought. I'm already here.

As Travis walked toward the front door, he wasn't sure how he would be received, but he would try to be discreet by standing near the back. Once inside, he realized he had few options where to stand, and he took a place next to the wall. A woman standing in front of him looked over her shoulder. "Good evening," Travis said politely.

"Evenin'," she murmured, and turned back toward the front.

The seated parishioners, led enthusiastically by a woman who stood on a platform at the front of the church, swayed back and forth, clapping their hands and praising the Lord. The crowd continued to swell, and Travis was pushed forward several feet while others squeezed into the building.

Eventually, the woman on the platform stopped chanting and clapping, and the parishioners followed her lead. She then read several passages of scripture, pausing only for the frequent calls of "Amen" from her rapt audience.

Travis noticed the woman next to him was quite vocal. Soon, he got caught up in the moment and uttered an "Amen" himself. Nobody seemed to mind.

The temperature in the building had climbed considerably since Travis had arrived. With the oil lamps lighting the interior, the crowd, and the night's late-summer heat, Travis felt beads of sweat begin to gather on his forehead and the familiar sensation of his damp shirt beginning to stick to his back. He looked around at the people dressed in proper worshipping attire, dresses and suits, and couldn't imagine how they could bear the heat. But then he remembered many of them worked all day under a burning sun.

After the Scriptures were read, the woman asked, "Does anyone want, I mean need, to testify tonight? Who needs to testify?"

Several hands went up.

"Come on up," she said. "One at a time, y'all."

Some began with a hymn and others just stood on the platform and started talking. Travis could barely hear the meeker ones. And some made more gyrations than noise.

One young man of about twelve got up and slowly walked to the front of the church. Travis could barely see him until he mounted the platform. A hush fell over the crowd.

"I got the Lord the day my momma died," he said with a bowed head.

"Oh, Jesus," a woman moaned.

"The Lord, he come to me when the first load of dirt hit the top of her coffin," the boy said. "I could feel him come inside me, touch my heart, and tell me it was time to become a man. I said, 'A man, Jesus?'" The boy was rocking side to side. "And He said, 'That's right, a man.' I said, 'I ain't ready.' And He said, 'Don't matter. It's gonna be all right 'cause I'm walking right beside you.'"

"Praise that baby," another woman said.

"And He walks with me every day and sleeps with me every night."

"Every night," someone said.

"And now I'm okay 'cause I got Jesus with me." The boy stepped down from the platform, and people clapped and patted him on the back. A woman who had kept shouting out during his testimony grabbed him and hugged him like she'd never see him again. He smiled, but with a pained expression on his face.

Travis felt the testimonies exciting the crowd. Everyone was moving, swaying, chanting, and Amening more and more.

An older man tried to testify, but he fell to one knee before he could get a word out and had to be led from the platform.

After the testimonies, a collection basket went around, the woman leading the service asking for "buffaloes" and "brownies." Songs and prayers continued while she encouraged the attendees to give a bit more, and then a bit more again. The collection was completed only when she pronounced herself satisfied with the amount.

Finally, after the collection, the woman took a seat on the platform. There was silence for a few moments. Once or twice someone cried out, "Jesus is in me," or "Praise the Lord." The woman in front of Travis shouted both.

Several minutes passed and everyone was in deep reflection, praying and shouting when necessary. Travis bowed his head, peeking every once in a while to see what was happening.

Then, shouts and screams rang out as a man who had been sitting in a chair on the platform stood and walked to the center. He looked over the congregation, raised his arms toward heaven, and shouted, "Amen, Jesus. Amen."

Travis jumped when several people around him immediately shouted out in response. The entire congregation began clapping rhythmically, in unison. Obviously, everyone had been waiting for this, and Travis smiled when the man gave himself over to the crowd's enthusiasm. This was what Travis had come for.

"My name is Reverend Taylor," the man said. "Reverend Taylor," he reiterated again for emphasis, raising his voice.

"Tell us, Reverend," a voice said from the crowd.

"Tell it all," another followed.

"Oh, I will brother," he said. "I will."

Another shout came from someone near the front.

The reverend looked out over the crowd. "I see a lot of ladies here tonight. That's good. But does that mean your men don't need saving?"

Some laughs were heard from the audience.

"Or maybe they've already been saved?"

Reverend Taylor took a handkerchief from his pocket and wiped his face. "It's warm tonight."

More Amens.

"But— not as hot as the Devil's house," he said.

"Oh no!" someone said.

"Not that hot," added another voice.

"But tonight, we're gonna cool it down," the reverend said, "because this is the Lord's house. And there isn't any place for the Devil in the Lord's house."

The crowd shouted in unison.

"Where is the Lord? Where is Jesus?" he said.

"Come to us, Jesus," a woman said.

"Can you find him?"

"Is he here?" He pointed to his head. "Here?" He pointed to his heart. "Here?" He pointed to a chair. Then a lamp, then outside. Then he swirled his arm over his head. "Where is Jesus?" Reverend Taylor paced across the platform, back and forth. "Where is He? Where is my Jesus?" Finally, he stopped. He turned, faced the crowd, and slowly raised his eyes.

"Did you find Him, Reverend?" a voice said.

"Oh, I found Him, all right," the preacher answered.

"Where was He?"

"He's everywhere. Here, here, here, here," he said, jumping up and down on the platform. Then Reverend Taylor moved around the room, pointing at adults, babies, chairs, the platform itself. "He's over here and there." He squeezed between people, touched them on their heads, and even went outside the building for a moment. His frantic motions whipped the crowd into a frenzy. They shouted and clapped and yelled, "He's here," as they pointed at themselves or their friends.

The reverend returned to the platform. He was breathing heavily. "Jesus is everywhere, my friends. He is everything."

Hallelujahs and Amens sounded all through the room.

The reverend took a sip of water and looked out over the congregation.

Travis noticed that although it was hot in the room, the reverend had not removed his coat. In fact, he still looked quite composed.

The crowd in its excitement had pushed farther into the room, though Travis had thought that impossible. The aisles were packed, the benches full, and Travis was holding himself stiffly to keep from pushing on the woman in front of him. Two people had already fainted and been carried out, overcome by "getting the Holy Ghost," though it looked like they had merely succumbed to the heat.

Now Reverend Taylor changed his demeanor, turning to the crowd and almost whispering, "And where is the Devil?"

"Oh no," someone said.

"Is he with Jesus?"

"No. Never," said the crowd.

"Is he outside?"

Travis noticed the crowd was tentative.

"Is he there?" the reverend asked, pointing to a baby who'd been sleeping by the platform.

"Oh no, not a baby," said a woman seated near the child.

"Is he here?" he said, pointing at himself. "And is he out there?" He pointed into the audience.

Only a few affirmatives came from the audience.

"You bet he is. He's in my heart, and he's in your heart. But he's not everywhere, oh no. He's not in the babies, and he's not in the animals. He's not in a mule, and he's not in a pig. The Devil's only in us."

The crowd pondered this while the reverend paced.

"So, if the Devil's in us and the Lord is everywhere, well then, what can we do? To the Devil?"

"Get him out," someone said.

"Oh yeah," the reverend said. "Oh yeah. Who said that? Who said that?" he asked, walking into the throng toward the part of the room from which the voice had risen.

A hand went up on one of the benches.

"You stand up, sinner."

A man stood up.

"Did y'all hear that? Did y'all hear that?"

Amens rang out.

"We're going to run that Devil off, because Jesus is everywhere and the Devil is hiding. He's hiding in our hearts and the Lord knows it. Like finding a weevil in the cotton, the Lord knows where to look for the Devil. And when the Lord finds him, oh the Devil's gonna pay."

"Gonna pay," the crowd echoed.

Travis could feel the reverend leading his flock just where he wanted them to go. The crowd was excited, almost wild, clapping, shouting out, praising the Lord. This was what they all had come for—to be infused with the power of the Lord—and the reverend knew just how to do it. He took them down, then up, then back down again. Now, he was building to the peak.

"He's gonna pay," the reverend said, swinging his arm down like he was chopping a chicken's head off.

The church members responded with their own condemnations of the Devil. They moved and sang and shouted, pushing the people toward the front of the congregation closer and closer to the platform.

"And how are we gonna make him pay?" the reverend said, moving back and forth across the platform, inciting the crowd into a religious fervor. "I'll tell you how, brothers and sisters. We're gonna sing, and we're gonna pray. That's how we'll pay that old Devil back."

Travis watched, fascinated. He glanced toward the front and noticed a woman wearing a long-sleeved dress, who earlier in the service had been seated in the first row, now standing as she clapped, sang, and prayed along with the reverend. Suddenly, she slumped forward, her body splaying out onto the platform as she lost consciousness. Her arm struck an oil lamp and sent it careening across the platform. The lamp's oil splashed across the wooden structure, onto some curtains, and instantly set everything in its path ablaze, the dry wood serving to spread the flames to the walls of the rickety building.

The reverend's back had been turned when the lamp fell, and the singing and clapping made it difficult to hear any of the commotion. In the moment before the reverend turned around, the fire was already burning out of control.

From where he stood, Travis could do nothing but watch it unfold.

Realizing it would be futile to attempt to extinguish the fire, the reverend tended immediately to several children who were sleeping near the platform, making sure their mothers picked them up and headed away from the flames. Next, Reverend Taylor turned his attention to the woman who had fallen. Two people were trying to help, but they weren't moving her away from the flames. In two steps the preacher reached her side, took her by the feet, and began to drag her away. But his progress was halted by the mass of people trying to flee.

The singing that moments earlier had filled the air had turned to screams. Smoke filled the room. The windows, really cutouts in the walls that looked like windows, were jammed with bodies scrambling to get out. Travis had been pushed away from a window into the middle of the room, carried along by those around him. The woman he had stood next to through most of the service was behind him now. Travis could hear her cries.

"Oh hurry, hurry, we've got to get out," she said. "I don't want to burn. Only people in hell burn."

Even in all the turmoil, Travis thought, she's still preoccupied with the sermon.

The crowd moved toward the door slowly, more and more people coughing and choking around him. When the man behind him started to cough, Travis found himself scared.

He turned to watch the blaze momentarily. The entire front portion of the building was now on fire.

No longer near a window, there was only one way out, and the mass of people surged toward it. Travis felt the woman behind him pushing him forward. By the time he realized she was falling, it was too late. She clutched his shirt on the way down, and her weight and the awkwardness of his position in the crowd also dragged Travis down.

They fell together, and as the people around them tried to make room for their tangled bodies, they began to topple in a domino-like reaction. The panic intensified as the smoke in the air thickened.

Travis lay near the bottom of a pile, and the woman who had pulled him down was actually now underneath him. He tried to rise, but the weight of others was too much. He lodged an elbow and a knee between him and the floor to protect the unconscious woman under him. People continued to fall, but now farther away from where Travis was trapped. He tried again to push himself up but could not budge those above him.

Then, he felt another body fall on top of him, this one with such force that it pushed Travis away from the woman he was protecting. He landed on his left side, and an arm from the massive body came down across the side of Travis's windpipe, restricting his breathing.

Travis couldn't see the man's face because he was slightly behind him, but he assumed the man had passed out. He tried to move the arm off his neck, tried to breathe, but he couldn't budge it. Travis tried not to panic. Then he realized the man was not unconscious but was in fact holding his arm tight against Travis's throat.

Unable to move, the smoke and heat overwhelming him, Travis began to gasp. The man on top of him moved his arm slightly, and Travis took a deeper breath, though he still could not move his head. Travis felt isolated and removed from the madness, like he was floating. Then he felt the man's mouth right next to his ear.

"Your daddy and all his friends wastin' their time," the man hissed, "trying to find out who killed all them niggers. So what if some poor white trash did it. He may go to jail, he may not. Nobody cares 'cept the white folks. He'll always be nothing, nobody, like the rest of us. And people will forget about those killings quick as they happened."

Travis moved his head to get some air, but the man on top of him forced his arm down harder. Travis relaxed.

"The man they ought be looking after is Vidla," the man continued. "Lot a people say he ain't doing right. But no nigger gonna say anything against a white man."

Travis felt the man's arm relax. Then he pushed up, off of Travis's shoulder, and got to his feet.

Several people who had been entangled with Travis also moved, and finally he was able to kneel. He looked up, but all he saw was the man's back before he disappeared into the smoke.

Finally, the fallen bodies started to clear. Someone lifted Travis to his feet. The woman who had fallen with Travis was already gone. He and a few remaining congregants stumbled outside and stood watching with everyone else while the flames engulfed the building.

Outside, family and friends reunited after having been separated in the panic, tears of joy and cries of praise spreading to all. A chorus of "Amen" and "Praise the Lord" rose amid the scattered coughs when it became clear that everyone had managed to escape the conflagration.

After a while, Reverend Taylor tried to refocus his flock, leading them in a short walk to a field about forty yards from the church. "Come on now," he said, urging gently. "Come to me."

"The Lord told us something tonight," the preacher said to his congregation gathered in the field. "He let us live to pray, and He let us live to take His word to others. To be His missionaries. To be His light."

"So, I want you—no, I *need you* to rise up tonight and spread His word—to your friends, your family, your neighbors, and your community. Remember where Jesus lives, and don't forget that the Devil is always lurking, waiting for you to forget that Jesus is in your heart. Now go and do His work."

The reverend's helpers began to take up the final collection of the evening. Travis watched from the edge of the group. The crowd, holding hands and praying as the flames leaped up behind them, created a picture that looked to Travis like heaven at the gates of hell. From heaven to hell—all on a small slice of Mississippi Delta. It was a revival no one would forget.

As Travis stood watching, the words that echoed in his mind were not those of the reverend but those of a man who had truly testified.

CHAPTER 26

Judge, don't ask me no questions.

—John T. Smith

SAM TACKETT SAT WITH HIS HANDS FOLDED IN FRONT of him and waited for Judge Bertram Long to begin.

"The first order of business is the schedule," the judge said. "We will only be in court today and Wednesday of this week. I have a federal case that I'm presiding over, and I must prepare for it on Tuesday with the federal prosecutor, and then I'm in Oxford Thursday and Friday. I'll return on Monday of next week to finish the trial. I apologize for the unconventional format, gentlemen, but it can't be helped."

Tackett stood and was recognized. "Your honor," he said, "this is most unusual, changing the days and times we meet. This is a murder trial, your honor, and altering the daily schedule is disruptive to the jury. I fear they won't be able to render a proper verdict with all these shifts in time."

"I *know* what kind of trial it is, Mr. Tackett. And I believe the jury can remember what's going on, even if we don't meet every day. This is not a complicated matter, and until you're sitting up here, and I'm down there, Mr. Tackett, we're doing this my way."

In reality, Tackett didn't care, but he tried to put on a good show for the jury, to demonstrate he was watching out for them. At least that's what he hoped they were thinking.

Judge Long turned to the jury. "Over the next few days, we will not be on a regular schedule. I will allow you to return home at night, but you must not discuss the trial or anything that goes on in the courtroom with anyone. Not your friends, not your wives, not your neighbors. No one. Is that understood?"

The jurors nodded.

Tackett looked down at his witness list. There were four witnesses left: Sheriff Collins, Bill Montgomery, Horace Johnson, who had been a friend of the victim, and Conrad Higson.

"Call your next witness, Mr. Tackett," Judge Long said. "We haven't got all day."

Tackett tried to ignore the comment. "The state calls Sheriff Frank Collins."

Collins was quickly sworn in and took a seat on the stand.

"For the record," Tackett said, "please state your name and occupation."

"I'm Sheriff Frank Collins, and I'm the law in Coahoma County, Mississippi."

"And how long have you been sheriff of Coahoma County?"

"Going on six years."

"Now, Sheriff, I've called you because we'll be discussing the crime scene today, to give the jury a sense of the crime and how heinous and vicious it was. We will also be introducing some pictures of the crime scene. As the sheriff, you're always one of the first people on the scene after a crime has been committed. Or at least discovered. Is that correct?"

"Yes, that's correct, Sam."

Judge Long cleared his throat. "Sheriff," Judge Long said, "please address the district attorney formally during your testimony."

"Mr. Tackett," Collins said. He slowly shifted in his chair and looked over his shoulder at the judge.

Tackett walked over to his table, picked up a piece of paper, and turned to Collins. "Seeing that you're usually at the crime scene before anyone else, could you please describe the circumstances that led you to the deceased?"

"I received a call late in the afternoon on Monday, the twenty-sixth. The caller indicated that a body was hanging out near 49. He gave me some general directions, landmarks, what to look for, then he hung up. That's when I called you and Mr. Montgomery, and we drove out there."

"And can you describe the scene?"

"He was hanging from a tree."

"Was he dead?"

"Yes, sir."

"Had you ever seen him before?"

"No, Mr. Tackett."

"Can you tell us anything else about the victim and his demise?"

"He apparently was a day laborer. Come to Clarksdale looking to make a little extra money during the picking season. We named him John Doe number five until someone came forward and identified him."

Collins hadn't finished his sentence when the judge's gavel slammed down so hard several jurors jumped in their seats. Everyone turned and faced the judge.

Tackett knew what was coming.

"Get to the bench, counselors," the judge said, his crimson face glaring at them.

Tackett and Usher stood like misbehaved schoolboys before the judge.

"What the hell was that, Sam?"

The judge was madder than Tackett thought he would be.

"I don't know what the hell you think you're doing, but I'm tempted to let Charlie move for a mistrial and grant it."

"That was my next request," Usher said.

"Denied, this time. Sam, do you have any explanation for this?" the judge said.

Tackett knew that referring to a dead body as number five would tell the jury that there were a slew of bodies in the morgue. And everyone knew that Luke might be related to some or all of them. "That's how the sheriff and others at the morgue were referring to the victims."

"Well we're only talking about one victim during this trial. And you had better start referring to that victim properly in my court or you're out. Got it?"

"Yes, your honor," Tackett said. He had tried to slip one by, but now it didn't seem so clever.

After the judge instructed the jury what to disregard, Tackett continued questioning Collins. "You indicated someone came forward and identified the body?"

"Yes," Collins said. "The victim's name was Milton Hibbs."

"And you found him hanging out near 49?"

"Yes, like I told you before."

"That's not unusual around here, is it? Was it a lynching?"

"No. I usually know about those. No one knew about this one. It wasn't a lynching."

Tackett picked up a set of pictures from his table and handed them to Collins. Then he continued. "Do you recognize these pictures, Sheriff?"

"Yes, they were taken at the site of the murder by my department's photographer."

"And they depict what you saw the morning the body was discovered?"

"Yes."

"And that man in the pictures was identified as Milton Hibbs?"

"Yes."

Tackett went on for ten minutes summarizing the details of the crime. "Is my description consistent with what you found when you investigated the crime scene?"

"For the most part," Collins said.

"What isn't?"

"It's consistent."

"Thank you."

Tackett offered the photographs into evidence, and Usher quickly objected because of their graphic nature. Judge Long overruled him and motioned for Tackett to continue.

"Sheriff, you're somewhat familiar with Mr. Williams's whereabouts over the past few weeks, is that correct?" Tackett knew not to mention that Luke had been in jail on other charges. Charlie would object immediately.

"Yes," Collins said. "I've been able to keep an eye on him sometimes."

"And so, can you tell us where Mr. Williams was on the night of the murder?"

"No, I can't."

"So, unless we hear otherwise from the defense, Mr. Williams cannot be accounted for on the night of the murder. Is that correct?"

"I don't know where he was that night."

Tackett leafed through some papers he was holding, studying them intently. The court was quiet. Tackett hoped they were all pondering his line of questions and Collins's answers. His next question needed just the right moment. "Sheriff, who killed Milton Hibbs?"

The sheriff started to speak Luke's name and point in his direction, but Charlie Usher rose to his feet. "Objection, your honor," he said, trying to drown out Collins's voice. Luke's name was barely audible. "Determining guilt is the province of the jury, not the county sheriff. And any deduction is completely without foundation. What exactly is the sheriff going to base his determination on? We haven't heard anything today that could possibly indicate the identity of the assailant? Maybe Mr. Tackett will provide an affidavit from the deceased, positively identifying the killer. I didn't see Sheriff Collins on the night of the murder; maybe he thinks I did it. Regardless, this is not the sheriff's responsibility. Unless he was at the scene of the crime during the murder, which he wasn't."

Charlie heard the snickers and watched a juror or two turn to his neighbor and smile. "Judge," Charlie continued, "I request that any statements or references from Sheriff Collins which were speculative or require a conclusion based on limited facts be stricken. This is ludicrous and is only Mr. Tackett's feeble attempt to create an impression among the jury that there is any real evidence in this trial."

"Your honor," Tackett protested. "I'm only asking the sheriff to provide an answer based on his years of experience as a sheriff and having been involved in cases like this before."

"Gentlemen," the judge snarled, tapping his gavel.

"Nonsense," Charlie said. "The sheriff has no more insight into this case, based on anything the prosecution has presented so far, than I do, your honor. What the prosecutor is doing is getting the sheriff to mutter my client's name within the context of this murder. Everyone in this courtroom could be a suspect."

"Your honor—" Tackett began.

The gavel descended again, louder than before.

"The objection is sustained," Judge Long said. "Mr. Tackett, present us with facts and keep the opinions of your witnesses out of my courtroom. Is that understood?"

Tackett raised his hand to speak, but the judge ignored him and then instructed the jury once again to disregard certain parts of the sheriff's testimony. "Mr. Usher, would you like to cross?" the judge asked.

"Yes, your honor," Charlie said.

Charlie positioned himself next to the stand where Sheriff Collins was sitting. "I only have a couple of questions. Did you inspect the body at the scene or wait until later?"

"We cut the body down," Collins said, "and checked it right there before we sent him to the morgue."

"Did you find anything? I mean on his person."

"A few things."

"Can you be more descriptive?"

"A ring, watch, pocketknife, and some money, a very small amount."

"You found all *that*?" He stepped away from the sheriff and faced the jury.

"Yes."

"Well then, it seems to me that robbery couldn't have been a motive for this killing. Now we're getting somewhere." He turned and faced Collins again. "So, if he wasn't killed for his belongings, then why do you think he was killed?"

"Objection," Tackett said. "Speculative."

"Sustained," Judge Long said.

Charlie nodded. "Okay, let's look at what we've got. One black man, a day laborer—not from Clarksdale—found dead with all of his personal effects. He'd been stabbed, beaten, and strung up. That's no easy feat for one man, almost couldn't be done. Now, I've lived in Clarksdale long enough to know this sure does look like somebody got lynched. Somebody did something that got him in a whole lot of trouble. I don't know what it was, but it could've been anything that offended the wrong person." Charlie glanced at the jurors. They were considering it. "Sheriff, you mentioned in your earlier testimony that you know about lynchings? Maybe where and when they take place?"

"I don't remember what I said."

"You said it. I'll bet Mr. Tackett remembers." Charlie shot a glance at Tackett. "So I've got to ask you, is it possible this was a lynching you just didn't know about?"

Collins quickly looked to Tackett for guidance.

"The answer's not with Mr. Tackett," Charlie said. "I'll repeat the question. Is it *possible* Hibbs was lynched and you had no knowledge of it—before or after?"

Collins wiped his brow and said, "Not likely, but it's possible."

"Possible, huh. That's all I have your honor." The defense attorney returned to his seat. A doubt in the jurors' minds was all he needed.

"We're breaking for lunch." The judge looked at his watch. "We'll reconvene at two o'clock."

By the time everyone returned to the courtroom, two hours had elapsed. Judge Long had eaten a quick lunch and then taken a nap to avoid falling asleep in the afternoon proceedings.

"All rise," the bailiff said. Judge Long entered the courtroom, which was only half as full as it had been this morning.

"Be seated," the judge said. The crowd seated themselves into the wooden benches and chairs. He sorted through some papers and looked up. "Well, Mr. Tackett, what do you have for us this afternoon?"

Tackett had the county coroner take the stand to discuss the autopsy procedures. Bill Montgomery reviewed the report that Tackett had presented earlier and indicated that some of the injuries were consistent with knife wounds. The bruising around the neck and crushed windpipe were undoubtedly caused by the rope. Montgomery vacillated on whether the victim died from the stabbing or asphyxiation. Whichever it was, both were attributable to the assailant. A number of pictures taken during the autopsy were also submitted as evidence.

Charlie had no questions for the coroner, so he declined cross-examination.

"The prosecution would like to call Horace Johnson," Tackett boomed.

In the back, a slight black man wearing a dark and somewhat tattered suit grabbed the seat back in front of him to pull himself up. He shuffled down the aisle and took the seat in the witness stand. The court was quiet, and all eyes were on this man with a pencil-thin mustache whose ebony face was adorned with lines and creases too numerous to count.

"Good afternoon," Tackett said.

"Good afternoon, suh," he replied.

Tackett knew that in order to convict a white man, he had to erase the victim's color. That's why Horace Johnson was on the stand. Horace would help humanize the victim as someone who could feel pain, could suffer, someone who had a family. Horace would help persuade the jury to think of the murdered field hand as a person, not a thing. Tackett quickly got to the point. "Did you know or ever meet the victim, Milton Hibbs?"

Johnson spoke slowly. "Yessuh, I met him once. We worked a cotton field together, but just one day. My row was next to his so we got to talkin', helped pass the time. I do remember he knew a lot of songs. A pretty fair caller and a hard worker."

"Could you tell us a little about what he looked like, his age, his size?"

"I guess he's about, maybe, thirty. Much younger than me. He was average size. Like you."

Tackett smiled. "What did y'all talk about that day you met him?"

"All sorts of things. Where he was from, his family."

"And where was that?"

"Up near Tupelo. Came for the harvest. Trying to get a little extra cash to put in his pocket. Heard the money was good here."

"He had a family?"

"Yessuh. Five kids, wife. Little place he was fixing up. Wanted to buy some more land, hoping to get a bigger crop so he wouldn't have to travel during harvest."

"Just trying to find a place in this world, wasn't he?"

"Yessuh. Just a little place."

"I think we're all looking for that."

Horace nodded his agreement.

"Could you tell us what you saw when you went down and identified the body at the morgue?"

Horace spent several minutes detailing the savagely beaten remains of Milton Hibbs. His description mimicked Collins's and Montgomery's testimony, but Johnson's hushed, scratchy voice, always seemingly on the verge of cracking, resurrected Hibbs's pain. "He must've been some hurtin'," concluded the witness.

Tackett looked at the jury. Some of them looked a little unsettled, almost queasy. The autopsy pictures were helpful, but Johnson gave the pictures depth and emotion. The jury had all seen death before, but usually only after the undertaker had performed his services, and rarely, if ever, so violently dispatched. Tackett was evoking their sympathy.

"You think he was in a lot of pain?" Tackett asked.

"Dun know 'zactly, but I hope he died quick."

"I hope so, too." Tackett glanced at the jury. "A man shouldn't have to suffer that much. One more question: Do you know what's being done with the body?"

"I heard they was gonna send him back to Tupelo, but the family ain't got the money. Don't know 'bout his insurance, and it's a long way by wagon. Just leave him, I guess."

"That's too bad. He won't get a proper burial. The family won't be able to say their final good-byes."

"Yessuh, that's a shame."

"That's all I have, your honor." Tackett took his seat.

"Mr. Usher," Judge Long said.

Charlie started to rise, but Luke placed his hand gently on Charlie's arm. Charlie turned. Luke wore a thoughtful expression, as though he were only now considering the ramifications of what he had done. Horace and Milton weren't much different from Luke. Only in color. Their pain was the same. What color drove apart, pain brought together.

No sense arguing with Luke. Charlie settled back into his seat. "No questions, your honor."

The judge tapped his gavel. "We're adjourned until Wednesday, counselors."

Tackett watched the judge disappear into his chambers, the jury file out, and the spectators start to disperse. Today had been a good day for him.

Charlie walked over to the prosecutor's table. "Maybe Luke would be better off without me," he said. "That way, at least, someone might feel sorry for him."

"Oh, don't worry," Tackett said, "they feel sorry for him all right. You can be sure of that. You see how they were looking at him. It's like they're looking in a mirror. He's one of them. But you know what, I need a conviction. We need a little justice. At least for those he killed."

"How can you *not* get a conviction? The defense is weak. No alibi, no witnesses to where he was that night. All I got is a white man who won't and shouldn't take the stand, and reasonable doubt. What else do you need?"

Could that be enough? Tackett thought. One more witness was all he had. "We'll see."

CHAPTER 27

Please take a walk with me.

—Robert Lockwood

TRAVIS HADN'T TOLD ANYONE ABOUT HIS NIGHT AT the revival. He figured nobody would have believed him anyway. He could barely believe it himself; caught inside a church aflame, pinned to the ground while someone whispered gibberish to him.

The Negro community in Clarksdale and throughout the South had always communicated by way of an undercurrent of gossip and news that penetrated even the most remote areas. Travis knew about this but had never experienced it until that night at the church. Its impact and the clarity it provided made Travis wonder what else he didn't know but should. And he wondered what to do with what he knew now.

On Tuesday morning, Travis decided to call Hannah.

"Hello," said the voice on the other end of the phone.

Travis hesitated in the instant it took to recognize her voice. "Hannah, it's Travis," he said.

"Hi," she said, her voice warm and friendly.

"You didn't go to the trial yesterday, did you?"

"No, I couldn't. I was helping my grandmother. She hasn't been herself lately. She's not sick, just not full of energy like she usually is."

"I'm sorry to hear that."

"Thanks, she'll be okay."

"Listen, Hannah." Travis dropped his voice conspiratorially. "I need your help tonight."

"What do you need me to do?"

"I need you to meet me behind the courthouse around nine."

"Behind the courthouse? That sounds rather clandestine. Can you tell me why?"

"Not right now. I'm in a hurry. I'll tell you when we meet."

"Nine?"

"Yeah, I'll see you there."

At a few minutes before nine o'clock on Tuesday night, Travis paused at the front door and told his parents that he was going to a friend's house. "Don't stay out too late," his father said from the easy chair where he was reading the newspaper.

"Just a couple hours," Travis assured him.

Margaret sat near her husband, reading a book and listening to the radio. "Call if it's going to be much longer, please, dear."

"I will, Mom." The screen door slammed shut behind him.

Travis walked toward the courthouse, but not along his usual route. Instead, he headed north on Yazoo Avenue for a block, then west until he reached the Sunflower River. There he turned south, walking along the riverbank until he could see the back of the court-house.

Travis felt certain no one had noticed him. Though it wasn't odd for someone to be out walking this late, a single individual near the courthouse or jail still might draw the attention of a police officer in the area—or worse, a bored neighbor. Travis didn't want any rumors circulating.

He walked to the back of the building and waited quietly for Hannah. After a few minutes, he heard the creak of a door opening. Startled, he stood breathless against the wall.

Someone rounded the corner and peered into the darkness. "Travis?" the figure called out softly.

He recognized the voice immediately. "Hannah! What were you doing inside?"

"Did you forget the curfew? I didn't want to be caught outside. Especially in the back of the courthouse. It was bad enough just trying to get here."

Travis slipped inside the building. "How'd you get in? I've got a key."

"Moses let me in."

They hurried through Moses Hooperman's tiny closet into the hallway where the janitor was working.

"Good evening, Mr. Travis," Moses said, looking Travis straight in the eye.

"He'd have waited outside all night if I hadn't gone out and got him," Hannah said.

"Good thing you did," Moses said.

"Now, what have you dragged me to the courthouse for, Travis?" Hannah said.

"Follow me. I'll tell you on the way."

Leaving Moses to his work, they walked toward the stairs at the other end of the building.

"What's all this about?" she asked again.

"You hear about the fire the other night at that revival?"

"Of course, my parents know some people who were there."

"Well, I was there."

"You were *there?*" she echoed, raising an eyebrow. "Lucky you didn't get hurt."

They went upstairs, and Travis recounted the singing, praying, and preaching. Then about how the fire started, how it spread quickly, and how people had tripped and piled up on the woman who fell. "Eventually, I fell, too," Travis said, his words tumbling out fast but quietly. "There were just so many people pushing and pulling on each other. But a funny thing happened."

"As if something funny could happen in a fire. What was that?"

"Someone grabbed me and kind of held me down. He was strong, because I couldn't move at all. And while he was holding me down, he said the sheriff shouldn't be worried about Luke. He said they should be looking for a Mr. Vidla, maybe. I couldn't hear very well with all the screaming and crying. Have you ever heard that name?"

Hannah shrugged her shoulders. "Mr. Vidla?"

"That's what I thought he said."

"But what are we doing tonight?"

Travis stopped in front of a door on the second floor. The word "Records" was printed on the glass.

"We're here," he announced.

Travis produced a small key ring and tried several keys before finding the one that unlocked the door. They stepped inside, and Travis locked the door behind them. He switched on the lights, walking quickly to the window to close the shade.

"Let's keep away from the window so we don't cast any shadows," he said. "You told Moses that we'd be here for a little while, right?"

"Well, I didn't know how long we'd be, but he'll watch out for us."

"We're going to dig through some records."

"We came all this way to review a bunch of paperwork?"

"Yeah, and I need you because I can't look through all the files myself. Now, I worked in records before, so I know the filing system and which records they keep where. We just need to go through them and see if we can find anything unusual."

"What do you mean?" Hannah said, looking puzzled.

"I mean anything that might be related to what I heard at the revival. Let's start with his name, Mr. Vidla. That should be easy enough to check. But if nothing turns up, then it's going to take a little more time. But if we're lucky, we might run across some documents that would lead us to him."

"We're going to have to be pretty lucky." Hannah surveyed the numerous cabinets and drawers. "Where do we start?"

Travis opened a drawer in a set of files against the wall. "I'm trying to remember where the property records are. These are birth records." He opened and closed another drawer. "And these are—"

"I think these are the property records," Hannah said, pulling a folder out of a different cabinet. "See, they're marked." She pointed to the label on the front of the drawer.

"They must have moved them recently." He removed another folder from her drawer and quickly looked through the contents. "You're right."

"What exactly are we looking for again?"

"A first name or last name that sounds or is spelled like Vidla, V-I-D-L-A. You start with property."

Travis walked over to another set of files on the opposite side of the room. "I'm going to see if I can find him in the voter registration records."

Hannah and Travis began sifting through documents, one drawer after another.

"I just finished the property records, and nothing," Hannah said.

"Not much luck in voter registration either," he said.

"Hey, Travis, this drawer's locked." She was down on one knee yanking on the bottom drawer of a four-file cabinet labeled "Miscellaneous."

Travis came over and pulled on the handle himself just to see if it was stuck. It wouldn't budge. Without hesitation, he opened two drawers at the desk nearest the cabinet and pulled out a set of keys. "Good courthouse security." He tossed the ring of keys to Hannah. "Try one of those."

"First one," she said, pulling open the drawer.

They continued searching, neither one speaking. The only noise in the room was the turning of pages and file drawers opening and closing.

"What was that?" Hannah whispered, turning quickly and dropping a handful of files on the floor.

"What?" Travis strained to hear anything at all.

Then, at once, they both heard it. The rhythmic click of heels on the wooden hallway.

His first duty was to keep Hannah out of trouble. Travis looked at her and then pointed under the desk. She kneeled down and started gathering the scattered papers, pushing them under the desk with her.

Travis moved to shut off the light, then saw a lone figure approach the door. There was no time to do anything but step to the side so that his outline wouldn't be seen and then hurriedly unlock the door because a locked one with him inside might bring suspicion. He waited.

The figure on the other side pulled out some keys. But instead of using them, he turned the knob. The door swung open and a man standing in the entryway stepped back.

"Travis, what the heck are you doing?" the man said, visibly surprised.

"Hello, Mr. Sampleton," Travis said, trying to appear composed. "How are you tonight?"

"I was doing all right until I opened this door. What are you doing here this late?"

Travis looked back into the room nervously and knew at once that he had made a mistake. The hem of Hannah's dress was sticking out from underneath the desk. Awkwardly, Travis stepped through the door into the hallway, blocking Sampleton's entry to the room. "I'm helping my dad out. He needs some death certificates, and I was collecting them for him. I forgot to do it today, and he needs them first thing in the morning."

While he spoke, Travis slowly inched the door shut behind him. He knew the older gentleman would back up if he got close enough. "What brings *you* up here this late?" Travis pressed.

It was a question all of Clarksdale might have asked. Sampleton was an assistant county supervisor, a widower whose grown children had all moved away years ago. Travis had heard he worked late some nights, but no one really knew why.

"Just finishing up some work from this afternoon. Some reports that are due tomorrow."

Travis had his doubts about that. Nothing in county government was due the following day except maybe paychecks.

"Well, I hope you got everything finished," Travis said. "I'm almost done myself."

"Would you like me to wait for you? Give you a ride home?"

Travis could hear the loneliness in Sampleton's voice. "I've got a bit more to do," he said, suddenly kind. "But why don't we have lunch sometime next week? You can fill me in on what Jim and Elsie are up to." Travis was thankful to have recalled the younger Sampletons' names.

"That sounds like a good idea," replied the older man with a shy smile. "Stop by the office during the middle of the week."

"Okay, I'll sure do that, Mr. Sampleton." They shook hands, Travis having his doubts about the commitment he'd just made. The supervisor walked away slowly, and Travis watched until he disappeared down the stairs. Then he listened for the creaky courthouse door's thud before opening the office door.

"All right, he's gone," Travis said.

"That was uncomfortable," Hannah said.

"It would have been a lot more uncomfortable if he found you hiding under the desk." Travis peered underneath the desk. "Are you coming out?"

"In a second. I'm reading something you might find interesting." Hannah scooted out from under the desk and stood up, brushing bits of dust off the front and back of her dress. "Take a look."

"What drawer is this from?" Travis asked, taking the file from Hannah.

"That one right there. The one that was locked." She motioned toward the open drawer with her hand. "There was a section marked 'FBI–Active.' It caught my eye."

The file was thin. Travis glanced over the first piece of paper while Hannah read over his shoulder. It was a standard county form listing the property, its location, and its valuation. Most of the form was left unfilled.

"I don't see a name, only the property description," Travis said.

Travis turned to the last sheet. He read the words typed in the middle of the page: "Restrictions on document content. Refer all questions to the Federal Bureau of Investigation, Jackson, Mississippi."

"What does that mean?" asked Hannah.

"I have no idea. I've never seen anything like this in these files. And look at the date." He paused. "It was filed this year."

Hannah picked the sheet up and turned it over. The reverse side was blank.

Travis quickly used the property address and searched through several other drawers for more information but found nothing.

"You could always drive by and see who lives there," Hannah said.

"We could do that," Travis said, "but maybe this is just some federal property, or the government is leasing space from the county."

"Well, a quick visit wouldn't hurt."

"We could drop by on the pretense of needing something."

"Or you could."

"Yeah, I guess." He winced at the thought of investigating alone.

"Of course, maybe we're just jumping to conclusions. This could be just some filing mistake. You know, the file being in the wrong place."

"Possible. But even if it's nothing, now I'm curious. I'd like to see why there aren't any of the usual property documents in the file." Travis spoke as though he was feeling more certain, more clear, than he had been in days. "I'll run out there tomorrow around noon, when the trial breaks for lunch. I'll look at the property and see who lives there. It'll only take a few minutes."

"You'd better be careful. Remember, the FBI's involved. That's not a good sign."

Travis looked at his watch. It was already half past ten. "We'd better get home," he said. He sat down at the desk, pulled a piece of paper from the trash, and quickly scribbled down the address while Hannah returned the files to their respective drawers.

When they were satisfied that the room was restored to its earlier condition, Travis opened the door. He peeked into the hallway and checked for anyone working even later than Mr. Sampleton. Finding no one, they returned to Moses's room, said their good-byes, and ventured out into the night.

Travis crept into the house and crawled into bed without waking anyone. But he stared at the ceiling for more than an hour, thinking about what he and Hannah had found, before he finally drifted off to sleep.

CHAPTER 28

Hear the thunder rumbling.

—*Maggie Jones*

BOB THOMPSON WAS PLANNING A HUNTING TRIP, from Wednesday through the weekend, and was scheduled to return on Monday. The casework had been slow all week, and Russ Kalman didn't have anything else for him.

Dan Mulevsky left the office early on Tuesday, then called in around lunchtime. "I'll be out the rest of today and tomorrow," he said when Kalman's secretary answered the phone. "I'm not feeling well."

"Sorry to hear that," she said. "What's wrong?"

"Sour stomach, headache. Maybe a fever."

"You want Russ to call you in the morning?"

"No, I'll be in bed all day," Dan said. "I'll try to sleep it out of me."

"Well, you get better and maybe we'll see you Thursday."

"Thanks."

Early the next morning, Dan dialed a familiar number. "You ready
to go?"

"Almost. You driving or should I?" Bob said.

"I'll drive."

"Be there in a few minutes."

Ten minutes later, Dan pulled up to Bob's two-story white house
adorned with yellow shutters. Large oaks covered the grounds.

"What time's the trial start today?" Dan asked.

"Around ten o'clock, I think."

"Good, then we've got plenty of time."

Dan headed north out of Jackson onto a slowly brightening Highway 49 and made his way over to Highway 61 because he liked the
scenery better. It led them straight into Clarksdale.

On the walk between his home and the courthouse, Sam Tackett
paused repeatedly Wednesday morning to chat with neighbors and
acquaintances who were planning to watch the day's proceedings.

Once in the courtroom, Tackett unpacked his briefcase and
arranged the documents he would need on the table in front of him.
Gruesome pictures and gory details always swayed a jury against
whoever was seated in the defendant's chair. Today's testimony
would probably finish Luke Williams for good.

Tackett turned and watched as spectators filed into the courtroom, settling into their places like children in a classroom. Travis Montgomery entered and took a seat next to his dad. Charlie
Usher and Luke Williams, present in their places before anyone else
arrived, were seated across the aisle.

Luke looked around for Elma, but he knew she wasn't there. She
had decided it was too hard for her.

Judge Bertram Long started the day with his usual discussion of timing. "This is the last day we'll meet this week," he said. "More out-of-town business. Are there any questions about our schedule?" He looked at the jury. All twelve stared back in silence. "Then we'll meet again next Monday. Today, Mr. Tackett will finish with his witnesses, and then Mr. Usher will have the opportunity to call witnesses for the defense, if he has any. Closing arguments on Monday." He looked around once more. "Any questions?" No one spoke. "Mr. Tackett, call your next witness."

Tackett stood and cleared his throat.

"Your honor," he said, "The State would like to call Dr. Conrad Higson to the stand."

At once, Tackett heard the room fill with whispers. Clarksdale had very few strangers, but somehow Higson had escaped the scrutiny usually lavished on most new upstanding residents. Except for the handful familiar with his cotton-harvesting project, almost no one would recognize the professor's face or his name.

In the back row, a lone figure rose and stepped into the aisle. All eyes turned toward him as the professor strode forward resolutely, like a man who had something to say.

Tackett watched him closely. Higson's clean-shaven face and well-worn gray suit rounded out his professorial appearance. His thin hair, cropped close to his scalp, and his bookish features were oddly offset by his unusually large hands. Put to good use assembling all those oversized machines.

Conrad Higson glanced at Luke when he passed the defense table. Then the professor stepped into the witness box and sat down. When asked if he would swear to tell the truth, he muttered "I do" in a voice so low no one but the judge and the bailiff heard him.

Tackett walked toward the witness stand. "For the record, please state your name and occupation."

"My name is Dr. Conrad Higson," the man said. "I'm a research scientist."

"Do you live in Clarksdale, Dr. Higson?"

"Yes. I have a small house in Clarksdale but spend most of my time in Oxford at the university."

"Could you briefly explain what you're currently working on?" Tackett said.

"I'm involved in several agricultural endeavors in the area. However, my most important project is the development of a machine that would pick cotton without the need for human labor. Eli Whitney and his gin had the easy part. This is a little more complex."

The slight murmur that arose in the courtroom quickly quieted with a stern glare from the judge.

"It's a difficult project, and I am still tweaking and tinkering with the design. But I haven't given up yet, although it's a little annoying for some. I think that's why I have so many nicknames. I've noticed that people in the South much prefer nicknames. Don't know if any of them are any easier to say than Dr. Higson, but I guess they are more interesting."

"I see," Tackett said, wanting his witness to stay focused. "You haven't lived in Clarksdale for very long, have you, Dr. Higson?"

"No, not long. Compared to most."

"Dr. Higson, I'd like to ask you a few questions about the defendant."

"All right."

"Have you ever met the defendant?"

"No," said the professor, looking at Luke.

"Ever spoken to him, maybe casually?"

"No."

"Have you ever seen the defendant before today?"

"Yes, I have."

"On how many occasions?"

"Two. Once in the paper."

"And the other?"

Higson was silent.

"You've seen him, but you didn't meet him or talk to him?"

"Neither."

"You just saw him?"

"Yes."

"Dr. Higson, would you please take a few minutes to explain the details of your sighting of the defendant?"

Higson began, his voice steady yet still almost inaudible. "It happened on Sunday the twenty-fifth of last month. I was taking an evening walk along the road near my house. It was about ten o'clock, and the moon was three-quarters full. There was some cloud cover, so at times it was dark. But mostly, if the moonlight was shining through the clouds, everything was plainly visible for thirty or forty yards. I was walking along, just thinking. I often do this when I'm having a problem with my research. The walk usually clears my head—helps me process my thoughts better."

Tackett nodded with feigned interest.

"I was about to return home when I heard some noise up ahead. Rustling and grunts and groans. I didn't know what it was, but I thought I'd investigate."

A hush had descended as the entire courtroom, barely daring to breathe, strained to hear Higson's voice. Tackett noticed that it hadn't been this quiet since the trial's earliest moments.

"I approached the noise," Higson continued, "and I was able to gain some cover near some bushes a few yards off the road. For a moment, I couldn't see very well because clouds had just passed over. But when they broke, I was startled by what I saw."

"And what did you see?"

Higson paused before he spoke. "I saw two men fighting, near a tree, about thirty yards away."

"Fighting? Can you describe the scene?" Tackett glanced at the jury to make sure they were paying attention.

"Fighting may not be the right word. I could see that one man was already on the ground and the other man was over him savagely kicking and punching him. He was also wielding a knife, which he used to stab him—twice. It was brutal. Awful."

"Was the man on the ground fighting back?"

"No. He was just holding up his arms, trying to cover his head."

"Could you see their faces?"

"Not from where I was. It was too far away."

"And did you try to intervene?"

"No. I was scared. I feared for my own life."

"Then what did you do, sir?"

"I wanted to return home, but I was worried this man would see me walking away. So I waited, and soon the man on the ground stopped moving. Then the other one took some rope and tossed it over a low tree limb. He wrapped one end of the rope around the neck of the man on the ground and tied the other end to the bumper of the car. He got in the car, started the engine, and moved forward a little. This pulled the unconscious man into the air so that he was hanging. Then the man in the car got out, untied the rope from the bumper, and tied it around another limb. When he drove away, I got a glimpse of him in his car."

Higson finished, and silence filled the room. Tackett felt the jurors losing Luke's presumption of innocence. This was the witness everyone on the jury thought would never come.

Tackett spoke again. "Did the assailant ever see you?"

"I don't believe so. He would surely have stopped if he had."

"But you definitely saw him?"

"Yes."

"I'll finish where we started. Is that man in the courtroom today?"

"Yes."

"Could you please identify him?"

Higson nodded briefly toward the defense table. "That's him. Mr. Luke Williams."

"What happened after Mr. Williams drove away?"

"I went right home."

"You didn't check on the body?"

"No. The man was surely dead."

"Did you report the crime?"

"Shamefully, no. The beast was still out there, and since I was the only witness, anything could happen. This is not a large town, Mr. Tackett. That kind of news becomes public very quickly. I thought that once he was in jail I would come forward, which is what I did."

"For the record, Dr. Higson, I'll ask you one more time. Are you positive it was Mr. Williams you saw that night?"

"Absolutely."

"I'll pass the witness." Tackett sat back down.

The judge broke Higson's spell. "Would you like to cross-examine, Mr. Usher?"

Charlie was staring down at the table in front of him.

"Would the defense like to cross-examine?" Judge Long said again.

Charlie stood and said, "Yes, your honor."

"Proceed."

Charlie picked up a piece of paper, walked over to the witness stand, and handed it to Higson.

"Could you please read this?" he said.

Higson reached in his coat pocket and pulled out a pair of glasses.

"Oh, you wear glasses?" Charlie asked casually.

"Yes, for reading."

"What's your vision without them?"

"I'm not sure. I haven't been tested in a while."

"Were you wearing your glasses the night of your walk? The night when you allegedly saw Mr. Williams?"

"No, I don't need them for walking. I need them for reading."

A couple of people in the gallery chuckled.

"But you've placed my client at the scene of a very serious crime and now, almost by accident, we find out you weren't wearing your glasses. You don't have perfect vision without your glasses, but we're to believe you clearly identified Mr. Williams at the scene of the crime. I guess no one was planning on informing the jury of this very relevant fact. I'm certainly glad I'm not the one on trial."

"Objection, your honor," Tackett said, rising to his feet.

"Sustained," Judge Long said.

"And what about the fact that it was dark, possibly very dark when the clouds moved in?" Charlie asked. "Was your view not obstructed? Possibly even when the car was passing by?"

"As I stated before, I saw Mr. Williams."

"What you said is that you got a glimpse of him. But is a glimpse enough to convict a man for murder? Let's talk about the car. Did you see the car? If you saw Mr. Williams, then you must have seen what kind of car he was driving."

"No, I was concentrating on the driver. It all happened very quickly."

"Yes, I imagine if the prosecution had been able to match any of the cars or trucks available to the defendant to one you might have seen, well, that would have been useful information—and not good for my client. But the fact that no one can identify the vehicle driven by the assailant further shows that Mr. Williams may not have been at the scene of the crime. This is a critical piece of information. Now, you've also indicated, based on your own safety concerns, that you didn't call the police to report the crime?"

"Correct."

"Someone had just been murdered right in front of you, yet you chose not to help, not to call the police, not to check on the body, not to cut him down, not to do anything."

"He was already dead, Mr. Usher," Higson said in a tone he might use when addressing a child. "He was hanging by his neck. It was pointless."

"Maybe for the victim, but not for capturing the suspect."

"He was gone. I knew I could identify him later if I needed to."

"What did you do on Monday? The day after the murder."

"I drove to Oxford on business."

"Went about your day? Just like you normally do?"

"We've been over this," Higson said, his voice rising slightly.

"Your honor," Tackett said, rising from his chair.

Charlie waved him off. "I'm done. Oh, but one last thing, Professor Higson. Would you please read what's written on the paper I gave you."

Higson slipped on his glasses and looked down at the paper. He shook his head in confusion and eyed Charlie.

"Read it," Charlie said.

"It says," Higson began, "'I can't read this without my glasses.'" He looked up.

"Keep reading, Professor."

"'So I probably didn't see Mr. Williams that night.'"

Tackett jumped up. "Objection, your honor."

The judge banged his gavel and turned to the jury. "You will disregard that last statement by Professor Higson. He was reading the note and that was not his testimony." He turned back to Charlie. "One more prank like that, and you'll be held in contempt. Do you understand me?"

"Yes, your honor," Charlie said.

"Is that all you have, Mr. Usher?" Judge Long said.

"Yes, your honor." Charlie glanced at the jury and smiled. A snippet of doubt.

Bob tugged on Dan's shirt. "We've got a long drive."

"I guess we know who Higson is now," Dan said as the two agents hurried down the stairs and out the side door they had entered earlier. "Should we call Russ?"

"I don't know," Bob said. "He thinks I'm hunting and you're sick. What would we tell him? Higson testified in a murder trial. No law against that. And what good would come of it? We can't do anything with what we saw today. Just by coming to the trial we've taken a risk that we'd spook the guy. We're not telling Russ. Not now. He can find out that Higson testified by talking to Collins or Tackett."

By now they were in the car. Dan started the engine.

"We'll just keep it to ourselves, then," Dan agreed. "Maybe it'll come in handy some time."

Ned rolled a penny back and forth between the fingers of his right hand, looking up every once in a while over the steering wheel at the courthouse door. Bo sat beside him in the passenger's seat, similarly dressed in dirty overalls, staring into the distance.

"What do you think Luke run for?" Bo said, shifting his stare to Ned's penny.

"I don't know," Ned said. "Maybe he got scared, missed his family. Could have been anything. But I know he still needs our help. He just hadn't figured that out yet."

"I bet you're right."

Shortly after noon, the courthouse doors opened and people spilled onto the steps.

"Are we getting out?" Bo asked.

"No," Ned said. "Stay put." Ned spied a boy of about nine crossing directly in front of the car. The adults he had emerged from the courthouse with remained near the door talking, ignoring him. "Hey, boy," Ned called out his window, his sneer and rough manner unchecked.

The boy looked suspiciously at Ned.

"You might think about running, but I wouldn't. 'Cause I'll catch you, then I'll whoop you."

The boy didn't move.

Ned slowly lowered his left hand out of the car. "Come here. I got something for you."

The boy craned his neck slightly to get a glimpse of what Ned was holding in his palm.

"Come on, boy. You're wasting my time."

The boy took one step, then another, till he stood next to the driver's side window.

"That wasn't hard, was it?" Ned said.

The boy shook his head.

"You in the trial this mornin'?"

"Yessuh," the boy said. He couldn't take his eye off the shiny nickel nestled in Ned's palm.

"You listen real close today?"

"Yessuh."

Ned's stare bored into him but the boy's gaze never wavered from the nickel.

"Who testified today?"

"Some doctor. He's a real smart man."

"What was his name?"

The boy beamed. "Higson. Doctor Higson."

Ned glanced over at Bo briefly. "What'd he say? You remember what he talked about?"

The boy narrowed his eyes, straining to recollect the testimony. "I don't remember everything."

"Well, you better try, or you ain't gonna get this nickel."

The boy was silent for a minute or so then he beamed again more radiantly than before. "He said he saw a man kill another man."

"Yeah, who done the killin'?"

"He said the man settin' down front killed a man."

"Down front in the courtroom? You mean Luke Williams?"

"Yessuh, that's his name. Mr. Williams done the killin'."

Bo slammed his fist against the dashboard. "That S.O.B.—."

The boy took a step back.

"You sure that's what the doctor said?" Ned asked.

"Yessuh. Positive."

"Don't be afraid, boy. You done good. Here, I'm gonna give you something."

Slowly, the boy extended his hand, and Ned dropped a coin into it. Then he started the car and pulled away. In his rearview mirror, he watched the boy look into his open palm then scowl at the car as he lifted but a penny from it.

A few miles later, Bo spoke up. "That was the wrong thing for Higson to say, wasn't it?"

"Yeah, he's not as smart as I thought he was."

"What are we gonna do?"

"Only thing we can do."

Bo beamed. Just like the little boy had done when he first spied the shiny nickel.

CHAPTER 29

I laid my cards on the table.

—Washboard Sam

JUST OUTSIDE THE COURTROOM, TRAVIS AND HIS DAD stopped and leaned against the wall.

"I'm gonna take the car," Travis said, "and get some lunch. Maybe stop by the house. Anything you want me to pick up?"

"No. Just have the car back by two."

Travis knew he had to hurry. Once he got into the car, he pulled the scrap of paper from his pocket to check the address. He headed southeast, and a few miles later he drove past an isolated strip of dirt road that led to the house he was looking for. He drove by slowly, glancing to his right at the house and looking for any movement or signs of habitation. But the house was set so far back from the road that he could barely see anything. One thing he did notice—no vehicle.

He turned the car around, and headed down the long, narrow driveway that led to the house. He bounced along the fractured dirt road strewn with sizable stones and drove behind the house so his car wasn't visible from the main road.

The house was one story, set up unusually high, and it was adorned with white shutters. There was a small porch that stretched across the front of the house. The front yard was vacant, and the door and windows were shut. There wasn't a trace of any living thing except for a droopy philodendron in the window to the left of the door. All was still, quiet. Travis got out and stood looking around at the property. He scanned the fields that butted up against the backyard. In the distance, the cotton stalks were bare, but the fields nearest the house were fallow. He could tell someone was living there, but they obviously weren't farmers. Not enough equipment, and the fields were barren. He walked to the backdoor, peered inside, and tried the knob. Locked.

A faint sound distracted him. As he held his breath to listen more closely, it grew into something he had hoped he wouldn't hear: the rumble of an engine and the crunch of tires turning onto a gravel road. He scurried over to the side of the house and peeked around the corner. A car filled the narrow lane, a fat tail of dust billowing behind it.

Before he could even think of what to do, Travis heard the engine shut off and a car door slam, followed by the sound of a rickety screen door closing. He stood, frozen, suddenly drenched in sweat. Seconds turned to what seemed minutes. He thought about jumping into his car and driving off, but the owner would either catch him or call the police. Finally, Travis dared to move, and he walked deliberately to his car. Before opening the door, he looked up at a window above his head. He saw a shadow of quick movement, and then the curtains parted.

Slowly a face came into view, blurry at first. It emerged from the dark backdrop in the house, and then, clearer, its features—its skin even—tight with a fury. Travis looked directly into the occupant's eyes.

Travis recognized him immediately as Conrad Higson. The professor disappeared, and then the back door opened abruptly and he reappeared. He walked toward Travis, who stepped away from his car and turned to face the older man.

"May I assist you, young man?" Higson said, extending his hand. "You do know you're on private property?" He wasn't as agitated as Travis expected him to be.

"Yes, sir, I'm aware of that," Travis said, shaking Higson's hand. "My name is Travis Montgomery, and I'm with the county."

Higson offered no name. "With the county? Oh, well, what are you doing on my property?"

"We're getting ready to start reevaluating the property lines, plots, and acreages in the area, and I'm helping with the initial assessment. Getting addresses, verifying whether folks are the owners or tenants, and letting them know we'll be out again so they're not alarmed when they see us next time."

"Do you usually do that without taking any notes?" Higson looked at him curiously.

Travis, without a pencil or notebook, tried to appear unfazed. "It's just preliminary today. I'll come out again in a few weeks, take some measurements, and record my findings."

Higson didn't look convinced.

"And what do you do, Mister—?" Travis asked, trying to sound inconsequential.

"You should know that already. Weren't you at the trial today?"

Travis fumbled for an answer when he realized Higson had recognized him. Fortunately, the professor didn't wait for one.

"I'm Dr. Conrad Higson, and I conduct farm research for the government. Every once in a while, I'll do some work for the state."

"Well, sir, that's something we definitely need. It must keep you very busy."

"Yes, you're right, it does. But shouldn't you have been working today instead of spending your time at the trial?"

"Probably. But everyone is following the trial closely, and I thought I'd stop by and see if anything interesting was going on."

"And was there?"

Travis didn't hesitate. "Yes, sir."

Higson offered to show him around the property so Travis could complete his preliminary evaluation. When they returned to Travis's car, the professor politely asked, "Did you get everything you needed?"

"Yes, sir, I did for now. There are no additional structures on the property, and the property lines look very similar to the ones on the map in my office. I'll come back next week and finish up. And I'll bring my notepad and the maps." Travis knew he didn't sound convincing. "Well, sir, I've got to finish my visits."

Higson grinned. "Maybe you can park in front next time," he said, extending his hand. They shook briefly, the older man squeezing a little too tight. "And don't forget to tell your father 'Hello' for me."

"Yes, sir." He drove back down the narrow lane, glancing often into his rearview mirror. Higson stood immobile in the yard.

Shortly before nine o'clock that night, the phone rang.

"I'll get it," Travis said, rushing to pick it up before anyone else in the house did. "Hello."

"Travis, it's Hannah."

"It's getting a little late for a call."

"I know, but I tried looking for you today and calling you down at the courthouse."

"Why? Is something the matter?"

"Well, I received some interesting news today. You were in court this morning, weren't you?"

"Yeah."

"Did you listen to the testimony?"

"Sure. I was there the whole time."

"I think I solved one of your little mysteries."

"Oh, really?" He shifted the phone to his other ear and grabbed a pencil. "What's that?"

"I was talking to someone today who had been at the trial, and I asked what happened and how it went. And you know what they said?"

Travis was silent.

"They said, 'The tinker testified.'"

"And I said, 'The tinker?'"

"'Yeah, the tinker, the guy that's building the machine. The fiddler.'"

"Did he say anything about the testimony?"

"Don't you understand?" Hannah asked. "Higson is known as the fiddler because he tinkers with all those machines. He fiddles, the fiddler. What you heard at the church was somebody mispronouncing it. Fiddler, Fid'la. Get it?"

"Yeah," Travis said. "F, not V. Yeah, I get it."

"Isn't this good news?"

Travis was silent again.

"What's wrong?"

"I went out to that house today. The address we found in the file."

"Oh, what happened?"

"Higson caught me snooping around."

"Higson lives there? What'd you do?"

"Tried to lie my way out of it."

"Do you think he suspects anything?"

"I don't know. I told him I'd be back next week to finish the work. But I was nervous, and he could tell."

"I'm sure it's okay. Anyway, that's my news."

"I'm glad you called, thanks." Travis hung up before she could say anything else.

He stood with his hand on the phone, his mind zeroing in on the evening at the church and the whispers of a man he never saw. "People say he ain't doin' right" rang again and again in Travis's head.

CHAPTER 30

Lord, grief will kill you.

—*Charlie Doyle*

BY THE TIME TRAVIS HEARD THE PHONE, IT HAD already rung three times. He sat up in bed, turned on a light, and squinted at his watch. It was well past midnight.

He heard his dad walk downstairs to answer the phone. Travis could hear his muffled voice. Then it stopped, and he walked back upstairs. He stopped at Travis's door and knocked.

"Phone's for you, son."

"Who is it?" Travis asked, now wide-awake.

"Hannah Morgan," his dad said gravely.

Travis leaped out of bed and hurried downstairs.

"Hannah?"

He listened but no one spoke. "Hannah? Hannah?"

Finally, she spoke. "Travis it's me." Her voice sounded strained and unsteady, as if she'd been crying.

"I know," he said in a soothing voice. "What's going on?"

"Travis, I'm sorry to call this late, but I need your help."

"Sure, sure. Anything."

"It's Gami. She's been feeling ill all day, and now she's in bed but can't sleep. We've been with her the entire time. We're not sure what to do for her."

"I'm sorry to hear that."

"She needs a doctor. But she won't see ours, the one we go to. She wants one of yours."

"Are you sure?"

"Oh yes, she's never liked our doctor. She might be sick, but she's still stubborn."

"And you want me to find someone?"

"Could you?"

"I'll try, but I don't know if he'll come out this late. Can it wait till morning?"

"I don't think so. She's never been sick a day in her life, and now she's not eating. She's just lying in bed, telling stories about when she was a little girl. I've never even heard some of them."

Travis twisted his head toward the top of the stairs where his father stood, arms folded, radiating disapproval. Travis turned back to the telephone. "I'll see what I can do," he murmured. "Where are you?"

"We're at her house. Five-twenty Sixth street. When can you be here?"

"Let me put some clothes on, and I'll be over right away."

"Hurry. Please."

Her voice had taken on a frantic tone, even in the short time they had spoken.

Travis hung up the phone and turned again to his father.

"I've got to go out for a while," Travis said, starting up the stairs to his room.

"What for?" his father asked, following him.

"Hannah Morgan's grandmother is sick, and she needs a doctor."

"Why the devil is she calling you?"

"We're friends, and her grandmother wants to see—well, I'm going to stop by Dr. Shelton's."

"I know you're friends, and it's something I've been meaning to talk to you about."

Travis met his father's eyes while he buttoned his shirt. "Can it wait until tomorrow, Dad?"

"I don't think so." Mr. Montgomery leaned against the door-jamb. "There are a few rumors around town concerning you and this Hannah Morgan. Are they true?"

"Depends what they are, I guess." Travis sat on the bed to put his socks on.

"You know what they are. And you know your mother and I are pretty lenient with you and Rachel—where you go, who you see—but there are some things we don't approve of. And this is one of them."

"What? Helping someone out."

His father stepped into Travis's room and closed the door. "It's not the helping that bothers us, it's everything else. I hope I don't have to tell you nothing good can ever come of it, especially for her and her family. Mr. Morgan works hard and makes a good living. Don't be selfish and make it tougher for them. You want to do Hannah and her family a favor, you really want to help them, then stay out of her life. In the long run she'll thank you for it; in fact, a long time from now, she may even love you for it. But you're a man and need to make your own decisions."

Travis finished tying his shoes and stood up. "I've got to go."

"Can I stop you?"

"Not this time, Dad."

"Remember what I said. I'm not the old, antiquated person you think I am." He opened the door for Travis. "And they can't just call another doctor?"

"Her grandmother won't see one of their doctors. She wants someone like Dr. Shelton."

Travis quickly headed back down the stairs. "I'm going to take the car. Okay?"

His father looked at him for a moment. "Be careful."

Travis rapped lightly on Dr. Shelton's front door. He waited a minute but didn't hear any footsteps. He could have telephoned ahead, but he knew that would've made it easier for Shelton to put him off until the next day.

He knocked again a little louder. Still no answer.

Finally, as he was about to knock for the third time, Travis heard footsteps on the stairs. A shadowy figure approached the door.

Travis stepped back. The outside light went on, and Dr. Shelton opened the door. He looked sleepily at Travis.

"Travis?" he said.

"Yes, sir, Dr. Shelton," Travis said.

"What's wrong?"

"I need your help, sir. Do you know Richard Morgan and his family?"

"Yes. I haven't met him personally, but I know who he is."

"His mother is quite ill and needs a doctor."

"I see. But why are you standing on my porch?"

"I'm a friend of his daughter, Hannah. She called me and asked me to help."

"Don't they have a family doctor?"

"I'm not sure, but I don't think the grandmother wants to use the family doctor. She wants you, Dr. Shelton."

"Oh, I see."

"And I know you're fair about these things, sir."

"Come on in, Travis, and wait just a moment while I get dressed."

Dr. Shelton was back down in five minutes, fully dressed and clutching his medical bag. "I'll follow in my car."

Hannah opened the door before Travis could knock. She looked exhausted, and her eyes were red. She grabbed Travis and hugged him tightly for a moment. Startled, he sagged backward under the weight of her body. Travis could feel the tension in the room escalate sharply at Hannah's display of affection.

In an instant, she let go.

The front room was small but nicely decorated with pictures and several paintings. The walls were beige, and an olive-colored rug covered most of the floor. A couch and several chairs were situated closely around a low table where a couple of unfinished cups of coffee and an empty plate sat.

"Dr. Shelton, this is Richard Morgan," Travis said.

Richard stepped forward. "Hello, Dr. Shelton. Thank you for coming."

"That's quite all right," Dr. Shelton said.

Richard quickly introduced Hannah, Hannah's mother, Cora, and Aunt Dot, all of whom exchanged handshakes with the doctor.

"Where's my patient?"

"She's in the bedroom," Richard said, opening the room's door. The family arranged themselves in a neat column, ready to follow.

The doctor turned and smiled faintly. "I'd like to evaluate her alone, please."

"Certainly, Dr. Shelton," Richard said. He ushered Hannah and the others back into the living room, then closed the bedroom door.

"Would you like some coffee?" Hannah asked.

"Please," Travis said.

Everyone found a seat and waited silently. Travis began to perspire under the gaze of Hannah's father. He thought uneasily of the man who had once accosted her and now walked with a limp. Hannah's embrace at the door—too brief for Travis even to enjoy—had altered the family's view of him.

It was Aunt Dot who broke the silence. "Travis, we'd like to thank you for bringing Dr. Shelton on such short notice."

Everyone nodded in agreement.

"That's quite all right. I'm happy to help, ma'am."

"I don't know why she won't see the family doctor, but we've all learned not to argue with her."

Travis smiled, grateful to relax. "Well, she's earned the right to be a little particular."

"And that she is," Richard said, chuckling.

Hannah returned from the kitchen with Travis's coffee.

Travis looked at each person's face. It was obvious no one had slept. They made small talk until the bedroom door cracked open and Dr. Shelton emerged. He came into the living room and set down his bag.

"How is she, Dr. Shelton?" Richard asked.

"She's about as good as she can be," he said.

"Do you know what's wrong with her?" Hannah said.

"It's possible she might have had a mild stroke, but she's still talking, very communicative. Hard to tell. There aren't any clear physical symptoms to indicate a stroke."

"Then what is it?" Cora asked.

"I don't think it's anything," he answered gently. "She's getting old, like the rest of us. I'm sorry. She's in no pain. And we really can't make her eat. Just make her comfortable."

Hannah sat down in her chair, hunching forward with her face in her hands. Her father moved next to her and placed his hand on her shoulder.

"I'm sorry," Dr. Shelton repeated. "At least you've got some time. I know it's of little comfort, but having time to say good-bye is a gift that not all of us get. Appreciate and enjoy it."

"How much time?" Cora asked.

"Could be days, a week," he said. "It's hard to tell. And if she starts eating again, then she might just perk back up."

"We'll hope for the best," Cora said. "Can we get you anything, Dr. Shelton? Coffee?"

"No, I'm fine, thank you. I've got to be going." He picked up his bag and walked toward the door.

"How much do we owe you, Dr. Shelton?" Richard said, opening the front door for him.

"Nothing at all. I really didn't do much."

"Thank you all the same, Dr. Shelton," Cora said.

"Yes, thank you very much," Richard repeated.

Richard closed the door behind Dr. Shelton. "Thank you, again, Travis," he said.

"You're welcome," Travis said. "I guess I should be heading home as well."

"Please stay," said Hannah. Everyone looked at her, but no one spoke up.

Travis looked to Hannah's father for guidance. "You probably couldn't get to sleep anyway after all that coffee," he said kindly.

"We're taking turns sitting with Gami," Hannah said. "Everyone else rests while someone sits with her. I think it's my turn. Why don't you help me? I think she'd like that."

"I don't want to intrude—"

"It's all right," Hannah said, rising from her chair.

Hannah filled a glass with water from a pitcher on the dining room table, and she and Travis went into her grandmother's bedroom. Hannah closed the door.

"I brought a friend, Gami," Hannah said. She approached her grandmother's bedside and placed the water on her nightstand. "Do you remember Travis from the picnic?"

"Oh, yes. Hello again, Travis," the old woman said in a high, thin voice.

"Good evening, ma'am," Travis said.

"More like good morning."

"Yes, you're right."

"I just can't seem to sleep 'cept every once in a while for a few minutes. But never longer than half an hour."

To Travis, she seemed to be quite aware of her surroundings, and very lucid. She knew exactly what she was doing, and maybe that's what was bothering Hannah the most.

Travis sat in a big chair with an ottoman while Hannah sat next to the bed. She spoke quietly with her grandmother for a few minutes. Finally, Hannah lay her head down on the bed.

Her grandmother rested her hand on Hannah's head. Then she motioned Travis over. "Why don't you put her in that chair?"

Travis picked up Hannah and placed her in the chair. Then he propped her feet up on the ottoman. She never made a sound or opened her eyes. Travis covered her with a blanket and started to walk toward the door.

"Travis," Hannah's grandmother called.

"Yes, ma'am, can I get you something?"

"Please come sit with me, child."

Travis felt awkward, but he obeyed, sitting down in the chair next to her bed. He scooted closer and rested his hand on the edge of the mattress.

Travis thought the old woman looked serene, peaceful. Although there was tiredness in her face, it wasn't like the exhaustion Hannah or her father felt. Hers was different; it would not be alleviated by a good night's sleep.

She placed her hand on his. Though her mind was sharp, Travis could tell that her physical strength was waning. It took real effort to lift her arm.

He turned his hand over so that hers rested in his palm, then placed his other hand on top of both of them.

Her hand was cool, and it shook slightly. He gently pressed his hands together.

"Your hands are warm," she said. Her voice was quiet. She would not wake Hannah.

"Yes, ma'am," said Travis.

"Travis, you can call me by my first name."

"What is it, Mrs. Morgan? Hannah's never told me."

"It's Adeline, but everyone calls me Addie. At least my friends do. Most of the family calls me Gami."

"That's a pretty name, Addie. I don't think I've ever known an Addie. My mother's name is Margaret and my sister's name is Rachel."

"I like the name Rachel. Hannah was almost a Rachel, but then my youngest daughter named her fourth child Rachel, so Cora and Richard decided on something else."

Travis rubbed the back of her hand. Her skin was darker than Hannah's, and it didn't feel at all like his own or Hannah's youthful, taut skin; Addie's seemed loosely attached to the rest of her hand. It resembled black tissue paper, creasing so easily that it looked like it might tear.

Hannah shifted in her chair and made a slight rustling sound, her body unconsciously seeking a more comfortable position. Travis and Addie both looked at her, Travis turning his head slightly and Addie looking in the direction of her feet.

"Hannah's very worried about you, Addie," Travis said, turning back to catch her shining gaze.

"Well, she's a young girl. She doesn't have much else to worry about yet. But she has to worry about something." Addie smiled a little, but even that seemed demanding.

"You should be feeling better in a couple of days. Then things will get back to normal, and Hannah will be her old self again." Travis caught himself being hopeful, not really believing what he was saying. His eyes met Addie's for a moment. She knew too well and caught him in his faithless thought.

"Travis," she said, forcing air from her chest to strengthen her voice. "I'm going to tell you something that my mother told me years ago when she was old. I've tried to tell Hannah, but she won't listen. She just talks about tomorrow and what we're going to do and who we're going to see and what we're going to eat. It's not that she doesn't want to listen; it's her youthfulness. She's always getting ready for tomorrow and the next day. Excited and hopeful. It's God's way."

She motioned for some water, and Travis helped her tip the glass so she could take a sip. He returned the glass to the table and took her hand again.

After a few moments she continued. "My mother told me that when you're born, your heart is pure and clean. Like a baby's skin, free of marks or cuts or bruises. But as we get older, go through life, we love and lose. Give and take. She said that every time we hurt it puts a tiny nick on our heart. Now, that nick heals, like a cut on your hand heals, but it leaves a scar. A scar on your heart, on your soul."

Travis listened closely, as intently as he had ever listened to anyone before.

"Eventually, you live long enough, and there's no place left for any more hurt. No place left for any more scars."

She paused.

"I've lost a husband, two children when they were babies, friends, and family. My heart's all covered with scars. The scars of living a long life. I'm not complaining. It's just the way it is."

Travis let his head hang, continuing to rub her hand. It had warmed since he started holding it. If he looked at her, he wouldn't be able to hide his tears.

"And when there's no more room on your heart for any more scars, then you must become a scar on someone else's heart. It's my time, Travis. Hannah has to understand."

Travis leaned over and lightly kissed the back of her hand. Tears escaped from both his eyes, and he massaged them into the creases of her skin.

Addie Morgan died that Friday. Her family was by her side, Hannah sitting on the edge of the bed and holding her hand. Addie had drifted in and out of consciousness for several hours. During her last waking moments, she called to her granddaughter. "Hannah, dear, dear Hannah," she said with a smile.

"Yes, Gami. What is it?"

But Addie didn't respond.

Then the old woman opened her eyes once more. "Daddy," she said in a child's high voice. "Daddy, will you swing me again? Please?" Her eyes closed again, and Hannah felt the life seep from her grandmother's body. Hannah shook her gently, but she had passed.

Travis's father had told his son long ago that you could tell the measure of a Southerner—black or white—by how many people of the opposite race showed up at their funeral. Addie had clearly been well liked.

After a short viewing in the morning, the service was held Saturday afternoon in a small country church just outside of town, where Addie had been baptized many years before. Inside the church were twelve rows of pews, the same number as the disciples of Jesus, and a narrow aisle ran down the center. Big wooden shutters, propped open, let in the light and a cross-breeze. The church was unusually cool, the large oaks outside providing continuous shade from the persistent sun.

The Morgan family filled the front pews, while distant relatives and friends took the middle pews. At the rear of the church, white mourners stood in silent respect or, some being elderly, sat in the last few rows.

Hannah sat in the first row, on the aisle, and Travis stood in the back.

A soloist sang, "What a Friend We Have in Jesus," Addie's favorite hymn, while mourners entered the church. Travis had overheard Mr. Morgan instructing the pastor several times that Addie's funeral service was to be short: no choir, no long-winded speakers, no collections for the family.

Mercifully, the pastor spoke briefly, and near the end of the service asked if anyone in the congregation would like to speak. Several people stood, and one by one told stories about Addie from different times in her life: girl, young woman, mother, grandmother, and, in the end, as the matriarch of her family. Some of the stories were humorous; others were poignant; all suggested how much Addie had meant to the speaker. Gradually, the gloom throughout the church lifted a little.

When the final story had been told, the crowd fell silent except for the occasional sniffle. Realizing that the reverend was about to conclude the service, Travis took a deep breath, grasped his grandmother's dog-eared Bible, and walked to the front of the church.

Hannah looked up, and for the first time that day, the tears briefly cleared from her eyes. Travis hadn't told her of his plans to speak.

Travis stepped into the pulpit and faced the church, looking out at all the faces of Addie's life, the people of both races whom she had loved or somehow touched. He wondered what the faces of his life would look like. Who would come to say good-bye to him?

"This was my grandmother's favorite passage in the Bible," Travis said. "I'd like to read it to you, and for Mrs. Morgan—or Addie, as most of you knew her. Today, it seems most appropriate."

But the souls of the just are in the hand of God, and no torment shall touch them. They seemed, in the view of the foolish, to be dead; and their passing away was thought an affliction and their going forth from us, utter destruction. But they are in peace. For if before men, indeed, they be punished, yet is their hope full of immortality; chastised a little, they shall be greatly blessed, because God tried them and found them worthy of Himself. As gold in the furnace, He proved them, and as sacrificial offerings He took them to Himself. In the time of their visitation they shall shine, and shall dart about as sparks through stubble; they shall judge nations and rule over peoples, and the Lord shall be their King forever. Those who trust in Him shall understand truth, and the faithful shall abide with Him in love: Because grace and mercy are with His holy ones, and His care is with the elect.

Travis closed his Bible and walked down the aisle to his place at the back of the church. He touched Hannah's shoulder briefly as he passed.

She could only nod and cry.

CHAPTER 31

District attorney sure is hard on a man.

—*Washington White*

JUDGE BERTRAM LONG RECONVENED LUKE WILLIAMS'S trial Monday at 10:00 a.m. People crammed tightly into the court-room, eager to hear the final statements from both attorneys.

Brusquely, the judge started the day by addressing the jury. "We are near the end of the trial," he said, "and today Mr. Tackett and Mr. Usher will give their closing statements. Subsequently, we will meet one final time when you are ready to deliver your verdict. It could be an hour after you begin deliberations or it could be—well, a little longer. Does everyone understand?"

The jurors nodded their heads, as did several people in the audience who were listening attentively.

"Mr. Tackett," Judge Long said. "You may proceed."

The prosecutor's closing statement reiterated the limited evidence he had presented. He reviewed details of the crime scene and the heinous nature of the murder. He mentioned Luke only when discussing Professor Higson's testimony.

"And he shows no remorse," Tackett said. "If he had any, his lawyer would have put him on the stand. But since he is not repentant, the defense is afraid to parade him in front of the jury, for fear they may find him callous and evil. Innocent men proclaim their innocence; the guilty hide."

Tackett walked closer to the jury box, focusing on his summation. He had momentarily forgotten this could well be the last term for the only Coahoma County district attorney who successfully prosecuted a white man for the murder of a black one.

"And so," Tackett continued, "you, the jury, have a difficult decision to make. Made even more difficult by the fact that you live in Mississippi."

Tackett could feel the anguish in the courtroom. One older man in the jury box gripped his handkerchief tightly. Tackett knew it would be hard for all the jurors.

"Can you do it? I don't know. But you will have to try. We all must serve justice. And while you deliberate, please remember that justice sees no color. Justice never conceals herself from her enemies, and her tears are only for the victims. You must not let yourselves be swayed by outside influences. You must do what must be done. Make the tough choices and don't look back." He paused. "Help me serve justice. If for no one else, then at least for Milton Hibbs's children."

Tackett walked back to his seat in silence.

"Mr. Usher," Judge Long said.

Charlie pushed his chair back and looked at his client. Luke's eyes were tired; they didn't dart around like they had at the start of the trial. The end was drawing near, and his look was one of sorrow.

Charlie had long planned what he wanted to say. "Gentlemen of the jury, you've heard a lot during this trial," he began as he walked slowly toward the judge's bench. "A lot to consider. You know, there have been a few times in my life when I honestly didn't know what was going on around me, what was happening. For instance, one time when I was at the University of Mississippi, I was playing in a football game—by the way, we beat Alabama." He saw a few smiles. "Well, I got hit so hard I had to sit out the rest of the game. I spent the entire second half in a daze. I didn't even know who won until somebody told me later that night."

Charlie stopped at the foot of the judge's bench and turned to face the jury. "The last couple of weeks have felt to me like I was back on that bench again, sitting in a daze. Accusations, but no motives. Witnesses who didn't see what they thought they did."

Charlie approached the jury box.

"I've been trained to do one thing in my life. To be a good attorney and defend the innocent and the guilty alike. Why do I do that? Because sometimes the guilty are not really guilty, and the innocent are not really innocent. But in the end, the truth is always the same. And don't confuse justice, which you heard about from Mr. Tackett, with truth. Because justice is served by men who have faults and make mistakes, but truth lies with a higher power. No matter who's guilty, and no matter who's innocent, the truth is always the same. I like to think that I protect that truth. At least, I try to. We all like to think that about ourselves, don't we? But that's hard, because sometimes it's hard to find the truth. Sometimes the truth can't be found. And no matter where we look, we can't find it. But why? Why can't we find it? Someone must know where it is. We know that God knows where it is. That's for sure."

Several jurors nodded their heads in agreement. One mouthed, "Amen."

"And if we can't find the truth," Charlie gestured with both hands, "it's because when men hide the truth from one another, it's very, very seldom found. Men know where to hide the truth from each other, but they can't hide it from God." He paused to let the jury absorb his words.

"Mr. Tackett," Charlie motioned toward the prosecution's table, "he thinks he's found the truth in this case. Maybe he has. And the judge, I bet he thinks he knows where the truth is. In fact, everyone in this courtroom probably has an idea of where the truth might be in this trial." Charlie swept his arm in a half-circle, trying to encompass the entire room full of people.

"But in a court of law, the only people who matter are you." Charlie spun back to face the jury, sternly pointing at one juror after another. "It doesn't matter where Judge Long or Mr. Tackett or anyone else in this courtroom thinks the truth is. You, the jury, are the only ones who can find the truth. Mr. Tackett and I have tried to help you find it, but we have only guided you based on what we know, which may or may not be right. Ultimately, it's yours to find."

When Charlie had finished speaking, he stepped back, away from the jury, never turning his back to them, and sat down at the defense table. He had said nothing about the evidence, the crime scene, witnesses, or any of the particulars of the case. But he had said something about Luke, Tackett, Judge Long, and himself. And about the legal system.

Charlie glanced at Luke, who looked satisfied.

Several minutes passed while Judge Long completed his notes and shuffled papers. At last, he looked up, peered at the jury, and gave them some final instructions. The trial was almost over, he said, and all that remained was for them to determine the verdict. Then Luke Williams would either be released or sentenced. "Seek the truth," Judge Long said. The jurors rose, filed out of the jury box, and were escorted to another room to begin their deliberations.

Twenty minutes later, after Luke had been led back to his cell and the courtroom had finally cleared, Charlie walked out of the courthouse and strolled by the Sunflower River on his way home. He declined an invitation to sip bourbon with Tackett and the judge. He had had enough of them for a while.

CHAPTER 32

I want to ride the Yellow Dog.

—Sam Collins

HANNAH WASN'T HERSELF AFTER THE FUNERAL. SHE moped around Monday and didn't bother to go out at all. She just sat in a chair in the living room, staring out the window most of the day. Her father offered to take her to Memphis for a day trip the following weekend, but she declined quickly even though it was days away. Her mother took her shopping Tuesday afternoon, but that didn't help either.

"Give it time," Cora said, rubbing the back of her hand across Hannah's cheek. "Your hurt will heal, sweetheart."

Travis now felt sure that any information they might find on Conrad Higson wasn't in Coahoma County. The only other place to look was in Jackson. At least that's what the records had indicated.

So, he decided to take a quick trip down to the FBI office. He'd get in and out in minutes and hopefully stumble across something useful. At least he'd find out if any files even existed on Higson. How he was going to do all that, he wasn't quite sure.

Travis was also thinking of Hannah. She needed a break, and he wanted to distract her from her sadness over Addie. He called her Tuesday evening and asked her to come to Jackson with him.

"No, I have to get back to work this week," she said. "I don't want to go all the way down there."

"Come on, Hannah. We can be there and back in a day. I don't want to go by myself."

"Well, I'll have to ask my parents."

"Okay, I can wait."

She returned to the phone a few minutes later. "All right. They said I could go, but only if we come back the same day."

"That's fine. But they know it'll be late when you get in?"

"They know."

"Great. I'll meet you at the train station tomorrow morning."

"What time?"

"Let's say half-past five. Too early?"

"No, that's okay."

"See you tomorrow."

Travis woke up early Wednesday morning. He got dressed quickly and packed a small bag for the trip.

"I'm going to Jackson today to see a few friends and maybe visit a couple of professors to ask for recommendations for graduate school," Travis told his mother.

"Your father knows you're taking the day off?"

"Yes, ma'am."

"Will you be home for dinner?"

"I'm not sure, but I doubt it, so don't wait for me."

He walked the short distance to the station and spied Hannah waiting near the "Colored" window. "Glad you could make it," Travis said.

She raised her hand to cover a yawn. "I really don't feel like going today," she said.

"I know, but I'm glad you are. I'll meet you on the platform."

While Travis walked over to the "White" window, Hannah made her way through the waiting room to the platform outside.

"May I help you?" asked the man in the ticket booth.

"Good morning. I'd like two tickets to Jackson, please."

"One way or round-trip?"

"Round trip."

"Illinois Central shouldn't be very crowded headed south today," the man in the booth said. "But it's always packed when it's headed north. Know what I mean? Seems almost everyone wants to go north. Chicago mostly. Not many whites, though."

"Yes, I know," Travis said, taking the tickets. "Thanks."

He walked to the platform where Hannah stood waiting. "Got the tickets," he said, holding them up so she could see them.

"Where exactly am I sitting?"

"With me."

"Really?"

Travis smiled. "You want something to drink? I'm going to get some coffee."

"No, I'm fine."

Travis stepped back inside and emerged a few minutes later. "How are you doing?" He took a sip of his coffee.

"Okay."

"Are you sure?"

"Don't ask so many questions. By the way, you never told me why we're going to Jackson."

"Oh, I don't know. Run a few errands."

"Errands?"

An announcement crackled over the station's speaker: Boarding for the train headed to Jackson and points south would begin immediately. They joined the line that was forming at the entry to one of the cars.

"Where *am* I going to sit, Travis? Really."

"I told you. With me."

"Why don't I just sit in the Colored car? Give me my ticket." Hannah put out her hand, but Travis didn't even look at her.

"No. Stay here."

Travis walked up to the front of the line, where a small commotion was holding everyone up because of a woman trying to board with her three unruly children. Finally, the nanny scooped up the noisiest one and grasped the hand of a second child and pulled him up the steps into the Pullman car beside her.

Travis breathed deeply with relief. She got in, he thought. This shouldn't be a problem.

The passengers continued to board, and Travis and Hannah slowly made their way up to the ticket taker.

"Ticket, please," he said. "One to Jackson?"

"No, two," Travis said, thrusting the tickets forward.

"Two?" He looked up and peered at Hannah. "You can't ride in this car. You have to ride back there." He motioned toward the rear of the train.

"It's all right, she's with me. I'm not feeling well, and my doctor has ordered that I be accompanied to Jackson. She was the only one who could go with me." Travis coughed gently into his hand in support of his argument.

"You seem to be able to take care of yourself." He squinted at Travis.

Travis ignored the man. "I'm in no condition to care for myself," he said, moving closer to the man. "I'm running a fever, and I'm on my way to a hospital in Jackson. I could lose consciousness at any time. I need her to assist me—to—to administer my medication.

Doctor's orders." He grabbed Hannah's arm feigning the need to steady himself.

By now the passengers standing behind Travis and Hannah were disturbed by the wait. "What's going on?" a woman called out from behind a large man who concealed her. "Let's get on the train."

The ticket taker snarled but did not speak. He stepped aside and let Travis and Hannah pass.

They climbed aboard and took their seats in the last row, where the seat backs rested against the rear wall of the car. Travis felt these seats were a bit more private than the others.

"That wasn't too much trouble, now was it?" Hannah said, turning her head and looking out the window.

"We're on, aren't we?" Travis tucked his bag under the seat. He knew he had made Hannah uncomfortable. He reached over and squeezed her hand.

They fell silent while the car filled. Several passengers stared at them but lost interest when the train began to move, chugging leisurely, soothingly, as it rolled along the tracks and out of town. With the window down, Travis and Hannah could hear the men of a work crew singing as they adjusted a rail on the adjacent track. The rhythm was deliberate, almost hypnotic. At certain moments in the songs, the men moved in unison to the cadence, their sinewy arms working the lever bars that in turn moved the massive rails.

"Did you know those bars are made by the Chicago Gandy Manufacturing Company?" Travis said.

"I didn't know that," Hannah said, clearly not interested.

"Those men are Gandy dancers. I used to watch them when I was a kid." He gazed out the window while the men heaved and wrestled the rails into place. "Those tunes grow on you," he continued. "They're all the same, in a way, even though the words are different. The men never sang any of the dirty ones, at least not when I was around."

"I've never paid much attention," Hannah said. "That's work I didn't plan on doing."

Travis leaned toward the window to listen better.

I don' know but I been told, my ol' gal is gettin' old.

Oh man don't ya ride that train, I say oh man don't ya ride that train.

Think I know what I will do, gonna git me somethin' new.

Oh man don't ya ride that train, I say oh man don't ya ride that train.

Whaaaooo!

The train picked up speed, and they settled back into their seats. "You never answered what I asked you about on the platform," Hannah said at last.

"I need to pick up my transcripts and meet with a couple of my old professors."

"Really?" She gave him a suspicious eye. "I need to go all the way to Jackson to help you get something that could have been done by mail?"

"I need to meet with them in person."

"What will I do?"

"Wait for me." He gently placed her hand in his and interlocked their fingers.

A few minutes passed.

"Please," she said.

Travis could tell she didn't want another frivolous answer. "I need some information."

"What do you mean?"

"Remember the file you found?" Travis stretched out his legs until his feet were underneath the seat in front of him.

"Oh, no, you're not thinking of trying to get more information on Higson, are you?"

Travis shifted his gaze to the passing fields outside the window.

"Do you just not have enough to do?" Hannah shook her head. "We're just going to walk into the FBI building and ask for a file that probably contains information we don't want to know, nor should we know? Is that what you think? Why are you so intrigued?"

"I don't know. That guy at the church got me thinking, and now I just can't get it out of my head. I want to know what's so secret."

"Does your dad know what you're up to?"

"No, I haven't told anyone."

"But you're confident the FBI will help answer all your questions?"

"That's the plan."

Hannah stopped prodding; they both sat back and let the train's rhythm take over. They read for a while, but soon the clack of wheels on the track put them both to sleep.

The train rolled on, rocking side to side between stops at a couple large towns that dotted the Mississippi countryside between Clarksdale and Jackson. At each stop Travis opened his eyes just a crack, watching as a few passengers disembarked and a new group boarded. Every new passenger snuck a second glance at Hannah.

Finally, Hannah and Travis were stirred from their slumber. "Next stop, Jackson!" came the call from the end of the car.

Travis stepped off the train and smiled at the comfortable feeling of knowing his way around. He had made the trip dozens of times in his four years at Millsaps.

The man who was helping passengers down to the platform eyed Travis and Hannah with contempt when they walked by.

"I'll be back for the return trip later," Travis said, pleasantly.

"I'll warn tonight's man," he snapped.

"I'm sure you will."

"I think the best time to get to the FBI offices will be early afternoon," Travis said, heading to the street outside the station. "Right after lunch is good because everybody's a little tired. Some of the staff won't be back from eating yet, and the heat today is just downright exhausting. I'm going to tell them I'm conducting a file review for the Clarksdale district attorney. How's that sound?"

"Are you sure about all this?"

"For now." Travis looked at his watch. It was just past noon. "Want some lunch?"

"I'm not that hungry."

"Well, I am. C'mon, I know a great little restaurant. We can pick something up and find a park where we can eat."

Hannah offered no resistance, though she waited outside while Travis went in to buy lunch. And when they boarded a bus to the FBI building, Hannah spent the trip across town riding in the rear. Travis sat with her.

"Why didn't you put up a fight on the bus?" Hannah asked.

"Did you want me to?"

"You did on the train."

"The ride was a lot longer."

"It felt long in the back of the bus."

"Sorry." Travis didn't know what else to say. He could tell Hannah was a little disappointed. He'd be more chivalrous next time.

Across the street from their final destination, they found a small park with several vacant benches. The many trees and bushes provided ample shade from the noonday sun. Travis chose a bench, and they sat down to eat the sandwiches and sip the cold sodas. People walking past the park glanced at them eating together and acting very friendly. But neither Travis nor Hannah noticed. She ate a little and fed the birds pieces of her bread. When she tossed some meat to them, however, Travis protested.

"I'll eat that if you don't want it," he said.

Silently, she handed him the rest of her sandwich.

Travis knew Hannah was still grieving, and he wanted to say something to comfort her. But he was afraid of sounding condescending. Besides, he had no real experiences to share. The relatives he had lost were no more familiar to him than the people in the park. Most had died before he was born or when he was very young, and none had held the place in his life that Addie had held in Hannah's.

Travis tossed some of his bread to the birds, but that wasn't enough to get Hannah's attention. She just sat motionless, gazing down at the birds.

Eventually, Travis broke the silence. "Are you ready to go?"

"Not really."

"Well, I need you, so there's no backing out now."

Hannah said nothing.

Travis threw the leftovers from lunch to the numerous birds now stalking their bench. He balled up the rest of the trash and tossed it into a can along with their soda bottles. Then he picked up his bag, placed it on the bench, and looked through it to make sure he had everything he needed. Together, he and Hannah walked quickly across the street and entered the front door of the FBI building.

A guard's desk was positioned at the entrance, but no one was seated at it.

"That's plain good luck," Travis said to Hannah. "Maybe the guard's still at lunch. Let's hurry before he comes back." He pulled Hannah toward the building's directory that was mounted on the wall near a large door. "Here it is." Travis pointed to a line on the directory. "Records, third floor. Let's take those stairs over there."

He pushed open the door for her, and they ascended two flights to the third floor.

"See how easy this is?" Travis said, coming to the third floor entrance.

"It's far from over. We're not even out of the stairwell."

Travis opened the door slowly and peeked into the hallway. "It's clear."

They stepped into the hallway and looked both ways.

"This way," Travis said.

No sooner had he spoken then a man emerged from one of the offices. Travis was stunned: he recognized the man from the public gallery at Luke Williams's trial. Suddenly, and for the first time, the fear of his plan falling apart crossed Travis's mind.

"What's the matter?" Hannah said, sensing his body tense.

The man approaching them was reading something. Travis looked around, panicky. He couldn't chance that the man might recognize him, too. Quickly, Travis did the only thing that presented itself: he pushed Hannah into the ladies' restroom, which was located near the stairs, and followed her in. They looked around, including under the stalls, and returned to the door to listen.

"What are you doing?" Hannah said.

Travis put his finger to his lips.

They listened as the man passed by. Travis assumed he hadn't noticed Hannah and Travis entering the ladies' room. Otherwise, he may have stopped.

"What's going on?" she asked.

"I recognized him from the trial." Travis still felt breathless. "That was close."

"No, no, on the contrary; everything's going *just fine*," said Hannah sarcastically.

Travis paid no attention. "Check if it's clear."

Hannah opened the door and peeked out. "All clear."

They stepped back into the hallway, and Travis immediately saw the door he wanted and hurried to it.

Seated behind a desk piled high with files was a white-haired woman of about sixty. Reading glasses were perched on the end of her nose, through which she squinted at the typewriter she was banging on. Each thump of a key made Travis jump a little. The woman's fingers must certainly ache.

They stood in the doorway for what seemed like minutes until the woman finished what she was doing. She turned her head and stared down her nose at them, just like she did at her typewriter.

"Close the door, please," she said. "Come inside or out, I don't care which, just close the door."

Travis closed the door and turned back to face her.

"What can I do for you?" she said.

Travis looked at her nameplate and cleared his throat. "Mrs. Beamer, my—"

"It's Miss," she said.

"Miss Beamer, ma'am, my name is Edward Barker and this is a friend."

"Good afternoon, Edward." She only glanced at Hannah.

"I've been sent by the district attorney of Clarksdale, Mississippi, to gather some information for an upcoming trial. This is the Records Department, isn't it?"

"Did you not read the door?" Without waiting for a reply, she answered, "Yes, this is the FBI Records Department in Jackson. Now, these are active records. Archived records are in the basement. Have you checked in with the guard downstairs?"

"Yes, ma'am."

"And you're from where?"

"From Clarksdale. Assisting the district attorney."

"Who is?"

"Sam Tackett."

"I'll need to place a telephone call to verify—"

"Oh, I'm sorry, ma'am, I almost forgot." Travis scrambled to get something from his bag. "I have a letter from Mr. Tackett requesting assistance from the bureau and giving me authority to bring the requested information back to Clarksdale." Travis searched for the letter in his bag.

"What kind of information are you looking for, young man?" Miss Beamer asked.

"Just some information on a couple of folks who live in Clarksdale. Personal information. Do you have those files?"

"Of course. Records are filed by region. Northwest Mississippi files are over there." She pointed to three filing cabinets in the back corner of the room.

Travis looked in the direction she was pointing, and then at Hannah, who was also looking at them. "Do I need to check them out?" Travis said, while he took his time finding the letter.

"Yes, indeed. Files on private citizens, with the proper authorization, can be checked out at eight in the morning but must be returned by two o'clock sharp. If someone wants to look at them after that, they have to review them here." She motioned toward a small table near the files. "We had some trouble this year with lost files. It's more like a library now."

Travis looked at his watch; it was 2:10 p.m. He finally pulled the letter from his bag and handed it to Miss Beamer.

She opened it carefully and began to read. Travis had typed it up last week and signed it himself. He was starting to believe he had thought of everything.

Miss Beamer looked up. "I'll still need to call Clarksdale to verify everything. Do you have the number?"

"Let me see." Travis picked up his bag and moved to a corner near the window. He pretended he needed the light to look inside his bag.

While he searched for the nonexistent number, Hannah sat down beside him.

"I'm still looking, Miss Beamer."

Suddenly, the phone rang. Miss Beamer answered it. Immediately, Travis could tell it was a friend, and he might have a little time.

"Hannah, did you see where the files were?" Travis asked in a hushed tone. Miss Beamer was laughing now, looking out a window on the other side of the room.

"Yes, I saw."

"If for some reason you end up in the room alone—"

"Alone? How will I end up in the room—"

"Just listen. If you do, I want you to go into the files and find anything you can on Higson. You know where to look, right? You remember the address? This is our only chance."

"What do I do if I find something?"

"Take it. Put it in my bag or something. Hide it."

"You mean steal it? Steal government property?"

"Yes. Steal it. We've got to take the files to Clarksdale. We need them. Without them, we've wasted our time, and we won't know anything more than we did this morning. It's all we've got, but we don't have the time to look at them here. Now go on, walk across the room. Get her attention."

Hannah stood up and walked toward a bookcase on the other side of the room. Miss Beamer's eyes followed her while she continued talking on the phone, engrossed in her conversation.

Travis pulled a small bottle out of his bag. He opened it and drank the contents. He had tasted syrup of ipecac only once, when he had eaten some rat poison as a young boy. It tasted just like he remembered—bad. He thought about the big lunch he had eaten.

Five minutes went by, then ten.

Finally, Miss Beamer said good-bye and hung up the phone. "I'm sorry. That was my aunt who I haven't spoken to since last year. Did you find the number?"

"No, not yet." Beads of perspiration had started to form on his lip.

"I'll get the number," Miss Beamer said, reaching for the phone.

"No, that's all right, I'll find it. But can I open a window? All of a sudden, I'm not feeling well." Travis unlatched the window and stood near it breathing in the warm air.

"Edward, why don't you have a seat? You do look a little pale. Do you need some water?"

"No, thank you. I'll just keep looking for the number in all these papers I brought."

Hannah looked toward Travis and walked back to him. "Are you okay?"

Travis looked at her intently. "Do what I told you. Please."

Travis pretended to dig through his bag, but eventually he leaned back in the chair and waited for the inevitable. Miss Beamer had resumed typing. After a few more minutes, Travis knew there wasn't much time left. "Do you have a towel or something, Miss Beamer?" Travis said.

"No, I don't. And I'm not supposed to leave the room. Security reasons. Can't she get it?" She gestured toward Hannah.

"Miss Beamer, I think the colored bathrooms are all downstairs, and I need a towel now."

"They are downstairs, aren't they? I guess I never thought about it. Can't you get to the bathroom?"

"No, ma'am, I feel too sick." He groaned. "Can you get it, ma'am? Please?"

"All right," she sighed, rising. "I really shouldn't be doing this. You two don't move until I get back. Do you understand?"

"I'll try," Travis said.

Miss Beamer walked out the door into the hallway. Travis could hear her heels clicking on the floor. When the clicking grew faint, he stood up.

"Find the files," he said to Hannah, stepping into the hall. "Lock this door, and make sure you get the letter back that I brought. I forged Sam's signature." He heard Hannah turn the latch, and he checked to make sure it was locked.

Travis's first convulsion was a dry heave. He felt his stomach churn and the onset of the queasy feeling he used to get whenever his mother made liver for supper. He was bent over in front of the office door, hands on his knees, when the first of his lunch hit the floor. Then he heard the clicking heels again, and a shriek.

He looked up at Miss Beamer. "Can you get some more towels? I'm sick to my stomach."

Miss Beamer turned and ran for more towels.

Travis heard several people gasp as they walked into the hall from their offices. He continued to vomit directly in front of the office door. Soon the mess spread across the entire entrance and began to seep under the door. This was even better than he had planned. Travis lay down and tried to block the doorway. He groaned and rolled from side to side as people approached, groaning louder when someone reached for him.

At last Miss Beamer returned, this time with two janitors. "Move him and clean this mess up," she ordered.

Five to ten minutes had passed, Travis figured. He hoped Hannah had found the files.

The janitors lifted Travis by his arms and placed him in a chair that someone had brought from their office. He leaned forward staring at the floor.

The door opened, and Hannah looked out.

Everyone looked up. She glanced at Travis, then down at the mess. Travis saw the bag in her hand.

"It must've been something I had for lunch," he said.

"Do we need to take you to a doctor?" Hannah asked with concern as she stepped around the mess and set the bag next to Travis.

"No, I'm feeling better already."

"Let's hope so," Miss Beamer said, scowling at the entrance to her office.

Travis rubbed a towel across his forehead. "Thank you, Miss Beamer. I do sincerely apologize for the mess." After a few minutes, Travis stood up. "I think we better get going. I'm feeling well enough to walk, and the fresh air will do me good."

"What about your information?" Miss Beamer said.

"Maybe we can come back tomorrow, when I'm feeling better, and try again. Thank you so much, ma'am, for all your help."

"Don't come back till you're fully recovered, young man," Miss Beamer said almost vehemently.

Travis and Hannah walked downstairs and out the front entrance to the building. The guard had returned to his desk but said nothing as they left.

"Did you find anything?" Travis asked, hurrying down the street.

"Everything I could. Are we felons now?"

"I think so."

"Maybe we're the ones that'll end up in jail."

"Let's hurry. We don't want to miss the train."

The return trip to Clarksdale was much more relaxed than the morning ride had been. Travis had cleaned up in the station's washroom, but he was still pale from his self-induced illness; the porter never questioned his need for a nurse-companion. If the porter from the morning had said something, this one kept it to himself.

Hannah sat next to the window, drew the shade, and went to sleep almost as soon as the whistle blew, signaling their departure. That's what most everyone did on the ride heading north. Travis never opened the files Hannah had taken. A man was sitting across the aisle, and Travis didn't want to attract anyone's curiosity, much less risk having to explain what he was reading.

The train rolled on, and Travis watched the sun settle onto the hazy horizon. Empty cotton fields stretched for as far as the eye could see. Dry, rotting stalks awaited the spring, with its renewal of the ritual that dominated the Delta for over a hundred years.

Then he heard up ahead of them a whistle that was more like a howl. With its engine's wailing whistle and its cars' yellow accents, the Yazoo and Mississippi Valley Railroad—formerly the Yazoo Delta Railway—was familiar and singular throughout the Delta. Travis knew the railroad better by its nickname, the Yellow Dog. As the train rumbled north toward home, a tune came to mind, and

Travis hummed W. C. Handy's "Yellow Dog Blues." He mouthed the last line of the song to himself.

"He's gone where the Southern cross the Yellow Dog."

A child in the car tried to emulate the train's whistle, but he could not match its pitch.

Travis's eyes closed with the setting sun, only to open again, hours later, when the train pulled into Clarksdale.

CHAPTER 33

Stay off of Parchman Farm.

—*Booker White*

JUDGE BERTRAM LONG REACHED OVER TO HIS nightstand and picked up the phone after the second ring. "Judge Long."

"Judge, it's Henry," the bailiff said.

"What do you need, Henry? It's almost midnight."

"Yes, sir, but I wanted to let you know. The jury's reached a verdict."

"Good. We've got to get this thing over with—but it's a little late now to reconvene."

"Yes, sir."

"Seven-thirty tomorrow morning, in my courtroom."

"Seven-thirty? We usually—"

"You heard me." The judge hung up. He quickly called his secretary, who called Sam Tackett and Charlie Usher. The latter then left a message with one of the jail guards to have Luke Williams in the courtroom by 7:15 a.m.

At 7:30 a.m., the courtroom was almost empty: Judge Long, Tackett, Montgomery, Usher, Luke, the bailiff, Sheriff Collins, and the jury sat in silence. The only other person in the courtroom was reporter Lewis Murphree. He sat alone, his notepad open, in the first row behind Tackett.

Judge Long was pleased. The last thing he wanted now was a crowd who might not like the coming verdict. He looked over the silent courtroom, then turned toward the jury. All twelve looked back, awaiting his directions. *With so few people, there isn't any chance of anyone expressing their dissatisfaction with the decision, doing as they've done so many times before, turning their emotional discontent into violent physical rage. They can always turn vengeful later, but by then, time will have abated the wounds, and individual reasoning will reign over collective, maniacal thought. If not, they'll be back in my courtroom. Sitting in Luke's seat.*

"Mr. Ellis," Judge Long said.

Ron Ellis, the foreman, stood up in the jury box. "Yes, your honor?"

"Has the jury reached a verdict?"

"We have."

"Could you please hand your decision to the bailiff."

Ellis handed a small piece of paper to the bailiff who immediately walked over and handed it to Judge Long. The judge opened and read it, then returned it to the bailiff. Henry handed the paper to Ron, who was still standing in the jury box. Judge Long looked out over the courtroom again. "Will the defendant and counsel please rise."

Luke and Charlie stood up.

The judge thought Luke looked like he hadn't slept well. "Mr. Ellis, will you please read the verdict."

"In the case of the State of Mississippi versus Luke Williams," Ellis said firmly, "we the jury find the defendant, Luke Williams, not guilty as charged."

The courtroom was silent. But all eyes slowly turned toward Sam Tackett.

"You may sit down, Mr. Ellis. Thank you." The judge picked up a pen. "At this time, the jury is dismissed. Thank you for your service to the State of Mississippi."

No one in the jury moved.

"You may go. Henry, please show them out."

Slowly, one by one, they stood, and Henry guided them through a side door out of the courtroom. When the last one exited, Judge Long returned to his work and signed several documents.

"What's going on?" Luke said, to no one in particular.

"You've been acquitted of this charge, Mr. Williams," Judge Long said. "Now we have to figure out what to do about the other charges against you. Mr. Tackett?"

Judge Long had hoped that Sam would drop the indictments and let Luke walk. That's what he'd have done, because they all knew the confession was inadmissible. And Charlie would make sure Luke pleaded not guilty. But sometimes Sam could be obstinate.

Tackett was infuriated that the jury had acquitted Luke. He looked up and almost sneered at Judge Long. "I just tried a case in which I had an eyewitness, and I couldn't get a conviction. Do you really think I should pursue the charges when I don't have any eyewitnesses and a possible inadmissible confession?"

"Did he admit to the crimes?" Judge Long asked.

"Not until after a deputy drew his weapon. Your honor, we can't move forward without an admissible confession. There's nothing else."

"Well, Sam, do I hear a motion to dismiss?"

The prosecutor stared down at his papers. Judge Long knew that Tackett didn't want to give up, but he had no choice. He might get reelected, now that Luke had been acquitted, plus there'd be other trials. Charlie and Luke were sitting at their table, unemotional, detached.

"I have no choice, your honor. The prosecution asks that the indictments against Luke Williams be dismissed because of insufficient evidence."

"Motion granted."

Judge Long watched Charlie lean back in his chair and breathe a sigh of relief. Then Charlie slapped Luke on the shoulder pulling him back from wherever he had gone in his reverie.

"You're free to go, Mr. Williams," the judge said.

"It's over, Luke," Charlie said. "You won."

"But how?" Luke asked.

"Because even with a witness," Tackett said, "I couldn't convict a white man of killing a black man in Mississippi. I'm either a bad prosecutor or there isn't an impartial jury to be found in this state." Tackett's words trailed off. He threw up his hands at Charlie and Luke, and packed up.

"Reasonable doubt," Charlie said.

"It's all speculation at this point," Judge Long said. "Save it for another venue."

"What do I do, Judge?" Luke said. "Where do I go?"

"You go home, Luke." Judge Long was stacking neat piles on his bench.

"But I'm not ready to go home."

"Well, I don't care what you do, but you're not staying in my jail one more day. You've been acquitted. Freed. Now go." The judge motioned for the bailiff to come forward. "Henry, please escort Mr. Williams back to his cell to collect his things. Ensure that he has everything, sign him out, and give him a few dollars to be on his way." Judge Long reached into his pocket and produced three one-dollar bills. He handed them to Henry. "This should get him started. I don't want to see him near my courthouse again. You got that, Mr. Williams?"

Luke nodded his head.

Judge Long looked at the small group left in his courtroom. "Court adjourned." He tapped his gavel one last time.

The handful of men watched while Luke was led through a door near the front of the courtroom. In an instant, he was gone.

"A killer's walking free," Tackett said.

"It doesn't go your way every time," the judge said. "Sometimes justice isn't always served the way you expect. But there's nothing you can do about it now, the jury's will is done." Judge Long looked at his watch. "Anyone want a drink?"

"How 'bout two?" Tackett said.

It was 8:25 a.m.

Since the judge had reconvened so early, Sam Tackett had gone straight to the courtroom without stopping by his office. When he returned after having had a shot of bourbon with the judge in his chambers, Tackett poured himself a cup of coffee and sat down at his desk. Positioned squarely in the center of it was a single file. The other items on the desk had all been cleared away. A handwritten note taped to the front read, "Urgent—Please Read!"

Taking a sip of the bitter coffee, Tackett opened the file and began to scan its contents. After a couple of minutes, he asked his secretary if she had set the file on his desk. She hadn't. Then he asked her to send for Sheriff Collins and Bill Montgomery. They each appeared within ten minutes.

They sat quietly while Tackett read excerpts from the file. He listed all of Higson's residences and his activities since he had arrived in the United States, beginning with his original work in New York through his transfer to Clarksdale. The most recent information described in detail how he had managed to pass military secrets to

Berlin through the German embassy in Washington, D.C. Every so often, Tackett handed a piece of paper to the coroner or the sheriff.

After a long silence, Tackett said, "He's not who we thought he was."

"Well, he's definitely not one of our most upstanding citizens," Montgomery said.

"Does anyone remember him moving into town?" Tackett asked. "I surely don't."

"He just kind of showed up," Collins said. "He ain't even been in Clarksdale that long."

"Yeah, but he's been busy," Tackett said.

"Why hasn't the FBI picked him up?" Collins said. "This really isn't our matter."

Tackett shrugged. "Good point. Maybe we should check with them."

"Don't you think they would have said something already if they wanted us to know?" Montgomery said. He sat back in his chair. "What are we going to do, Sam?"

Tackett rubbed his brow. "Nothing, it's not our jurisdiction. We're just going to wait for the FBI to call us or come up here to arrest Higson. Frank, why don't you have someone drive by his house every so often. Just to make sure he's still around. Or if the professor does head to Oxford, we know of his whereabouts. If I don't hear from the FBI in a day or two, and Higson's just going about his business, I'll call them. The guy's got no reason to think he's under suspicion, does he? No reason to run?"

"Not that I know of," Collins said.

Elma heard the knock and opened the door to find Reverend Coulter standing with his hat in his hand.

"Hello, Elma," he said. She peered out, not opening the door all the way. "May I come in?"

She didn't answer, but opened the door wider to allow him to pass. She prayed he wasn't there for one of his compassionate visits.

"You're not going to offer me a cup of coffee?"

"Sorry, Reverend. What can I get you?"

"Water is fine."

Elma poured a glass of water and placed it in front of him at the kitchen table. Then she stood near the window and watched the children out in the yard.

"Elma, have you heard the news?"

"Yes, I know. Luke's coming home."

"How did you hear?"

"Just did." Elma stood with her arms folded, staring out the window. "He's been gone so long. I'm not sure what it'll feel like to have him home. Kind of strange at first I guess." She dabbed at her eyes with the back of her hand.

"Are you worried?"

"'Bout what?"

"What he's done."

"What he's done? They set him free."

"Doesn't mean he didn't kill anybody, Elma. He confessed to the killings."

"But the jury—." She turned to face the reverend.

"Somebody saw him do it. But I guess it doesn't matter now. What's done is done, and when he comes home, you'll be living with a man that's sinned against God. The only reason he's not going to Parchman is all those poor souls were black."

Elma sighed heavily.

Reverend Coulter stood up and took a step toward Elma. "You know there are some things that happened while Luke was away that he shouldn't know about. You know that, don't you?"

She folded her arms in front of her again.

"How you strayed, fell outside the favor of the Lord." He took another step toward her. "Luke would not look kindly on you seeking comfort elsewhere."

She moved her foot backward but her heel hit the wall.

Coulter grabbed her wrists and brought her arms down to her sides. She tried to struggle free, but her frail arms were useless.

"Please, Reverend."

They could hear the children outside playing a raucous game of tag. He glanced out the window, then at her.

"You never know what Luke would do if he found out. Maybe hurt one of the children."

"No, he'd never."

"You never know what could happen." One hand was now moving down her back, the other grabbed her tightly around the neck. He pulled her ear to his mouth and ran his lips over it.

She felt sick.

"We'll get through this," he whispered. "But believe me, like you believe in the Lord, Luke should never know what happened. What you did."

She could feel his hand move to her hip and then behind her. She pushed on his wrist. It didn't help.

He shoved her against the wall.

Not with the children outside. Not now.

Finally, he relaxed his grip and stepped back.

She quickly straightened herself. The children might be in for lunch at any moment.

"I'll keep in touch." The reverend opened the door. "You and Luke make sure to be at church."

Just get out. Please, please, just get out, she thought.

"Oh, I almost forgot." He pulled an envelope from his coat pocket. It was a ritual now. He threw the envelope on the kitchen table. "Just a few dollars for the children. And don't worry, Elma, even with Luke back, I'll still be around every once in a while to bring you comfort."

As he drove away, Elma could hear the kids out back now, so she went out on the front porch and sat on one of the steps her neighbor had recently repaired after he'd tripped on the old ones. She put her face in her hands to hide her tears.

CHAPTER 34

North wind has began howling.

—Walters Davis

CAPTAIN JOHANN KESSLER WAS STANDING OUTSIDE the bridge of the Liberator, a general service cargo ship, waiting for his orders from Germany. They'd been moored in New Orleans for several days, where the youthful crew enjoyed the nightlife and the cynical captain enjoyed heckling them when they stumbled back to their berths early each morning.

Kessler leaned on the railing and watched the dockworkers, puffing at his pipe. Suddenly, the bridge door opened and a sailor appeared at his side.

"Captain?"

"Yes," Kessler said.

"I've received an emergency communication from the German embassy in Washington."

Kessler straightened up. "Let me see it." He read the single line of transcription carefully. "Spider's web is broken. Get the spider out."

Kessler looked up. "When did you receive this?"

"Just now, Captain. What does it mean?"

"Never mind. Tell Neumann I need to see him immediately."

Neumann was outside the bridge with Captain Kessler in less than a minute.

"Neumann, how close are we to being ready to leave?"

"We can be ready in a day."

"Contact Perry Fontaine in Pilot's Town and tell them we need someone to guide us back out to sea. Send him soon. Have we finished off-loading cargo?"

"Yes, Captain, but we're still loading supplies on board." Neumann motioned toward the labor and equipment being used to load containers of cotton, sugar, canned foods, and some chemicals into the cargo hold. They also needed provisions for the crew during the return trip.

"We may not be able to finish reloading."

"What's the hurry, sir?"

Kessler stood closer to his first mate. "The network is broken. It's only a matter of time before Higson is arrested. We've been ordered to get him out of the country."

"Where is he now?"

"Clarksdale, but we'll see if he can meet us somewhere in between, maybe Vicksburg. We certainly can't risk having him lead the Americans to us. Have the ship ready for departure as soon as you can."

"Yes, sir."

Kessler turned and leaned on the railing again. To the north he saw storm clouds drifting in.

CHAPTER 35

Special agents up the country.

—John Estes

RUSS KALMAN WALKED INTO HIS OFFICE AFTER A late-afternoon meeting and stood at his desk, gazing at the surface strewn with papers.

"Mr. Kalman," his secretary said.

He looked up.

"It's Washington on the phone."

"Who is it?"

"Robert Haynes."

The chief sat down, propped his feet on his desk, and picked up the phone.

"Afternoon, Robert."

"Hello, Russ."

"How are things up there?"

"Oh, pretty good. The weather's starting to cool off, so that's a relief. A little too hot for us Yankees in the summer."

"Well, it hasn't cooled off down here yet. And I doubt it will for a few more weeks at least. What can we help you with today?"

"Actually, nothing. But I'm going to help you."

"Oh, really?"

"We've broken Higson's network," Haynes said.

Kalman sat up in his chair and positioned himself over his desk. "Say again."

"Just what I said. We cracked the network."

"I thought there was no hard evidence."

"There is now. Just a little while ago, we apprehended a man from the German embassy named Albert Thums. He worked for the ambassador, and we found out he carried some information back home a few months ago. He'd probably been doing it for a while, but that was the first time we could actually confirm he was carrying intelligence. We searched his bag today and found what we were looking for. A pile of documents—some originals, some copies, and all classified—about military projects that various universities and some private organizations have been working on. All of them had contact with Higson, and all of them said they had sent or loaned him things that were never returned."

"How'd you know he was carrying anything?"

"Little bit of instinct and a lucky guess. We'd be turning our badges in if he was clean."

"Has he implicated Higson?" Kalman asked.

"He didn't have to. Higson had written notes on some of the documents, and he included a cover letter discussing the scientific concepts and principles of the documents. He had signed the letter."

"Then we can pick him up?"

"Absolutely."

"Do I need to send someone tonight?"

"No, tomorrow morning's fine. We arrested Thums, his driver, pilot, and a couple others. By the time the embassy realizes they're missing, Higson will already be behind bars."

"I'll make sure Thompson and Mulevsky are up there first thing in the morning. Maybe even get the good professor while he's sleeping. Thanks, Robert. I'll call you when we have him in custody."

The men hung up, and Kalman walked out of his office into the hallway. "Thompson, Mulevsky," he said loudly. "Where are you two?"

Bob Thompson walked into the hall. "What's going on, Russ?"

"I want you to head to Clarksdale and pick up Higson tomorrow morning."

Thompson stood, stunned. "Why? What happened?"

"Washington's broken the network. They've taken someone into custody, and they've got evidence implicating Higson, linking him to the network. They've given us the go-ahead to pick him up."

"Mulevsky," Thompson shouted.

Dan Mulevsky emerged from the restroom. "Can't I even get a few minutes alone?"

"You're going to Clarksdale to arrest Higson in the morning," Kalman said.

"What?"

"You two better go home and get some sleep. I'll call Sheriff Collins to let him know you're coming. You should be back here around noon."

The chief reentered his office but quickly popped back out into the hallway again. "Hey, guys. Be careful with Higson. He knows he's going to spend a long time in prison, or worse, so he doesn't have much to lose. And remember, he can lead us to his other accomplices. So if you can get him alive, that would be best."

"We'll see you tomorrow afternoon, Russ," Thompson said.

Once more the chief returned to his office and called Sheriff Collins.

"Sheriff's office," the secretary said.

"This is Russ Kalman in Jackson. I need to speak to Sheriff Collins."

"He's already left for the day."

Kalman looked at his watch. "Any deputies there?"

"No, sir, they've also gone home."

The FBI division chief reconsidered the consequences of notifying Collins. What if the sheriff himself decided to pick up Higson? Or worse, what if he spooked Higson? He needed this arrest. Even the slightest mistake would certainly make the bureau look bad and possibly ruin his career. But what did Collins care?

"Should I have him call you in the morning?" she said. "Or, I can give you his home number."

"No, I don't want to bother him. It's not urgent. I'll call back tomorrow."

He hung up the phone and considered his next promotion.

CHAPTER 36

Going to Germany.

—Noah Lewis

HIGSON STUMBLED FROM HIS BED IN THE DARK TO answer the ringing phone. He grabbed the handset roughly, unsteady on his feet.

"Higson," said the voice.

The professor recognized the accent as German. "Hello?" he replied in German.

"You've got to get out immediately," the voice returned in German.

"Who is this?"

"A friend. You've been compromised."

"What should I do?"

"Your orders are to travel to Vicksburg as quickly as you can. You need to leave *now*. But don't take the train or drive your car.

The train stations and roads may already be blocked or under observation. You must travel by ship to Vicksburg."

"But won't they be watching the docks also?"

"It's less likely. They wouldn't expect you to take such a slow means of escape. Can you get there?"

"I believe so. There's one out of Helena across the river."

"Don't *believe so*. If you are caught, your trial will not be pleasant."

"Where will I meet you?"

"At the docks. If we don't contact you there, go on to New Orleans any way you can and find the ship *Liberator*. We'll wait for you, but we can only wait so long. You must hurry."

"How will I recognize you in Vicksburg?"

"We'll check the passenger boat schedule and watch for you. Liberator is the code word. If we don't find each other in Vicksburg within an hour after you arrive, proceed to New Orleans. How long will it take you to get to Vicksburg?"

"I'll leave at daylight. Depending on when the ship leaves, it'll be a day at least. Where am I going once I board the *Liberator*?"

"Home, Professor."

The line went dead.

Higson was stunned. Finally, his requests had been answered—he was going back to Germany. Back to his homeland, and the work he was meant to do. They finally understood how important he was to the Party. He would be vindicated.

The professor pulled up the floorboards in his bedroom and went down into his lab. He quickly rummaged through the trash and pulled out the local paper. Rifling through the pages, he finally found the advertisement he was looking for.

The *River Belle* would leave at 4:30 the next afternoon from Helena. En route to New Orleans, she would be stopping at several places along the way, including Vicksburg.

Higson circled the listing with a pencil, took the newspaper back upstairs, and tossed it on the kitchen table. Although he hurried through his house getting ready to leave, he was nonetheless methodical in packing his suitcase with clothes, shaving kit, and the rest of his important papers. He did not want to risk overlooking anything he might need on his trip. In the kitchen, he found several small cans of food; he placed them in his bag along with a can opener. Then he placed the paper and the brown suitcase next to his black doctor's bag by the front door.

He had just clicked out the light in the front room when he heard something through his open windows. Sound travels far on a still night, and wafting in, faint but unmistakable, were voices.

The four men stopped talking and stood at the edge of the field behind the house, lugging their heavy cans.

"What do you think?" Wyatt asked Ned.

"I think these cans are heavy," Edgar said.

"I think you should keep your voice down," Ned whispered while motioning to Bo with his hand.

Bo was back in less than thirty seconds. "Bastard's car's still there."

"Good. Everybody clear about what he's supposed to do?" Ned said, throwing his cigarette on the ground near an old clothesline post.

They each nodded their heads.

"It's time this S.O.B. paid for his big mouth," Bo whispered. "In fact, it's *past* time."

"Don't shoot till he's outside the house," Ned said. "We don't want him running back inside and shooting back at us from the safety of the house. Let's go. And be quick." Ned could tell Bo's finger was twitching.

Ned stayed in the backyard while Bo crept around to the front and Wyatt and Edgar took their positions on either side of the house. The two took their lead from Ned, and when he moved so did they, in unison, soaking the outside of the house and the porch with gasoline.

The wind caught the fumes, and they swirled through the yard. Ned breathed deeply, enjoying the sweet smell of the gasoline.

When they were done, Wyatt signaled to Ned they were ready.

Calmly, Ned struck a match and touched it to the base of the outside wall. In seconds, the flame raced around the perimeter of the house. Moments later the dry timbers were ablaze, and the men watched as the fire quickly moved up the walls and to the roof.

Ned stepped around to where he could see Bo. The light from the fire danced across Bo's evil grin.

Higson has to be awake by now, Ned thought, and he wondered which exit he would take. He looked from the door to the window and back again.

Suddenly, sounds of broken glass and pistol shots filled the air. They seemed to come from all directions, and Ned looked around before he bolted toward the front of the house.

"What happened?" Ned asked, running up to Bo, Wyatt following in his wake. "Where is he?"

"I saw him at the window. Right up there." He pointed at a large window to the right of the front door. "He was wearing a white undershirt."

"I told you to wait till he got outside." They stepped back as the heat from the fire intensified and the drapes billowed like burning flags from the windows.

"I know, but I couldn't wait. I jus' had to kill him." Bo rubbed his hand over his pistol.

"Well, it would have been nice to see the body," Wyatt said. "Now it's gonna be all burned up."

"We better get outta here," Ned said. "This fire might attract some attention. Where's Edgar?"

"He was on the other side of the house," Wyatt said. He and Ned started in that direction.

Ned looked back. "Come on, Bo."

Bo was still staring at the window. "I'm coming." He moved slowly.

Edgar was sitting near the edge of the yard holding his shoulder when they walked up.

"Edgar," Ned said. "You okay?"

"Yeah, I guess so."

Ned moved Edgar's hand and looked at the wound. A chunk of flesh had been taken from his left shoulder. It was bleeding profusely. Ned took out his knife and cut a swath from Edgar's shirt, then packed the material into the wound. Edgar grimaced in pain.

"Hold it down," Ned said.

"When I heard the shots," Edgar said, "I thought somebody was shooting at me, so I fired. Caught one of my own shots after it bounced off that pipe sticking out there." He pointed to a pipe jutting out from the house.

"Come on," Ned said. "Let's go get you fixed up."

"Did we get him?" Edgar asked.

"Yeah," Bo said. "I shot the bastard when he came to the window."

"Good."

Wyatt and Bo helped Edgar up, and the men shuffled out into the field toward their car parked several hundred yards away. Halfway there, they heard a rumbling and turned around just as one of the walls tumbled into the center of the house.

"We done good," Bo said.

Higson reached down and picked up one of his bags while searching for the newspaper he thought he had stuck between the two. It wasn't there, but it didn't matter; he knew the schedule. He picked up his other bag, all the while staring at the blaze in the distance, a volcano erupting in a cotton field. With his car still there, maybe they'd think he had died in the fire. No one would be looking for him as he headed for his rendezvous. It was all working out better than expected.

The professor started down the main road that ran parallel to his house, one he had traveled so often. The only thing on his mind was getting to Helena and catching the *River Belle*. "I'm not long in Mississippi," he said, softly. "Not long at all."

CHAPTER 37

The blues and the devil.

—*Lonnie Johnson*

THOMPSON ATTEMPTED AND SUCCEEDED IN SETTING a personal record on his drive with Mulevsky to Clarksdale. Even though the driver thought they were going pretty fast, his passenger never flinched. They talked about Higson, but only briefly. Most of the conversation was devoted to their families, sports, Roosevelt's Works Progress Administration, and why the Democratic Party kept supporting urban labor. It made Thompson's stomach turn.

Thompson brought the car to a halt in front of Clarksdale's courthouse. He looked at his watch. It was 6:15 a.m., and still dark. They quickly got out of the car and headed for Collins's office, but the courthouse doors were locked. They wondered why Collins wasn't there to meet them. They banged on the doors but no one answered, so they returned to their car and waited.

"Where have you been?" Thompson called, when Collins finally arrived in a squad car.

Collins looked over, raising an eyebrow. "Home in bed. What about you?"

The two FBI agents stepped out of the car as did Collins.

"You got the call from Russ, didn't you?" Mulevsky asked.

"No, I didn't. When did he call?"

"Russ was supposed to call you yesterday," Thompson said, "and let you know we were coming to arrest Higson."

"On account of his being a spy?"

"That's right. How'd you know?" Thompson looked at Mulevsky, who shrugged his shoulders.

"Just do," Collins drawled. "Don't worry 'bout Higson, though; we've been sending a car past his house. He's not going any-where."

"Then let's get out there and arrest him."

"Before we go, I need to let Sam Tackett know what we're doing. He'll probably want to come along. Let me call, and I'll meet you boys back down here in a couple of minutes."

"Hurry up." Thompson clapped his hands together. "We're wast-ing time."

Collins disappeared into the courthouse and emerged a few min-utes later. The three men spoke by the vehicles until Tackett arrived with Montgomery right behind him.

Collins, Tackett, Montgomery, and two deputies loaded them-selves into two different vehicles.

Mulevsky rolled his eyes and nudged Thompson.

"It's only one guy," Thompson called out from his window.

"We want to be careful," Tackett said, smiling.

"You know where you're going?" Thompson asked the sheriff.

Collins shot him a stare. He led the caravan of three law enforce-ment vehicles—the FBI agents' car sandwiched in the middle—through downtown and toward Higson's house.

Thompson looked ahead and saw a thin black plume of smoke rise above the shimmering horizon, which was already glowing with the risen sun. "Somebody's burning something over there." He stepped on the gas and passed Collins.

"What're you doing, Bob?" Mulevsky said.

"I hope that's not what I think it is." Thompson accelerated steadily.

Thompson turned sharply right, onto the road that led to the house. The glowing embers and wisps of smoke came clearly into view. Speeding down the drive, Thompson skidded a few yards from what remained of the front door.

He stepped out of the car, but climbed right back in, his arm raised to shield his face from the heat of the smoldering ashes. He backed the car up another twenty yards and got out a second time.

Without saying a word, he shook his head, laughed to himself, and leaned against the hood of his car. He lit a cigarette, offered one to Mulevsky, and watched while the charred remnants continued to be transformed into ash.

Mulevsky took the cue and climbed up on the hood. "What do you think happened?"

"I don't know. We could've gotten this guy weeks ago. And now we got nothing. Washington was dragging their feet and now they only have half of what they need."

"Think he was inside?"

Just then, Collins pulled up and parked behind Thompson. The other Clarksdale police vehicle was parked at the entrance to the road leading to Higson's house to stop any curiosity seekers who were bound to come along as day broke.

"I thought you'd been keeping an eye on things," Thompson said in a challenging tone when Collins and Tackett walked up.

Montgomery wandered past the two agents and closer to the ruined house.

"We were," Collins said. "Now, maybe if you had called us a little sooner, we might've had him in custody."

"Where do you think he went?" Montgomery asked.

"If anywhere," Thompson said. "The S.O.B. might still be in there, because I'll bet that's his car." Thompson flicked an ash in its direction.

Collins walked over and looked inside the car.

"We'll wait till this burns out," added Thompson, "and then we'll see what's left. Right now, I'm going back to your office to call my boss. He's not gonna be happy. And neither will Washington."

Collins had a pained look on his face.

Thompson threw his cigarette down and ground it into the dirt. "We'll see you guys back at the office." He climbed into his car and slammed the door. Mulevsky followed.

"We'll be back shortly, Bob," Collins said into the dust swirling around Thompson's open window as he drove away.

"Hey, Frank," Montgomery called out.

Collins and the others turned.

"We got a body."

CHAPTER 38

The lowdown dirty deacon.

—Luke Jordan

CONRAD HIGSON SPENT THE NIGHT RESTING FITFULLY as he hid in a ditch. Soon after daybreak, he started his walk toward Helena, turning to thumb down a ride. But he had a single stop to make before going to the dock.

"Yeah, I can drop you near there," the driver said in answer to Higson's stated destination.

Perched in the cab of the truck, the professor stared out the window thinking that this would be one of the last times he would have to look at a cotton field. He was sure he would miss them at some point in the future, but not right now.

An hour after they started, which included one twenty-minute stop to unload some flour at a country store, the driver let Higson out. There had been no roadblocks. No trouble.

"Thank you," said the passenger. "Your kindness is appreciated." He handed the driver some change for the ride, then grabbed his bags from the truck's bed.

"Much appreciated," the man said.

Higson watched the truck drive away and then walked down a dirt road leading to a small cabin with a new set of porch steps tucked away behind a clump of trees. Coming to a stop, he watched while several children played in a large oak a couple of hundred yards away. He tried to recall his own last days of innocence. He could not.

A car was parked next to the house. Higson wondered if Elma had borrowed it from a neighbor.

He walked up the steps onto the porch and set his suitcase down near the front door. He kept a tight hold on his doctor's bag. Just as he was about to knock on the door, he heard Elma's voice coming from inside the house. She was pleading, crying.

Higson opened the door and looked into the kitchen. No one was there, but the voices were clearer. They were coming from the bedroom.

"Please, Reverend," he heard. "Just go."

Higson heard a slap, and a woman's voice cried out in pain followed by muffled sobs.

"I'll go when I'm good and ready," a man's voice said. "Now take off that dress, or I'll take it off for you. We don't have much time."

The professor stepped into the bedroom to see Reverend Coulter—stripped down to his undershirt, his pants unbuttoned—standing over the bed where Elma lay. There were drops of blood on the sheets and on one of Elma's hands, which she held over her face.

Reverend Coulter turned in surprise. "Who are you, and how dare you come into my house uninvited? You need to get the hell out."

"What's going on, Elma?" asked the visitor, ignoring the pastor.

"I'm having a discussion with my wife." His voice was louder now. "I told you to get outta my house. This is none of your business."

"This isn't *your* house, and I think this *is* my business." Higson observed a welt rising under one of Elma's eyes.

Coulter followed Higson's glance toward Elma, and then he looked back at the professor. "Mister, are you calling me a liar? If so, I suggest we have this conversation outside."

Higson set his bag down in the doorway, and Coulter took a step toward him.

Coulter was thin and had to look up at the intruder. This didn't even seem fair.

"You'd better pick up that bag," Coulter said. He took two more steps and was reaching for the bag when he rose up and swung a fist at Higson's head. The professor feinted to his left, then recovered and grabbed Coulter by the throat. His meaty hands gripped Coulter's neck tightly, and Higson spun him around and slammed the man's head against the wall.

"Did you enjoy what you were doing just now?"

Coulter couldn't speak.

"Who is this, Elma?"

"Our reverend."

Higson sneered. "Look at her." Coulter didn't respond. "Look at her, I said." Coulter's eyes darted in her direction. "Are you proud of yourself, *Reverend*? I wonder where her husband is?"

Coulter gurgled.

"Do you know where Luke is, Elma?"

She shook her head.

"You know, my father beat my mother like that a few times. He was always drunk. You haven't been drinking, have you, *Reverend*?"

He sniffed Coulter's breath.

"You don't even have that excuse. Of course, my father would also beat us. Do you like to beat children? Look at this scar over my left eye." Higson brushed his finger over it.

Coulter stared straight ahead.

Higson lifted Coulter's head, tilted it forward, and slammed it into the wall again to make sure he could see it.

"Do you see it?"

Coulter looked right at it.

"My father, he took his belt buckle, placed it in the palm of his hand, like so." Higson pushed his palm under Coulter's nose. "And then he hit me three, four, five times. It's not so bad now. And I'm not sure how it healed so well. But even that really didn't hurt as much as the beatings he gave to my mother. He would lock me and my brothers and sisters in the closet, and we would sit in the dark, all together, holding each other, sometimes covering our ears so we couldn't hear. And then we would wait and listen to the yelling and the screaming, which eventually turned to shoving and punching. He would throw her around our small house, much like a doll, until she was either unconscious, or he passed out from his incessant drinking."

Her rescuer turned and looked at Elma. She lay on her side, not moving. He relaxed his grip on Coulter throat. Coulter brought his own hands to his neck, gasping and choking. He tried to breathe deeply. Staggering, he took a step forward.

"Where are you going?" Higson snapped, bringing a knee into Coulter's stomach. Coulter went down to his knees, gripping his abdomen. "Reverend, you can't leave just yet. You haven't been punished for your sins. Are sinners not meant to suffer? To be punished?"

He hoisted Coulter onto the bed and positioned him facing Elma. He kneeled against the pastor's back to keep him in place. Then he removed his belt and wrapped it around Coulter's neck. "Is there anything you would like to say to Mrs. Williams? Anything about your sins?"

Coulter swallowed hard. His voice was hoarse and tears spilled from both eyes. "I've got the Devil in me, Elma," he gasped. "I—"

"You don't sound very convincing, reverend. Besides, I'm in bit of a hurry and must be on my way."

With a single, violent twist, Higson tightened the belt around the preacher's neck. Seconds ticked by while Coulter coughed and sputtered, trying to inhale, trying to swallow. His arms flailed, and the attacker readjusted his grip, cinching the belt tighter.

Higson watched Coulter's face turn from white to dark red. Coulter tried frantically to slip his fingers in between the belt and his throat. When he couldn't, he reached madly for Elma, but she sat frozen, just beyond his fingertips, staring at him through her swollen, discolored eyes. Slowly, Coulter's limbs stopped jerking and his body went limp, silent and still.

The professor held onto the belt and dragged the body to the front door. He dug into Coulter's pants pocket and found the keys to his car. He opened the front door and looked for the children. They must still be in the trees, or playing in the fields somewhere. He dragged the body down the steps and across the yard. He opened the car's trunk, loaded the body in, and slammed the lid shut.

Higson returned to the bedroom, picked up the bag he had brought, and sat down on the edge of the bed. "Elma."

She said nothing. She hadn't moved since he first began to tighten the belt around Coulter's neck.

"Can I get you a doctor?"

She mouthed no. She had no voice.

"He won't be bothering you anymore." Higson looked at his watch. "But I cannot stay. I'll be taking the preacher's car, with him in it, of course. I hope that's okay."

Her eyes looked into his. "Who are you?" Her voice was raspy and tired.

"An acquaintance of Luke's."

"Luke never said—"

"This is for you." He patted the side of the bag. "Open it when I'm gone."

She looked at the bag. "Why?"

"For you and the children."

"Why?" She couldn't say anything else.

Higson hesitated. "It's not important. I've got to go now. The reverend is waiting." He smiled and gently moved strands of hair from her bloodied face. "Don't ever mention that he came here. They'll eventually find his body, but you never saw him. Do you understand?"

She nodded.

He placed a hand on her cheek. "Good-bye, Elma. Watch out for your children. They need their mother most of all." Higson stood and walked to the bedroom door.

"Thank you," Elma said.

He smiled at her and walked out.

Half an hour ticked by before Elma unbuckled the bag and pulled it toward her. It toppled over, and several neatly wrapped stacks of twenty-dollar bills tumbled onto the bed.

CHAPTER 39

I got to ride this new highway.

—Sonny Boy Williamson

TRAVIS WAS READING AFTER HAVING EATEN LUNCH when the phone rang. His mother answered.

"Hello, Anita," Margaret said. "No, I haven't heard of any fire. Whose house was it? Higson? The one from the trial?" Margaret laughed. "Slow down, Anita, you're speaking too fast." She listened intently for a moment, her smile fading into a worried look. "I'll talk to Bill this afternoon. He'll know all about this. Yes, of course, I'll call you when I know."

"What was that all about?" Travis asked.

Margaret hung up the phone. "Anita Thornton was rambling on about the FBI. Have you heard anything like that?"

"No. Did she say they were looking for Higson?"

"I don't think so." She returned to dusting the dining room table. "She was difficult to understand."

Travis got up from the table, put his lunch plate in the sink, and was tucking his shirt in at the front door when his mother walked into the foyer.

"Where are you headed?"

"I've got to run by the courthouse. I'll be back later."

"Don't be late for dinner," came her customary admonition.

"Yes, ma'am." He opened the door and hurried out.

Thompson and Mulevsky were standing by their car in front of the courthouse when Travis walked up. He recognized Thompson from both the trial and the hallway outside the Records room in Jackson. Travis waited while Thompson finished his conversation on the two-way radio.

"If you can't tell, then get the damn body back here so we can figure out if it's Higson or not. If he's already dead, we can save ourselves a lot of trouble." Thompson turned the radio off abruptly.

"Hello, sir," Travis said. "Are you gentlemen with the FBI?"

"Yeah, that's us," Thompson said, tossing his cigarette on the ground.

"I'm Travis Montgomery. My dad's Bill Montgomery, the county coroner." They looked blankly at him. If they remembered him, it didn't show.

"Yes, we know him."

"I've heard a few rumors today. What's going on?"

"Shouldn't you be asking your father that?"

Travis paid no attention to the comment. "I'm sure I'll hear all about it at suppertime, but I'm really curious about what happened to Higson's house. My mother just received a call from someone, and I'm checking on it for her. "

"See that faint trickle of black smoke over there on the horizon?" Thompson turned to look back southeast. Travis's eyes followed.

"Yes, sir."

"That's it. His house."

"Was Higson in it?"

"Good question. They found a body, but we won't know any-thing about the identity until your father conducts the autopsy. The body was pretty well charred. It could take a couple of days. In the meantime, we're gonna call every sheriff's department within a hundred miles and ask them to be on the lookout for Higson. We've got a good description, and he shouldn't be hard to find with that British accent of his."

"Did you see—"

"That's enough questions, son." Thompson ended the conversa-tion. "You need to run along; we've got work to do."

Thompson and Mulevsky left Travis in the parking lot, staring at the wisp of smoke in the distance. He knew as much as anyone about what was going on. Why wouldn't the sheriff want his help? This wasn't some two-bit thief stealing chickens, after all; this was a man who was wanted by the FBI. A man who was Clarksdale's version of John Dillinger.

Travis looked toward the parking lot. His dad's car was gone. Without hesitation, he turned and started walking south, slowly at first but picking up his pace to a jog. His breathing quickened and beads of sweat started to form on his brow. He turned up a street in the Brickyard, ran up the steps to a familiar house, and knocked on the door.

Hannah answered. "Hi, Travis."

"Have you heard the news?" Travis asked, still breathing heavy. She looked inquisitive.

"Higson's house burned down last night." Travis leaned forward intently. "They have a body."

"Is it him?" She stepped out onto the porch.

"They haven't identified it yet, but I'd like to go out and take a look."

"To the house? What for?"

"See if it's him, or if we can help."

"Help do what?"

"Find him. Look for clues. I don't know, something. We'll figure it out on the way."

"Travis, why don't you let the police handle it?"

"I will, I just want to take a quick look." He was getting impatient. "We need to borrow your dad's car."

"What!" Her eyes narrowed as she came to a realization. "Now I know why you want me to go."

"That's not the only reason. We've got to get out there fast, and I don't know where my dad's car is. Plus, I need you."

"My dad will never let us have the car."

"Come on, get the keys. The house will be rebuilt by the time we get there."

"Travis, I—"

"Please."

Hannah studied him closely for a moment, and he knew she understood. Reluctantly, she went back inside.

Travis started pacing back and forth in front of the door. He could hear her speaking with her parents, but the sounds were muffled. There were no raised voices, which was a good sign. Finally, the door cracked open and she emerged.

"Yes, ma'am," she said, speaking through the opening in the door. "Before dinner, I'm sure. If not, I'll let you know." She shut the door behind her.

"What'd they say?" They stepped off the porch and headed for the street.

"That I could go. My mother would have come to the door, but she was shucking peas for dinner."

"No, about the car?"

"I didn't ask them."

"We need the car. You need to go back—"

She lifted her hand, and a set of keys dangled from her index finger.

Travis stared at them. "We're just going to take it?"

"You were the one who wanted the car. How bad do you want it?"

Travis stood silently, being thoughtful for a moment. "Won't you get in trouble without asking?"

"Travis, he would never have let us take it. And don't worry; we are *definitely* going to get in trouble. We probably won't be seeing each other for a while, and I'm sure my dad will talk to your dad."

Travis looked at the car parked in front of the house. Then he looked back at Hannah's front door. Is it worth it? All this trouble for something we shouldn't even be involved with in the first place. He thought of several other people who might have access to a car, but there wasn't enough time.

The door opened, startling both of them.

"If you'll be late, don't forget to call," her mother called out.

"Yes, ma'am."

"Where are my keys?" Mr. Morgan said from inside the house, his voice booming.

Her mother looked back inside but left the door open.

Hannah looked at Travis. "What's it going to be, boy?"

Travis smiled and quickly opened the passenger's side door for her. She jumped in, reached over, and pushed the driver's door open slightly.

"Hannah, why are you getting into your father's car?" Mrs. Morgan shouted from the porch.

"We'll be back shortly," Travis said. "We just need to borrow Mr. Morgan's car for a little while." Travis jumped in and shoved the key in the ignition; the motor rumbled to life.

"Hannah!" Mr. Morgan yelled from the porch, now standing next to his wife.

She waved mightily and smiled back at her parents as if she and Travis were headed off on a lovely outing. She turned toward Travis. "We're in so much trouble."

Mr. Morgan was quickly moving down the steps and was much more nimble than Travis expected. He shifted into gear and pushed the pedal down hard. They could still hear Mr. Morgan yelling halfway down the block.

A line of cars had already formed along the highway by the turnoff to Higson's house. Travis steered onto the shoulder and pulled up behind the last one and shut the engine off. A good number of bystanders were huddled together to one side. Others had remained in their cars, hanging out their windows trying to catch a glimpse of something gruesome. It wasn't quite chaos, but it was Clarksdale's equivalent.

"Is this where you met Higson?" Hannah asked.

"Right around back. Let's see if we can get a closer look." He got out of the car. "C'mon." He tapped the hood.

Hannah followed Travis toward the deputies guarding the drive. They were only a couple years older than Travis, and he knew both of them, but not by name. He tried to walk past them.

"You can't go any farther," one of them said, leaning against a squad car. "Sheriff's orders."

Travis was ready. He removed an envelope from his pocket and held it up. Only he knew it contained a blank piece of paper. "Yes, but I was instructed by the sheriff and my father, the coroner, to deliver this letter immediately to—" He scanned the scene for a familiar face. "— Mr. Birdsong. He's right there." Travis pointed toward a man standing on the corner of the property. "We won't get in anyone's way."

"Sheriff Collins didn't say anything to us about you or the letter. Maybe you could wait until Mr. Birdsong is done."

"Let me call in and check with the sheriff," the other deputy said, climbing into the squad car to use the radio.

"We don't have time for this. I was here the other day, and all I need to do is give this letter to him. He's right there. Let's go." Travis beckoned to Hannah. He walked past the deputies toward the house.

Hannah followed quickly, eyes on Travis.

"Let me talk to the sheriff first," the deputy called after them. Travis kept walking.

When Hannah walked past the deputy standing next to the car, he grabbed her arm. "You're not going anywhere."

Travis turned around quickly. "Let her go."

The deputy didn't move; the other one was already talking on the radio.

Travis took one step forward. "Now."

"Our orders were that no one goes in."

"I told you I was asked to deliver this letter."

"Well, what's she doing?" The deputy tugged on Hannah's arm.

"She's with me. That's all you need to know."

The deputy let go of Hannah. She rubbed the spot on her arm where he had gripped her while she and Travis proceeded down the dirt road.

"Let's hurry, I don't know how much time we have," Travis said, glancing over his shoulder at the deputies.

They walked quickly, eyes darting around the property

"What am I supposed to be doing?" Hannah asked.

"Helping me."

"What about the body? Doesn't it make sense to find out whether it's Higson first before we start digging around? I can't believe you talked me into coming here."

They eyed the smoldering timbers, circling around to the back of the house where Travis had met the professor. They both noticed the sheets covering something near the back door.

"You look around," Travis said. "I'm going to check with Bird-song about the body."

Travis returned to Hannah's side a few minutes later.

"Well?"

"It's not Higson."

"How could that be?"

"Mr. Birdsong said my dad didn't want to confirm it until after he conducted the autopsy, but the body they found was missing most of its teeth. Higson had all of his. And he said the corpse was shorter than the professor appeared to be. He wants to be a hundred percent sure before he releases the information, but he's almost positive."

Travis looked up; the deputies were approaching. "Here they come."

"I just talked to the sheriff's office," the one who had been on the radio said. "He said no unauthorized personnel are allowed near the house. No one. And your *daddy* wants you back at the courthouse." The deputy smirked.

Travis and Hannah started to walk back to the car, followed closely by both deputies, when Travis noticed an old trash pile that workers were using for the few remains from the house. "I need to throw this away," he said veering off quickly, holding up the letter he was supposed to have delivered to Birdsong.

"Hey, I told you to get back to your car."

Travis ignored him and walked over and tossed the envelope onto the heap. Bottles, rags, a wire spool, and an assortment of burned building materials made up most of the items. Then someone tossed a board on the pile, knocking over an old wooden chair with only three legs. Something caught Travis's eye. A newspaper, completely intact, lay near the back edge of the pile. The chair had been covering it.

"Let's go," the deputy said, moving closer to Travis. "You're coming now." He reached out to grab Travis.

Hannah screamed loudly. Everyone who had been working around the house stopped what he was doing and turned toward her. Suddenly, it was quiet. The deputies froze.

Travis used the opportunity to bend over the pile and pick up the folded newspaper. It was dated two days ago and had been opened to a page with travel information. Something was circled. He tucked it under his arm.

"What's going on over there?" one of the investigators said from across the yard.

"Nothing, sir," one of the deputies said. "We're escorting these people to their car."

The four of them walked back to the car in silence. One of the deputies gave Travis a sour look. "You make sure to bring *your daddy* when you come back, you hear me, boy?"

Travis started the car, turned around in the middle of the road, and headed back to town.

A quarter mile down the road, Travis said, "What's circled? In the paper."

Hannah picked up the paper that Travis had lain on the seat between them. "It's a schedule."

"What kind of schedule?" Travis tried to read and keep the car on the road at the same time.

"*River Belle*'s."

"The riverboat out of Helena? We need to make a call."

"Not from my house."

"No, mine either."

Early's Diner on the south side of Clarksdale was mostly vacant, but its dinner crowd would start arriving shortly. Travis pulled into a parking space behind the restaurant.

Hannah waited in the car while Travis went in the back door to use the phone. "It'll just take a minute to check whether the schedule in the paper is right," he assured her.

"Hello, sir," Travis said when a man answered the number Travis had secured from the paper. "Is *River Belle* running today?"

Travis listened while the man on the other end of the line spoke. "About half past four?" He looked at his watch. It was 4:10. "You don't think I'll make it, but maybe I could, if the boat doesn't leave on time? Yes, sir. Thank you, sir."

Travis hung up the phone and hurried back out to the car.

"They said if the *River Belle*'s late departing, we just might just catch her."

"I don't think we should be doing this, but if I don't go, you may do something really stupid."

"That's the spirit." He backed away from the restaurant and accelerated toward Helena. On the outskirts of town, he looked at the speedometer. The needle wouldn't go any higher.

CHAPTER 40

I heard the Helena whistle blow.

—Charlie Patton

HIGSON PARKED REVEREND COULTER'S CAR IN AN empty lot across the street from where the *River Belle* was docked. He paid the attendant.

"When will you be returning, sir?" the attendant said.

"In about a week."

"Do you need help with your suitcase, sir?"

"No, I've got it." The professor crossed the street and entered a small two-story whitewashed building a short walk from the dock. He joined a line of travelers. He kept his eyes on the ground and spoke to no one.

When the man behind the counter asked, "May I help you?" Higson muttered a simple yes, knowing the less he said, the better.

He also knew that no one would forget his accent, so he tried to disguise it. "One to Vicksburg, please."

"And when will you be returning?"

"I haven't decided."

The cashier glanced up, but said nothing. He stamped the one-way ticket and took Higson's money. "Will you need someone to carry your bags?"

"No."

With a languid wave, the cashier directed Higson toward a walkway that led to the ship. Passengers and well-wishers crowded the pier, the walkway, and the deck. This suited him just fine. It would be easy to go unnoticed in a large crowd.

The professor boarded, weaving through the mass of people, jostling and bumping his way through the narrow aisles. When he found his room, he shoved his suitcase under the foot of his bed.

The ship's whistle sounded, and Higson looked at his watch. It was 4:25 p.m. He was relieved that the departure would be prompt. What was left of his house would be swarming by now with law enforcement officials from the FBI. He wondered what was happening with Thums and his other associates in Washington. He had a long way to go before he could relax and look forward to his return to Germany.

Higson strolled out on deck and leaned on the railing with the other passengers awaiting their leisurely voyage down the Mississippi. For almost everyone but him, New Orleans was the final destination. He gazed idly to shore. He saw two men emerge from a police car in front of the office where he had just bought his ticket. One was dressed in a dark-blue uniform, the other in a suit. They stared at the ship for a moment, took a couple of steps toward her, and surveyed the passengers from afar. Then they disappeared into the building.

He looked down from the upper deck and watched as several men loosened the massive ropes that secured the boat to the dock.

They manhandled the ropes on board, secured them, and quickly vanished below deck.

A cheer went up when the engine roared and the horn blasted, once, twice, three times. The *River Belle* began to move and passengers lurched backward, grabbing a handrail or a fellow passenger for stability.

Higson kept his eye on the building's door until, a moment later, the two men he had spied walked out and got back into their car. He watched the dock recede, holding his breath while he waited for thc current to take hold and push the boat into deeper water. There was no turning back.

The professor relaxed and ordered a drink. *Prost*! he said to himself, draining his glass immediately after the waiter had departed.

CHAPTER 41

Down Highway Sixty-One.

—Charlie Pickett

HANNAH HELD ON TIGHTLY AS TRAVIS STREAKED north on Highway 61. He hit the cutoff about twelve minutes after they'd left the diner and squealed around the corner, heading for the bridge that spanned the Mississippi River between its east bank and Helena's downtown. The bridge came up fast, and the impact of a small elevation in the road was magnified by Travis's speed. Hannah shrieked when the car's tires momentarily left the ground.

"Are you all right?" Travis asked. His knuckles ached from gripping the wheel.

Hannah nodded. Her eyes were wide.

"Which way?" Travis called out.

"Turn right. I think that's the way to the boat dock."

Travis finally slowed when they neared the city limits.

"Thank goodness," Hannah said, relaxing her grip on the dashboard.

Once they entered the city, it wasn't long before the dock came into view. Travis skidded on the gravel as he came to a stop in front of the office, the dock just up ahead. A Helena police car pulled out of the far end of the parking lot and onto the main road.

Travis shut off the engine and slumped back in the seat. His eyes scanned the dock. He didn't want to believe they were too late.

"Looks like we just missed the *River Belle*," Hannah said.

"Yeah," said Travis, looking at his watch. "They left on time after all."

They stared while the boat slowly entered the rapid waters of the river's main channel. As the *River Belle* pulled away from them, she hardly seemed to move at all, but within ten minutes she turned a corner and was out of sight.

"What now?" Hannah said, breaking the silence.

"Let me check the travel log." Travis stepped out of the car. "I'll be back in a minute."

Travis walked to the building's door and disappeared inside.

"May I help you?" a man said.

"Yes, sir. I'm looking for someone. I was hoping to say good-bye before the boat left, but it looks like I'm a little late. Is there any way to make sure my friend is on board? I need to give him something from his mother. It's important."

"Do you have a name?"

"Yes, sir, of course. His name is Conrad Higson."

The clerk shuffled the papers before him, then opened a drawer and removed a ledger. He scanned down several columns on different pages. "Good news, I don't think he made it. You can certainly catch him before the next departure."

"When is that?"

"Next week."

"Do you mind if I take a look?" Travis pointed at the book.

"Those are private. We're not supposed to let anyone look at the ledger."

Travis stared at him and waited a few awkward seconds. The man sighed. "Be quick." He flipped the book around for Travis to read. Travis scanned the sheets but Higson's name was not on them. He looked up at the man.

"What's this mean?" Travis pointed to one of the columns on the sheets.

"That indicates whether someone bought a one-way ticket or a round-trip."

Travis counted ten one-way tickets, including one purchased immediately before the boat departed. "Do you remember this gentleman, sir?"

"Oh yes, Mr. R. Coulter. He was quiet. Didn't want any help with his suitcase. Most folks like the assistance."

"Hmm, I've heard of a *Reverend* Coulter. Did he have an accent?"

"No, I don't think so. But I couldn't tell you. Like I said, he was quiet."

Travis pushed the ledger back toward the clerk and thanked him. He opened the door to leave, then turned back. "Where does the boat stop next?"

"Greenville."

"And what's her name again?"

"*River Belle.* B-e-l-l-e."

"Thank you, sir, much obliged." Travis walked out the door.

The squeak of the car door opening roused Hannah. She had dozed off. "Find anything out?"

"No. There's no record of a Conrad Higson buying a ticket."

"What do you want to do, now? Maybe it's a good time to contact the police?"

"I think he's on that boat. But we've got to make sure before we go to the sheriff."

"Why don't you let them find out for themselves? We'll tell them what we know, about finding the newspaper. Then they can board wherever the boat stops next and arrest him."

"But Higson could get off anywhere between here and Greenville. That's just where she stops next."

"Really, Travis. How would he get off in the middle of the Mississippi River?"

"He could jump. Or someone could pick him up before the boat docked. Maybe he's already planned that."

"Do you really think so? Listen, Travis, the police will send someone out to the *River Belle* and search from stem to stern if we notify them. But we have to tell them first. "

"No, I don't want to risk it. He's on that boat, and he's not very far away right now. We can't let him get away this time. Should we just drive to Greenville?"

"There must be something not right in my head, because I can't believe that I'm even going to utter these words. Higson's a fugitive, running from the law, and I should know better even if you don't." She took a breath. "My uncle has a small fishing boat."

"Where?"

"At his cabin south of Moon Lake. Not much there: just a few supplies, a bed, a stove. But couldn't you just board in Greenville?"

"I don't want to wait that long. Besides, it's too obvious. He'll be watching for police and anything else that seems suspicious. And he knows what I look like, remember? He sees me, and he'll know something's wrong." He shifted into gear and stepped on the gas.

Travis tried to stay parallel to the river, along back roads, short-cuts, and makeshift bridges. The river's meandering path wandered two or three miles for every one they drove. Soon they reached a rutted road—more a path than a road—that was wide at its entrance but tapered gradually to the car's width farther ahead. Tree branches and undergrowth reached inside the windows at the narrowest part when Travis finally stopped the car.

"It's up the trail another quarter mile," Hannah said, setting out confidently. Travis followed. "My uncle used to come here quite a bit, but not so much anymore."

"Who owns the land?"

"I don't know. My uncle kind of found it one day and built the cabin. He said he never saw anyone come out this way, so he figured nobody would care if he did."

"What about the road?"

"He cleared the way originally, and then all his trips to the cabin kept it that way." She stepped gingerly over fallen trees and carefully bent branches back as she made her way forward. "There it is." Hannah pointed along the path toward a barely visible structure in the distance.

Travis strained to see the cabin through the underbrush, but only when they came within fifteen yards of it did the cabin come into full view.

Travis stood behind Hannah while she fiddled with the doorknob and then pushed it open. "Whew, what's that smell?" Travis said, stepping through the doorway.

"Uncle Roger must have left some fish somewhere."

"Or maybe something crawled in and died. Whatever it is, let's don't stay too long."

Hannah quickly opened and closed several drawers.

"What are you looking for?" Travis asked.

"A key. The gas for the boat is outside, locked up in a shed. We need a key to get in."

Travis started doing the same, opening, searching, and closing several drawers. "Are these the right keys?" He held up several that were all tied together on a string.

Hannah squinted across the small, poorly lighted room. "Good, you found them."

Travis tossed her the keys then they headed outside to the shed behind the cabin.

Inside the shed, Hannah immediately spotted the gas can and a toolbox. "Take this." She passed the can to Travis. "And this." She handed him the toolbox. "All right, let's go get the boat." She closed the shed door but left it unlocked.

Hannah pulled back a tarp that covered the small boat, which was lying twenty feet from the water's edge. "What do you think?"

"It looks a little small for two people. But it'll do."

"Who's driving?" Hannah asked.

"You drive, and I get on the *River Belle*. Then you come back here, get the car, and contact the police. Tell them where we think Higson is and to pick him up in Greenville."

"And if you're wrong, and he's not on the boat?"

"We'll add that to the list of things we're in trouble for."

Hannah and Travis dragged the boat to the water. Hannah inspected the engine, filled the tank with gas, and then pulled a wrench from the toolbox.

"You know what you're doing?"

"My uncle showed me how to get the boat ready a few times." She tightened several bolts. "He does the same thing every time he puts the boat in." She closed the toolbox and handed it and the gas can back to Travis. "Could you put these back in the shed, please, and then lock up and put the keys back in the drawer?"

"Sure."

After locking up the shed, Travis went back inside the cabin and started opening drawers, trying to remember where the keys had been. At a small makeshift desk, he pulled so hard on the top drawer it flew out and landed on the floor with a thud. He stared down, startled by its contents. Travis picked up the revolver and peeled back the oily handkerchief it was wrapped in. He cracked the cylinder; it was fully loaded. He tucked it in his belt, making sure to cover it with this shirt. He replaced the drawer, threw the keys in another, and left the cabin.

Hannah was waiting in the boat. "Push us off."

Travis pushed the boat away from the bank and quickly jumped in.

"Get your foot wet?" Hannah asked.

"Just a little." Travis picked up the oar that lay in the boat and dug it into the river bottom to propel the tiny boat into deeper water.

"Once we get out a little farther, I'll drop the motor in. It's still too shallow."

Travis rowed hard until Hannah finally eased the propeller into the water. The small motor sputtered and coughed, but when it finally started, it ran effortlessly.

"We probably should have started it closer to shore," Travis said. "I would have hated to row all the way back."

"I wasn't worried. Not about the motor, anyway. Where are we heading?"

"We've got to figure out some place where we can wait for the *River Belle*."

"How long do you think it will take to get here?" Hannah trailed the fingers of one hand along the water's surface.

"I don't know. By the time you figure all the bends and turns, it may be dusk before she reaches this part of the river. Just depends how fast she can travel."

Travis looked toward the sun, still visible on the horizon. It was descending quickly. Soon it would be dark on the water, and if the moon was waning or covered by clouds, seeing anything or navigating would be difficult.

"I know a place where we can wait," Hannah said. "I can almost see it from here. It's a small cove with some cover."

Hannah turned up the throttle and the boat bounced gently through the water from one side of the Mississippi to the other. They arrived at the cove a few minutes later. It was set back slightly from the main body of water and allowed good visibility both up and down the river. The foliaged branches of several large trees growing near the banks provided a canopy.

Hannah shut off the engine, and Travis rowed the boat against the bank. Once in place, they made themselves comfortable and watched for the *River Belle*.

While they waited, the clouds that had been forming all day up and down the Mississippi finally began to release their contents in a slow, warm drizzle. Although the trees provided protection, some water trickled through their leafy roof.

"This isn't what I had hoped for," Hannah said, trying to make herself comfortable.

"Don't worry, I don't think we'll have to wait long."

CHAPTER 42

The storm is rising.

—Lonnie Johnson

TRAVIS DIDN'T KNOW HOW LONG THEY'D DOZED, BUT he awoke with a start when vigorous waves beat the small motorboat against the roots of a giant tree that was growing half in the water and half on the bank.

For a split second, he didn't remember where he was. He squinted in the darkness to get his bearings, then looked at Hannah. She was on her side, her head resting on her arm, her breathing heavy.

He looked up and out toward the middle of the river. Chugging along at her leisurely pace was the *River Belle*. She was fully lighted and glittering in the drizzle.

"Hannah," Travis said. "Wake up." He nudged Hannah with his foot.

She lifted her head wearily and almost fell backward when Travis pushed off from the bank. "Whoa," Hannah said, rubbing her eyes and repositioning herself in the boat. "What are you doing?"

"*River Belle*." Travis pointed behind her. "She's here."

Hannah peered through the rain toward the brightly ornamented boat. "Hard to miss that."

"Kind of looks like a Christmas tree floating sideways on the water, doesn't she?"

Hannah started the engine.

"Let me drive," Travis said.

They carefully switched places, Travis moving to the stern to control the boat's direction and speed, and Hannah to the bow. The wind and rainfall had picked up, and water started dripping from the tip of Travis's nose. He revved the engine, and the boat slipped into the rushing waters of the Mississippi. The noise of the rain, along with the roar of the engine and the constant smacking of the little boat every time she rose and fell against the river's now rough surface, made talking difficult.

"Are you worried about someone spotting us?" Hannah shouted.

"No. The rain should keep everyone inside. And keeping to the backside of the boat will make it easier to move alongside without anyone seeing us." Travis wiped the rain from his face, then maneuvered the boat behind *River Belle* to ride her wake. Travis cupped his hand around his mouth. "When we get close enough, I'll try and get on."

"I still think you're crazy."

The few droplets that had fallen gently an hour ago had now turned into a torrent. Lightning streaked through the sky, and the crackle of thunder silenced any further talk on the small boat. Travis looked at their skiff. She had seemed so adequate a short time ago, but now she existed at the whim of the elements. He knew the river would decide their fate. He held the engine at full throttle and slowly edged closer until he could read the name *River Belle* painted on the back of the boat. The passenger ship was traveling much faster than Travis thought she would be. The motorboat moved dangerously close to the *River Belle*, but Travis pushed on. He eyed the huge paddle wheels that propelled the larger vessel and could demolish their diminutive craft in seconds. He had left any good sense on shore.

Drawing nearer, Travis yelled out to Hannah, "Let's trade places!" He motioned with his hand for her to move back to where he was sitting. "Then I want you to pull up alongside so I can get up the ladder. Okay?"

She looked at him blankly.

"Come on back."

The boats weren't moving that quickly now, but the torrential downpour, the noise from the engine, the darkness, and the sheer size of the *River Belle* made maneuvering more difficult than it should have been.

Hannah hadn't moved.

"What's wrong?" Travis shouted above the roar.

"I want to go with you. On the boat."

Travis looked at her incredulously, and shook his head.

She nodded in rebuttal, and pointed toward the deck, urging him to move next to the larger vessel. He knew her expression was that of someone who wasn't backing down. He could sit and argue with her, turn their tiny craft around and head back, or he could let her come along. Travis pulled the throttle arm to the left and their boat moved right, hopping over the steamer's wake. Their speed was fractionally faster than the larger boat's, allowing them to slowly creep from the stern toward the bow.

"Watch it," Hannah called when Travis veered too close, bumping the *River Belle*. They could feel the tug of her hull trying to pull them under. Hannah was clinging to the edge of their boat to keep from being tossed toward Travis or into the river.

Travis looked at her and sensed her fear. He leaned toward the larger riverboat and pushed off from her enormous side, then steered their boat away and slowed the throttle to regain control.

"Sorry," Travis said, resuming full throttle. He pulled alongside the *River Belle* once more, steadying their boat near a ladder that extended almost all the way down the bow. He made sure not to get as close this time.

"Hannah! When I get near the ladder, you're going to have to grab the lower rung and pull yourself up."

She nodded, still gripping the sides of the boat, and moved to the left side of their small craft.

Travis again sidled up to the riverboat, but this time he carefully steadied his boat within a foot of the ladder. Hannah reached out and grabbed the second rung with her left hand. Then she quickly reached out for another rung with her right. The rungs were slippery from the rain, but she managed a firm grip. She pulled hard to lift herself up, and slowly their boat was inching toward the heaving *River Belle*, her massive frame starting to catch the edge of their tiny craft and push her down. A splinter sheared off, and it crackled above the storm. Travis steered right to avoid being pushed under, but he drifted too far, and suddenly Hannah was out of the boat.

"Go!" he yelled, wiping rain from his face.

Hanging onto the rungs, her legs dangling, she started to pull herself up using just her hands. Hannah managed merely two rungs before she stalled. Her legs and knees were still searching for a foothold but couldn't find one.

Travis could see she was struggling, the strength in her arms already waning. He once again turned toward the larger vessel until he was right below Hannah. He reached up and grabbed the bottom of her left foot. Using his palm as a step to push off from—while

Travis was trying to control the smaller boat—Hannah moved skyward.

"Keep going!" Travis shouted encouragingly.

Once she landed a foot on the lower rung, Hannah climbed the ladder quickly. She turned and waved him up.

Travis steered back toward the larger boat and positioned himself next to the ladder. He got into a crouch position and reached unsteadily for the first rung while keeping his other hand on the throttle. His fingertips wrapped around the slippery rung, but he couldn't quite get his thumb around and his hand slipped away. He fell back into his seat, rocking the small craft.

Hannah yelled something, but he couldn't hear it.

He reached a second time for the rung, and this time he securely found his mark. He gripped the rung tightly, but the shift in his weight caused the left side of his boat to dip. The larger vessel's hull caught the edge.

"Get out!" Hannah screamed.

Travis jumped and held on with one hand while the other flailed helplessly. For a second, he panicked, unable to find another rung with his free hand. But just as his grip started to slip, he grabbed another. He turned back toward their boat just in time to see her crushed under the riverboat. He scampered up the ladder.

"Where've you been?" Hannah teased when Travis slung his leg over the top.

Their noses touching, she wrapped both arms around him and smiled.

Travis could see her exhaustion and fear. They quickly ran to the *River Belle*'s stern and scanned the water's surface. Pieces of their boat were strewn across the Mississippi behind them.

"You owe my uncle a new boat."

"I thought this was your idea." He didn't bother to check her expression. "Come on. Let's go see if we can find Higson."

Travis had heard that the *River Belle* was no ordinary riverboat. Built only two years earlier, she was the largest passenger ship traveling the Mississippi River from the headwaters in Minnesota to the Gulf of Mexico. The paddle wheeler, because of her size, housed main and auxiliary dining rooms and several large game rooms, formal parlors for quiet conversation, a ballroom, and sleeping quarters for three hundred passengers and crew. There were also day-travel accommodations for another fifty passengers.

Travis and Hannah slipped through a door near the stern and stood silently for a moment, leaning against a wall and letting the rainwater drip off of them. It pooled beneath their feet, forming a large puddle. They looked at each other, breathing a sigh of relief that they were finally on board. But neither smiled.

"The first thing we have to do," Travis said, "is find some dry clothes."

Hannah nodded, and they descended the nearest set of stairs to the lower deck.

"It's still dinnertime," Travis said, stepping onto another landing. "I'll bet most everyone is in one of the dining areas or playing cards in one of the game rooms. And that means the crew is busy serving and cleaning up."

Travis and Hannah crept along a series of hallways and stairwells that finally led to a sign directing them to the sleeping cabins of the ship's employees. Without hesitation, Travis knocked on the first door they came to. He waited for an answer but heard nothing. Slowly, he turned the doorknob, but it was locked. He moved to the next door in the hallway and repeated the process. Again, the door was locked. And yet again. On the fourth try, Travis turned the knob and the door opened. He and Hannah slipped into the room.

"Women's clothes," Travis said, opening a closet door and removing a dress. "Try this on." He tossed the dress onto the bed. "It looks like an employee's uniform. You'll fit right in."

"What if it's not my size?" She held the dress to herself. "I want to look my best. Although I guess it doesn't matter, because my daddy wouldn't allow me to work on a passenger ship anyway."

"Snob." Travis laughed. "It looks about the right size, and we can't be picky about the wardrobe. Try it on, I'll bet it's warmer than what you're wearing. I'm going across the hall to find something for me."

He opened the door to leave, and Hannah picked up a flowery hat that had been sitting on a chair and turned teasingly to Travis. "I think this'll fit you."

"And please get some shoes," he reminded her, closing the door.

Travis entered the room across the hall while Hannah was changing. From the things scattered about, it was evident the room housed men. He quickly found a steward's uniform that fit well enough. Before returning to Hannah's room, he inspected the revolver he'd been carrying since they left her uncle's cabin. He couldn't believe he hadn't lost it. Carefully removing the bullets, he made sure they were dry then he reloaded the gun and slipped it back into his belt. He hoped he wouldn't have to find out whether the rain had rendered it useless.

Travis stepped into the hallway, closing the door behind him. He rapped lightly on Hannah's door.

"Where to?" she said, cracking open the door. She looked him up and down. "Don't you look handsome. Why can't I wear a nice dress so we can have dinner?"

He grabbed her hand. "Let's see what we can find."

"Wherever we go, let's stay inside."

Travis grinned. "Deal."

They found some stairs and started their ascent. They emerged onto the main deck and quickly blended into the mix of passengers and crew.

"Are you hungry?" Travis asked, realizing he was ravenous.

"Yeah, sort of."

They easily found the kitchen, and Travis requested two plates of the evening's entree. They sat down at a small table in the rear of the kitchen.

"You don't know what Higson looks like, do you?" Travis said.

"No, I've never seen him. I never went to the trial, remember?" Hannah ate quickly but delicately, the very proper product of a lifetime of training in good table manners.

"That's right, so I guess there's no sense describing him. With so many people on board, you'd never find him."

"Or, I'd see a lot of people who looked just like him. What about going to the captain and see what information we can obtain on passengers?"

"I thought about that, but Higson's not registered under his name. And if the captain wasn't discreet, and the professor found out someone was looking for him or he saw me, he might get spooked. Let's keep looking together until we find him."

"And if we don't?" Hannah said.

"Well, then, we'll have a nice trip downriver. You want something to drink?"

"Please."

Travis got up from the table and returned with two glasses of tea. "Don't you think Higson needs to be caught?" Travis asked. "He's not a very upstanding citizen."

"Sure I do, but not by me. I only came along so you don't get into trouble."

"You don't have to worry about me. I can help you get off the ship right now, if you want." Travis smiled at her, and she smiled back. He didn't want her to leave.

"Really, what are you going to do when you find Higson?" Hannah asked.

"Notify the captain that he has a fugitive on board and have him contact the authorities. We just have to make sure Higson's on board."

"And when the captain asks who you are and how you got on the ship?"

"I'm hoping he forgets about that when he realizes Higson's a fugitive."

"Glad to hear you're leaving the actual arrest to the authorities, but being a stowaway still has its consequences."

"Just leave all that to me."

Hannah shrugged her shoulders. "Okay. I hope you're right."

Travis finished his tea, then picked up their plates and placed them in a sink that was already stacked with dirty dishes. "Are you ready to go?"

"I guess," Hannah said. "I can't just stay in the kitchen?" She stood up and ran her hands down the front of her dress, smoothing the wrinkles. "How do I look?"

"Like the ship's best employee."

"That's what I was afraid of."

They left the kitchen and walked out into one of the dining areas. It was filled with people lingering over their sumptuous evening meal. The weather had eliminated walking around the deck as an option, leaving nowhere to go except boisterous game rooms, a quiet parlor, or one's own cabin or berth.

"Why don't we split up?" Travis suggested. "I'll meet you back here in half an hour."

"What am I looking for?"

"Well, since you don't know what he looks like, just get a feel for the layout of the different rooms. It might come in handy later."

Travis watched Hannah walk away. She hadn't taken ten steps when someone at a table handed her a water pitcher and asked her to fill it.

She passed Travis on her way back to the kitchen. "I'll never get out of this room."

Travis wondered whether the uniform had been a bad idea.

He left the main dining room and began to circulate through the other rooms looking busy and occasionally delivering a cocktail or a cigar to a passenger who requested it. Card games seemed to be particularly popular tonight, and all the game rooms were brimming with active and prospective players. The parlors were also filled to capacity with people enjoying the trip, but Higson was nowhere to be found. He'd be better off staying out of sight, and Travis figured he knew that.

Twenty minutes later, Travis returned to the room where he had left Hannah and motioned her back to the kitchen.

"Did you see him?" she said.

"No. Did you ever get out of the dining room?"

"Once, but not for long. I had to go right back to the kitchen to get something else." She tugged at her dress. "And this uniform is uncomfortable."

"I know, I know, but let's try this." Travis looked around the kitchen and found a piece of paper and a pencil. "You walk the tables," he scribbled something on the paper, "and say that you have a message for Dr. Conrad Higson. He probably won't respond immediately, and maybe not at all. But if he's out there, it'll get his attention. Hopefully, he'll be curious enough to ask about the message."

"Aren't you afraid this'll tip him off?"

"Maybe, but we need to find him soon. If we can't find him now, we can always get off the ship first and try to spot him when he leaves."

"What are you going to do while I'm table-hopping?"

"I'll follow you to each room and keep an eye on the tables you visit. It's so crowded, it won't be hard for me to be inconspicuous."

Travis folded the paper and handed it to her. She walked out of the kitchen, and he followed her a few moments later.

Hannah moved methodically through the main dining room, making her announcement at each table. "Excuse me," she said after being acknowledged by someone at the table. "I have an urgent message for Dr. Conrad Higson. Is he here?" Again and again the diners shook their heads, indicating that no one by that name was at the table.

After making the rounds in both dining rooms, she did the same at each of the tables in the game rooms and parlors.

An hour later, Travis was convinced that Higson was keeping himself hidden in his room. Hannah headed back to the kitchen, Travis trailing behind her.

"You didn't see him, did you?" she asked when they were alone.

"No. I thought for sure he'd be having dinner or walking off his meal. Playing cards. Something."

"What do you want to do now?"

"I don't know."

"We should go to the captain."

"No, not yet."

"Then when?"

Travis looked at her. He wasn't surprised at her temper; he just didn't know what to say. "I'm getting something to drink. Do you want something?"

"No."

Hannah pushed through the door and returned to the dining room. At last, all the diners had finished, and the room was empty except for a few waiters who were clearing tables. She sat down in a corner and realized at that moment how tired she was. Her legs ached from her struggle onto the boat and from walking table to table in shoes that didn't fit well. She was overwhelmed with a desire to lie down. Her eyes were half shut when someone spoke into her ear.

"Do you have a message for Dr. Higson?"

Startled, she leaped up and bumped into the table before her, upsetting two half-full glasses of water. "Yes. I mean, no. I did, but not anymore." She fumbled for words while trying to right the glasses and clean up the spilled water.

"I'm a member of the staff," the man said, "and I want to make sure this message was delivered. Where is it?"

By now Hannah had regained her composure. "I gave it back to one of the ship's stewards. I looked everywhere, but I couldn't find Dr. Higson." She quickly sized up the man before her. He was in his fifties, she guessed from his thin, graying hair and nondescript features. His clothes were strange, his dark suit unlike the attire any other employee wore.

"Would you like to assist me in searching for Dr. Higson?"

"I'm sorry, sir, I can't." Her manner was fully deferential now. "I have to help clean up the dining room, and then go to bed. We're up early tomorrow to prepare for breakfast."

He looked over toward the kitchen. A voice could be heard above the rattling of dishes and glassware.

It was Travis, Hannah thought, feeling a little safer.

The man started to fidget. "Well, if you find the note, please let me know." He turned abruptly and walked away.

"Where can I find you?" Hannah called, but he didn't answer. By the time Travis emerged from the kitchen a moment later, the man had turned a corner and was gone.

"Travis, someone just came up and asked me about the note."

"Who?"

"I don't know. He said he was an employee, but I don't think he was."

"Was it Higson?"

"I don't know."

"Where'd he go?"

"Over there." Hannah pointed toward the exit he had taken.

Travis rushed to look down the hallway, but no one was there. He walked back to Hannah.

"Do you think it was Higson? What else did he say?"

"I don't know who it was, Travis." She was trembling slightly. "He just said that he wanted to make sure the message was delivered. I told him that I gave it back to one of the stewards. Then he asked if I wanted to help him find Higson."

"What did he look like?"

"Fifties, gray hair. He was wearing a suit, not a uniform, unusual for a ship's employee."

"Well, so much for being inconspicuous. Even if it was someone else, he must know something's up."

Travis noticed Hannah's uncharacteristically wobbly demeanor. "Are you all right?"

"Yeah, he just caught me off guard, that's all. I was half asleep when he appeared out of nowhere. Then he asked me to help him find Higson and that made me nervous. Are you sure we can't just go to the captain?"

"You'll be okay?" Travis put his hands on her shoulders, peered into her eyes, and then wrapped his arms around her. She leaned into him, nestling her face into his chest. A lone tear crept down her cheek. She turned her head and wiped it on his shirt. She didn't want him to see her cry.

A waiter carrying dishes back to the kitchen walked by and looked at them oddly. Otherwise, the room was empty.

After a long minute, Travis said, "Let's find you a room to rest in. It's late, and I don't think we're going to find him tonight. Heck, he's probably already asleep himself."

Hannah mustered all the energy she had left. "Okay."

They walked downstairs to the crew's cabins and returned to the room where they had found Hannah's uniform. Travis knocked. There was no answer. He opened the door and peeked inside. "No one's here. Why don't you lie down for a while?"

"What if the other residents return?"

"There are two beds. Just tell them you—I don't know, make something up."

Hannah was too tired to argue. She sat down on the bed nearest the door and leaned her upper body toward the pillow, her legs bent and feet still on the floor.

CHAPTER 43

Hellhound on my trail.

—Robert Johnson

TRAVIS WATCHED HANNAH FOR A MOMENT, THINKING she might speak or move. She didn't. He walked over and lifted her legs onto the bed, then covered her with a light blanket. He brushed her hair back, then turned out the lights and left.

Back in the dining room, he walked over to one of the many windows that separated it from the elements. The rain had stopped, and a stillness seemed to have enveloped the sky and the water. The great Mississippi no longer churned in the winds, and the *River Belle* glistened prettily while the moon, no longer shrouded by clouds, cast her beams upon the deck. A lone chaise lounge secured to the dining room's exterior wall caught Travis's attention.

He went outside, unfolded the chair, and wiped the water from its seat. He positioned it in a corner, out of sight from the dining room windows. The rain had cooled the air, a welcome relief.

Travis lay down and looked up at what had become a starry night. The only hint of the storm was off to the east, and he could see flashes of lightning in the distance. But without the associated thunder, which was now too distant to hear, the intermittent flashes reminded him of the lighthouses he had seen in movies, warning an ocean vessel's crew of a rocky and dangerous coastline.

Travis's eyelids were leaden. He could no longer think of Higson or anything else. His limbs became heavy, his breathing shallow.

Travis didn't notice the first kick to his chair. Some innermost part of him thought it was the ship's jerky movement. But when the kick came again, then again, he stirred at last from his slumber. He opened his eyes but was disoriented. He couldn't tell whether it was early morning or still the middle of the night. His vision was blurred.

"Mr. Montgomery."

Travis heard the voice, but could see no one. He had slid down in the lounge chair but slowly raised himself to a seated position.

"Are you awake?"

The accent was familiar.

"Yeah, I'm awake," Travis said into the night.

"Are you still evaluating property lines?"

Travis didn't answer.

"Where's my message? Do you have it with you?"

Travis couldn't think of anything to say. This was *not* how he had hoped to find Higson.

"No, I didn't think so. Mr. Montgomery, what exactly are you doing aboard this ship? Illegally, I suppose."

"I'm just enjoying a quick trip downriver. Much like yourself, sir."

"Why do I doubt that?"

"I don't know."

"You know, I wish that I had never come to America. I've had nothing but trouble since I arrived. I should have stayed in England."

"Then why did you?" Travis hoped desperately to keep the professor talking.

"Oh, it's a long story. But we're near the end. Very near. In fact, I'm on my way home right now."

"I doubt you're going to make it back." Travis was fully awake now.

"Why is that?"

"Because the police and the FBI are searching for you all over the Delta. Probably all over the state. Every train station, every major road, every dock." Travis wasn't sure, but he hoped it was true.

"Do you think so? They don't think I might have died in the fire?"

"No. It didn't take my dad long to figure out it wasn't you. So many dissimilarities between you and whoever that was."

"Someone knocking on the wrong door looking for a meal, perhaps. Does it matter?"

"Maybe to some of his kin," Travis said. "Be assured, Professor, they're already looking for you."

"But nobody knows where I am, and I'm so close to my final destination."

"*I* know where you are. And isn't it quite likely that I would have told someone where I was going beforehand?"

"Possibly, but why would they have sent you instead of the police? No, this appears to be more like you were playing a hunch, and it's probably not going the way you had expected."

"My friend who you met earlier is speaking to the captain right now. I'll bet he finds this all very interesting, which he can quickly confirm with the authorities."

"Do you know how late it is, Mr. Montgomery? The captain's asleep, and he won't be up for several hours. And I'm certain he does not wish to be disturbed by *anyone*. I don't know where your friend is at this moment, but I know she is *not* speaking with him."

Travis saw a match light up in the darkness and the tip of a cigarette start to glow.

"Why were you sending classified documents back to Germany, Dr. Higson?" Travis continued to stall.

Higson hesitated for a moment. "I guess it won't hurt to tell you now. You won't be telling anyone. Simply, I wanted to go home, and I knew that by providing this type of information, I might be allowed to return. And my assumption was correct. I've done all I can do here, and I've helped the German war effort immensely. America's technology, while advanced on paper, is years away from any working prototypes. By then, Europe will be under German leadership, and the Americans will see too much risk in getting involved. It'll all work out as planned."

"Why would you want to return to a country that didn't want you?"

The professor blew smoke into the air. "Why do you live in Mississippi?" Higson didn't wait for Travis to answer. "Because it's your home. It's what you know and believe in. It's part of your identity."

Travis moved his elbow, feeling for his revolver. He thought he had placed it on his left side but now he couldn't remember.

"I can see you very well, Mr. Montgomery. Can you see me?"

"Not as well."

"If you are looking for your weapon, I'm sorry to say that I had to confiscate it. I'm surprised you did not wake up when I removed it from your belt. You must be very tired."

Travis looked hard and saw it in his adversary's hand. Why hadn't he listened to Hannah?

Then, at once, they both heard footsteps approaching. Turning the corner, a familiar face stepped out of the shadows.

"Luke?" Higson said, startled.

Travis looked from Higson to Luke and back again. The former was nervous.

"Hello, Dr. Higson," Luke said.

"What are you doing here? How did you—"

"I know, but I can't go back. I can't do it."

"What on earth do you mean? I've provided for you and your family."

"I can't sharecrop anymore."

"You don't have to, you can do whatever you want. That was the point."

"But I don't know nothing else. I don't know what to do. And people look at me funny now. They're scared of me."

"I told you they would. Do you remember?"

"Yeah." Luke looked down.

"That was part of our deal. I've kept my word."

"What do you mean, Luke?" Travis asked, eager to intervene.

"I mean, I'm no killer."

"Then who is?"

Higson laughed, and stepped back against the railing. "This is all becoming so complicated."

"You?" Travis asked, incredulously. "But why?"

"I've told you. I wanted to go home. In addition to passing the research and military documents that were needed, I wanted to give them real proof of my commitment to the Party. Do you know what happened after the Negro Americans came to Berlin a couple of years ago for the Olympics and won all those medals?"

Higson waited, looking at Travis and Luke. "The führer was enraged with these Americans. And what better way to show my loyalty than to sacrifice a few of America's equivalent to the Jews— the mongrel, the Negro. When my superiors found out what I had done, they were very pleased. The führer himself was said to have smiled. Of course, I sent the newspaper articles back as proof."

"And Luke?" Travis asked.

"A desperate man, willing to risk his life for a better one for his family. The world is full of people who barter their lives, just in different ways. I met Luke in town one day, and I offered him a ride home. He told me so much about himself, and I knew his plight was not unlike that of a hundred others I have known. I understood his limitations, but also his vast hopelessness and what he would give up to create a better life for those closest to him. And I needed someone to accept responsibility for the murders, so the police would discontinue any investigation." Higson shifted uncomfortably. "Elma, who never knew anything about our deal, would read him the accounts of the murders from the paper. That's all he needed to know. And we decided that I would be an eyewitness to the final murder, to place him at the scene, so there would be no question as to who committed the crimes. For his cooperation, I promised to replace the chains of a plow for a prisoner's chains, but freedom for his family. His life for the life of his wife and children. It was an easy decision for him given the alternative of sharecropping, which is really just another form of slavery for you Americans. You see, Travis, we are all chained in some way, all living in a state of incarceration."

"Why were the victims killed in different ways?" Travis asked.

"Enough questions," replied Higson abruptly. He rubbed his jaw with his free hand as he turned to face Luke. "And now here you are, Luke. Why?"

"People still think I killed all those men, even though they let me go. I can't go back there. Folks will always look at Elma funny if I'm there, especially in church. She's better off without me. Maybe I can go with you."

"My dear man, after all this, the money just wasn't enough. You want something else. Something I cannot give you. Why are you Americans so greedy?" Higson quickly slipped the revolver into his belt, and pulled out something shiny in its place. He tossed his cigarette into the water.

"Please," Luke said stepping forward.

Higson's motion was fluid, effortless. Travis didn't even flinch as the assailant's arm slashed twice at Luke's throat. The large blade in Higson's hand glinted in the moonlight, and Travis watched as Luke clutched his throat, blood seeping between his fingers. Luke's unintelligible dying words gurgled out in gasps of escaping air. Luke tried to lean against Higson, but he stepped aside, and Luke fell over the railing into the water below. The splash was quiet, and Higson looked back as the body floated in the riverboat's wake. He tossed the bloody knife into the water, then removed the revolver from his belt.

"For some people, nothing is ever enough."

Travis shifted slowly in his chair so as not to startle Higson. "Does that not bother you?"

"What? Killing? Maybe a little. But it's so simple. Some lives are worth less than others, Mr. Montgomery. Isn't that the way things are in Mississippi? And if some lives of lesser value must be sacrificed for one of greater value, then logic dictates the course of action. Are you a man of science? I assume you are not. Maybe it is your immaturity. If you haven't learned it already, some day this reasoning will become apparent to you. For now, though, we must decide what to do with you. It'll be light in a few hours. Why don't we take a walk to the rear of the ship?"

Travis didn't move. Higson stepped into the half-light; Travis could see the revolver pointed at him.

Higson motioned with the weapon. "Get up."

Travis noticed that the man's voice had lost any hint of casual conversation. It was harsh now, angry and desperate.

Travis slowly rose from the chair and began to walk toward *River Belle*'s stern. Hannah's suggestion had been the best one after all. The captain could have taken care of Higson already, and Travis and Hannah would be enjoying a free trip to Greenville. Instead, Travis was shuffling toward an uncertain future.

They approached the stern, and the roar of the engines grew. Now Travis knew why they were heading this way: the engine noise would conceal the gunshot and throwing his body overboard would be easier. He could imagine only three choices. He could jump the railing into the river, hope that Higson's shot would miss, then swim to shore and alert the police. But that would leave Hannah on board, and Higson would look for her. Or he could stall and hope that someone would happen upon them, forcing Higson to either hide the gun or kill two people, which he would probably do. Or he could try to wrestle the gun away from Higson, and likely get shot in the process.

Travis glanced back at his captor. He was walking only a step and a half behind him, looking over Travis's shoulder toward the stern. When Travis took a half step, Higson took a whole one. That put the revolver almost in Travis's back. Travis turned quickly and with a sweeping motion knocked the revolver from Higson's hand. It slid thirty feet across the deck and bounced against the base of the ship's guardrail. Almost simultaneously, Travis swung wildly at Higson, but he was off-balance and missed. He figured he'd get another chance because the German was at least twice his age.

Before Travis could regain his balance, Higson opened his hand and clamped it around Travis's throat. It was nothing like Travis had ever felt before.

"Yes, I am strong, Mr. Montgomery. I worked for several years in a coal mine. I used to win strength contests back in Germany. But I did not win because of my physical strength. No, it is anger and rage that win a fight."

Travis reached up and with both hands tried to pry Higson's grip loose. But he was not only overpowered; he was fearful of the inhuman strength in the man's hands.

All at once, Higson let go of Travis's neck and roughly threw him to the ground. Travis struggled in the direction of the revolver, but Higson stomped down on the outside of his knee. The knee bent unnaturally, and a pain shot up Travis's leg. But he knew he must get to his feet if he wanted to live.

He hobbled up before his attacker could strike again, and this time Travis's fist found its target: the bridge of Higson's nose. The German staggered back a step, and blood streamed from both nostrils and cascaded down his lips, into his mouth, onto his teeth. Travis stood panting and watching while Higson wiped the blood with the back of his hand and studied it. A calmness appeared over him as he looked up at Travis.

"That's the first time I have tasted my own blood since I was eleven or twelve years old. It brings back bad memories."

Travis lunged for the gun, but his knee would not carry him fast enough. Higson was on him again. He grabbed Travis's injured leg and dragged him back to the rearmost guardrail. Travis cried out, but it was useless. The engines were so loud they muffled all other noises near the stern. As Travis tried to get up, the man grabbed his throat again and lifted him, this time bending Travis back over the stern's guardrail, Higson's fingers digging into his neck. Travis felt the desperate man squeezing the life out of him.

He was transfixed by the soulless look in Higson's eyes. They were vacant. Unrepentant. Guiltless. His head became light; he was dizzy. Blood dripped onto Travis's shirt, neck, and face as Higson leaned over him.

"After you are gone," Higson said, "I will find your friend and kill her, too. It must be that way. You never should have followed me."

Travis wasn't concerned with his own death, but he was with Hannah's. He knew he was responsible. Now, it was too late. Travis had no more air. He felt he was losing consciousness, but he also felt at peace. He knew that at some point you must resign yourself to die; this he had done in these last few minutes. But Hannah had not resigned herself. He prayed, and his last thoughts were of her. Involuntarily, his eyes closed.

Travis vaguely heard a series of shots. At first he wondered if he was dead. Then he realized he had just been unconscious.

Travis fell onto the ship's deck. He rolled over and crouched on all fours, coughing and gasping for air. He knew a gun had been fired; the smell of burned gunpowder hung in the air. Travis looked to his left and saw Higson lying sprawled on his back, his legs and arms spread wide. Then, like he was moving in slow motion, Travis turned his head to the right. He squinted to make out a lone figure in the darkness. It was approaching him. Then it kneeled down next to him.

"Travis, are you all right?"

Travis couldn't answer. He just nodded his head, and lay down.

Hannah sat down, crossed her legs, and gently pulled Travis's head into her lap.

Travis reached up and felt for her hand. What he found was the warm barrel of his revolver. She had not let it go. He pried it from her hand and put it next to him. "I'm sorry, Hannah," he said. His voice was raspy, his throat in pain.

"Sorry for what?" Her voice was calm and steady.

"Sorry that you had to do that."

"Somebody had to. It just happened to be me."

They said nothing for a few moments. Travis gradually caught his breath and spoke when he could. "What made you come outside?"

"I was sleeping where you left me when the legitimate occupants eventually returned. They weren't happy to see me in their bed or their clothes. I left as quickly as I could. Instead of finding another room, I decided to get some fresh air up on deck, especially since it had stopped raining."

"Good thing," Travis said. "Good thing."

Their state of suspended animation snapped when a crewman rounded the corner, whistling while he made his nightly rounds. He stopped and gasped loudly when he saw Hannah, Travis, and Higson.

"What's going on?" he said.

Without moving, Travis answered. "That man lying there is Dr. Conrad Higson. He's wanted by the FBI; they're probably looking for him all over Mississippi."

"Is he dead?"

"I believe so."

"How did he die?"

"I shot him," Hannah said.

Travis looked up at her. "I could have told him I did it."

"It's a little late now."

The crewman turned and ran. "Wait here," he called back over his shoulder.

"We're in a mess now," Travis said.

"And we weren't a little while ago?"

Travis and Hannah watched the paddle wheeler's wake for just a minute before a swarm of people arrived and surrounded them and Higson's body.

Travis was escorted to the cabin of the ship's doctor, who examined the young man's neck and knee. Travis's neck was severely bruised, the marks where Higson's fingers had been wrapped around it an angry bluish red. Travis's knee was sore and swollen; it would need to be more thoroughly examined once the *River Belle* docked. Travis was released with some aspirin and told to rest.

Meanwhile, Higson's body was taken to the ship's morgue, where it was prepared for off-loading in Greenville, the next stop.

The ship's captain questioned Hannah and Travis for an hour. Calls were made from the bridge, and the captain confirmed Higson's identity and his "wanted" status. Travis also told the captain of Luke's fate.

"We're going to keep this quiet until we get to Greenville," the captain said. "If we don't, you'll never get any rest, and neither will we."

"Sounds good to us, Captain," said Travis.

"And we notified the sheriff's office in Clarksdale, and the FBI in Jackson. They'll be waiting in Greenville."

Finally, Travis and Hannah were taken to a pair of small rooms— not the crew's quarters. Hannah observed dryly that they weren't the luxury staterooms either. They said their good nights, although it was almost morning, and each slept for several hours.

When they awoke, the captain arranged for Travis to be given a shirt with a high collar, which he buttoned completely to hide his bruises. A suitable dress was found for Hannah to wear so she no longer had to masquerade as one of the ship's employees.

Rumors of the night's events spread quickly among the riverboat's passengers, who talked incessantly about the shooting and the victim—who he was and what he had done. But only a few people knew the details, and those crew members remained silent.

The captain had been discreet: no one knew that Travis or Hannah had been involved. Not able to spend time together in public places, they ate breakfast and lunch in the back of the kitchen, played a few card games in a room adjacent to the captain's, and debated what would happen when they docked.

It was early afternoon, about twelve hours since Higson's demise, when the announcement came: the *River Belle* would be landing in Greenville within two hours. At 3:45 p.m., the big ship's engines slowed, and the captain steered her toward the dock in Greenville. Fifteen minutes later the riverboat was tied up and her passengers were disembarking.

Travis and Hannah watched from inside, near the bow, and saw the large collection of police and FBI vehicles waiting for them and the "special cargo" in storage. They could see Sheriff Collins, the FBI agents, Travis's father, mother, and sister, and Hannah's parents.

"That's quite a welcoming party," Travis said.

"Maybe we could just keep going all the way to New Orleans."

"Not today, I don't think."

They watched while Higson's body was carried on a stretcher down the gangplank and then placed in a waiting ambulance. One of the agents got into the truck and briefly inspected the body. He got out, apparently satisfied, closed the door, and signaled for Higson to be whisked away to Clarksdale's morgue.

Travis turned to Hannah when the last passenger had walked down the gangplank. "Are you ready?"

"Let's get it over with."

Travis took her hand, and they walked down from the upper deck and started their descent. When they approached the dock, the crowd began to converge at the end of the ramp. Travis saw Lewis Murphree and a couple of other men, notepads and pencils in hand. They must also be reporters was Travis's first thought. I'll give Lewis a story later he'll never forget. Murphree and the other reporters were pushed back from the gangplank by one of the deputies.

At the end of the ramp stood Sheriff Collins. Even though he was outside his jurisdiction, the sheriff's icy glare, intimidating posture, and hands stuck firmly in his belt all testified that he was in charge.

Travis's hand went to his neck; he unbuttoned his collar, wanting everyone to see exactly what had happened to him. By now, his neck had deepened into a continuous purple bruise that could have come from only one thing.

They hadn't reached the bottom of the ramp when Margaret Montgomery pushed past Sheriff Collins and threw her arms around both Travis and Hannah. She squeezed them tightly and kissed Travis on the cheek. Then she turned to Hannah, kissed her cheek, and whispered in her ear, "Thank you, dear."

Now Travis knew their story was out, that Hannah had saved his life. The tale would be told again and again for years to come, because things like this just didn't happen in the Delta.

Mr. and Mrs. Morgan rushed forward as well and hugged Hannah, pulling her away from the crowd and toward their car, albeit one borrowed from a neighbor since theirs was still at the cabin. Her father looked relieved, but not very happy. Travis made a mental note to retrieve Mr. Morgan's car the next day.

Travis watched as Sheriff Collins approached Mr. Morgan and said something while motioning toward Hannah. Then he watched Hannah wave to someone else in the crowd. He spied his sister waving mightily in Hannah's direction. They would talk later.

Mr. Morgan opened the car doors for his brood, and then they were gone.

Meanwhile, Bill Montgomery put his hand on Travis's shoulder. "I'm not even sure what to ask first, son."

Travis shrugged his shoulders.

His father gave him a look that said the price they had almost paid was too high. Then he stepped forward and hugged his son. "I'm glad you're all right, but stealing Hannah's father's car? Along with Hannah? He was very upset. Took your mother to calm him down."

"Borrowed, Dad."

Rachel reached up and gave him a hug. "I guess I'm glad, too."

Murphree and several other reporters from other towns were shouting out questions above all the commotion, but Collins hushed them and said they weren't getting any information until he had time to speak with both Travis and Hannah.

"Travis," Collins said, "I want you down at my office at nine tomorrow morning. I want to hear your story along with Hannah's."

Travis acknowledged him with a simple, "Yes, sir."

Sam Tackett came over to shake Travis's hand and inspect his bruises. He suggested to Bill and Margaret that Travis get checked by a doctor on the way home. They couldn't have agreed more.

"We'll see you tomorrow morning, Travis," the district attorney said. "Try to get some rest."

The crowd started to break up when everyone realized they weren't going to hear any more about the wild tale that day. Travis was glad; for once, he couldn't wait to get home. He recognized Bob Thompson speaking to Collins about the next morning's meeting. He was close enough to eavesdrop.

"We'll be by about eight-thirty," Thompson said. "Russ will drive up with us and fill you in on what happened in Washington. We have a few questions ourselves. They could have some details that are important to the investigation. As far as Higson is concerned, not much left to talk about. We still have people in custody in Washington, and I'm sure the German embassy will be getting a visit from our folks up there."

Thompson and Collins parted ways. Travis was vindicated. He had done the right thing. But he also knew there was still a price to be paid—for borrowing Mr. Morgan's car without permission, for turning Hannah's uncle's boat into a pile of floating wood and putting the motor at the bottom of the Mississippi, and for almost getting himself and Hannah killed. A price to be paid.

On the way to their car, Travis's mother suggested a special meal to celebrate his safe return.

"Can we start with a julep?" Travis said.

"Oh, I suppose."

Rachel rolled her eyes. Still Mama's favorite—a Southern son. He'd never relinquish that title. Nor could he.

CHAPTER 44

Going to leave this southern town.

—Charley Jackson

CAPTAIN JOHANN KESSLER AND HIS FIRST MATE, Neumann, were ashore in Vicksburg doing what they always did when they arrived in a new city: they found the most interesting bar close to the dock and went in. First, they would order what the bartender recommended, and then they would choose for themselves. The only problem was that Mississippi was still under Prohibition. They'd have to find someplace that had relaxed its interpretation of the law. That was usually pretty easy.

The sign hanging above the door of the third establishment they came to read, "Dockside Dave's." Kessler and Neumann figured that was interesting enough. They walked inside and took two seats at the bar.

"What'll you have?" asked the bartender, looking at Kessler. A well-groomed, slender man with dark black hair, the bartender could easily have worked in a bank.

"Anything local?"

"Nothing that I can sell legally."

"You decide."

The bartender eyed them suspiciously, but Kessler's accent told him they weren't agents looking to enforce the law. "And you?" the bartender said to Neumann.

"The same."

"Thanks," Kessler said, after the bartender placed the drinks in front of them.

"My name's Rick when you're ready for another."

The interior of Dockside Dave's looked like a hundred other bars he and Neumann had frequented during their travels around the world. Peeling paint on the walls, tables scarred from cigarettes left unattended, faded watercolors of seafaring men and ships hanging crooked on the walls, and the ever-present haze generated by chain-smoking patrons. They felt right at home.

"Do you think he made the boat?" Neumann said.

"I don't know. We'll see soon enough."

"And if he's not on it?"

"Then let's hope he can make it to New Orleans. But we won't wait long."

"What about those men we talked to? Do you think they'll keep an eye out for him?"

"Maybe. They know there's a reward for the first person who leads us to him. Or him to us. It's to our advantage that Vicksburg is a small town with a small wharf. He will be easy to find."

In the corner behind the bar, a radio with the volume turned low played popular tunes that some customers tapped their feet to and others appeared not to hear at all. Twice an hour, the music stopped for five minutes and the national and local news was read.

Kessler and Neumann savored their beer, talking idly about what they would do when they arrived home. Neumann planned to visit Munich, where his sister was getting married, and Kessler had promised his wife a short trip to Switzerland.

When the news had been read the first time they missed it, not because of their conversation, but because the bartender had turned the volume down before it started. He was in the back taking a delivery when the news was broadcast a second time.

Kessler's ears perked up. He thought he recognized a name. "Did you hear that?"

"What?" Neumann said, straining to listen.

Kessler rose from his chair and walked around behind the bar. He turned up the volume.

"Hey, turn it down!" someone said from the back of the bar. "We don't want to hear any of that." The man was slurring his words.

"One moment, please," Kessler said.

"I said turn it down," the voice said.

"Wait a minute!"

The edge and sound of his voice startled Neumann. No one else said a word. Only the radio could be heard.

"I repeat, Conrad Higson, a noted agricultural scientist in Mississippi, has been found dead aboard the *River Belle*, a passenger ship based out of Helena, Arkansas. The Federal Bureau of Investigation had been conducting a massive manhunt up and down the Delta for the suspected spy. We will bring you more information as it becomes available."

Kessler turned the radio down and returned to his seat. He finished his drink and put some money on the bar. "If we don't get out of here, they'll be looking for us. Let's go."

Neumann took his last swallow of American beer then followed Kessler out the door.

CHAPTER 45

My baby's gone.

—Tampa Red

AFTER A FEW DAYS, THE DOCK ATTENDANT IN HELENA called the local police about a vehicle in the parking lot that had an odd odor coming from it. A heavy-set police officer pried open the trunk, then covered his face as Reverend Coulter's rotting corpse was exposed to the daylight. He sent the body to Clarksdale for identification and burial.

An editorial in the paper by Emmett Wilson pondered Coulter's tragic meeting with Conrad Higson on that fateful fall day. A moment in time that might have been avoided had the reverend needed to perform a baptism, wedding, or have an extended conversation with a grieving mother. "But the Lord has a plan," Wilson wrote.

Coulter's wife, children, and many of his parishioners attended the three-hour funeral. Long sermons extolled his wisdom, his compassion for the downtrodden, and his tenacious faith in the Lord, his Savior. Rivers of tears flowed that day, but none came from Elma Williams. On the other side of town, she was shedding hers for Luke.

After his body had washed up on shore and had been recovered, the church immediately offered to place Luke right next to Reverend Coulter.

"Oh, no thank you," Elma said. "Luke didn't go to church that much. We'd just as soon have him in the backyard as in the cemetery." Even if Luke was buried next to the reverend, she knew they wouldn't be seeing much of each other in the afterlife. They had different makers.

Luke's funeral was held on Sunday, and Travis and Hannah arrived early at Elma's. They played with the children in the front yard while Elma finished getting the food ready. A viewing had been held the night before, and Travis thought the funeral home had done a good job mending the weary sharecropper. Dressed in a new suit Elma had purchased, Luke, for once in his life, looked peaceful.

"Can you say a few words, Travis?" Elma said, lightly touching his arm after the preacher asked for any words from the small crowd who had assembled.

"I didn't know Luke very well," Travis began his eulogy. "But what I do know now, as you do, is that he was a law-abiding man, a just man, who didn't do the things people said he did." He looked at Luke's boys. "His only crime was wanting a better life. He knew sharecropping would never amount to anything, so he gave the only thing he had—himself. For his wife, his children, his family. And he was brave in the face of death, yes he was." Travis saw the boys grin. "Mighty brave."

That sleepy Clarksdale would be the hub of a scandalous, international incident involving the FBI had gotten the town's collective tongues wagging. Over bridge games, in barbershops, on street corners—nowhere was safe from the raging epidemic of gossip about Travis, Hannah, and Conrad Higson, the quiet newcomer to Clarksdale who had barely caused a ripple even after testifying against Luke. "Who would have thought!" exclaimed every interested party.

A couple of weeks passed before the fervor surrounding Higson's escape and capture started to die down. Over the course of those weeks, Lewis Murphree wrote a series of articles about the murders for the local paper. Headlined "Dead or Alive," the last article discussed the FBI's investigation into Higson's espionage activities. The FBI, right up to the director, had wanted the German spy any way they could get him, the reporter wrote.

Sam Tackett was one of the many sources Murphree interviewed for the story. "Why do you think Higson went on this murderous rampage, District Attorney?"

Tackett shrugged his shoulders. "I don't know. I guess some people are just no darn good."

Hannah knew that what she had done was going to have repercussions. A girl like Hannah couldn't kill or truly love a white man in Mississippi and expect to get away with it. She had done both.

When Sheriff Collins and Russ Kalman questioned Hannah, Travis sat next to her and corroborated everything she said. With Travis at her side, she might as well have been quoting the Bible. They asked about her marksmanship, and she told them that her uncle who owned the boat had taught her to shoot. They all remarked that her uncle was a fine teacher.

Yet even after Hannah was vindicated, the talk would not stop. She knew that for those who cast their world in only two colors, what she had done could not be forgiven. From the afternoon she and Travis stepped off the *River Belle* together, the Morgan family had been receiving telephone calls—always anonymous, sometimes threatening, sometimes just menacingly silent. Sometimes the caller mentioned Hannah's suspected involvement with Travis. Travis could easily defend himself against innuendo and hearsay, but he wasn't able to shield Hannah. Even though she was leaving some-time next year, she knew what her father would do now. There was no waiting out this storm.

Hannah's last day in Clarksdale proved to be the first cool day of fall. Travis stepped outside and felt the change at once. He knew what was coming—the biting winter cold. Mississippians resided either in the sweltering heat of summer or the damp, deep chill of winter. They felt most comfortable at these extremes, because Mississippi was always either black or white. Hannah had several relatives in Atlanta, and Mr. Morgan thought that was the best place for her. She would still be close enough to visit, but distant enough to be removed from the town's anxiety.

On her last night, she sat with Travis on her porch swing for hours.

"Do you want to stay?" Travis asked.

"Of course I do. But you said it yourself, Travis, the night of the party when we ran down to the river."

"What was that?"

"You don't remember?"

"No."

"You said, 'Things won't change in time for us.'"

"And you believed me?"

"You were right." She leaned over and put her head on his shoulder. "Unfortunately, you were right."

"I wish I wasn't."

He kicked the porch floor and the swing started to sway. They rocked and gazed at the stars that filled the cloudless night sky. They talked into the night, teasing, laughing, at times silent for a while, at other times crying. They recalled the hours they had spent down by the river where their love ran deep like the water, binding them as the river ties the east bank to the west. They would judge every love by this one.

On Sunday morning, Travis skipped church with his family and went to the train station to see Hannah off.

Hannah's family had gathered already; they were standing together outside on the platform, chatting, hugging, and wishing Hannah well. It was not a happy occasion, but they were used to saying good-bye to friends and family heading north, or west, or somewhere that would offer a better life.

While Hannah's family mingled and talked, Travis walked around to the side of the train that faced away from the station and climbed on board. He found a seat next to a window and watched Hannah step onto the train and take her place in another car.

It was only a minute—but a long one—before the train whistle sounded, announcing the start of their journey. Travis felt the train stir. He slipped into her car and walked to her seat.

She looked up and smiled. "I thought you weren't coming to see me off?"

"I didn't get to give you a proper send-off last night since you fell asleep on me."

"And this is my proper send-off?"

Travis looked outside. The train, though still moving slowly, was picking up speed. He had to hurry. He removed a small velvet box from his pocket and handed it to her.

"What's this?" she asked.

"Open it."

Hannah opened the box. Inside lay a small golden cross.

"It was my grandmother's. Wear it. It'll keep you safe."

"Don't you need it?"

"Not anymore. You kept me safe."

She picked the cross up by the chain and suspended it in the air.

He took it from her, gently placed it around her neck, and fastened it. He pulled his hands from around her neck and cradled her face. "I won't soon forget you, Hannah Morgan. Remember that." He kissed her deeply. Someone in the car gasped.

"You better not."

By now her tears had mixed with his. He glanced outside. The train was moving faster.

He removed his hands from her face. "Good-bye," he said. "I expect some letters."

"And responses."

He walked to the back of the car, bumping into the porter who was making his way through the car checking on passengers.

"May I help you, sir?" the porter said.

"That was my stop. I'll just get off here."

"You can't get off now."

"Sure I can." Travis brushed past him and entered the open space between the cars. Looking up and down the track, he took a deep breath and jumped.

He was in midair, and he thought of Hannah, that night by the Mississippi. How he had chased her into the woods and had landed on the soft banks of the river. He thought of the gentleness of her soul. He would miss her more than she would miss him.

Travis landed on his feet but instantly curled up, rolling several times before coming to a stop. He stood up and made sure he hadn't injured himself. Squinting at the train as it chugged toward the sun, he could see the outline of a passenger hanging out a window. She was waving wildly.

He waved back.

When the train was out of sight, he took a shortcut through a cotton field on the way home. He wanted to finish that application to Emory University in Atlanta before his father returned from church.